Revenge of the Bakeneko

VB Scott

No Barrier Publishing

Contents

Dedication V

Content Advisory VI

Preface VII

Pronunciation Guide IX

Map of the Nikkō Kaidō X

Part One - Life and Debt 1

1. A Little Coin 2

2. Fathers 11

3. In The Moment 22

4. Reverse Course 32

5. Melee 43

6. Fake Estate 53

7. Blood Money 62

8. Hurt 72

9. Of The Same Mind 78

10. Gratitude 90

Part Two - Paid in Death 95

11. No Rest For The Ambitious 96

12. Principles	106
13. Marks	114
14. Too Easy	124
15. Battle Bond	134
16. Regrets	146
17. Prices to Pay	156
18. Ghosts	167
19. Skewered	178
20. Bumpy Road	187
Part Three - Bloodlines	192
21. Rewards	193
22. Understanding	202
23. Honor	210
24. Curiosity Piqued	219
25. Cold Blood	229
26. Holding Back	238
27. Discontent	247
28. Heart to Heart	256
29. Bakeneko & Tanchōzuru	264
30. Brushstrokes	275
Glossary of Japanese Vocabulary	282
Takana's Haiku	286
Special Thanks	287
About VB Scott	288

Dedication

Dedicated to my college roommates at Western Washington University. Without their insistence that I experience Japanese culture, I would have never discovered a love and respect for Japan that led me to live along the middle of the *Nikkō Kaidō* and meet my wife.

Also dedicated to Richard, Roger, Hiroshi, Yoshie, Lilly, and Howard.

Gone way too soon.

Content Advisory

The following book contains:
    Graphic, bloody violence
    Brief strong language
    Sexual content (non-graphic)
    Attempted rape (non-graphic)
    Suicide and suicidal ideation
    Sex trafficking
    Gambling
    Tobacco use

Preface

When Westerners rewrote the history of Japanese culture before the Meiji Restoration, the rest of the world adopted the idea that samurai warriors were exclusively men. Even modern Japan believes this to be the truth, as its own history was taken from it and reshaped by the West.

The heroics of women warriors, the *onna-bugeisha*, *onna-musha*, *kunoichi*, and the Empresses that forged military victories and mythic bloodlines, were buried or erased, and Japanese women were portrayed as submissive, subservient, clad in *kimono* and *obi*, and confined to the home.

From Empress Jingū to Tomoe Gozen to Nakano Takeko, and the thousands of women warriors throughout the country's history, Japanese women were —and are— much more than the reductive narrative forced on them by the outside world and modern culture.

Revenge of the Bakeneko is a fictional account of fictional people in the early Edo period (whole period refers to the years from 1603 until 1868). Artifacts and most customs at the time should be historically accurate, as are the towns and cities represented within. It is highly recommended to keep in mind that this is a work of fiction for the purpose of entertainment, filled with characters one could certainly wish existed, but, in fact, did not.

The main character's given name is Takana, which can be represented by a number of different kanji combinations. Our Takana can be broken down into multiple meanings: "Taka" can mean "respect for parents and ancestors" and/or "mourning," and "na" can mean "beautiful," "peaceful," "doubt" and/or "contradiction."

Pronunciation Guide

Takana — Tah-kah-nah
Tomoe — Toe-moe-ay
Iwakuchi — Ee-wah-k`-chee
Kochiya — Koh-chee-yah
Taiga — Tah-ee-gah
Tetsuo — Tay-tsu-oh
Chiyo — Chee-yoh
Fusa — Who-sah
Shinkichi — Shee-n-kee-chee
Sōkichi — Soh-oo-kee-chee
Natsu — Nah-tsu
Genjirō — Ghe-n-gee-roh-oo
Chise — Chee-say
Hana — Hah-nah
Yoshimatsu — Yoh-she-mah-tsu
Itarō — Ee-tah-roh-oo
Kameya — Kah-may-yah
Manhachi — Mah-n-hah-chee
Kunō — Koo-noh-oo
Aoi — Ah-oh-ee

NIKKŌ 日光
今市 IMAICHI
HATSUISHI 鉢石
大沢 ŌZAWA
TOKUJIRŌ 徳次郎
宇都宮 UTSUNOMIYA
TOCHIGI 栃木 PREFECTURE
雀宮 SUZUMENOMIYA
ISHIBASHI 石橋
小金井 KOGANEI
SHINDEN 新田
小山 OYAMA
MAMADA 間々田
野木 NOGI
KOGA 古河
中田 NAKADA
KURIHASHI 栗橋
IBARAKI 茨城 PREFECTURE
SATTE 幸手
SUGITO 杉戸
春日部 KASUKABE
SAITAMA 埼玉 PREFECTURE
越谷 KOSHIGAYA
草加 SŌKA
千住 SENJU
TOKYO 東京 PREFECTURE
日本橋 NIHONBASHI
江戸 EDO (TŌKYŌ)

Part One – Life and Debt

Chapter One

A Little Coin

Kiseru: A pipe used for smoking finely shredded tobacco. Samurai and subordinate classes carried them in a special case, called a kiseruzutsu, during the Edo period. They were considered status symbols due to their precious metals and intricate designs, and the high cost of tobacco. Cigarettes and tobacco were introduced in the late 16th century by the Portuguese.

June 1, 1708
Kurihashi, Saitama Prefecture

TAKANA GOZEN INHALED THE AROMAS wafting from the kitchen, and her undernourished stomach growled. She sat in the boisterous *tatami* room in the back of a restaurant, holding a respectful position on a *zabuton* while boorish gamblers and drunken *yakuza* thugs placed their bets over a game of *Chō-Han*.

She needed a cigarette. Or a satisfying drag from her grandfather's pipe. There were at least a dozen tobacco clouds circulating the room, each man seated around the long, rectangular table providing a different scent. It did well to drown out the rank smell of the men's sweat. Unfortunately for Takana, the dealer wasn't allowed to smoke or eat during a game, which often went on for hours, well into the early morning. With the first major downpour of the rainy season pounding outside, no one would choose to step out early unless they lost all their money. It was going to be a long night.

Every participant was distracted by food, drink, waitresses, and most of all, her—exactly the way she liked it when she needed to juice their bets. She wore her upper-back-length raven-black hair in a loose ponytail, with several strands dangling in front of her blank, dark eyes. Her painted red lips remained pursed between rounds. The *kimono* she borrowed from the House's daughter hugged her waist. She wore a plain, white *sarashi*, wrapped around her chest. Though she wrapped it tighter whenever traveling, the looseness garnered the right kind of distraction from the men crowding around the table. If the men were to see her without the linen, though, they'd be turned off by the visual effect of malnutrition in her chest. The wrap provided an illusion that at least doubled its size.

More than her fabricated feminine attributes, it was the elaborate *irezumi* of a *bakeneko* covering her collarbone, upper right breast, and upper arm, along with a frog covering her back shoulder, that earned the most attention; the tattoo kept most of the men in line. The markings indicated she wasn't some commoner to harass or, perhaps, accost after the game—the House and game were under the protection of a *yakuza* clan. While the fearsome, ugly cat in the front was meant to mock her when her owners forced it on her, it most often had a desirous effect of making drunk men think twice about laying hands on her.

Takana grabbed the bottom of the cup that covered the two dice and swirled it around, picking them up inside the rim, expertly harnessing their velocity. She shook it vigorously as she lifted it above her head, yelling *"Chō-Han!"* before slamming the cup down onto the fabric-lined block of wood on the table. The men placed their bets for an Even or Odd outcome. After all bets were placed, she paused for a brief moment to heighten the room's anticipation, then yanked the cup up, revealing a two and six beneath.

"Chō!"

The men who bet on the Even outcome cheered, while the ones who bet on Odd cursed and slapped their thighs. Takana collected five percent of the winning bets for the House, then divided the rest of the winnings to the successful bettors.

Waitresses brought forth more *sake* to those who still had the coin. Takana met eyes with one of the waitresses, then directed her gaze to a particular man who seemed to be in some sort of rivalry with another at the opposite corner of the table, and the waitress had caught their eyes throughout the night. She acknowledged Takana, then caressed the man's shoulder while she leaned over to pour his *sake*, glancing her torso against his arm. She whispered something into his ear, then verified the identity of the rival, who stared at the display with clenched teeth.

She did the same thing to the rival, causing the men to glare at each other. They traded verbal barbs when all the wait staff left. It could become violent after the game—Takana hoped outside, so the rain would wash the blood away if things escalated. During the next few betting phases, the two men brought their rivalry into their wagers, attempting to one-up each other. Once the golden *ryō* coins made an appearance on the table, several other men's greed caused them to up their bets, too.

One of the rivals favored betting the Odds, and most of the other gamblers would bet on his side, so Takana needed to ensure the dice came up Odd to earn a larger sum of the winnings.

Aggressive dialogue and derisive laughter distracted them while Takana loosened the sharp *kanzashi* sticks holding her ponytail up and pretended to tighten all the loose hair that had been hanging in her face. She retrieved two dice secured beneath the ponytail and hid them in her palm. Finished with her hair, she picked up the cup, swirling the original dice inside. When she tilted the cup, she squeezed a concealed mechanism at the bottom designed to grab the two dice inside. At the same time, she put her other hand over the mouth, dropping the trick dice inside and clattering on as if nothing had changed.

She shook the cup over her head, matching the men's attitudes, as if she was just as invested in the outcome as they were. She yelled "*Chō-Han!*" and slammed the cup down, but not so hard as to lose her grip on the mechanism holding the original dice in place. All the chest-beating and insults resulted in a heavier-than-usual wager for an Odd outcome, so that's exactly what her trick dice revealed.

"*Han!*"

One of the dice had only the numbers one, three, and five, while the other die had only twos, fours, and sixes, so there could only ever be odd combinations. Since the human eye can only see three sides of a die at once, she didn't worry any of the men would be able to detect the cheat unless they snatched them from her. No one was allowed to move around the room during a roll, either. It was a simple cheat with low risk of getting caught.

The five percent take included multiple *ryō* and change for the House, alongside some elated men, and murderous looks from a couple of the others. Takana snapped her fingers. The head waitress came into the room and knelt behind her.

"Bring these fine men a free round of *sake* and *gyoza*, on me," Takana said for the room to hear.

The "free" amenities cooled down most of the table, except the man in the rivalry who'd lost the wager along with the seeming affection of the waitress who'd played the two off of each other. Takana hoped the loser would come closer to breaking even before the night was out, or there would be bloodshed later.

While the men enjoyed their free food and drink and took up genial conversation, Takana prepared for the next round. She slid her hand over the block to gather up the trick dice, and released the mechanism for the original dice to clatter inside the cup as if all she had done was cover them up before the next round. She pretended to wipe the sweat from her hands onto the fabric covering her inner thighs, where she deposited each trick die into small hidden pockets.

After a few more rounds of inebriated betting, most of the gamblers had enough and raised their bets for the last roll. The wagers had increased in Odd betting because of the large hit she'd forced earlier. She anticipated the last bet of the night would also tip that way as many men chased their losses. Takana had one more hidden set of trick dice, in a small pocket in the *sarashi* that she'd wrapped so it would lay between her cleavage.

Pretending the humidity was getting to her, though sweat among the room attendees ran thick and pungent long before the final round, she grabbed a cloth behind the *zabuton*. She dabbed at her brow and neck. The men lost track of their conversations and observed the cloth as it descended further south. She smiled at their lascivious grins as she exaggerated wiping between her cleavage. She let the looseness of the *sarashi* expose a little more skin so her fingers could nab the trick dice, then slipped them into the cup as before.

After dividing the final winnings, Takana waited for all the men to stagger out before securing the second pair of trick dice into her hidden pockets. The head waitress came in to direct the other staff to clean the room. Takana gave her a *ryō* coin and pocketed her trick cup while handing the House cup back to the waitress.

"Here's a second *ryō*, *nēsan*. Divide it among the staff, please. This was a good night."

Takana slipped the top half of the *kimono* back over her shoulders and delivered the night's take to the back room. She dispensed with the formalities of announcing herself once she heard the proprietor snoring from the other side of the *shoji* door. She entered and found him lying on the floor.

"Wake up, Ito-*san*."

When he didn't respond, she dropped the bag of heavy coins on his desk, which startled him awake. His eyes widened as he spilled the money out and stacked it for counting. He divided out ten percent and slid it across the table to Takana.

"Sorry, Ito-*san*, but it's twenty percent now. The clan's raising rates again."

"Twenty percent? Why didn't you tell me before you started?"

"Didn't want to argue with you and have to cancel the game. I *still* don't want to argue. You know what will happen if you make me explain how your gambling racket works with the clan's protection, don't you?"

"*Kuso!* I heard about what you did down in Kasukabe."

"Heard what?" She crossed her arms.

"Kenshi wanted out of the protection; you dissuaded him after killing his *rōnin* bodyguard."

"I was attacked first. Anyway, if Kenshi had simply accepted the *oyabun's* new terms, he wouldn't have incurred an even *higher* rate for refusing in the first place, and he wouldn't be minus one bodyguard."

Ito slid another ten percent across the table, tempering his frustration so it wouldn't come off as defiance.

"You act like you had to do a lot of work to earn all that," Takana said. "You can train one of your waitresses to do what I do the next time you're running low on income, so you won't have to request my presence again."

"No, no, Gozen-*san*. You do good work. I'm angry at the situation, not you. Thanks for helping out tonight with the game."

"Of course. Are you heading to bed so I can get dressed and on my way?"

He nodded, slid the rest of the coin in a bag, then shuffled out of the office. Takana retrieved her travel attire from the closet. She removed the elaborate *kimono* after putting her trick dice into one of the pouches she wrapped around her thighs. She re-wrapped the *sarashi* tighter around her chest and slipped on a warm, hip-length *haori*, taken from the *rōnin* she'd dispatched in Kasukabe. It kept her shoulders warm and let her wear less fabric underneath to avoid hindering her movements.

Next, she pulled a torn, half-length *hakama* over her legs. The ends of the fabric tickled her knees. It bore mud, sword cuts, and hundreds of kilometers of travel, walking through all terrain and weather, but she could never afford to replace it. The look didn't bother her, and it was useful, allowing her to reach the pouches wrapped around her thighs with ease. The less fabric she dealt with overall, the better.

Finally, she tied a set of *daishō* around her waist, consisting of a pair of *katana* and *wakizashi* blades—also taken from the *rōnin*. Her own ornate, master-smithed *daishō*, gifted to her by her *onna-musha sensei* after completing warrior training at age twenty, had been sold off by her father as he fell further into *yakuza* debt. It was his last act of desperation before selling his wife and daughter.

The memory of coming home to see the *katana kake* empty of her second-most prized possession still angered her. She was unable to face Tomoe-*sensei* from then on out of shame for what her family had become, and for her plunge from a serious warrior to a part-time mercenary and full-time *yakuza* pet.

Without honor, she took the *daishō* of defeated *rōnin* or wannabe *samurai* punks. When she wounded or killed the next one, she'd keep or swap blades depending on whichever had the least amount of molding, denting, weak points, and coagulated blood. She rarely spent any money on herself, instead funneling nearly every coin she earned back to the *yakuza* clan that owned her and her mother. Though the debt was unlikely to ever be paid off, Takana earned special treatment from the clan for all the trips she returned from with coin—often exceeding the actual *yakuza* ranks' individual hauls.

Before leaving the office, she spotted a flat case on the edge of the desk. She took half of the pre-rolled cigarettes inside and slid them into one of her many pouches. The waitress responsible for closing was the only one left in the building when Takana slipped on her *geta* at the front entrance. She held up her hand before the waitress could blow out the last lantern near the door. Takana pulled a thin candle out of a pouch and lit the wick with the lantern, then nodded and stepped outside.

She lit a cigarette and sat down on the steps as the rain refused to abate beyond the building's overhang. Takana lit her traveling lantern and set it to the side, blew out the candle, returned it to its pouch, then tied the chin strap of her *kasa*, positioning its padded ring atop her head. Rope tassels hung in little loops around the rim of the bamboo-woven, cone-shaped hat.

She'd rather smoke from her grandfather's *kiseru*, but she'd used the last of the rich tobacco a month before. The cheap cigarette was a godsend, though, especially after being around the mishmash of tantalizing smoke in the tight quarters of the gambling room.

The waitress offered a hand-sized rice ball to Takana as she left the restaurant, then clacked away under her umbrella. Takana consumed the rice ball in three ravenous bites. The cigarette grew shorter as she waited for a break in the storm. Finally, as the stub burned her tobacco-stained fingers, she accepted that the rain wasn't going to let up. She sighed and got to her feet, attaching the lantern to a loop on her belt.

With her free hand reposing on the hilt of the *katana*, she went into the rain and turned up the road that would lead her back to the *Nikkō Kaidō*. The heavily travelled highway started in Edo and snaked north to Utsunomiya before breaking into the mountains to Nikkō in the west. The journeys north always ended in Utsunomiya, where her clan and parents lived.

Over the rain beating on rooftops and in the muck of the road, muffled cries came from the space between the restaurant and the neighboring building. Takana entered the alleyway and found a body in the mud. She recognized the robes of the man who'd won the large wager she manipulated. His pockets had been emptied, she discovered. A hushed struggle continued further down the alleyway and around the corner to the back of the building.

The man who'd lost the rivalry was busy trying to tear away the *kimono* of the waitress that had flirted with the two of them during the game. A few coins spilled out of his purse as he hurried to pull down his *hakama*. In the downpour, he didn't hear Takana approach from behind. She tossed a handful of mud into the back of his head. He'd dropped his *daishō* in his haste to take the waitress, so Takana stooped to pick up the blades.

The man rushed to pull his *hakama* up and cursed at her, threatening her even though she'd disarmed him. She ignored his words and tossed the *daishō* at his feet, challenging him. He sputtered and ripped the *katana* out of its scabbard, then squared up, preparing to charge her.

Takana tilted her head at the waitress to leave. The waitress only straightened her *kimono* and stood on the back step of the building beneath the small overhang of the roof, a look of confident retribution in her eyes.

The man flexed, making more threats like he thought that might scare Takana off. She stood poised with her hand on the hilt of her *katana*. She could stand there all night. Her *kasa* protected her head and shoulders, and the *rōnin's haori* kept her warm. She was much more comfortable than he looked, and she didn't have a bad case of blue balls.

He charged towards her with the blade high above his head. She stifled a laugh at how he left his torso open for her. A swift draw would end him, and in his drunken state, he wouldn't even know what happened until his face hit the mud. But Takana bore responsibility for the situation, thanks to juicing the bets and inflaming the rivalry with the dead man in the alley.

When he got close enough, and right before he started his downswing, Takana extended the hilt of the *katana* beneath the man's chin, instantly knocking him out without having to unsheathe the *katana* fully from its scabbard. The blade snuck back into its home as quickly as it escaped.

The waitress clapped once in excitement before regaining her elegance when Takana looked to her.

"What do you think, *nēsan*? I could kill him right now, or we can drag him to the local *samurai* to deal with for the murder."

"I assume you mean *after* we relieve him of what he robbed from that other poor bastard?"

"Naturally."

The waitress chose the latter option. After splitting the coins from his purse, they both dragged him down the road to the *Dōshin* on patrol at the edge of town. Takana left the waitress to clean up the rest of the mess with the local police and once again set off on the *Nikkō Kaidō*.

Chapter Two

Fathers

Yakuza: Originating in the 17th century, the yakuza began as two organizations: the tekiya (peddling illicit, stolen, or shoddy goods) and bakuto (involved in or participating in gambling and loansharking). Most yakuza groups were composed of misfits and delinquents. Tekiya were held in such high regard that they were granted near-samurai st atus.

June 7, 1708
Utsunomiya, Tochigi Prefecture

A WEEK AND THREE GAMBLING houses later, Takana prepared to knock on the door of her father's *yakeya* after dusk. The small space could never house more than one person, but he didn't have that worry since he sold Takana and her mother to the *yakuza*. It was located in the back of a larger building through tight alleyways. *Samurai* resided in the front of the building with far more space. Takana's family had lived for her first twenty years in an opulent estate resembling the *ryokan* of the most elaborate *onsen* hotels. How far her father had brought the family down in such a short period of time...

Before Takana could knock on the thin slatted door, it opened to reveal a shabby *yūjo* of about twenty years. She backed into Takana as she exited and cowered when she turned around. Her short hair was an unkempt mess; the back part looked like it had been in the clutches of a fist. She smelled of *sake* and shame. The rags she would consider "clothes" were torn and stained.

"What are you doing outside of the *yūkaku*, *nēchan*?" Takana whispered.

The prostitute glanced around to be sure no one else saw her, then down at Takana's feet.

"No one chooses me. I can only make money by coming to these kinds of houses…"

"Did the man inside pay you?" Takana asked, even though she could assume the answer. If he had money to spend on women, she would like to know where he got it.

"He says he'll pay when he can. He's said that the last three times…"

Takana sighed and pulled out one of the *ryō* from her part of the journey's take. Judging by the way the girl's dull eyes lit up, it would be more than enough to settle the debt. Takana fumed that the bastard continued increasing debts she had to pay on his behalf.

"Take this and tell Chiyo no girl is allowed to come to this house anymore. If he ever makes his way to your *yūkaku*, do whatever the hell you want—if he's got the coin."

The prostitute bowed, making Takana uncomfortable—it was far too deep. Takana watched the girl hurry off into the darkness in poorly thatched straw shoes, then stepped into the doorway and removed her muddy *geta*.

"You want a little more, sweetie?"

"I think she's had enough, *chichi-ue*."

"Ta-*chan*?" Her father rolled out from his disheveled bedding and covered himself with his robe. "Is it time for our monthly visit already?"

Takana came into the small living space and sat on her calves. She pulled out a *ryō* and slid it across the moldy *tatami*. Her father looked at it and huffed.

"Is that all?"

Takana's face burned, but she hid its redness beneath the rim of the *kasa*.

"If I give you more, you'll only spend it on booze and girls. It smells like a *sakagura* in here. And...whatever you were doing with that *yūjo*."

"I'm surprised you can smell anything beyond the tobacco coming from your shitty clothing."

Takana kept her head low to avoid his furious gaze. She knew what was coming and braced for it.

He flipped the *kasa* off her head and slapped her.

"You have *more*. I heard it scrape against the others in your pouch."

"If I don't bring that to the *oyabun,* his son will punish *kaasan,* if he doesn't punish me instead. You know this, and always demand more. You're...such a bastard," she whispered the last part, not committing to hurling it at him, but not able to hold back completely anymore.

He struck her with his fist. Though his abuse didn't pain her physically in his drunken state, and her hardened skin could take it, she rolled with the punch and fell over. He always stopped when she fell down. Many years before, she'd meant to prove her strength with a show of defiance, taking hit after hit, which served to make him angrier the longer she stood there. The bruises had taken a month to clear up, and she'd had to take jobs that could only be carried out in darkness.

She reached into the sleeve pocket of her *haori* and pulled out the *ryō* she had hoped to use to buy a pouch of the expensive, special tobacco her grandfather always smoked the next time she traveled to Edo. The tobacco reminded her of a better life, when they were protected by wealth. Besides training with Tomoe-*sensei,* the happiest times had been sitting at her grandfather's knee while he regaled her with stories of the *onna-musha* and *onna-bugeisha,* Empresses and women warriors who defended Nihon and the clans for millennia. His breath smelled of *sakura* and vanilla, with a cinnamon backing. It was like dessert, even in the mornings. She delighted in the way he told stories with his hands, accentuating action with invisible blades. Tomoe-*sensei* taught her in the ways of actual blades.

Takana cried at her father's feet. He would think it was from the beating, but really it was because she'd never come of age before her grandfather died—they could have smoked together in the sunroom of the old estate, watching the sun set over Fuji-*san*. She missed him dearly and would give anything to spend one evening with him, sharing the tobacco in contented silence. All she had left of him was his *kiseru* housed inside an ornate *kiseruzutsu*. After her *daishō* had been sold off, it was the only treasure she had from the time before *yakuza* creditors took the estate and she and her mother were dragged away. If anyone had touched the pipe case, she would have cut off their hands.

Her father picked up the *ryō* coin and mumbled about how expensive she and her mother had been, how if they weren't around, he would have never lost everything and gone into crushing, lifetime debt with the *yakuza* in the first place. Takana didn't correct him, that if he didn't have two women to barter, the *yakuza* would have killed him instead. It was clear to the clan he could never clear the debts on his own, and it was even clearer to her.

Takana picked herself up and sniffed blood back into her nose, regaining her composure. She bowed parallel to the floor, waiting for him to dismiss her. Instead, he grabbed a fistful of her hair and flung her towards the door.

"I don't want to see you until the month is over. You'd better have double next time, or you'll have to walk around the city with that ridiculous *kasa* covering your face for another month."

She slipped on her *geta* and stepped outside, sliding the door closed behind her. The skin around her upper cheek tightened, and she pressed her fingers against the spot that would mar her face over the next few days. Her father hadn't hugged her since his panicked embrace before the *yakuza* pulled them apart. The only way he touched her since was with his palm or fist.

She put her *kasa* back on and walked up the road to the blacksmith. The light from his residence flickered, even at such a late hour, so she picked up his hammer and tapped it against the anvil twice before placing it back where she'd found it.

After a few minutes, the blacksmith came outside, wrapping himself in a light jacket. Takana bowed to him.

"Good evening, Inoue-*san*. I apologize if you were close to sleep. I wouldn't have come if your light was off."

"It's okay, Taka-*chan*. Another fifteen minutes would have been another story. What can I do for you?"

"My *kasa* needs a couple *kunai* replaced beneath the rim, and I'd like you to verify the broken *katana* pieces beneath the bamboo aren't loose before I head out again."

"A couple of *kunai*, eh? Had some trouble your *katana* couldn't solve? You look like you've been in quite a scrap recently," he said while holding his lantern up to her face. She shrank back from his scrutiny.

"Something like that. I might have starved to death if I couldn't take out a couple hares along my last journey. I...lost the *kunai*."

"Mm-hm. Must have been some mighty strong rabbits..."

Takana smiled miserably at his insinuation.

"Regardless, here's a little something extra for your trouble."

He returned an earnest smile when she laid the *ryō* coin in his palm.

"I'll be back around midday to pick up the *kasa*. Good night, Inoue-*san*."

Inoue flipped the coin in his hand, testing its weight, as she continued up the road.

"Taka-*chan*," he called. "Do you need a place to stay tonight?"

"No, thank you. I'm heading home now."

She'd made the mistake of taking him up on that one night years before when he'd had too much *sake*. He wasn't rough with her, but the way he guilted her into a different form of payment stuck with her. She resolved to never again come to him unless she had coin in hand, no matter the weather outside.

Takana walked until she was out of sight of the blacksmith, then entered a public bath. She paid the lady in the front, who told her the hour of allowing *yakuza* into the baths was almost over, then breathed a sigh of relief that the end of another trip was finally upon her. She removed her clothing and equipment, washed the two-week journey off her body, then soaked in the hot water, dozing off several times as her muscles let go of all the tension she'd built up along the way.

A couple of women entered and relaxed themselves at the other end of the bath. They wore intricate, full-bodied *irezumi*—they were the wives of senior members of the *yakuza*, but Takana didn't recognize them from her own clan. The two giggled at Takana's small tattoo, and other things, compared to their own, but otherwise left her alone.

Still, she quit dozing for fear of what they might try if her eyes were closed. When they left, she exited and re-dressed, then asked the lady in the front if she could sleep in one of the waiting chairs overnight. The lady huffed and told her to get out.

If Takana wanted to lay in a *futon*, she had a tiny one in the clan headquarters, but the *oyabun's* son would be around. If he didn't try to take her, many of the lower ranks would. She wanted to sleep, not fend off their aggressive advances, so she opted to find a spot between some random buildings that provided cover from the rain and couldn't be seen from the streets. Sleep eluded her for a few minutes while she replayed the visit to her father's house. She drifted off to the sound of rain battering the roofs of the surrounding buildings.

Many people came in and out of the Kochiya-*kai* headquarters as the day passed. A long staircase led into the lobby, where a rotating set of *yakuza* wives acted as receptionists for the days' visitors. Takana's status guaranteed she'd be waiting until the end of the day to speak with the *oyabun*, Tetsuo Kochiya. She ignored the looks from uncouth and uncivilized *yakuza* as they went about their business. She sat with her legs crossed and the *haori* covering most of her body.

When she realized they couldn't be looking at her body, it became clear they were sneering at her swollen eye. Close to the end of the day, Tetsuo's son, Taiga, sat next to her.

"How'd your little dice trick work this time, *ane-san*?"

"As well as always, *ani-ki*. And stop calling me that. Besides the fact that I'd sooner kill than marry you, the clan would never allow it."

"Once the old man dies, it doesn't matter what anyone will *allow*. When I run the place, *I* make the rules."

Takana would deride his cockiness if she didn't know how quick his temper was. She'd spent years testing his boundaries, and he still surprised her.

"Can I be present when you explain that to the neighboring clans, or the head of Utsunomiya? I'm sure they'll be delighted to learn about your rejection of a hundred years of tradition."

"It'll be a simple matter to take over the city. Then I'll make you my wife. You won't be able to hide behind my old man's protection anymore. Besides, you're resourceful—think of it as a fast-track. You'll more than make up for your father's debt in my bedroom, after we get some damn food in you."

"I can't wait, *ani-ki*." Takana maintained a neutral expression and stared out the windows lining the hallway, concentrating on the lush greenery.

"Your dismissive attitude won't last long once I'm *oyabun*, bitch."

He backhanded her. Her hand went to the *wakizashi* at her waist, regaining her senses before her fingers wrapped around the hilt. She'd be executed if she raised a hand to him, or any of the other *yakuza* in the clan, no matter their seniority. Even Tetsuo wouldn't be able to save her. Taiga noticed where her hand went and slapped the swollen spot where her father had hit her the night before.

As if he could feel the escalating situation from the other room, Tetsuo emerged from his office and scowled at Taiga.

"You should be happy, *oyassan*," Taiga said without hiding his bitterness, "Taka-*chan* has plenty of *ryō* for you to go along with her shitty attitude."

Taiga bowed slightly, disrespectfully, to his father, then left the room. Tetsuo sighed and shook his head, then motioned for Takana to follow him into his office. As he lowered himself with aged dignity into his *zabuton* at the other side of his table, Takana emptied her pockets of all the remaining *ryō* she'd collected over the two-week period.

Unsurprised and disinterested by the large stack of coins laid out on the desk, he asked how the increase in rates played with Ito and the other Houses.

"They understood that times are tough and agreed to pay the new fifteen percent rate."

"Did you have to kill that bodyguard to get the point across?"

"*Oyassan*, I deeply apologize for Kasukabe. If I could have—"

Tetsuo chuckled and held up his hand.

"How much did you *actually* quote them, Taka-*chan*?"

Takana's eyes nearly fell out of her head, and she lowered her *kasa* quickly to hide her shame.

"...twenty, *oyassan*..."

Tetsuo's chuckle turned into a quick belly-laugh.

"I wish I had more men like you. You don't need to apologize when you bring such prosperous results to the clan. Consider it the cost of business and forget it ever happened. Keep that five percent and start eating better."

Not sure how to proceed, Takana bowed, waiting for him to dismiss her. Instead, his robes rustled around a box at his side.

"Rise, Taka-*chan*. I remembered your birthday last week. It's too bad you were on the road, or we could have celebrated properly."

"Was it my birthday? I've...stopped counting..."

It was hard to say what was more surprising—that she'd missed her own birthday, or that such a busy affluent had remembered it instead.

"I understand. I stopped counting twenty-five years ago, although I was still more than twice your age at that point. Hard lives don't give people the chance to prioritize such trivial matters. I always remember because your birthday coincides with the rainy season."

Tetsuo slid a small, unadorned pouch across the table. Takana didn't need to open the bag to know what it contained—the delicious aroma invigorated her senses. A small pressure throbbed behind her eyes, but she held it back.

"Your grandfather was a great man. Paid his protection money on time, and never threw away his fortune on anything that didn't increase his value, or the value of his family. The only thing he ever 'wasted' his money on was this. Expensive, for something that disappears so quickly and never provides a return. But I think you and I understand this can be more valuable than all of this gold you've brought me."

"Yes, *oyassan*," Takana managed once she could trust her voice wouldn't crack.

"Would you be open to sharing?" the old man asked, pulling his own *kiseru* from a sleeve pocket.

The sun set over the mountains in the west while they sat side by side on the balcony. The *kiseru* had stopped smoking, and Takana regarded Tetsuo as a long silence extended between them. He'd always said he was never personally involved in her father's debt terms, and she knew, as with all heads of the clans, they couldn't bend the rules when they pleased—she wouldn't be pardoned, no matter how much Tetsuo favored her.

It was the same as how she couldn't bend her duty to her father, drunken brute that he'd become—she couldn't force him to change, cut ties with him, or stop the world from crashing down around him. Despite their disparate status, there were restrictions on both her and Tetsuo, preventing them from taking charge and doing the things they thought were right—or at least, bending the world into something more just.

"*Oyassan*," Takana whispered. "Why are you so nice to me?"

A small frown crinkled his features, and he exhaled a frustrated breath, but he kept his eyes on the mountains. Despite the pleasant surroundings, Takana's skin tightened around where she'd been struck by her father and Taiga.

Tetsuo turned his head a degree towards her and lowered his voice.

"Do you wish you could have chosen your family, Taka-*chan*?"

Her eye pulsated.

"I...never think about it, *oyassan*."

She was sure that sounded like a lie, but dwelling on the truth did her no good.

"I imagine for you it would be more complicated, being a dutiful daughter. It's an easy answer for me."

"It doesn't benefit us to think on such things. It's the one luxury even the richest heads of the clans can never buy. Right now... I'm only thinking about how I can possibly thank you for—"

Tetsuo held up his hand.

"Don't overthink it."

"Are you certain you don't want...anything else from me?"

Despite his status as an octogenarian, his continuous, unexpected kindness didn't make her uncomfortable the way other high ranking clansmen's attention did. Tetsuo was genuine, not looking for a reward from her that she could discern. Still, she ran a finger along her outer thigh in view of his periphery, and she didn't even cringe when she did it.

He chuckled and turned his gaze back to the mountains.

"Is that your plan to finally kill me? A heart attack for this old man?"

"Not at all. I don't know how else I could thank you. But I certainly don't want to kill you. The longer I can keep Taiga away from your position, the better."

"I don't blame you, Taka-*chan*. I wish he wasn't an only child, too. Anyway, I appreciate your gesture, all the same. Even with your thinness and the bruising you always carry with you, if I was sixty years younger, I would happily take you up on such a generous offer from one as striking as you."

Takana emptied the *kiseru* over the rail outside before returning it to its case, then went to the table and packed the gifted pouch of tobacco into the inside pocket of the *haori*, all the while reflecting on how good he could make her feel, despite how she felt about herself and her terrible life.

"I'm going to look for work. But if you need me to do anything for the clan, I'll be traveling the *Nikkō Kaidō* towards Edo."

"I'll send a courier if you're needed. Were you ever going to tell me what happened to your face?"

"Just a little dust-up with a drunk outside Ito's restaurant. I handled him. Nothing for you to worry about, *oyassan*."

It impressed her how he could sense the truth of a situation without betraying any excessive expressions on his weathered face. Why did she bother lying to him anymore? Because lies were her currency, and the truth was as unaffordable as a new wardrobe.

Takana kissed Tetsuo's forehead and left the office before he had a chance to respond.

Chapter Three

In The Moment

Yūkaku | Yūjo : The legal red-light districts walled off outside cities, and women of pleasure, respectively. Prostitutes were restricted by law in the early 17th century to the red-light districts. One could enter or be forced into the profession for various reasons, including to pay off debts, to earn dowries, to work in slavery, and to entertain through music and other traditional arts. They filled a need for the low social classes who would otherwise not be able to patronize the more expensive and exclusive Oi ran and Geisha.

June 8, 1708
Utsunomiya, Tochigi Prefecture

ENTERING THE PERIMETER OF THE *yūkaku* that had been constructed outside the city-proper's walls, Takana clutched her *haori* around her torso and lowered the rim of the repaired *kasa* she'd picked up from Inoue. She moved around the district prostitutes as they made their way to the bathhouses, and the lower ranks cleaned the stalls and rooms.

Outside the small room that served as the pleasure quarter's office, though it was nothing more than a fancier version of the other rooms and often used for the same purposes, she found the overseer of the *yūjo*, looking over the bloodied face of one of the newer girls. The overseer, Chiyo, dropped a few coins in the girl's hand and instructed her to visit the back-alley doctor near the entrance of the city.

"You'd think she'd have learned by now not to argue with anyone who has a tattoo..." the older woman said, then sighed when she peered at Takana's face beneath the *kasa*. "Looks like a lesson *you'll* never learn either, Ta-*chan*."

"*Ohayō, kaasan*. Any deadbeats you need me to chase before I head back out on the road?"

"Is it too much to hope that my daughter came by to speak about anything other than business?"

Chiyo smiled a little bit and pulled a small box out of a pocket inside her sleeve. "*Otanjōbiomedetō*."

Takana opened the box, noticed a flash of gold, then snapped it shut.

"I can't accept this, *kaasan*."

"You can and you will. Buy yourself a new *hakama* that doesn't look like a tattered skirt; clothing that isn't stolen. Eat something! Or have a thousand cigarettes. *Sofu*'s tobacco..."

Takana pushed the box into her mother's hand.

"I still have a good supply left; that's all I need. Please keep those coins for yourself."

"Ta-*chan*, you will take these for your twenty-ninth birthday, or I'll give them to your father."

"...if you do that, they'll only end up back in your hands via your prostitutes, or in the *sake*-merchant's. If you give them to me, I'll give them to the *oyabun* to pay down the debt."

"It's almost nothing... Why won't you accept a gift without—?"

"I don't deserve it!" Takana snapped.

Her mother took a step back, then put the box back in her sleeve. If she wasn't forced through her profession to wear make-up and look presentable during all operating hours, Chiyo would have bags under her eyes that betrayed how weary she'd become. She'd tried giving love and care to young women who perpetually wouldn't accept it. Takana was no different than Chiyo's charges on that account.

A commotion came from one of the filthier, lowest-ranked stalls. A girl was thrown out by someone. Her meager rags were torn up, and stray bits of hay stuck out of her hair.

"The clan's doing an inspection. You'd better get out of here," Chiyo urged.

"I'm not afraid of them..." Takana muttered.

"What did you—?"

One of Taiga's underlings stormed out of the stall, yelling at the young girl that Takana had run into the night before.

"What the hell is this? No one would ever spend one *ryō* for your ugly ass! Have you been holding out on Chiyo?"

The girl cowered. He delivered a kick to her stomach, then marched over to Chiyo, waving the *ryō* in her face.

"What are you going to do about this, Chiyo? She either stole this or she's not handing over the payments every morning like she's supposed to. You're not keeping your bitches in line!"

Before Chiyo could answer—and before Takana could decide whether or not she should speak up for the girl—Taiga and a few more of his underlings came into the central area, having finished their own rounds. Takana backed up, hoping to get out of sight before he noticed her, but she was a few steps too slow as he made quick eye contact. Taiga then demanded to know what the hell the commotion was about with his underling. After the relay, he loomed over Chiyo. Takana gripped the hilt of her *katana*. The creak of her fist tightening over it caught Taiga's attention again.

He smirked, then turned back to Chiyo.

"Did you know about this, whore-runner?"

"Of course not, sir."

"Do I need to station my men in this disgusting quarter to keep you and your whores in line?"

"No, sir. Please let me handle her. It won't happen again."

Taiga surveyed Takana while he addressed her mother.

"Show me. Handle her." A dangerous glint in his eye flashed at Takana before he turned back to Chiyo. "Prove to me the old man wasn't even more of a fool for allowing you to run this place to pay down your husband's debt."

Taiga didn't pick up on the pain behind Chiyo's eyes, but Takana knew it all too well. Chiyo raised her painted face and cleared her throat.

"For theft, she'll be paraded through the city naked."

Taiga laughed and shook his head.

"A whore of her status has no shame. Try again."

Chiyo grimaced. Takana wasn't sure if it was at being disregarded, or the awful suggestion she'd have to offer next to appease him.

"I...I will flog her. Thirty lashes."

The girl cried out and begged but one of the underlings kicked her back down into the mud and told her to shut up.

"A whore that can't earn for months while she heals isn't going to cut it, Chiyo. If that's the best you can come up with, maybe I'll have you whip the girl, and you can take her place in the hay stalls while she convalesces. You run a loose operation. It's clear it needs a man's oversight. This is your last warning before I start stationing men across the district."

Chiyo got on her knees to bow. Taiga put his muddy *geta* on her shoulder and kicked her away. The little box fell out of her sleeve and scattered its contents into the mud: three golden *ryō* coins. Taiga picked them up and smiled. He ambled over to Takana, lifting the *kasa* up so he could look into her eyes. They were furious, and the one was badly swollen from where he'd struck her. He wiped the coins off on the chest of her *haori*.

"And *you, ane-san*?" Venom dripped from his smile. "What would you do about this?"

"That's a stupid question, *ani-ki*. I'd kill all five of you and burn this place to the ground. But if I was someone like *you*..." Takana straightened her back, watching the rage build in his eyes, then she whispered, "...I'd rape them both."

Taiga blinked in surprise, and his fury turned to curiosity. Takana walked with purpose to the girl still cowering in the mud. She picked her up by the back of her rags and shoved her to the ground beside Chiyo, hiding a wince when a rag tore from her hand and exposed too much.

"Do it, *ani-ki*. You and the others."

Takana almost believed she'd bluffed the two women to safety—no one moved for a moment. But eventually Taiga grinned. It wasn't a solution he would have accepted from anyone else. The punishment was nothing to a whore, but it was everything to a daughter that would have to watch. Taiga saw an opportunity to hurt her, and he took it. He shoved her aside while three of the other men fell upon the muddy women. Two underlings held the women down by the shoulders while Taiga and the next high-est-ranked lieutenant positioned themselves, kneeling between the women's legs. The girl flailed futilely, while Chiyo braced to take it with quiet dignity.

The men slid down their *hakama*. As they were about to move in, Takana unsheathed her *daishō*. The man standing watch didn't react fast enough; too distracted to react at all. She held the end of the *katana* and *wakizashi* blades steady between both men's legs. The coldness of the steel froze them. She needed less than a flick of her wrist to castrate them.

"Are you insane?" Taiga seethed from his prone humiliation.

She couldn't see his face, but the hairs on the back of his neck raised and his skin burned bright red.

"You can't touch us. You'll be executed. Horribly. The old man won't be able to protect you anymore."

"Maybe today's the day I chose suicide over paying back the debt, *ani-ki*. You can either leave us to our jobs, or you can delight in my execution as a *kangan*."

The men holding down the two women got the message and let go. Chiyo helped the girl up and shuffled back against the wall of the office, unsure how the *yakuza* punks would take the massive hit to their pride. Takana acknowledged Chiyo's quiet plea to leave well enough alone but ignored it.

Once the two men stood and straightened out their clothing, Takana smirked at Taiga, matching the look he'd given her when he came upon them a few minutes before.

"I'll bet that's not how you dreamed I'd touch you there for the first time, *ani-ki*."

Taiga squared up, inches from her face. She straightened her posture and met his eyes with equal intensity. If he was intimidated by her, it was overpowered by his twisted sense of amusement. His rage morphed to mirth, which struck Takana as all the more dangerous.

"Enjoy your protection while it lasts, *ane-san*. Tetsuo won't live forever. You just bought yourself the most painful wedding night in history."

"Looking forward to it, my love," she called after him as the men turned to leave.

Out of their view, Takana let out all her breath, stumbling backward in shock. Chiyo and the girl caught and steadied her, although each of them were still shaking.

"For someone who's too good for my money, you sure bought something with it," Chiyo muttered.

Takana pulled out one of the cheap cigarettes from its pouch and lit it from a hanging lantern overhead.

"Rain's coming again, *kaasan*. I want to get on the road; put this shit behind me."

Why did she say that aloud to someone confined to the slums?

"Want to switch places?" she asked in order to put a smile on Chiyo's face.

"I'd be too afraid for my girls with how you'd run the place. Especially after that little display," Chiyo put her hand tenderly on Takana's swollen cheek. "The only thing that makes me happy anymore is knowing you get to live a life outside these walls. It's not the life any of us wanted, but I'd sooner die than see you in a cage."

"I will free you from yours, *kaasan*. I promise."

"Sure." Chiyo smiled facetiously. She'd resigned herself to her fate long ago. "Anyway, you came here for a job, didn't you? The baker's son didn't pay for two nights..."

Takana threatened the baker's son with far less theatricality and marched him to the red-light district to pay up. Once he parted with his coin, Takana nodded down the path at her mother before getting back on the road.

She pulled a small loaf of bread that she'd stolen from the bakery, hiding it in her sleeve, and took a few bites before returning it to the pocket. The rain began pouring in earnest as she walked along the *Nikkō Kaidō* south to Ishibashi. The route typically took about three hours, but with the rain and mud, she'd arrive closer to dinner time. That worked well enough for her—she could either solicit a dice game at a busy restaurant or force an establishment under the clan's protection to run one. She preferred the former because she could set a higher percentage of the take, but it was also riskier when the restaurant didn't have time to advertise the game beforehand to the right people. The spontaneous games often had the wrong people, and things could get even bloodier than that mess in Kasukabe.

When one traveled alone on the highway, it was important to watch one's back. Horses carrying merchants or *rōnin* sometimes hit pedestrians; the riders didn't look back and the walkers didn't get up again. Noble processions and *samurai* were often slower, but no less dangerous if one got too close to them as they passed in their columns. The best one could hope for was a kick further out of the way. Some *samurai* still practiced *tsujigiri* even though the abhorrent behavior had lessened in the previous century. They always claimed it was to test the sharpness of their blades. Some killed for no other reason than the foulness of their mood in the moment.

There was also the risk of highwaymen robbing travelers. They gave Takana a wide-enough berth because of her *daishō*, but most people couldn't afford them and travelled the highway at their own risk.

Takana noticed someone in a shroud behind her. A few kilometers later, they were still there. She was being followed, unskillfully. Whenever she turned her head to look back, the figure stopped. Their poor stealth skills weren't enough to worry her. For a moment she thought it could be a courier from Tetsuo, but a courier wouldn't keep such a distance, or stop when seen, if they wanted to be paid.

It was odd the figure didn't have an umbrella, or at least a hat. Through the rain it looked like their shroud was nothing more than a blanket. Takana peered ahead to see a pair of horses in full gallop racing in her direction. She backed off the path and watched them pass. The shrouded figure barely noticed them, raising its head and throwing itself out of the path at the last moment.

Takana grew tired of guessing who was following her and also pondering the "why." She trudged briskly down the road and stood over the figure, still laying in the mud. She couldn't see who was beneath the hood, but they saw her and cowered upon her approach. Takana unsheathed the *katana* and tapped against the body.

"Please don't hurt me," a frightened, familiar voice rose from the tattered heap.

Takana sheathed her weapon and picked the figure up, then pulled back the shroud. The girl who'd tried to hide the *ryō* coin—the girl Takana had given that very coin to outside her father's hovel—winced and braced, conditioned to expect punishment.

"Why are you following me?"

"I...I don't know. I heard your conversation with your mother, and...and I ran after my turn in the bath house."

"What were you expecting by following me?"

The girl looked puzzled, as if she never had the opportunity to expect anything but what was thrust into her. Her eyes watered, and she fell to her knees in supplication.

"Please take me with you. I have nowhere else to go."

"You can go back to the *yūkaku*. I'm not looking after you."

"I'm not asking you to. I'm... I can't take what they do to me anymore. I'm at the bottom of the ranks. I'm ugly and cheap, so the things I have to—"

"All of those women went through the same, at some point. You're not special."

"Don't you think I know that? I have to look at those beautiful faces every day and night, knowing I'll get passed over again and again until we're at capacity and some of the men have no other options."

"So, you think because of what you saw me do to those men, you'd just follow me, and I'd protect you from this shit world? Look at my face," Takana stooped down and lifted her kasa so the girl could see the bruises and swelling. "Does it look like I'm having an easier time than you? I'm trapped in a different kind of cage, but a cage no less."

"I'll earn my keep!" the girl pleaded as she got back to her feet.

"There's nothing I need from you. I've been working these roads for over eight years. You'd only be in my way."

She turned to walk away.

"Don't you get lonely out here?"

Takana paused.

"Not in any way *you* would be able to cure."

"That's not even... I can sew. I know that doesn't sound good, considering what I'm wearing, but... What about food? Look at you!" the girl reached out to open Takana's *haori*. "I can see your ribs. And your chest... I'll bet those were bigger when you were younger."

Takana closed the *haori* to cover her torso and scowled, eager to stop talking about it.

"Your mother keeps our diets top of mind. Men won't pay when they see them all shriveled up. See mine? I may be at the bottom of the ranks and too ugly for most, but these still earn."

Takana's stomach chimed in with a loud growl at the worst time, cutting her off from any further argument. The girl smiled as Takana sighed.

"What's your name?"

"Fusa."

"Alright, Fusa-*chan*. Another hour and we'll be in Ishibashi. Don't expect me to slow down for you."

Takana pulled out the remainder of the small loaf of bread and broke it in half, giving Fusa the unbitten end. She meant it to be a display that she didn't need anyone else to help her eat, but the sight of Fusa's naïve smile warmed her to the idea of a companion...at least until she proved herself not to be useful after all.

Scrimping and saving every coin in order to expedite paying off her father's debt often took precedence over her desire to eat. A rice ball here, a bit of bread there, even if spaced over a day or two, was all she needed. Fusa brought to Takana's attention her state of near starvation. She'd been using her figure to distract men while she dealt dice for so long... She didn't think it was anything but necessary in order to keep earning.

If she hadn't been neglecting her body, perhaps she could have been earning even more money.

After the bread was gone, Fusa asked how Takana knew Iwakuchi.

"...that was my useless father."

"Oh... I'm sorry."

"For what?" Takana asked.

"I'm not sure. It just felt right to say in the moment."

"If you don't have any reason to talk, it's okay to *not talk*."

"I'm sorry, Takana-*san*. I'll remember that."

As they walked in silence, Takana thought about meeting Fusa the first time, then the events of the morning with Taiga.

"Fusa-*chan*, what was your plan with that coin I gave you?"

"...I don't know. I'd never held a *ryō* before. Only the high-end girls get those. Last night, I held the coin in my hand beneath the hay, dreaming of something new—a different life. It made what was happening to me at that time hurt less."

Takana cringed, both for Fusa, and the quick, unwelcome thought of how it would feel if Taiga ever made good on his threat to marry her.

"I'm...sorry, Fusa-*chan*."

"For what?"

"It just felt right to say."

Chapter Four

Reverse Course

Dorobō: Thief—When the Edo period brought peace to the formerly warring nation, samurai were left masterless, wandering the land as Rōnin. Some became police or bodyguards, while others took on mercenary work. Still others roamed as highwaymen, robbing the main roads t hroughout the country.

June 8, 1708
Ishibashi, Tochigi Prefecture

TAKANA SURVEYED EACH OPEN RESTAURANT along the main road as dinner time began. Fusa grew restless as the glorious aromas wafted out into the air. The rain had finally died down, and the enticing smells overpowered the muddy thoroughfare. Takana stopped near an entrance, lit her second-to-last cigarette with the thin candle from her pouch and lantern, then walked on. Fusa grumbled but continued to tail her.

"Why aren't we stopping at any of these places, Takana-*san*?"

"I'm not looking for food."

"Aren't you hungry? I'm starving!"

"That bread wasn't enough?"

"Of course not! I didn't eat breakfast this morning. Because of *you*, I might add. Can't we at least buy some rice?"

"I don't have any money."

"What? How is that possible? All you do is make money! Your father says it all the—"

Takana wheeled on Fusa and stared her down. Fusa cowered and averted her gaze to the ground.

"You said you didn't know that was my father until I told you. Did you lie to me?"

"No, Takana-*san*! He never named you; he only said all his daughter did was earn money, but you...never earn...enough..." Fusa's timid voice trailed off as she realized she was relaying an insult.

Takana fumed at her father's words, not Fusa's honesty. She took a drag on her cigarette to turn her anger to smoke.

"Anyway... Maybe you can tell me what else he's said, later. Right now, I'm looking for work."

"As a waitress?"

"No. I'll walk up and down the road, looking for a full, loud restaurant with the most punks, hoodlums, and gangsters. Then I'll get a game started if the owners agree. I take my own percentage off the clan's cut of the House's winnings. I was here a few days ago at a protected House, but I'm going blind tonight."

After an hour of perambulating, one restaurant seemed to be full of the desired occupants. Takana went into an alley, where she adjusted her *sarashi* to accentuate her cleavage. Fusa pulled Takana's hands away and helped arrange it in a way that was flattering *and* comfortable. They went inside and sat close to the kitchen. She tilted the *kasa* to hide her bruised face and focus the eyes down, where she'd flung open the *haori* to hang off her shoulders.

When the head waitress came to them, Takana asked to speak with the owner privately. Fusa tried to order two bowls of rice, but Takana silenced her, bidding the waitress to ignore her and fulfill the previous request.

"They can take the price of the food out of your take, right?" Fusa asked, confused but hopeful.

"Yes. They could. But they often give me free food at the end of the night. Paying is unnecessary if you're patient."

"Okay, Takana-*san*. I'll remember that."

While they waited for the owner to come out to greet them, Takana pushed the *kasa* off onto her back, then pulled out the *kanzashi* holding her ponytail up. She balanced the *kanzashi* and a pair of *hashi* between her fingers, over and under, making the sticks appear like boats on floating waves. Fusa followed the display in awe. Takana put down the chopsticks, retrieving a pair of trick dice from the pouches around her thighs while keeping the show going in her other hand. She hid the dice in her palm and worked them into the base of the new bun she tied up in the *kanzashi* with added flourish.

Most of the men in the room were looking at her. One man sitting with his wife earned a slap on the arm. Takana pretended to sweat and aired out her *sarashi* playfully, seductively while she worked the next set of trick dice into the hidden pocket between her cleavage.

The owner tapped her on the shoulder. She smiled at the men before getting up and following him to the back room. She laid out the take and percentages and made sure the house had plenty of *sake* and *gyoza* to manipulate the mood as necessary. She requested to borrow a *kimono* and a place to keep her things. Finally, she asked that Fusa be allowed to help in the kitchen during the game.

While the back room was being set up for the event, Takana asked the head waitress to spread rumors of the game around the restaurant.

The game went off without a hitch. It was one of the best nights Takana had in a while, and by far the best in an unprotected house. Deep in the early morning, she changed back into her traveling outfit, pleased with the weight of the *ryō* in a small bag the owner supplied. She thought about celebrating with a pinch of the special tobacco when a commotion came from the kitchen.

Takana hurried to find Fusa cowering before the head waitress and owner, both furious. She had tried to sneak food and *sake* while going through the final clean up. It sat on a nearby table like a display of damnable evidence. Takana walked to the table and picked up a couple of pork buns and the *sake* bottle, asking if they were what Fusa tried to steal, to which the waitress nodded.

Takana grabbed Fusa by the hair and pushed her towards the entrance of the kitchen, then turned to face the owner and bowed parallel to the floor. It was good she could only see his feet, because he would have seen her eyes wet while she held the bag of *ryō* out for him. She sensed his hesitation—she'd made so much for his family that night—but she couldn't let his gratefulness absolve them of such dishonorable behavior. Takana apologized and demanded he take her percentage for the trouble they caused. When he wouldn't take it, she placed the bag on the floor and backed away while maintaining the bow.

She bumped into Fusa hiding around the corner, then grabbed her by the back of the neck and forced her outside. Takana dragged her by the elbow up the road while she cried and apologized, then threw her into an alley with an overhang to protect them from the rain that had kicked up again.

"Stop your crying!"

"I'm so sorry, Takana-*san*! I thought it would be covered, like you said—"

"It doesn't work like that. Most of the time it's freely offered. I never ask for anything from them but my take. It builds trust so the next time I come to town the owner will be *happy* to see my face. Now I can never set foot in that restaurant again."

"I'm so, *so* sorry, Taka—"

"Stop apologizing." Takana sighed. Of all the things she expected Fusa to do wrong, misinterpreting her words hadn't been one of them. "You screwed up. It's your first time. It won't happen again, will it?"

Fusa shook her head, then bowed down onto her knees. Takana tightened her lips so as not to smile and pulled a pork bun out of the sleeve of the *haori*.

"Here, Fusa-*chan*."

Fusa sat up from her bow and looked at the bun, wide-eyed. Takana offered it, then took out the other bun.

"How did you—?"

"If you're going to stick around with me, you're going to learn 'how.' Then I won't have to worry about you wasting my hard work."

Takana sat down against the building next to Fusa.

"This is going to be the most expensive thing I've eaten in my life…" Takana muttered before devouring it in a few quick bites.

Fusa ate hers slower, with more reverence than she had with the bread earlier in the day, then got up.

"Where are you going?" Takana asked.

"To find some water."

"We can look after sun-up."

"I'm thirsty after that bun…"

Takana reached into another pocket and pulled out the *sake* bottle. Fusa sat back down and smiled that cute, naïve way that Takana couldn't help forgiving.

A headache pounded against Takana's temples as she pushed herself up from the dirt. Fusa wasn't lying next to her anymore. Panic rose as she gained clarity, no longer feeling the familiar weight of her tools. Her pockets were empty. The *daishō* were gone. A stabbing pain struck her heart when her hand found nothing in the pocket that housed her grandfather's *kiseruzutsu*. Everything could be replaced but that. She leaned back into the building, holding her forehead with her hand, cooling off her rage. It was gone, but…what could she do? She sniffed to temper the feeling of loss. Crying about it wasn't going to get it back.

The only things she still had were the clothes she wore and the *kasa* hanging off her back. She tried recalling anything from when they started drinking the *sake*, but she'd fallen asleep a short time later. She almost never drank but had felt so bad about losing the money that she welcomed the opportunity to fog up her mind. Was Fusa the thief? Takana threw that idea out—there was no way the girl could have stolen so much without waking Takana with her clumsy hands.

The tracks in the alleyway led out into the thoroughfare to be lost among hundreds of other prints from merchants and horses that had come through since sun-up. Takana fumed and repositioned her *kasa* over her ponytail. She didn't think she'd get anywhere searching the town; she could be searching for days. Without her trick dice, it would be a waste of time trying to run more games and even *think* about replacing all she'd lost.

Dejected, she walked towards the town gates. She'd go back to Tetsuo, *kasa*-in-hand, and ask for a small loan to get back on track. It infuriated her to have to add to the debt. It was worse that she may never see her grandfather's *kiseru* again.

If only she'd accepted her mother's gift the day before, none of it would have happened. Fusa wouldn't have—

"Psst! Takana-*san*!" a voice came from a thicket of bushes outside the gates.

Takana approached and was surprised to be happy to see Fusa. She had left the blanket behind in the alley and only wore her shabby, tattered, low-rank prostitute clothing, held together by weak, sloppy threading.

"What are you doing here? Why did you leave?"

"This morning, I woke up to someone leaning over you. I didn't know what to do, so I pretended to be asleep. Soon his hands were all over me, too, but I didn't have anything to take, so he left. I followed him to a little hut hidden in this forest. I was just coming back to get you when I saw you approaching the gate."

Takana put her hand on Fusa's shoulder.

"Take me there."

They hiked for a couple of kilometers before the hut came into view. It wasn't much bigger than her father's back-alley room. There could be no more than two people living there. Takana hoped it was only one, at least until she got the *daishō* back. She picked up a thick tree branch and flung it into the little clearing in front of the hut's entrance to catch the occupant's attention.

A man about her age emerged, carrying the *daishō* in each hand, still within their scabbards. When no one else came out behind him, Takana materialized from the trees and squared up at the edge of the worn dirt path. He yelled at her to leave or he would cut her in half.

"*Dorobō*!" she yelled back. "I will have my things returned. Give them over and I won't report you to the *samurai*."

"They aren't your things anymore."

"They are until I'm dead."

Her expression seemed to frighten him, even though he was the one holding her blades. She mimicked Taiga's venomous smile, hoping to push the man to turn tail and run.

He hesitated and took a step back before standing his ground. His fear turned from desperation to determination—clearly intimidation through expression wasn't her forte.

"I need your things. You can't stop me."

He unsheathed the *katana* and squared up, then waited as if she was going to decide to walk unarmed, torso-bared, into his range.

"I can wait here all day, too, thief. But I'd rather be on my way. So, either charge me or move aside while I take back what's mine."

His grip wavered and shook. It was easy to tell he'd never killed anyone before. She surmised he must be new to crooked life; perhaps he'd taken a fall from a formerly comfortable one. Most thieves she'd come across at least knew basic weapon-use, and they never bothered talking to their marks.

Takana moved towards him. His shaking increased, and the katana dipped. As she took a step past him, his breath changed—a sharp inhale. A coward, waiting to hit her from behind; at least that part of being a thief he'd picked up on already.

She turned and ducked so the *kasa* took the brunt of the downward swing. Fusa cried out from the clearing's edge. The blade clanged against one of the many broken pieces of former *katana* that Inoue had inlaid beneath the bamboo covering. All the attack did was knock the *kasa* askew, but Takana fell to the ground to convince him it had been a fatal blow. Her hand fell onto the *wakizashi* that he'd dropped at his feet when he'd unsheathed the *katana*.

Fusa let out a desperate cry and jumped onto the man's back, pounding her fists on his head. Takana shot to her feet and grabbed the thief's sword hand while bringing the *wakizashi's* blade to his throat.

"Drop it," she said.

"Takana-*san*!" Fusa got down from the man's back and picked up the discarded *katana*.

"Go see if my things are inside. I'll keep him out here."

"Please don't—!"

Takana pressed the blade closer to his throat.

"I've heard enough out of you. Another word and you get a new mouth."

Fusa went into the hut and rustled around some things, then gasped. Takana looked towards the entrance as Fusa came out empty-handed.

"Takana-*san*, you need to see this..."

"What am I going to find in there, thief?"

His eyes pleaded with her, but he didn't speak. She led him to the entrance and peered inside. Most of her possessions were there, but a little further past was a basket. Takana sighed.

"Is that baby really yours? Or did you steal it, too? Answer me, thief!"

"Um, Takana-*san*," Fusa said, "you told him not to say another word."

Takana lowered the *wakizashi* and loosened her grip on the man's clothes. He covered the basket with his torso.

"She's mine," the thief said. "Her mother died a month ago. Killed by a wild boar while foraging for mushrooms."

"*Kuso*!" Takana swore as she put her things respectively back in their pouches or hanging off her belt. "Where the hell is the *kiseru*, thief?"

His expression changed, indicating he meant to keep it, but then thought better of hiding it and pointed at a box in a corner. Fusa found it and brought it to Takana. She ran her fingers over the ornate, colorful draconic patterns and lost some of her edge as she remembered what it was like to love someone so dearly.

"I'm sorry to hear about your wife, *Dorobō-kun*," Takana said as she left the hut, Fusa trailing close behind.

"Shinkichi."

Takana turned to find him standing in the entrance with the baby in his arms.

"My name is Shinkichi. Not 'thief.'"

"I don't care," Takana said as she walked away.

Once they got back to the road, Fusa tugged on Takana's sleeve, biting her lip. Takana shot a look around for danger. When she didn't find any, Fusa only shook her head.

"Takana-*san*... When I saw the baby, it looked...sick. Its color was wrong."

"So what?" Takana muttered as she lit her last cigarette using a nearby brazier.

"So...that's it? You'll turn your back to—"

"Turn my back to a baby? It's not mine. It's not yours. Mind your own business. That's how you survive out here with no money. No one cares about us. Let it go. We need to focus on earning back what you lost last night."

"But..."

"Enough. Either follow me and shut up about it or go save their lives yourself. I hope you don't run across an orphanage on the way."

Takana walked back into Ishibashi. There were no sounds of footsteps close behind. She turned towards a restaurant and looked inside, then pretended to check for a pebble between her foot and *geta*. Fusa wasn't in her periphery, either.

The rational part of her laughed callously; that she cared. The dumb girl had been following her for a day. She'd lost a large amount of coin. She couldn't be trusted not to blow their cover until she had serious training.

Indeed, Fusa'd had a hard life. Takana would never deny that for any of the *yūjo*. Though she was barely over twenty by the looks of her, she'd been used in every conceivable way already. But...she hadn't been broken, like so many of the other prostitutes that Takana came across when she visited her mother. Fusa's smile was never forced—she had genuine cheer left in her, even after people had tried to beat it out of her. She still had dreams, or at least the kernel of a dream that told her to run away, follow Takana, and find something—anything—better.

Takana hated to admit that it was kind of fun having someone walking with her on the road. The *sake* was so much more enjoyable with someone to share the bottle, even if it was from a dirt alleyway. Fusa had made her *forget* she was eating, drinking, and sleeping on the ground.

Takana sighed, flicked away half of the cigarette, and turned back towards the forest.

Outside the hut, Fusa sat on the step holding the baby with Shinkichi beside her, cooing at it, making an oblivious fool of herself. Shinkichi had fallen under her spell, as well. Takana could see why he'd have been married—his smile conveyed he was a good husband and father.

The smile disappeared when Takana approached.

"Please! You got everything! I promise! The dice, the cigarette, the *kiseru*! I'm not—"

Takana held up her hand and tried smiling, knowing how forced it must look. She was out of her element and it was uncomfortable.

"Look, you know we don't have any money, or you wouldn't have taken everything else. I can't offer you anything, but I know of a doctor in the back alleys of Utsunomiya. Take your baby there. Tell him that Chiyo sent you, and it belongs to one of her girls. The doctor will help you for free."

Shinkichi regarded her with justifiable skepticism.

"Why would he help me for free?"

"Because Chiyo pays him a monthly fee to help...others. Fusa-*chan*, has the doctor seen you?"

"Many times..." Fusa said with a pained, far-off look.

"Tell the doctor the baby belongs to Fusa, if he insists to know which girl the baby's connected to."

"Why are you...helping me?" Shinkichi asked, his tone changing from suspicion to awe as it sunk in that Takana wasn't playing a trick on him as payback.

"I don't know, honestly. Thank Fusa-*chan*. The walk is about three hours. Can you make it there by yourself? I'm afraid playing bodyguard to a broke thief and sick baby aren't in my plans for the rest of the day.

"Fusa-*chan*, I'm going back into town. Take Shinkichi-*kun* to Utsunomiya, or you can find me in Ishibashi tonight in one of the restaurants."

Takana didn't wait to hear which option she'd pick, or care to linger any longer on Shinkichi's wet, thankful eyes. She hiked back to Ishibashi.

It wasn't long after she crossed through the entrance again that Fusa appeared, trailing closely behind.

"Fusa-*chan*, if you're going to walk with me, walk to my side. I'm not nobility, I'm not *samurai*. You're not my property."

It was a little annoying, though a little cute, that Fusa brought herself up to Takana's periphery but didn't align herself completely side-to-side. Fusa's lifetime of subservience would be hard to break, but Takana had a long road ahead of her, and she was growing fond of having company while she travelled it.

Chapter Five

Melee

Doku: Shinobi used poison in many situations, using various natural ingredients, such as strychnine, cyanide from several types of fruit seeds, poisonous leaves from tomato and rhubarb, pufferfish venom, and the deadly amanita phalloides, a mushroom ten times more powerful than cyanide. The poisons were administered in many ways, including dipping weapons and slipping into food and drink.

June 9, 1708
Koganei, Tochigi Prefecture

THOUGH FUSA PROVED TO BE a pleasant companion outside of her clumsiness in the kitchens, Takana was even more thankful to have another person carrying the weight of the coin. The only problem was that Fusa didn't have the best clothing to hide much.

During a stop in Koganei, Takana chose one of the roughest bars in the region to run her game. She singled out an aggressive *yakuza* thug from another clan. She played up his frustration throughout the game with smirks and sneers, using her trick dice to make sure he lost, even though it resulted in a smaller percentage of winnings for her in the end.

After midnight, once all the other patrons had trickled out, they left the bar with their spoils. Fusa carried the bag of *ryō* as she walked by Takana's side, still a step behind. The *yakuza* thug paced in the street, waiting for her. Takana grabbed Fusa's sleeve, pulled her into an alleyway and told her to wait down at the further end.

The man followed them into the alley, stopping halfway when he saw Takana squared up at the end. The brim of her *kasa* covered her eyes, and a sheet of rain poured off the edge. She didn't need to see to be able to follow his footsteps, though, and she had learned long ago that men acted foolishly when they thought they weren't "seen."

He charged. His footsteps grew closer. Fusa gasped. Takana reached up for one of the loops hanging from her *kasa*, pulled on the rope, and brought a *kunai* down from its hidden compartment beneath the rim. She looked up only enough to locate his feet and threw the blade through the wood of his *geta*.

The thug crashed at her feet. Fusa emerged from the corner to grab the *katana* out of his hand. Takana's *katana* was already held down to the man's neck as he whimpered.

"Fusa-*chan*, take his *haori*."

She obliged.

"*Kuso ama-tachi*! Do you know who I run with?" the thug said through clenched teeth.

Takana used the point of the *katana* to push back the man's robes, revealing his tattoos.

"Shingo-*kai*. Your clan is shit. Your tattoos aren't finished, so you're still low in the ranks. No one will care, except they'll laugh that two women robbed you of your *haori*. Were I you, I would keep my mouth shut about this, or you'll never rank up. Do I make myself clear, *ani-ki*?"

She delighted in flustering *yakuza* scum by using their own terms against them. Though she would never be accepted in her own clan's ranks, no matter how useful she proved herself to be—even if she gained high-enough regard to be respected above the vapid, do-nothing *yakuza* wives—she knew how much reverence the region had for her clan. She'd developed a certain pride when she flashed her tattoo in the back rooms, in a position to decide the monetary fates of others.

It didn't bother her in the least to humiliate and rob them. She knew what they did to earn their way, knew what they did all day—dirty work and heinous play—acting as if the world belonged to them.

It appeared Fusa knew that as well, as she took the opportunity to kick the man in the face.

"*Yakuza* asshole!" she spat.

Takana raised her eyebrow. Fusa grinned at the first act of power she'd ever experienced in her life.

"Don't take it too far. Kill one of them and it's a whole different story."

"Okay, Takana-*san*. I'll remember that."

Takana couldn't put her finger on why she found it so cute that Fusa kept saying that. The burden of teaching the girl could only get lighter if Takana saw that wide, careless smile more often.

On the road south towards Oyama, Takana and Fusa walked off and sat next to a tree, snacking on rice balls that they'd earned after their second night in Koganei. After eating, Fusa tried waving half-a-*hashi* over and through her fingers.

"You don't really need to know how to do that yet, Fusa-*chan*. Start smaller. Here." Takana pulled out a thin glass vial from one of her pockets. "Practice keeping this hidden behind your fingers. Move them from trough to trough. Hide it in your palm."

"What good will that do if no one can see—?"

"What I was doing with the *kanzashi* was to distract the eye. First, you learn how to keep things hidden. Distraction comes later."

Fusa practiced keeping the vial hidden. With each clumsy fumble, her determination intensified, which brought out a small smile from Takana.

"What is this for?" Fusa asked before dropping the vial to the ground, then picking it back up.

"Poison powder. It doesn't slosh around like a liquid, giving away the movements behind your fingers."

"You poison people?" Fusa's face twisted in disgust.

"No... There's no reason to do that for my job. I only practice it because..."

How much of her life did she want to share with Fusa? Often—usually after Taiga struck Takana—she fantasized about poisoning him on their "wedding night." If she could manage to slip it in his *sake* unnoticed at the ceremony, before he could enact his threats in the bedroom, it would be the happiest day of her life indeed. It would have to be a perfect move. She practiced it while resting on the side of the road.

"Because what?"

"I'm...not sure... I guess you'd also have to ask why I spent most of my life learning how to fight. I haven't used nearly half the moves I was taught by my *sensei,* but if I needed it, that knowledge is there."

"I think I understand. Some of the friendlier higher ranks in the *yūkaku* would share techniques that sounded less painful. I never once got to use them, though. Being ranked lower, there're only a couple ways men use me."

The conversation had grown far too awkward. Though they both had hard lives, Takana would choose her own infinitely over Fusa's, or any other prostitute's unfortunate existence. She didn't quite understand how Fusa could be as upbeat and curious after going through all that. Most girls were broken within months.

Takana dozed off and on for about an hour while Fusa played with the vial. People passed on the road, taking no interest in them. Takana noticed a man tailing a woman carrying a large bag. She knew what was going to happen but didn't want to involve herself when she was carrying so many *ryō* of her own.

Fusa had no such preoccupation. When the man snatched the bag from the woman and ran out into a rice paddy, Fusa yelled after him and made to stand up. The woman looked in the direction of Fusa's exclamation. Takana sighed and lifted herself up by Fusa's shoulder to keep her seated.

Takana shook off the heavy *haori* and burst across the road into the rice paddy. She ran the way Tomoe-*sensei* taught her while carrying *daishō,* freed from the awkwardness of running in a full *hakama.* Hers was torn and frayed above the knees, allowing her to run faster than she ever could during training.

The *kasa* blew off her head but the chinstrap caught on her neck, and it fell onto her back. When she got within a couple meters of the fleeing thief, she unfastened the *katana* but kept it in the scabbard and threw it into his legs. He tripped over it and landed face first into the mud walkway lining rows of rice paddies.

Not ready or willing to hear another sob story, Takana snatched the bag and *katana* and ran back towards the road. When she reached the edge of the field, she looked back, and the thief was already gone. Fusa waited next to the victim, who bowed deeply in appreciation at Takana's effort. When she rose, the woman beckoned them all to get off the road so they might speak further out of the dangers of traffic.

"Thank you so much. Both of you."

The woman's reaction to seeing Takana's tattoo was so unusual that it gave her pause. Most people acquired a fearful or distrustful look when they saw her markings, but the woman seemed fascinated.

"Kochiya-*kai?* Is that your clan? Are you married to one of them?"

Takana slipped the *haori* back on with help from Fusa, then lowered her shoulder so the woman could get a closer look at her markings.

"My connection to them is complicated. I'm more interested in how you so easily recognized the patterns."

Without elaborating, the woman continued in her observations.

"One doesn't often see a frog and *bakeneko* together. I'm guessing you earn a lot of money for them, signified by the frog. The *bakeneko,* though... Seems dangerous to display that to your own clan..."

"Dangerous?" Fusa asked as she leaned in to get a closer look. "Why's that?"

Takana pulled the fabric back over her shoulder to put an end to the conversation.

"Which clan do you work with?" Takana asked the woman.

"Oh, I don't. But there are a lot of individual members where I work. There's a kind of truce, to protect the business."

"Do you work at a restaurant?"

The woman made sure no one was nearby on the road, then untied the bag Takana had retrieved from the thief. Fusa peeked into it, then promptly turned around and threw up. Takana raised her eyebrows, regarding the woman more seriously. She was a couple years older but looked like any other peasant walking the *Nikkō Kaidō*.

"Bounty hunter?"

The woman nodded and tied the bag closed.

"Ten *ryō* per head."

"You ever take them alive?"

"If the client asks, sure."

"You almost lost your heads. Is there some kind of recovery fee?"

"There would have been, if you hadn't just confirmed you set that whole thing up."

Takana stared into the woman's accusing eyes. She hadn't wanted to get involved in the first place and now she had to defend herself. Instead, she shook her head while rolling her eyes, then brushed hard past the woman's shoulder, getting back on the path towards Oyama.

After a few minutes, Fusa caught up and tugged on Takana's sleeve.

"I told her the truth, and she believed me after I said we don't want her money. Then I asked for information about that business she was talking about. She gave me the address."

Takana had noticed Fusa's eyes lighting up after hearing the price per head, miraculously recovering from the unexpected, grotesque sight of them. Takana whapped the back of Fusa's head.

"I see what you're thinking, Fusa-*chan*. I'm no killer."

"Are you sure? After seeing you fight since Utsunomiya—"

"Out of the question. I'll stick to dice."

"She said they take some alive, though... Doesn't hurt to check it out, right?"

"It might, if she's correct about all the other clans that could be there. Maybe you can look into it while I visit a *dōjō*?"

Fusa relayed the location again before they parted within the city gates, a worrying level of excitement in her voice. Takana pinched a bit of the special tobacco into the *kiseru* and smoked while walking the streets. It soothed her travel-weary bones and readied her mind for training.

Deep within the city was a *dōjō* she frequented often. The landscaping was exquisite, but Takana waited outside the gates. One of the men cleaning the wooden veranda noticed her and nodded, then went inside. Takana walked to an open area off the road nearby, removed the *daishō* from her hips along with the *haori*, and waited for a few minutes.

The student came out with four others, all carrying their wooden practice swords. Takana bowed to the eldest student, the one she hoped would come out, then offered a *ryō* coin from her hidden-percentage fund. She maintained relationships with at least one *dōjō* per town along the *Nikkō Kaidō*. Most of them didn't allow women to train, but there were a few with open-minded students who understood that battles weren't exclusively the domain of men, and wisely viewed any type of practice as valuable. Even if they could only fight with her off the premises to avoid angering the *dōjō* masters, she didn't complain about the arrangement or hush payment.

To keep up the relationships, she never stormed the *dōjō* in challenge, or sought to humiliate anyone. She needed the practice, not the prestige or pride of beating a man. Humility and supplying gold to poor students were the best ways to foster her training.

The elder student offered one of their wooden swords, and she took it reverently. Once the swords were raised and the pomp finished, she didn't hold back, and neither did they. She recognized four of the five students from her last visit. They already knew how dangerous she was and provided almost no openings for her to attack. The unfamiliar student "died" within seconds.

After a few hours of training, progressing from one-on-one to many-on-one, she offered another *ryō* in thanks and handed back the practice sword. They all wore new bruises on their arms, shoulders, and backs. Takana was grateful for every throbbing welt she received and considered them new, valuable lessons in survival.

She noticed their disappointment when she covered her torso with the *haori*. Some of the more dedicated students didn't get out much, it seemed.

The eldest student, Sōkichi, was closest to her age and acted more courteously, averting his gaze unless they fought. He treated her with respect, as an equal, since they'd first clashed, years before. He'd never held back, as if she were an actual *samurai* worthy of that respect. Initially overpowering, she grew to deal with him better, and that knowledge saved her life more than once in alley fights with disgruntled gamblers and *rōnin*. Tomoe-*sensei* could only train her so much without live battle.

The students bowed to leave. Takana asked Sōkichi to wait a moment. He handed his and her practice sword to another, as well as the two *ryō* coins.

"Sōkichi-*san*, thank you for training me today." Takana bowed again. "Can I ask for your help locating a building?"

"Certainly, Gozen-*san*."

He guided her to the address the woman on the road had given. Fusa stood outside and approached them once she saw Takana. Takana introduced Sōkichi and Fusa. Fusa was conditioned to flatter and fawn over men, but Sōkichi's good looks and strong shoulders seemed to elicit a genuine attraction on top of the usual forced formalities. He remained stoic through her blather, only reacting to thank her for her many compliments. His eyes flitted to Takana as he returned Fusa's flattery.

"Thank you, Sōkichi-*san*, for the escort. Let me pay you for your time—"

He held up his hand to stop her from reaching into her *haori*.

"You've paid enough today. But allow me to continue the escort if you plan to go inside that building. It's a rough place, I've heard."

Takana already recognized some of the men entering and exiting—*yakuza* thugs, *rōnin*, and other uncouth men she'd hosted at dice throughout the region. She didn't see anyone from her own clan, thankfully. She wasn't in the mood to come across one of Taiga's hangers-on, or worse, lieutenants. Not that the other men in the building were any less dangerous, but she preferred the devils she didn't know.

Upon entering, a blast of thick tobacco smoke hit them. It hung in the air, a cloud disguising the faces of those standing. It seemed if you wanted to speak to someone, you had to be sitting at a table with them. Waitresses served all sorts of food to the tables, including some of Takana's favorite items, making her mouth water. Fusa wiped her mouth with the back of her sleeve.

Loud and boisterous noise filled the place, more than any gambling room she'd come across. Men and women spread throughout the room while citizens of all social classes solicited the people sitting at the tables. The lower-class citizens were despondent, unable to afford the mercenaries. They begged with pity and sympathy over coins, to which nearly all mercenaries are immune.

One such peasant woman shouted at a large, boorish man as he exited the room they had been occupying. He was still putting his clothes back on while he walked away, ignoring her. She followed and cursed him for promising to help her after she "paid," then reneging after the act. He laughed on. When she put hands on him, he backhanded her, then continued back to his table where a few similar-looking men joined in laughing with him.

Fusa took a step towards the woman before Takana grabbed her sleeve and pulled her back.

"Stop making other people's problems your own. I'm already regretting where your latest act of compassion has led us."

As they walked deeper into the room, the familiar clacking of dice in a cup came from behind one of the sliding doors, followed by the mixed cries of victory and defeat after the cup slammed to the table. The sounds of various games of chance came from the other rooms lining the main space.

A man crashed through one of the sliding doors, followed by the man that must have thrown him. They wrestled on the ground in front of Takana. Sōkichi grasped Fusa's shoulders and pulled her away from the fray.

The fighting men rolled into a table, knocking expensive-looking food all over the floor. More joined the scrum. In the chaos, Takana spotted the man that had cheated the peasant woman, about to slam his fist into a much smaller man's face. He raised his arm, then cried out. He reached behind, trying to remove the *tantō* sticking out of his back, courtesy of that same peasant woman.

A high-pitched note from a *shakuhachi* pierced the din of the melee. Punches stopped flying, and people picked themselves up—except for the man who regretted the way he treated women in the afterlife.

A man lowered the *shakuhachi,* then stood at attention to the side of the top of a grand set of stairs. An elegant, middle-aged woman appeared from one of the rooms. She overlooked the floor below from the railing. She glanced at the dead man for a brief moment, then addressed the room.

"It appears a spot at a table has opened. Spread the word that the table will be filled after one week, and the mercenary that offers the highest payoff to the Inn will earn it. Money is money, I care not how you get it. Happy hunting."

The woman disappeared back into her room and chatter picked up all around them. A few people bolted for the door, eager to get a head start on collecting funds to buy in. Not knowing what any of that meant, Takana decided she'd seen enough of the place. It was time to leave.

She motioned towards the entrance with her head and the other two nodded. Before they could step outside, a woman appeared to block their path. She was going to ask them something. Even if Takana wanted to hear no part of any offer, Fusa would be all ears.

Chapter Six

Fake Estate

Kunoichi no Jutsu : Evidence came to light in the late 17th century of female shinobi. Their training and activities could often differ from their male counterparts, but they were no less deadly and effective. In fact, they were even more feared because they could disguise themselves as any form of harmless woman in order to gain access to places shinobi couldn't, assassinating high-status men and women in almost any setting. Some scholars believe there were no female shinobi—only "women b ehaving as women."

June 10, 1708
Oyama, Tochigi Prefecture

THE WOMAN WAS A COUPLE years younger than Takana and wore her burnt orange hair up in a high ponytail. In the few steps from Takana's periphery to where she blocked their path, her nimbleness was evident. Takana tensed up in case the woman meant to rob them. Only thieves and *shinobi* moved like that.

"Greetings, travelers! Leaving so soon?" The woman smiled, but Takana couldn't tell if there was any venom behind it.

"Yes, I think we've had enough," Fusa piped up from between Takana and Sōkichi.

"You certainly look like this isn't your kind of place. But *this one*," she said while looking Takana over, "I think you could do very well here."

"I'm not interested. I don't kill for money."

"Neither do I, my lovely, bruised friend. There's more than one way to make money for the House. I happen to know of one such opportunity. Would you like to hear it?"

"The lady said she's not interested," Sōkichi said. "Please step aside and allow us to leave."

"Oh, sorry! I'm not trying to intimidate you. I simply know a thief's hands when I see them, and the clink of all those coins prove you're an exceptional one."

"She's amazing." Fusa beamed.

Takana closed her eyes. She didn't appreciate Fusa speaking for her, but her innocence was hard to get too worked up over.

The woman smiled at the exchange. The mirth behind her eyes shone through, and Takana relaxed.

"I guess...there's no harm in listening."

Her smile widened, and she bowed formally in greeting.

"My name is Natsu Jingū. It's a pleasure to meet you."

They each introduced themselves, then Natsu motioned for them to follow her outside. Fusa's stomach growled loud enough to hear in the cacophony of noise emanating from the Inn. Natsu went back inside, motioning to a waitress and holding up fingers in some sort of code. They moved to the veranda and took in the fresh smell of rain that absorbed the overwhelming mixture of tobacco smoke. Takana loved tobacco but didn't enjoy all the different aromas blending together.

She didn't want to use up the special tobacco so soon, but she needed a cheap cigarette after being in that room.

"I don't suppose you smoke, Natsu-*san*?"

She shook her head and gave a little sneer at the thought. Takana shrugged and leaned back against the wall as the waitress rounded the corner with four seaweed-wrapped rice balls. Natsu paid, then whispered something in the waitress's ear. She nodded, handed over a pair of cigarettes from within her apron, and left. Natsu passed them to a grateful Takana. Fusa and Takana ate their rice balls hastily, but Takana could tell they were much higher quality than the end-of-the-night, stale rice balls they were often gifted after the dice games.

Sōkichi ate his reverently, while Natsu split hers and gave a half each to Takana and Fusa. Fusa devoured it without hesitation while Takana held up her hand in refusal so Natsu could at least partake.

"Alright, Natsu-*san*, before we start incurring even more debt, what's this opportunity you mentioned?"

"That's a unique way of describing a gift. Well, there's an estate between Ishibashi and Utsunomiya, owned by a noble courtier. He posts a few guards outside at night or when he's at court. I've seen many boxes and bags change hands at the gates—from all kinds of people. I disguised myself as a male courier and was allowed to carry a heavy box inside a storage area. From what I saw, there were expensive goods and chests I believe to be full of *ryō* inside."

Fusa's eyes widened while Sōkichi furrowed his brow.

"That's...not the kind of thieving I do," Takana said.

"I only need your help subduing the guards. And perhaps your friends here can help carry out the goods?"

"What's our part of the take?"

Natsu looked around the veranda's corner to make sure no one was eavesdropping.

"Do you understand what a spot at one of those tables means? You didn't seem to when the Mistress made the announcement. You can pick and choose mercenary jobs. You kick ten percent to the Inn and keep the rest. I've been here for a few days looking for a partner to help take this estate, but everyone wants too much.

"Help me with this, and I'll grant you three favors once I get a spot at a table."

Takana was taken aback by the suggestion of such an odd payment. Natsu seized on the hesitation to say "no" to the offer.

"I *knew* that would get your attention. As soon as you came in the door, I saw you were different from all the other lowlives and bloodthirsty mercs that frequent the Inn."

"I'm not much higher than any other lowlife," Takana said.

She planned to say "no" next, but Fusa interrupted her.

"That's not true, Takana-*san*."

Natsu offered to give them time to talk it over then come back in a few minutes. Takana lit the second cigarette and leaned over the railing.

"What do you think, Sōkichi-*san*?"

He folded his arms and breathed, deep and calm.

"If you decide to help Natsu, I'll join you. It would be nice to take a break from studying and practice. I've been at it for three weeks straight now. Anyway, favors are a valuable thing to have—from the right people. I'm unsure if she's one of them. I can't get a read on her."

"I like her."

"You seem to like everyone, Fusa-*chan*."

"Not everyone..." Fusa trailed off. Takana regretted forgetting about Fusa's profession.

The only favor Takana could think of asking for would be coin to pay down the debt to her clan. The closer she got to the end... It might be nice to have an option in her back pocket to expediate the final stretch to the finish line.

...Assuming Natsu wasn't exaggerating or outright lying about the lucrativeness of the enterprise on the other side of the wall: The Inn. There was always the chance that whatever they stole still wouldn't be enough to earn a seat at the table. It was a lot of effort for potentially nothing in return.

When Natsu came back, Takana stipulated that Natsu must share half of the take if she didn't win her place at a table, otherwise they agreed on the three favors if she did. Natsu eagerly accepted.

It was a six-hour trek back to Ishibashi. Natsu's fingers were even more nimble and gifted than Takana's, and she taught Fusa several beginner sleight-of-hand tricks while they walked north on the *Nikkō Kaidō*. Takana and Sōkichi practiced swordplay with their blades sheathed. When it rained, Natsu shared her umbrella with Sōkichi while Fusa huddled close to Takana under the umbrella-like *kasa* on her head.

In Ishibashi, Natsu stopped outside a public bathhouse.

"This is the last of my coin," she said while dividing it among the four of them. "But we need to be clean before we get to the estate. Don't want the guards to smell us. Even in all this rain I can smell all of us."

Inside the bathhouse, Natsu gasped when she saw Takana and Fusa's bodies. Bruises and scars from practice, duels, and years of beatings from Taiga and her father covered Takana. Fusa's scars told an incoherent story of abuse for most of her life. Natsu bore no such hardships on her body, and she seemed embarrassed to be in their presence, whereas Fusa looked upon her, envious. If only she were half as attractive and clean as Natsu, perhaps she'd have been treated better in the red-light district. Getting beaten for being "worth less" was a vicious cycle to which Fusa had fallen victim.

The hot water stung Takana's fresh scrapes and bruises, but soon her whole body relaxed beneath the surface. She craved the special tobacco to complete the calming experience, but she was already pushing her luck. If an average citizen came in to find her *irezumi*, they'd get thrown out by the bathhouse staff. When she allowed herself to dream of a life out from under the thumb of her clan, a private *onsen* that she could use however she liked was always part of her vision.

Natsu stared at the tattoo while she relaxed on the other side of the bath but said nothing. Fusa fell asleep, slipping down until her face hit the water and she splashed awake. Natsu laughed and Takana couldn't help smiling, partially because of Fusa's theatrics, but mostly because she couldn't believe she never tried to recruit a traveling companion before. Loneliness on the road was almost as crushing as the debt that drove her to walk it.

They met with Sōkichi outside and Natsu led them out of the town towards the estate. A kilometer away from their target destination, Natsu stopped near a thicket of trees and bushes. She beckoned for them to crawl inside, then moved some loose shrubbery to reveal a hole hiding a cloth bag.

"Sōkichi-*san*, can you turn around, please?" Natsu asked.

He complied, and she unwrapped the bag to reveal a black *kunoichi* outfit with a belt of *shuriken* and *kunai* lined up evenly. Natsu changed out of her traveling clothes. She tied on wooden slats with sharp points to the back of the forearms and side of the calves that could be used as climbing tools, or weapons if the need arose. She checked the sharpness of a *tantō* and fastened it to her lower back inside its sheath.

She left the head-covering off for the moment and allowed Sō-kichi to turn around.

"Now, you two," she said to Fusa and Takana. "There's no way they won't be able to hear all that coin clattering in your *haori*. Deposit your coins in this bag and we'll keep them hidden in here."

Fusa complied immediately, but Takana didn't like it.

"Why do I get the feeling we're getting played? You could have been playing us since you saw how our jackets were weighed down when we entered the Inn."

Natsu looked into Takana's eyes with what seemed like true sincerity. Assessing the mood of the group, she met Sōkichi's eyes, Fusa's, then landed back on Takana's.

"I promise on all the lives of my family, I will not rob you."

Takana still hesitated despite Natsu's voice cracking in the middle—the robbery of her most precious possession was still fresh in her mind. But that thief, Shinkichi, had proven to be desperate, not dastardly. For some reason Takana couldn't quite understand, she wanted to believe Natsu would prove her mistrust wrong. Takana removed the *haori* and placed it in the bag. Her pouches were tied tightly enough at her thighs that nothing else would make a sound on her unless the scabbards of the *daishō* clacked together.

Sōkichi only had on a simple warrior's practice garb and his personal *daishō*. Fusa carried nothing on her once the jacket was off. All three of them dropped their *geta* into the hole and stood barefoot.

"Hurry," Natsu said as she led them out of the thicket. "We have only a small amount of light left to look over the estate."

Guards patrolled the front gate, so they made a wide circle around the outer wall. After putting the black head-covering on, Natsu climbed up one of the tall, overhanging trees faster than Takana thought was possible. Sōkichi followed. He wasn't as quick, but he was mindful of making excessive noise. Sneakiness wasn't a high priority in his combat training. Once they had a look, they came back down and whispered their findings to the group.

"There are more than 'a few guards,' Natsu-*san*." Sōkichi frowned, which Takana matched.

"I'm not the only one after the treasure. Maybe someone got caught and they increased their security? I don't know. I didn't mean to deceive you. But we only have a few days to do this and get back to Oyama in time to sell off anything we take besides the coins. If we wait, they might increase the guards again...

"If it makes you feel better, we can wait a couple days, then try, but if security gets tighter, it would only be harder. I think we can do this tonight."

Takana assessed the other two for hesitation. Sōkichi didn't seem bothered beyond the initial annoyance. He asked Fusa if she was sure she wanted to join. She scoffed and said she would help however she could. Takana liked seeing Fusa taking charge of her life, despite the danger.

"Here's my plan," Natsu said, "I'm going to distract and lead them away from their stations. When you three get inside there should be no one guarding the valuables, at least not while I'm out here causing confusion. Get everything you can grab over the wall, and we'll meet at the thicket. If I'm not there by daylight, I'll look for you in Oyama. Any questions?"

"No killing, right? You said you don't—"

"I don't. But I'm not going to tell you not to defend yourselves. Are you ready? Let's go!"

Natsu sprang over the wall, her feet whispering along the tree branches. Takana went over next, while Sōkichi helped Fusa, who'd never climbed a tree in her life. Takana scanned around, body tensed. Natsu disappeared, but if that outfit she wore was for anything other than show, no one would see her unless she wanted to be seen.

Once they safely scaled the wall, a whistle pierced the silence from the front gate. Was the sound cut off abruptly or did it stop naturally? Takana went on high alert, drawing her *katana* alongside Sōkichi. They ran to and climbed over the veranda of the ostentatious estate. Footsteps pounded the wooden floors inside, accompanied by the unmistakable, rushed unsheathing of swords as they raced towards the front of the building.

The three of them stalked along the back until they came to a door. Inside, they crept down the hallways in search of the treasury. The alarm had caused great upheaval with open doors and bed linens dragged along the floor. They found drugged women in the rooms. Takana recognized a few of them from Utsunomiya.

Fusa swooped in to check on their health while Takana and Sōkichi continued searching rooms.

As artwork increased in frequency and resplendence, they figured one of the rooms at the end of the hallway must house the treasure. Natsu had been right about the items they would encounter—most of it would sell for several months' worth of dice trips.

The silence in the building was deafening, but infrequent cries from outside punctuated it. Takana focused on the task at hand and continued on. They were too far in to turn tail and run with nothing to show for it. At the end of the hallway, muffled noises came from behind a closed sliding door: rustling fabric and whimpers. Sōkichi pulled it open and Takana entered to find an old man on top of a distressed prostitute. She had bruises on her face severe enough to be seen in the poor light, and she was restrained in an excruciating position, wrists and ankles twisted in rope. The old man had tattoos covering his body.

"This isn't a noble's estate," Sōkichi whispered behind Takana.

"Get off her," Takana said, katana pointed at the old man's shoulder, then down to his groin. She wasn't above killing people as quickly as possible, but what he was doing to her was unconscionable, and he'd earned a slow death.

He scrambled off the woman and fumbled for something in his discarded robes. Before Takana could reach him, he withdrew a whistle and blew it. She pulled a *kunai* from beneath the rim of the *kasa* and threw it into his hand hard enough to send the blade through the palm into the *yakuza's* neck. Sōkichi brought his blade down on the head of the first man to come running at the sound of the whistle while Takana cut the prostitute free. Footsteps stormed the wooden floor, all coming back from the entrance. Natsu's distractions must have run out of steam, or the old man was more important than leaving the entire rest of the estate unguarded.

Fusa peaked out of a room just as half a dozen men rounded the corner of the hallway. She withdrew and slid closed the *shoji* door, as if the rice paper and thin wood would protect her from swords and daggers. Takana and Sōkichi sprinted down the hallway to get between the men and Fusa's room.

At the sound of the initial whistle, the men must have been occupying the rooms with the drugged prostitutes—they didn't have their robes on, and they all had full-body tattoos. Before Takana could process how bad the night was turning out, the six men charged.

Sōkichi sliced through the first two with powerful, fluid blows. Two more dodged around his attacks to go for Takana, leaving Sōkichi to engage the last two.

The men that set their sights on Takana ran at her from opposite diagonal angles, their swords pointed forward to skewer her chest. She pulled the *wakizashi* and waited for them to be within a meter, then dove and rolled between them, slashing their legs with both blades. They fell down in a heap; thick arterial blood sprayed the white walls.

Takana verified that Sōkichi didn't need help, then turned back to her crumpled opponents to deliver slashes to their necks. There were no more guards following that they could hear, so Takana opened the red-spattered door to Fusa's room. Fusa cried out, expecting to be attacked. After calming her down, Takana asked her to help the girl at the other end of the hallway. She nodded and ran off in that direction, holding her mouth as she skirted around the bodies littering the floor.

Takana and Sōkichi wiped the blood on their blades onto the dead men's scant linens. Takana's lips trembled, and her stomach heaved when she looked down at herself. Her *sarashi* and the tattered *hakama* that exposed her legs to her lower thigh were soaked deep red, but it was the blood on her that shook her, to see in such sharp contrast against her skin—she had as much blood on her as the men on the floor. The sight was far worse than the *rōnin* she'd killed in Kasukabe. They had both been fully clothed, and those clothes hid the mortal damage well.

In only her torn *hakama* and *sarashi*, it was a much different visceral sight. She turned her back to Sōkichi and threw up against a wall. He put his hand on the middle of her back.

"Are you alright? There might be more outside."

Takana stared at the rice sliding down the wall, turning pink with the blood on the floor. The rice, courtesy of Natsu.

Chapter Seven

Blood Money

Ryō: Introduced in the 12th century, ryō was a unit of value attributed to an oval, gold coin, weighing about sixteen and a half grams when it became widespread throughout Japan in the 16th century. The value of each coin fluctuates wildly depending on the time period due to the various metals and weights used, as well as the extreme difficulty of attributing value in both modern Yen and US Dollars, in both nominal and practical terms, and there is often disagreement among historians of their true value at any given time. For some context within this book: In 1695, the coin weighed almost eighteen grams, but the value of the metal was cut nearly in half by the time of these events.

June 11, 1708
Ishibashi, Tochigi Prefecture

TAKANA'S STOMACH SETTLED AS THEY proceeded down the hallway to the front door. They descended the stairs to find unexpected carnage strewn about the grounds. The men hadn't been "distracted." They weren't wounded or moaning or writhing. Even with all their fallen blades next to their bodies, it would be inaccurate to call it anything less than a massacre. The dead silence constricted Takana's heart. It wasn't so much the men themselves, the loss of them. She hated most *yakuza* and wouldn't grieve for a single one, except, perhaps, the *oyabun* of her clan if he should pass before her.

But the murder around the grounds was on another level. She considered herself to be battle-hardened for the relative peace of the era. Whether or not she was capable of stomaching what had transpired didn't negate the fact that it *never* should have happened.

Takana shook her head, only then remembering Fusa and the prostitutes. She ran back inside with Sōkichi trailing. Some of the prostitutes emerged from the rooms in a daze. They gasped and hid when they saw the six dead men in the hallway. The sight of Takana covered in spatters of blood didn't help, either.

The two of them raced down the hallway to where they'd found the old man. The prostitute lied in a pool of blood spreading over the *tatami* floor. The old man stood with his back to the wall, holding Takana's *kunai* against Fusa's throat. The blade Takana had thrown hadn't gone far enough into the man's neck—thanks to his hand being in the way. Non-fatal as it was, the wound still drew a lot of blood down his body.

The old man shouted for them to drop their weapons. When they only looked at each other and didn't move fast enough, the old man pressed the point of the *kunai* into Fusa's throat as a warning. A trickle of blood flowed down her neck.

"Okay," Takana said, then dropped her weapons. Sōkichi did the same.

"And the hat!" he yelled, pressing the blade the furthest it could go before it would truly pierce Fusa's artery.

Takana winced at Fusa's whimpering. She took off the *kasa* and tossed it on top of the weapons.

"Who sent you? Kochiya-*kai*? We had a deal!" the old man cried.

What deal? Maybe he recognized her tattoo, but she hadn't seen any on the slain men that resembled an allied clan. That only raised her hackles further. Her mind raced for how she could save Fusa, but she had no more ideas. It would take too long to pull the *kanzashi* from her hair to use as a throwing weapon, and she hadn't practiced with it enough to use it that way—she could just as easily kill Fusa with an errant throw.

A shadow appeared behind the *shoji* wall. An arm thrust through the paper, wrapping around the old man's jaw, then another arm burst through the other side with a *tantō* and ripped the blade across his neck in the blink of an eye. Fusa fell to the floor as his hold released. The unfamiliar *oyabun's* blood sprayed over her back.

"Natsu!" Takana yelled, thinking too late it wasn't a good idea to confront a person that was capable of what she'd witnessed in the courtyard.

Sōkichi bent to comfort Fusa through her terrified sobbing. Takana turned around, ready to run after Natsu, when a door slid shut from the other side of the hallway—a door they hadn't checked yet. She put her *kasa* back on and grabbed her weapons, then went to investigate. She slid open the door to a trembling *yakuza* holding up a spear that rattled in his grip.

"Put it down," Takana said. "There's no one else."

He summoned his courage and charged her. She spun around the tip and grasped the wood with both hands, driving his momentum into the floor where the spear stuck. The other end jammed into his solar plexus. He curled up on the ground, squirming, desperate for air.

Before she could decide whether or not to end his life, Natsu was already past her, holding the man flat to the ground with one hand around his neck as she thrust the *tantō* between his legs. It sliced up through his groin, stomach, then ended at his heart where she stabbed deeper, putting her whole weight onto the blade to end his ear-splitting wails.

Natsu rose, utterly spent. Blood dripped off her black clothing, staining the *tatami*. Before Takana could grab a sleeve to stop her, Fusa brushed past and embraced Natsu, thanking her for saving her life. Natsu placed her hand on the back of Fusa's head. Sōkichi shared Takana's fury and stood by her side.

"Natsu, what have you done?" Takana said through clenched teeth.

"I've made you rich," she said. Her voice shook while she regained her breath.

Fusa let go of Natsu, coming away covered in blood to match what had sprayed on her back. Natsu pointed towards a chest against the wall. Fusa approached it and lifted the lid, then gasped and backed away. Takana saw the gold's reflection in her periphery, but she didn't remove her death stare from Natsu.

"You said no killing, *kuso ama*," Takana seethed. "Why did you—"

"This fucking *yakuza* scum destroyed my family. Made my brothers and father watch as they raped me; my sister; my mother. Then killed them all. They laughed while they did it. They all pissed on me before leaving me to be consumed in our burning house.

"I was ten."

Natsu collapsed to her knees, pressing her palms to her eyes as two decades of suffering and catharsis escaped. Fusa embraced her again. Sōkichi sighed and relaxed his aggressive stance, then placed his hand on her shoulder. Takana crossed her arms and turned away from the group hug, unsure how to feel anymore. So much had happened in fifteen minutes. Natsu's confession hit her harder than anything, but she had still been used. If she had heard Natsu's story before deciding to help, she would have refused and gone on with her life. She didn't want to help people with their shattered lives. She could spend the rest of her life doing so and only lighten the tiniest fraction of all the suffering in the country, let alone the region.

Takana caused enough suffering on her own. She didn't deserve to feel good about helping others—she was marked by the evil she committed, all in the name of personal freedom and money.

And where was Takana's eager savior? The person who would come out of nowhere to end her debt so she could move on with a real life and escape the *yakuza*?

The dueling thoughts twisted up in her head, infuriating her further. She left the room and sat down on the steps outside the front door.

The stench of death couldn't get worse than walking through the hallway, but it was thicker in the air of the courtyard as it mixed with the mustiness of mud. She needed something to comfort herself, so she pulled out the *kiseru* and special tobacco. The smoke calmed her down, but the death around her tainted the aroma. She stepped around pools of blood and viscera spread throughout the courtyard, until she was outside the gate.

The fresh air allowed her to take in her favorite smell, cleansing her mind and filling her lungs. She wondered what her grandfather would say if he saw her that night. He had filled her head with so many stories of brave, heroic women warriors in Nihon's history. Would he approve of Natsu's journey of revenge? Would he chastise Takana for being so selfish about helping others, regardless of what was in it for her personally? Give her a speech about using her power and training for good causes? That seemed like the lesson at the end of so many of his stories, yet it never occurred to her until that moment that maybe he had been directing them *at her*, not merely recounting history.

The rain kicked up again. Her *kasa* protected the *kiseru* as the smoke lingered beneath the rim. Absorbed in her thoughts, her feet absentmindedly carried her to the thicket. The trees protected the hole from flooding. She put on her *geta, haori*, and made sure nothing had fallen out. She decided to leave Fusa and Sōkichi behind.

Takana picked up Fusa's *haori* and reached for the *ryō* within its pockets. She could leave them for Fusa, but all Fusa had to do was reach a hand in that chest for a fistful of enough money to take care of herself for years. Sōkichi, as well.

"And you were worried about *me* stealing your money." Natsu's voice startled Takana, causing her to drop Fusa's *haori*.

Natsu laid on her stomach in an oddly comfortable-looking position over a thick branch. She'd removed the mask. Drying blood streaked her burnt orange hair, visible from Takana's lantern. All of it was incongruous with her bewitching smile.

"How do you do that?" was all Takana could manage.

"Seventeen years training with the best *kunoichi*-clans in Nihon. We're like monkeys."

Takana pocketed the rest of the *ryō* and made to leave the protection of the thicket.

"Aren't you even curious about—"

"I'm sorry, Natsu-*san*, for your childhood. For what you've carried with you. But you used me. You said no killing except in self-defense. Almost every kill in that estate was in *their* self-defense!"

"So, I didn't *lie*..."

"Don't get cute with me. Keep your money. Share it with the other two. I don't want anything to do with you. Don't follow me."

Natsu dropped effortlessly from the branch to block Takana's path. The feeling of déjà vu almost made her physically sick.

"You're not leaving things like this. Running away. You and your friends saved my life tonight. I really wasn't planning on there being that many of them. They must have been having a party. I was nearly spent clearing the courtyard; vulnerable. You took out seven and distracted two more for me to dispatch easily. I thought I was going to have to attack over multiple nights. You've helped me end it all inside a half-hour."

"Okay. Can I leave now? Are you done?" Takana made a step around, but Natsu put a hand on her shoulder. Takana glared as if one more move would result in losing that hand.

"I understand your hostility, but I wasn't lying about the money," Natsu said. "Take the chest. Clear out the art and decorations. It's all yours. And your friends' of course. I never wanted it."

"What about Oyama?" Takana crossed her arms, not slackening her stance.

"Believe me, even with all the money you can scrounge from this estate, it wouldn't have been enough to earn a place at one of those tables. A lot of them simply murder each other to consolidate all the work they do during the week. It's allowed since there are no rules, and the mistress doesn't ask questions. It's all about the totals to her. Even if I did get that much money, I don't want to be part of her organization."

"So, what will you do now that you're done tricking people into helping you enact revenge?"

"I was hoping..."

"I don't really care. I just want this conversation to be over. Will you stop blocking my path so I can leave?"

"As I said, Takana-*san*, you saved my life. I like...you three very much. Can I follow you?"

"Follow *me*? What value is there in that for you? You obviously don't need my protection. If you like Fusa, no one's stopping you from following her wherever you want. You'll probably make a better companion for her anyway; you can help her enact her own little revenges whenever she sees an injustice happening. Just a warning—she likes to get involved. A lot.”

Natsu sighed and went around Takana to the hole. She stripped out of the blood- and rain-soaked *kunoichi* outfit and changed back into her traveling clothes. Blood smeared over her face and in her hair.

“Aren’t you even curious about how much money was in that chest?”

“It’s blood money, twofold. It’s bad luck.”

“Says the *yakuza* warrior with the *bakeneko* decorating her skin. You can’t think of anything in the world worth spending that money on? If you want to take the blood off of it, donate it to a hospital. An orphanage. A temple, I don’t know. Give it all to Fusa and Sōkichi. I talked to them before I chased after you—they think it’s yours to decide. At least give them closure on your decision, either way.”

When Takana first glimpsed the golden tint glowing from the chest, she believed it was simply *lined* with gold. She was very wrong. The *ryō* were stacked neatly in layers, filling the chest dozens of rows across and deep—easily ten years’ worth of debt. The thought of it being unlucky blood money fled her mind.

Fusa only marveled at holding it. She practiced a few sleights-of-hand with the *haori* Takana brought back with the *geta*, but she put every coin back in the chest when she was done. Sōkichi seemed disinterested in the chest’s contents.

“Takana-*san*, you can pay off your debt with this, right?” Fusa asked.

“I never mentioned anything about that debt to you.”

“No, but you said something about it when you were about to slice Taiga. This would clear you, wouldn’t it? No one could carry this much debt.”

Takana exhaled miserably. If it was worth selling his wife and daughter, it wouldn't pay off all her father's debt. It would certainly speed things up and she could leverage more special favor for her and her mother. One thing was certain, though: If she didn't get the money to the *oyabun* before the title passed to Taiga, it would be worthless.

"Fusa-*chan*, can you escort the women back to Chiyo?"

"What if your clan is watching? They'll throw me right back into the hay stall."

"Take them to the doctor, then. They'll know the way back to the *yūkaku* from there."

"What about...?" Fusa asked while glancing across the hallway.

"I'm sorry for what happened to her. Maybe you and the women can fashion something to carry her out with all this bedding. Be careful getting through the gates so you don't get picked up and blamed for her death."

"In that case, they'll need my help, Takana-*san*. I'll go with them," Natsu said.

"Leaves you and me for the worst of it, Sōkichi-*san*."

He nodded and opened closet doors to find the two long poles used to carry the chest. They placed the chest in a protective outer box and draped bedding over their shoulders to keep from bruising. As they reached the gate of the estate through the rainy night and muddy courtyard, Takana was already winded from the weight.

Sōkichi looked at her with a little amusement.

"I'm sorry," Takana huffed, "I haven't had reason to carry this much weight before."

"No doubt your smoking doesn't help."

"Sōkichi-*san*, are you taking this opportunity to say you don't like the way I smell?"

"No. But I would be worried about getting into a fight you can't win quickly."

"Well, perhaps..." Takana started, wanting to finish with "you'd be by my side" but thought better of it. They were wasting enough time, and she resolved to make a better show of endurance the rest of the way.

When Takana and Sōkichi reached the front gates of Utsunomiya, a guard approached them in the pre-dawn light. She was miserable, sweating, soaked from the rain, muddy from the knees down. Her shoulders ached terribly. They'd even stopped several times along the way, but the stretch of trails they'd taken to avoid thieves had been slippery and brutal. The only good thing came from the rain washing the blood from their clothing before it could stain.

"*Ohayōgozaimasu.*" Takana greeted the guard while sucking in air and resting both hands on her knees. "Delivery for Inoue-*san*, the blacksmith. Bricks of iron."

"I'll need to check that for myself, *nēsan*," the guard said as he stooped down for the lid.

"Sir, we're so tired that I just want to get this to the shop and fall asleep in the bathhouse for a week."

Normally she would have put on a better show, but her weary irritation demanded a different tact.

"Perhaps this can speed us through?"

She pulled five *ryō* from the *haori* sleeve and greased his palm out of sight of the other guards. He nodded and waved them inside. To help sell the lie in case the guard changed his mind, they stopped in front of Inoue's, pretending to wait until he opened. After about twenty minutes, Fusa and Natsu joined them.

"I'm going to get an audience with the *oyabun* immediately," Takana told them. "They usually make me wait until the end of the day. If I can get us in earlier, I'll come outside and wave you to bring it in."

Takana climbed up the steps to the Kochiya-*kai* headquarters. One of the clan wives manned the front door. She sneered at Takana's disheveled appearance. Takana ignored the attitude.

"It's very important I talk to the *oyabun* this morning."

"They're in a meeting. You can wait until the end of the day as usual."

"Please get a message to him that it's urgent."

"I said wait your turn, bitch!"

Taiga stormed down the hallway having caught a whiff of insubordination; Takana's signature scent.

"What the hell is going on out here?"

"I told this bitch to wait her turn, and she won't shut up."

Taiga, who didn't have what one would call a "good mood," looked farther from it than usual.

"*Ane-san*, wait like normal. Nothing you can say or do is more important than clan business. If I hear another word from either of you during this meeting, I'll display your heads to the other wives outside their quarters. Got it?"

The wife was shocked but bowed in understanding. Takana shook her head and left the building. Guarding the money all day wasn't ideal, but it didn't look like they had a choice. They made themselves more comfortable outside Inoue's and Takana set them on a rotating guard basis: three stood watch while the fourth went to the public bathhouse. When Inoue opened his doors to find three people and a large chest, Takana gave him a friendly smile and two *ryō* for using his shop to loiter.

Takana assigned the task of gathering food to Sōkichi, since he wouldn't overspend or overindulge like Fusa might. When Natsu and Fusa were together, they played with more sleight-of-hand tricks. Takana did the same when it was Natsu's off-time. When Fusa had her free time, the remaining three practiced parrying *wakizashi* and *tantō* in close quarters.

About an hour before they planned to carry the chest to the headquarters, a group of five men from the clan, all lower ranks, ran full bore through the street in a near-panic. They came all the way from the city gates, hard-travelled and sweating. The men ran straight up the steps of the clan building and burst through the front doors—something Takana could never get away with.

"Wonder what that's about..." Fusa mused.

Standing close to Inoue's furnace warmed them pleasantly against the wet chill in the air. Inoue replaced the two *kunai* that had been used on the trip and verified the integrity of the *katana* pieces inside the *kasa*. When he finished, the four of them picked up the long rods, hoisting the burden of the chest together, and made their way to the headquarters.

Chapter Eight

Hurt

Tsuyu, or Baiu: The rainy season, between May and July throughout Japan. In the Kanto area where the book takes place, the season would go from early June to late July. Monsoons, flooding, mudslides, lightning storms, and consistent downpours plague the island during this distinct fif th season.

June 12, 1708
Utsunomiya, Tochigi Prefecture

THE KOCHIYA-*KAI* WERE MORE ANIMATED than usual, especially for the end of the workday, when things were most often downright boring. The squabbling and loud conversations throughout the entrance, hallways, and the room before the main office all quieted when they saw the four companions carrying the heavy chest on their shoulders.

The procession stopped in front of Taiga, the last person in the way before the office doors.

"*Ani-ki*, may we pass?" Takana dropped the accustomed hostility. Since they never spoke to each other in any other way, he was taken aback. Or maybe he couldn't justify berating her without provocation, not with so many eyes on them during the dramatic end to the day.

He stood aside and opened the door for them. Takana expected to meet with Tetsuo in private. Money exchanging hands was important but uninteresting to the rest of them. However, Taiga and all the lieutenants crowded into the room while the lower ranks huddled outside, pushing and trying to get a look into the office.

Undeterred from the unexpected audience, Takana held her head high, eager to display how she handled her responsibilities. She would show all of them, not only Tetsuo, what she was worth to the clan.

They placed the box down in front of the desk. Takana couldn't understand the furrow in Tetsuo's usually placid demeanor, but she imagined the look would change once she opened the lid for him. Natsu and Sōkichi lifted the heavy chest nestled inside the traveling box. Tetsuo's expression hardened when he saw the seal over the latch.

"Taka-*chan*, what have you done?" he whispered.

She couldn't understand the confusion, or the smug sense of satisfaction emanating from Taiga, or the strange amalgamation of looks from the rest of the clan. None of it made sense. *They didn't even know what was in the chest yet!*

Takana straightened her back and lifted the lid. The golden glow reflected off Tetsuo's face and the gilded wallpaper behind him. The men from the doorway gasped. The lieutenants remained grim-faced. Taiga's smug grin grew wider. Takana couldn't tell if Tetsuo's eyes were wet from the display of wealth or old age.

Tetsuo turned his back to her.

Taiga grabbed her by the elbow and dragged her outside the office, throwing her down on the floor. The lieutenants did the same to her companions. The lower ranks laughed and jeered before Taiga cut them all off with a look. The underlings scurried out of the building while he and the lieutenants stayed behind, encircling the group of four confused coin couriers.

"Do you have any idea what you've done, *ane-san*?" Taiga said. "We had just brokered a deal with that clan. This was their payment—to become our ally. The whores were a gift before the meeting we were to have today. Instead, you slaughtered their ranks and stole it from them."

Takana shook her head and raised her hand in a defensive position. She'd only ever been insubordinate with Taiga, never to the whole clan. The potential punishment was unthinkable.

"I'm...I'm sorry, *ani-ki*! I didn't know!"

"How could you have? That doesn't surprise me, *ane-san*. What surprises me the most is I never thought you had it in you. You threaten and talk a mean game, but after hearing the scouts report what they found at the estate? I'm almost sorry I can't make you one of my lieutenants."

The others in the circle didn't appreciate that comment, but Taiga didn't notice. He was too absorbed in the cruel delight of the spectacle; of Takana losing.

"It wasn't her—" Natsu started before Taiga backhanded her. Sōkichi made to get up but three of the lieutenants grabbed him and pushed him back down.

"Street scum don't talk in here."

Taiga went back into the office and slammed the doors behind him. Fusa hugged Takana from behind, trembling. Takana looked back at the angry welt rising on the side of Natsu's face.

"Didn't hurt, did it?" Takana arched her eyebrow.

"Not even a little bit." Natsu half-smiled.

Takana liked a girl that could lie through pain. She'd been doing it ever since she had the misfortune of meeting her "future husband." What truly hurt were the ineffectual, drunken beatings from her deadbeat father. She wondered if Natsu had felt much pain at all during her *kunoichi* training, or if it'd all gone numb since the night her family died.

"I was just thinking how I'm glad to share my first real bruise with you," Natsu said.

A lieutenant kicked at her back to prompt her to shut up, but there wasn't much force behind it. They didn't like being belittled by Taiga, and he wasn't shy about doing it in front of others.

They waited in uncomfortable, miserable silence before Taiga burst through the doors again. He flipped Takana's *kasa* to her back and picked her up by the hair. The lieutenants removed her *haori* and *daishō*, as well as Fusa's *haori* and Sōkichi's *daishō*. They rattled out all the coins that they'd earned before the estate massacre and divided them among each other.

"No," Takana whimpered.

"Shut up," Taiga said before punching her in the stomach, knocking the air out of her.

Sōkichi broke free from two of the lieutenants and almost leveled Taiga but the other lieutenants caught him and held his arms back. Taiga punched him several times in the stomach and about the face. Natsu struggled against the painful armlock one lieutenant held behind her back. Fusa shrank and cowered without a need for restraint. Taiga grabbed her by the neck once he was done with Sōkichi.

"After Takana's punishment, I think my lieutenants and I will finish what we started in the pleasure quarter before you ran away. This time, Takana won't be able to stop us, you ugly whore. Make it good, and we might let you live through it."

The lieutenants stood to immediate attention when Tetsuo appeared through the open doors. Takana feared his sad expression more than if he'd been angry.

The lieutenants marched all four of them back inside the office, then stood to the sides. Taiga shadowed over his father's shoulder while Tetsuo sat back down on his *zabuton*. Takana dropped to her knees and bowed with her arms pointed at Tetsuo.

"*Oyassan!* I'm so sorry for what I've done! I never would have gone near that place if I'd known!"

She only cared about Tetsuo. She didn't worry how begging made her look to anyone else in the room. Her heart burst with sorrow for hurting him—both his reputation and his view of her.

Natsu pushed Takana to the side and prostrated herself before him.

"Sir, this was all *my* fault! I used her! I lied to her! It was my idea. I killed all but seven of them. Takana and Sōkichi killed those men in self-defense, only after I lured them into the dangers of the estate. I didn't tell them about the chest. I didn't tell them those men were *yakuza*! Please don't punish them for my treachery!"

Fusa did the same.

"None of this would have happened if it wasn't for me! It's my fault Takana acted outside her normal duties. Please spare the others!"

Tetsuo glanced at Sōkichi.

"Anything to add?"

"Natsu and Takana tell the truth, but Fusa's only trying to protect them. She had nothing to do with any of it."

"That's not—!" Fusa started before Tetsuo raised his hand for them to be quiet.

"Stand up, Takana."

She did, but maintained a deep bow, unable to meet his eyes.

"Taiga and I couldn't decide on one punishment, so we will give you a choice. You will commit *hara-kiri* in front of the headquarters for the city to see. There will be no dignity of *seppuku*. Or you will behead this lying *kunoichi* and the two accomplices for all to see, and we will apply what you've stolen towards your debt. Choose one."

It was an impossible choice, meant to humiliate her either way. Takana had tried putting herself in Natsu's *geta* since learning of her story. She hadn't lied about it. No actor could have conveyed her anguish or relief when it was all over. If those scum had been stupid enough to leave her alive, Takana would have taken the same path of revenge as Natsu, though she wouldn't have involved others if she could help it.

"*Oyassan*, if you would entertain a third choice..." Takana's voice cracked as tears spattered her *geta* and the *tatami* below her. "Take the chest, don't apply it to the debt, and start a new debt of my own for all that I have destroyed of your alliance."

Tetsuo paused to consider. Taiga fumed in silence when Tetsuo didn't squash the idea immediately.

"You realize it will be impossible for you to ever repay such a debt on top of what's already owed?"

"Yes, *Oyassan*."

"You realize that by offering this solution in front of Taiga, he will hold you to the debt after I pass?"

"...Yes, *Oyassan*."

Tetsuo stood and walked over to the door that led to the balcony, looking out as the sun set over the mountains. After the sun disappeared and he let out a deep sigh, he nodded.

"From now on, you may never set foot in this office again. You'll turn in your payments to the lieutenants instead."

Of all the punishments he could have come up with, that one hurt as much as her father's beatings.

The lieutenants picked up the other three and led them out. Taiga held Takana by the back of the neck, pushing her through the headquarters. At the top of the stairs, he pulled her back, bringing the side of her face next to his. Her companions looked helplessly up at them from the ground.

Taiga bit her ear, then whispered, "did you really think it was going to be that easy?"

He shoved her down the stairs. She landed at the bottom hard, and her *kasa* fell off her head. Her old bruises would have new bruises. Her companions stooped to pick her up before Taiga shouted at them to get their hands off her. Four of his lieutenants marched down the stairs and lifted her up. They dragged her through the street, yelling and making as much noise as possible. In a large, open space near the town center, they pushed her under a wooden tower, then tied her hands around one of the pillars so her back was to them.

A crowd had followed them and gathered around the tower. Taiga made a torch from the flames of a nearby brazier. He held the torch behind her, then slid a dagger up her back and cut the *sarashi* with a quick stroke. He shouted a speech to the onlookers about what would happen if they went against his clan—Takana was only a taste.

She took quick, panicky breaths, understanding what was about to happen. Bracing for it wasn't going to help. Neither was going limp. She would feel foolish for believing anything could ever hurt more. Her father's beatings were child's play. Not seeing Tetsuo or her grandfather again was inconsequential.

Fusa screamed from the crowd, overpowering all the strangers' murmurs and cries of pity. Takana's screams drowned out everything around her; her ears filled with ringing, her nose with burnt hair and flesh. All senses narrowed to nothing but one singular, searing point.

Her tattoo was on fire.

Where was the rain?

Chapter Nine

Of The Same Mind

Bakeneko: A supernatural cat—not that cats need much embellish-ment to their many supernatural abilities. The bakeneko has some truly evil mythology—heralding strange events, shapeshifting into humans, speaking, cursing, manipulating the dead, possessing humans, and be-friending wolves to attack travelers. Cats with long tails were thought to bewitch people (leading to the custom of cutting off their tails). Above all, bakeneko kill their masters. Many spooky, superstitious events around felines could be boiled down to "cats being cats."

June 14, 1708
Utsunomiya, Tochigi Prefecture

THE HORRID SMELL OF BURNT flesh and hair stung Takana's nose before opening her eyes, then a lovely aroma of incense over-powered it. Her vision was too bleary to see where she was. She hissed and reached for her shoulder, but a hand swatted it away. Clearing the sleep from her eyes, she found herself in the back-al-ley doctor's room. Dozens of needles stuck out from around her burned tattoo. The doctor slid in another one.

Takana needed to scratch the itch of the healing, burned skin, and the acupuncture needles weren't helping. She reached up again, but another hand pulled it back from the other side. Fusa smiled, then leaned in to hug around Takana's waist awkwardly.

"How long was I out?"

"A couple of days," the doctor said. "From what your friends said, you didn't pass out until nearly half a minute after the torture started. They continued until the *samurai* patrol came by and chased them off."

"How bad is it, *sensei*?"

"It's bad but could have been much worse. They got your back shoulder and upper arm. Your hair and underarm were singed. Your collarbone and chest were spared."

The doctor spoke curiously, more to himself than Takana. "It's strange, the application of the heat—they didn't press the torch into you so much as let the flames lick off the top layers of skin. Cracked, blistered and burst, but not melted. Brutal, certainly, but more precise than I'd have thought could be done…"

Fusa frowned. In the back of both their heads Takana knew they were hearing Taiga's speech about how damaged whores can't earn.

"The frog is gone, the *bakeneko* remains…" Takana sighed as the itchiness of the frog's absence drove her crazy. "Where's Nat-su-*san*?"

"She's spent most of the last two days selling anything valuable from that estate," Fusa said. "She and Shinkichi-*san* have been working together to—"

"You mean Sōkichi," Takana corrected her, confused. She'd been beaten and burned but she hadn't hit her head that hard. Had she?

"No, *he's* been standing guard outside since we brought you here. *Shin*-kichi was the thief with the baby, remember?"

"Oh, right. Where's the baby, then?" Takana looked expectantly at Fusa's arms, then the corners of the room.

The doctor sighed.

"There was nothing more I could do," he said. "She was too far gone by the time he reached me…"

Fusa sniffed and busied herself with some fabric on a table across the room.

"*Sensei*…" Takana asked, "would a more…specialized doctor have saved her life?"

The doctor scoffed and jabbed a needle into her shoulder a little too far, sending a shock through her nerves.

"*Itai*! I didn't mean it that way, *sensei*. I meant, if...if he had money and found an infant doctor..."

"I know what you're getting at. How could a doctor who only works on whores save a baby, correct? What does that make *you*, then? Understand without my help you'd be in far more pain than you are now."

"I only meant..."

"She feels guilty she didn't do more to save the baby," Fusa said without looking up from her work.

Takana wanted to deny it, but Fusa spoke the truth. She had been clinging onto her grandfather's pipe for so long. Would allowing the thief to sell her priceless possession have saved a baby's life? Was her ephemeral memory more important than a living human being? What would her grandfather think about that?

"Ah! Finished!" Fusa said, then brought her work to Takana. "Natsu-*san* found this beautiful *kimono* at the estate. I cut and fashioned it so it would only drape over your left shoulder, allowing your right side to heal easier. Half of your new *sarashi* will be exposed, but you never seemed shy about that before. Then I cut the bottom up to your lower thighs so your legs would be free, as you like them to be. You can still reach your pouches easily.

"Finally, I got rid of the *obi* and used a simpler belt to hang a new set of *daishō*. The belt is reversible and should be easy to move around your waist, so if you decide to train your left arm while your right heals, you'll have that freedom, too."

Takana regarded Fusa's handiwork. The *kimono* itself was pinkish white, with ornate wheels of blue, gold, and red, sakura, along with other flower petals, and a curious green ink splotch on the front left shoulder. Takana focused on it and realized it was a clumsily painted frog.

When she was growing up and her family seemed to have all the money in the world, her mother spared no expense in dressing Takana in the finest warrior-gear and the most striking *kimono* and *yukata*, treating her much like a doll.

None of the cuts on Fusa's garment were hemmed or bordered. They were already fraying at the edges. After a few weeks of travel, it would look as tattered as her old *hakama*. Takana pretended to wince in pain to muffle a smile at the sight of the cut lines not even being straight. It would have been more accurate if Takana had slashed at the fabric with a dull *katana*.

"I added some pockets inside the sleeves, too." Fusa beamed.

It was the most beautiful garment Takana had ever seen, and she showed Fusa her appreciation with an extra-long and tight hug. The doctor muttered about moving her right shoulder too much. She didn't care.

With the "new" *kimono* on and the acupuncture needles removed, Takana stepped outside to greet Sōkichi and thank him for standing guard. He bowed, then walked around the corner of the building after beckoning. She found him unwrapping a long piece of fabric. Inside was a set of *daishō*. The scabbards were worn, but he displayed the blades inside to her and they appeared new.

"These were the best from the estate. It didn't have any legendary sets on display. They were more into crafts and clothing than weapons."

Takana handled each, getting the feel for their weight and dimensions. The emotion of what Fusa had done for her, and learning Sōkichi had stood guard over her for two days, then this gift on top... Her face flushed, and she decided to play a little with him.

"Sōkichi-*san*, *sensei* said I shouldn't move my right arm too much, so I can't fasten these to my hip. Would you...?"

He nodded and leaned over to adjust her belt according to Fusa's design. His hands touched her waist, hips, lower back and abdomen as he worked, careful not to brush her shoulder. He was bent, his face close to her nearly bare right torso but for the *sarashi* wrapped around her chest. She could faintly smell his hair. Though he hadn't bathed since the altercation, and her sense of smell was dulled by a decade of smoking, he smelled good. Of course, anything was better than the smell of her own burnt flesh and hair, but above all that, his sweat was more pleasant with the understanding of *why* he smelled that way.

Like Fusa's fashion skills, Takana thought as she ran her fingers casually through the freshly shorn section of her hair that had been burned around her shoulder.

When Sōkichi finished tying the *daishō*, Takana caught him by the side of the neck with her left hand, so he couldn't stand at his full height or remain stoically distant as he was apt to do. She gazed into his eyes and recognized something of what she felt behind them. Her hand slid from his neck, down through the fabric of his practice robes, resting it over his chest.

They knew each other's bodies from sparring matches, measured one another's breaths, assessed each other's intent of movements for years. It took a lot to quicken Takana's pulse, but it rose, and beneath her fingertips she felt his as well.

His hand moved to rest on her upper hip, and the other rested in the mess of her hair that Fusa had cut a few minutes before to minimize the burnt smell. Their heads came forward by agonizing millimeters. Takana relished the thrill as she moved closer, rather than rushing together too soon. She valued that Sōkichi proved to be capable of the same restraint. It would feel that much better when their lips actually m—

"Takana-*san*! Natsu-*san* is back!" Fusa cried from the end of the alley.

They pulled apart and looked at Fusa. She shot her hand up to cover her mouth and averted her eyes.

"*Honnnnn—tōni gomen-nasai!*" Fusa bowed quickly, cutely, her face bright red as she disappeared from view.

Takana smiled. Sōkichi cleared his throat and straightened his robes around his torso, then walked down the alleyway. She followed back a few paces, practicing unsheathing the *daishō* with her left arm. It would take some time getting used to it, but Tomoe-*sensei* had taught her to use both arms. She only needed to practice reminding her muscles how to do it again.

Natsu and Shinkichi stood around the doctor's entrance when Takana rounded the corner. Upon seeing Takana, her lopsided hair, and the new outfit, Natsu almost exploded into a full belly laugh, sputtering and pretending to cough instead when Fusa emerged from the door. Natsu clapped Fusa on the back.

"That's a job well done, Fu-*chan*."

"I'm going to fetch Chiyo-*san*," Fusa said. "She asked us to let her know when you woke up."

"That's not really neces—" Takana started, but Fusa had already taken off.

Takana met Natsu's eyes and thanked her with them, followed by a respectful bow.

"What are you thanking me for? You saved my life, Takana-*san*. Twice! You'll never be rid of me now."

Takana put her hand on Natsu's shoulder.

"I'm glad of that, my lovely, bruised friend."

Natsu smiled, crinkling up the black eye that Taiga had given her. Their eyes would match for a couple weeks at least.

Takana approached Shinkichi and bowed deeply at the waist.

"Shinkichi-*san*, I'm eternally sorry for your loss. There's no replacing your daughter, but I will make it up to you, I swear."

"What are you talking about? I followed your advice and *sensei* did all he could for her. He made her last days easier. If you hadn't been there, she would have died in pain out in the wilderness, and I would have stood over her believing there was nothing more I could do but let her suffer until the end."

Takana straightened with wet eyes and a tight jaw. She couldn't tell if he was only softening the blow for both of them or if he was sincere. Natsu cut short the awkward moment and motioned for them all to go into the doctor's building.

"We've finished sweeping the estate for valuables, and I helped Shinkichi clear his hut of anything worth selling. Once my fence sells it all off, we could have another chest of *ryō* as heavy as the one we dragged into your clan's headquarters."

"When do we take back *my* chest?" Takana asked.

"We were waiting until whenever you woke up. If you're up for it, we're doing it in a few hours. I scouted that balcony your *oyabun* stood at when he sentenced you. That's where we're going to lower the chest with ropes."

Takana loved that Natsu went into forming a plan without skipping a beat, as if she knew exactly how Takana was going to feel when she woke up. She wished she could have met Natsu sooner—they would have made an unstoppable, debt-reducing machine.

"Fu-*chan* has already arranged with Chiyo-*san* to use some of the prostitutes to distract any of your clan that happen to be inside after midnight. They don't post many guards at that time. I don't see much going wrong."

"*I* didn't see much going wrong with setting a giant chest of gold in front of the *oyabun*," Takana muttered.

Fusa came into the office with a *tantō* held against her throat by Taiga's main lieutenant.

Everyone but the doctor reflexively put their hands on their weapons' hilts.

"There's no need for that," the lieutenant said. "I was only getting your attention. Taiga put me up in the pleasure quarters to relay a message to you once any of you were seen. He wants Takana to meet in the main office. Alone."

"I'm not allowed in there," Takana said. "You heard the *oyabun* as clearly as I did."

"Things are different. When the *oyabun* found out what Taiga... What we did to you..." The lieutenant trailed off.

Takana couldn't help feeling a sense of satisfaction that Tetsuo either changed his mind, or he'd shamed them all for the excessive violence. She earned more than many of the higher ranks. Damaging her tattoo ran the risk of ruining the dice games, of her losing the air of authority and privilege to demand more from all the businesses she was involved with along the *Nikkō Kaidō*. She was his reach into many far-flung sources of income; his most trusted muscle that understood dead men can't pay back debts.

That Tetsuo had developed such a quick change of heart—that he valued her enough to see past the fact that she wasn't one of them, in more ways than one—elated her.

"Okay, I'll follow you up there. Please let my friend go."

He obliged and backed out of the office. Shinkichi pulled Fusa into his arms as she shuddered from another blade being held to her throat.

"This is a trap, Takana-*san*," Sōkichi said while Natsu nodded.

"Probably so...but if I get the chance to kill Taiga *and* steal back my gold, I'm going to take it. You should still set up beneath the balcony and be ready to climb up when I signal it's clear. I'll see you all soon. Fusa-*chan*, time to send in the prostitutes."

The lieutenant opened the doors to Tetsuo's office, let her in, then closed them behind her. No one was in the room. Why wouldn't Tetsuo be there to oversee the meeting? If it was just her and Taiga, in her condition... She cursed herself for being so cavalier about coming back, but it was too late to turn back and leave.

She took a cautious look around the office. Rounding the desk, she found Tetsuo's *zabuton*. It had red splotches dappling it. There was a scrubbed, pink area around the *tatami* beneath the cushion.

"Sit down." A poisonous voice startled her from behind. Her hand went reflexively to the wrong hip, grasping air instead of the *katana* and shooting pain through her shoulder.

Taiga grabbed her left elbow and turned her around, but with less force than she expected. He had been on the balcony the whole time, catching her off-guard.

"Sit on the *zabuton, ane-san*."

She would have liked to disembowel him on the spot, but he carried his own weapons, and she'd witnessed him practicing at *dōjō* in the city over the last eight years. He was no one to trifle with, unless she was absolutely sure she had the upper hand.

"Please don't make me sit there, *ani-ki*."

"Sit!"

He let go of her arm and she lowered herself on the cushion, sitting on her calves. Uneasiness and growing fear wracked her nerves.

Taiga paced in front of the desk.

"You've broken me twice, *ane-san*. I meant what I said about wishing you could be one of my lieutenants. You're more competent than all but a couple of them. When I heard your screams, I... My heart broke. I realized what I lost by taking your tattoo, financially and personally.

"You and I... We insulted each other and played rough when we first met. It turned into something uncontrollable on my part. I pushed you away at some crucial point—crossed a line—that we couldn't come back from, and our relationship curdled. Early, I really did want to marry you. Once the moment to genuinely court you came and went, I kept that line up, hoping maybe someday you would hear the sincerity—"

"Enough with this manipulation, Taiga," Takana said. "Don't you dare start blaming me for the way you've treated me. There was never love there—it was always about dominating what you couldn't control. Your father wouldn't let—"

"My father is the second way you broke me. When he learned what we did to you the other night... He shared his true feelings about me. He told his only son he wished you had been born to him, as a man. Not because he doesn't value you as a woman, but because he would have given over control of Kochiya-*kai* to you without hesitation if you were his son.

"Do you know what it's like for your own family to wish you hadn't been born?"

"...Yes." Takana's voice cracked.

"That's unbelievable to me. Your father wishes the only one trying to save his ass was dead? What a cowardly piece of filth."

Takana cleared the lump in her throat and set her eyes on him. She blinked to keep them clear and focused. She couldn't lose sight of his true self, hidden below the confessions and flattery.

"Why did you bring me here? Why are you telling me all this?"

Taiga sat down cross-legged in front of the desk and sighed.

"I guess I needed to unburden myself to someone. I can't talk to any of the men like this."

"You should try talking to some of your men instead of insulting them all the time. You might get somewhere on a deeper level with them. Maybe they'll give you a chance to make it up to them, like the one you'll never get with me."

"Oh, no? The other reason I asked you up here was to tell you I'll erase your family's debt if you marry me, once I'm officially the *oyabun.* All this talk could bring us to an understanding—one that doesn't need to lead to a violent marriage. And...I told you I don't care about rules. You'd be my right hand as well."

Takana couldn't believe part of her was being swayed. His powers of manipulation were another discipline he'd been honing alongside his martial arts training. He talked about Takana seeing the truth behind his words—but there was never a doubt in her mind that he hated her. It was all bullshit. The marriage was going to be a cage of misery whether she agreed to it willingly or not. The meeting was his last desperate attempt to get her inside that cage.

"You serpentine, worthless—" she seethed as her hand went to the correct hip, but Taiga pushed the desk into her stomach, trapping her legs beneath it. She couldn't stand up.

She shot her hand into the *kasa* and pulled out a *kunai*, flinging it towards his heart the moment it cleared the rope. He used the scabbard of his *katana* to deflect the blade. She flung another one, but he dodged so it sliced the outside of his bicep. In a moment he stood on the table, his *katana* raised to slice off her head in one quick slash.

He was mid-swing when a flash of metal flew into the back of his hand from the balcony. Takana had already put her arms beneath the desk, and she used all her strength in lifting it. The incline unbalanced him and sent him tumbling backwards. Her burned shoulder cried out in agony, but she pulled her *katana* out and stood, then threw it like a spear into the door before he could reach the handle. Two more *shuriken* flew past and stuck into the door, backing him away from it.

Takana rushed to grab him from the back and slid the *wakizashi* beneath his chin. She pulled it up a little bit, meaning to get his full attention.

"No, wait!" he cried.

Something spattered the *tatami*, sprinkling against her legs. She wondered if she pulled too much, unused to the strength of her left arm. Had she slit his neck open by accident? But when she looked down, the liquid splashing between his feet wasn't red.

"What are you waiting for?" Natsu asked as she sauntered in from the balcony, holstering her last couple *shuriken*. "You wanted to kill him, didn't you?"

Sōkichi entered behind Natsu, then grabbed away Taiga's weapons. Takana pulled Taiga away from the spot, getting annoyed thinking about the puddle of piss touching her *geta*. Sōkichi slid between Taiga and Takana, reaching around and grabbing Taiga's arm in a lock behind his back.

"All I have to do is yell, and all my lieutenants will storm through that door," Taiga said.

"No, they won't." Natsu sighed in mock sympathy. "We have some friends running some...distractions. Your lieutenants have more important matters on their mind than protecting an ungrateful leader. *Irete hoshii!*" she continued in a high, vapid, sexy voice, "*Kimochi ii! Gaman dekinai! Ikisou!* Ah, *ani-ki! Iku~u~u~u!*"

Takana burst out laughing. Natsu's voice and words tickled her, distracting her from the itchiness in her shoulder. She took in the momentary ceasefire to brush against Sōkichi's arm—strong, firm, and holding her would-be future abusive husband in a diminutive position.

"You all want the chest, right? It's in the closet on the left. Take it!" Taiga cried, struggling to no avail from Sōkichi's grip.

Takana slid the door open and gasped. Tetsuo's body slumped in the corner behind the chest, his throat slit from ear to ear. She wheeled on her heels and punched Taiga in the face. She did it twice more before her hand got too sore to ball in a fist and the skin on her shoulder felt as though it were going to crack open. She put the *wakizashi* below his chin again.

"You will give that man proper funeral rites, Taiga. I don't give a fuck about your feelings, you disgraceful child! Take care of him, or I'll tell every one of your lieutenants how you treated our clan's *oyabun*. Whichever way you decide to handle it, they'll treat you the same way."

"Wait, so, you're *not* going to kill him?" Natsu asked as she dragged the chest out of the closet.

Takana glared into Taiga's frightened eyes.

"Who else is going to tell the clan my debt is erased?"

"It's gone," he whimpered. "Your family is free."

Sōkichi released him, and Takana held the blade at Taiga's neck while he slumped against the wall. Sōkichi and Natsu negotiated ropes around the chest to be lowered down to Shinkichi and Fusa below.

"You know, leaving the *bakeneko* part of my tattoo unburned was fitting. When the clan inked me, you chose the ugliest creature you could think of as my front-facing spirit. I don't think you ever looked into the mythology beyond that."

Takana lowered herself in a crouch.

"*Bakeneko* kill their masters, *tonchiki*. Remember my mercy, and above all, remember my spirit animal before you get it in your head to hunt me down. You leave me alone; I leave you alone. Are we clear, *ani-ki?*"

He nodded miserably.

As she gazed upon him, she came to an understanding about what he'd said earlier, about how seeing his enemy break before him also broke his heart. He was pathetic, near sobbing, covered in urine, fatherless, soon to be leading men that resented him and would sense his weakness soon enough. And if his talk was all to be believed, the 'love of his life' had been the one to humiliate him.

She pulled the *shuriken* from the door followed by her *katana*, and a strong urge to put him out of his misery bubbled up from her chest. However, she took it as a sign that while all of their backs were turned to their tasks, he hadn't moved a muscle away from the wall. He was more broken than he'd proclaimed to be before—*three times*...because of *her*. She didn't know how far her mercy could go for someone so loathsome and venomous. If they crossed paths ever again, would there be a second's hesitation?

She didn't look back on him as she joined her friends beneath the balcony and helped carry their treasure out of the city.

Chapter Ten

Gratitude

Kaeru: Frogs are a symbol of fertility, good fortune, and prosperity. They are often linked to things or people returning to their place of origin. Small frog charms can be put into suitcases for traveling, hoping to return home safely, as well as wallets and purses to attract money. Frogs both jump and look forward, symbolizing a positive meaning of advancing and moving in the right direction.

June 14, 1708
Utsunomiya, Tochigi Prefecture

CHIYO WAS SURPRISED TO SEE Takana so late at night and so soon after the injury. She fussed over the burned shoulder with Takana's hand lantern like any mother would. She ran her fingers over the new *kimono* and smiled, then laughed aloud, like Takana hadn't heard in over a decade. The prostitutes and clients milling about couldn't believe the sound came from the overseer and cast baffled looks their way.

"*Kaasan*, Fusa-*chan* worked very hard on this. I only love *sofu's kiseru* more."

"Well, it's still an improvement over that filthy wardrobe you were wearing before. What's this? A little...frog?" Chiyo covered her mouth, her eyes watering as she tried holding it all back.

Takana crossed her arms, winced at her shoulder, and waited for the laughter to die down.

"I'm so sorry, Ta-*chan*. It's...so cute..."

It wasn't the frog that wouldn't let Chiyo stop laughing—it was because she hadn't laughed in so long, it was like a dam of mirth broke open. Takana wished she'd hurry up through the fits, though, so she could share the real news.

"Are you okay, now, *kaasan*? I have something more serious to discuss."

"Do we need to go into my office?"

"No. Do you remember what I said when I saw you last?"

"When you threatened the second-in-command of our clan, after you encouraged him to rape me? Yes, I remember a little bit about that day."

Takana smiled and took her mother's hands.

"They're not our clan anymore, *kaasan*."

Chiyo processed that for a moment. Several moments. Her eyes grew wider with each one that passed.

"How did... Did you—?"

"Do you really want to know? Or do you want to start packing your things and follow me to our new estate?"

Chiyo frowned.

"I don't like this kind of joke, Ta-*chan*. Cut it out."

"Well, if you won't believe me, that's fine. But will you do me a favor? Gather all the girls you know want to get out of this trade and come to the estate where Fusa-*chan* rescued some of them. If those girls don't think they can handle going back there, it's all cleaned and stripped of furnishings. It won't look like how they remembered.

"Any other girls, any number, I don't care, if they want out, bring them to the estate. I'm going to offer them real jobs."

"You're... Wait a moment, Ta-*chan*. You're being serious?"

Takana beamed and nodded. Chiyo embraced her tight, lifting Takana off her feet while she returned it. Takana was surprised she had so much strength left. When they parted, Chiyo's cheeks were streaming with joy, and her shoulders had risen a few centimeters.

"Pack your things and talk to the girls, *kaasan*. I'll meet you all at the estate."

"You're not going with us?"
"I have one more visit to make."

Takana let herself into her father's house. There were empty *sake* bottles strewn about the room. The place hadn't been cleaned in… She couldn't guess how long. He never had to when they were rich and he hadn't gotten into the habit afterwards, either. Mildewy *tatami* and worse smells forced her to cover her nostrils with the back of her wrist. When that didn't help, she pulled off her *kasa* and wafted all the horrid smells away from her face like a fan. She almost wished for the smell of her burnt hair. A whiff of her singed armpit hair made her regret the idle thought.

Her father wasn't there, so she waited. His cushions were soiled. There was a tiny window on the wall. She opened it for what must have been the first time in years and stood close to it. It wasn't much better, but she could give her wrist a rest from fanning.

It wasn't long before the door slid open. Iwakuchi entered with another shabby prostitute. As much as it hurt Takana to make such a comparison, she believed the girl must have been Fusa's replacement in the cheap hay stalls.

"What are you doing here? It hasn't been a month yet," Iwakuchi muttered.

"*Nēsan*, did you get a chance to talk to Chiyo in the last hour?"

The girl shook her head meekly. She trembled at the sight of Takana with her *daishō*, and the *bakeneko* tattoo staring at her from beyond burned flesh.

"Go to her, now, before it's too late. I don't want you to miss the good news."

She nodded and left in a hurry. Iwakuchi sighed and scrounged around the apartment, flipping items in search of a new *sake* bottle.

"Did you bring what I told you to last time? You'd better not have come here without it."

"Or what? You'll slap me? Punch me? Rape me?"

"I never—"

"No, but get a few more bottles of *sake* in you, get increasingly angry at me for telling the prostitutes to stop visiting you, grow more frustrated at your lot in life—I'm not naïve enough anymore to think you hadn't thought about it, or that you're a better man than to do it."

"What a horrible thing to say to your father!" His exclamation dripped with denial.

"More horrible than selling your—" Takana stopped herself and held her hands out as if to stop the freefalling conversation. She breathed and collected her poise.

"*Chichi-ue*...I brought what you asked."

She pulled four *ryō* out of one of the poorly sewn pockets inside the *kimono* sleeve and fanned them out in front of his face.

He snatched them from her hand, showing no gratitude whatsoever.

"There's another reason I came by earlier than our 'monthly visit.'"

His mind had already gone to how he planned to spend the money, and he didn't seem to be listening.

"This is my last visit. This is the last time you'll ever see me. No more coin."

"What? You have to!"

"No. I don't. The debt's cleared. We're free."

He looked up into space as it slowly sunk in, the clouds over his eyes dissipating a tiny bit.

"We're... I thought I'd never hear that word again..."

"Yeah... Well, enjoy it. Good luck with your life, *chichi-ue*," she said with as much dismissive venom as she could muster.

She turned to leave, but he caught her by the arm and pushed her against the wall. She felt a section of her blistered skin tear open, but she took it without a whimper. He hadn't noticed her injury; he wouldn't notice if she made a sound for the pain.

She let him hit her once. Then twice. Then her blade pressed beneath his chin, backing him off her and into the other side of his room.

"You know why I let you hit me all these years? Because it's the only way you would ever touch me after you sold us. I'm almost sorry that this is the last way you're going to see me; touch me; remember me. But you had eight years to earn better memories."

A trickle of blood escaped from the side of her mouth.

"Goodbye, *chichi-ue.*"

She got all the way onto the path out of the city before her father caught up and called out to her.

"You really meant it? We really got out of the debt?"

Takana didn't look back or stop walking, but she replied over her burned shoulder.

"'*We?*' What did *you* do?"

A procession of former prostitutes walked about half a kilometer ahead on the road.

Takana pulled out the last of the special tobacco and stuffed it in the *kiseru*, trailing sweet puffs of smoke along the *Nikkō Kaidō*—to her new home.

Part Two – Paid in Death

Chapter Eleven

No Rest For The Ambitious

Dōjō: The practice facilities for Japanese martial arts. The student body supports and manages the grounds and building through ritual cleaning and care. The building itself was most often reserved for symbolic or formal occasions and decorated with various artifacts, while the grounds were used for the actual training.

June 18, 1708
Oyama, Tochigi Prefecture

IT RAINED AS TAKANA AND Fusa walked to Oyama. Natsu, Shinkichi, and Sōkichi went ahead to deliver the two chests with a few hired hands while Takana and Fusa helped Chiyo settle the rejuvenated former prostitutes into their new home. They paid a few *rōnin* to guard the estate until their return.

Fusa's sleight-of-hand practice progressed, and Takana found it fun playing together with different objects on the long walk. Fusa managed to swipe a handful of cigarettes from a shop in Ishibashi without alerting the owner. Takana left their value in coin on the counter with her own sleight-of-hand so Fusa could enjoy her success with a clear conscience.

On the road they were given a wider berth than normal from passing commoners, thanks to Takana's exposed tattoo. The burned flesh on the back of her shoulder didn't put people any more at ease. They didn't come across any thieves, either, which made for one of the most relaxing journeys she'd ever taken south.

A man ran up the road from Oyama. It took Takana a moment to recognize Shinkichi through the rain. Fusa waved him over.

"Takana-*san*, Fusa-*chan*, there's a problem with the money."

Takana imagined a hundred things that could have gone wrong. She chastised herself for taking the gold back. With Tetsuo's body touching the chest in the closet, his blood running along the bottom, it was blood money thrice-over. She'd been counting on being rid of it forever with the purchase of a better way forward.

"Catch your breath, Shinkichi-*san*," Takana said.

In his hurry to get to them, he forgot to bring water. Takana and Fusa held out their water containers. He looked at each skeptically, almost rudely, imagining sharing a container with the mouth of a former whore or a decade-long smoker. He decided not to hurt either of their feelings and pretended not to need water at all. Fusa shrugged and thought nothing of it. Takana rolled her eyes.

"Both chests are at the inn, safely in front of the mistress. It seems all who've come to pay for the table have arrived. We're three *ryō* short of winning."

Takana scowled, pulled the cigarette out of her mouth, and spiked it into the mud. If only she hadn't given the man who ruined her life those four *ryō*.

"That bastard continues to..." she muttered. "How much time do we have?"

"Until sundown."

"Two hours... How long did it take you to run to us?" she asked as she picked up their pace.

"Twenty minutes."

"Fusa-*chan*, how fast can you run?"

"Let's find out."

Takana was capable of good speed over short distances, but her lungs couldn't handle much more than that. She led them on a light jog to Oyama.

Sōkichi met them outside the inn about an hour before sundown. He filled them in that they had nothing more to sell on them besides their weapons, and those weren't worth four *ryō* combined. Fusa pat down her clothing but didn't come up with anything.

"I could steal from one of the shops on the main road," Shinkichi offered.

"I could, too," Takana said. "Fusa-*chan* and I could also use our... No! That's not what we're going to do. Come on, let's walk for a bit. We still have some time. Maybe an opportunity will present itself. It's better than standing around here."

Takana sighed when she accepted the futility of manifesting three *ryō*—if it was that easy, she'd have been out of debt eight years ago. She considering allowing Shinkichi to go ahead with the theft plan, then repay the shop owner once they secured the table in the Inn. She dismissed the thought. With a new, debt-free life, getting back into petty criminal behavior so soon was off-putting.

They had split up, anyway. She wouldn't be able to find him in time for a heist and get back to the Inn before the sun disappeared.

She stopped in the middle of the main road, ready to give up, when a shop caught her eye. It bought and sold used goods. Awareness of a certain pocket in her *kimono* sleeve grew heavier the longer she looked at the shopfront.

The last legal card she had to play...

The *kiseruzutsu* and its contents weighed even more in her hand as she tried to get used to the idea of never holding them again. She ran her fingers over the draconic design. She'd taken such good care of it. It had no scratches or dents. Its color hadn't faded. Surely the shop owner would appreciate that from an artifact that was at least one-hundred-fifty years old. Her grandfather received it from his grandfather, and who knew how old it was *then*.

She didn't care about its age. Her grandfather's strain of tobacco could be smoked in any pipe, if she were lucky enough to find another pouch to purchase. What she feared most was losing him, that she'd forget him if she no longer had something physical to spark her memories.

But...

It could be the currency to a better life: reunited with her mother at a new estate, new friends, two enterprises she couldn't wait to sink her teeth into, no debt for the rest of her life, future relationships with men she didn't expect to hate and abuse her, who weren't also men in the later stages of their lives.

Perhaps...

A hand grabbed her left shoulder before her next step would have put her in the shop. She turned around clutching the *kiseruzutsu* tightly to her chest and looked up into Sōkichi's eyes. He held up four *ryō*.

"How— Where did you—?" Her question was a whisper.

"All those *ryō* you paid us outside the *dojo* over the last eight years... We put them in our treasury. We've spent most of it on new practice swords, gear, food. There was almost nothing left, but I convinced the students I only needed these for a short time."

"I...I don't know what to say, Sōkichi-*san*. You just saved me from..."

While her hand remained tight around the *kiseruzutsu*, she reached the other up to his neck again. No one was going to interrupt them this ti—

"Takana-*san*! Sōkichi-*san*!" Fusa cried from down the road. "The sun!"

Sōkichi grabbed Takana's hand from his neck, then led her in the run to the Inn, never letting go until they reached the front door. Fusa took over from there, putting her hand in the small of Takana's back to speed her up the stairs to the mistress's office, filled with gold and hopeful mercenaries.

Natsu sat in front of their two chests, sweat dripping from her brow. Her smile lit up the room as the sun set over the mountains through the window.

Takana never thought she'd see so many people upset that they hadn't lost whole chests of gold. Then again, she never thought she'd be so happy to be rid of hers. The other mercenaries cursed and grumbled as they left the office with their hauls.

The mistress formally welcomed Natsu to the Inn from her ornate desk.

"This is my partner, Takana Gozen," Natsu said. "She and I will share the table."

The mistress maintained a neutral expression.

"Partnerships aren't unheard of, but it's rare for one of them not to kill the other for any number of reasons. We don't care if your partnership sours. If you kill one or the other, the living keeps the table. If you both die, the table opens up for another event.

"As far as the Inn is concerned, we get ten percent of whatever you make. There are no rules regarding the types of jobs you take. Reject or accept them as you like. If you go two weeks without a job taken, though, your table will be forfeit, with no refunds of your buy-in here.

"Do either of you have any other questions?"

They shook their heads and bowed together.

"You may take up your table immediately. Good night."

Takana and Natsu met Fusa and Shinkichi downstairs.

"Where's Sōkichi?" Takana asked.

"He went back to his *dōjō*," Fusa replied. "Said he needed a lot of sleep after helping carry those chests so far, especially after keeping guard at the doctor's office for so long."

"How rude of him not to invite Takana-*san* to share his *futon*." Natsu had a lewd little smile to go with the comment.

"What are you talking about? Why would—?"

"Sorry, Takana-*san*," Fusa said. "I told Natsu what I saw the other day."

"Oh. Well... Nothing happened. Thanks to *someone* in this room..."

Fusa blushed and bowed in apology again. Takana smiled, then reached into a pouch for a pair of trick dice.

"Your punishment is to learn how to hide these on your person, two at a time. Shinkichi-*san*, show her what you know. Then meet me at the gates at dawn."

"Where are we going to sleep?" Fusa asked.

"In the same conditions the three of us met in Ishibashi. We're broke, after all."

"What are you going to do, Takana-*san*?"

"Get this enterprise rolling. I'll see you in the morning."

In one of the rowdier restaurants in Oyama, Takana earned a different kind of distracted look from the gamblers and thugs. They couldn't seem to take their eyes off her burnt shoulder and colorful bruising all over her torso and face. They murmured questions and conspired between dice rolls.

Takana didn't fear that news from Utsunomiya—how she'd ended up in such rough shape, absconded from the clan—would have traveled so far so soon, but perhaps a rumor from the night she was burned could have.

She assessed the surrounding company. Some of the faces were notably piss-drunk and didn't care about anything else in the world but getting drunker or winning bets. Some looked like they wouldn't have cared about the protection that the full tattoo had afforded her before. They saw vulnerability, a softened target. If they saw an opportunity after the game was over and everyone had gone home—they were going to test her.

An aggressive-looking man, with a scar across his cheek—who wasn't as careful in his whispering—met her eyes before a dice roll. She stared back without fear. The room grew silent as his sneer twisted and his breath shortened; everyone focused either on the man or on Takana's face or burn. Not a soul watched her fingers do their magic with the cup and dice.

Most of those sorts of threats were diffused when the men won, so it was worth manipulating for a lower payout. When she rolled the Odd outcome and he won a large payout, his demeanor lost its hostility. Her take would be slightly less, but it was worth avoiding a street fight later. She needed to get her right arm back to full functionality, or her left arm up to speed, before she started looking for fights again...

In the owner's office she gathered her gear while he divided the take.

"Here you go, Takana-*chan*. Twenty percent."

Takana sat at the end of the table and offered him one of her cigarettes, then lit her own.

"I talked the *oyabun* back down to ten percent. Times being what they are."

The owner raised his eyebrows. No one ever lowered the take after raising it. She kept her serious "*yakuza* representative" face on.

"Only thing I'm going to ask is that you open yourself to more games during the month. I can usually only get here once, maybe twice. We're branching out, though. The *oyabun* is allowing me to hire some new girls. That means more money for you, my friend. I'll even improve our communication and send a courier ahead to alert you when a dealer will be in town. Gives you a little more time to prepare your staff and the late nights."

"I'm having trouble getting my head around this, Takana-*chan*. I've dealt with a lot of clans since I opened this restaurant forty years ago. What do you want from me?"

Takana took a puff of her cigarette and tossed her head in the general direction of the Inn.

"You know that merc inn? A few roads over there?"

He nodded. "Never needed to use it, but everyone in town knows of it."

"You...have the 'ear' of everyone in town?"

"I'm no politician, but many important people come into my restaurant. We're famous locally, and we've hosted processions from Edo."

Takana smiled at what she had hoped to hear.

"There's a new girl at the Inn. Orange hair. Pretty face, better smile. Black eye, currently, but that'll go away soon enough. If anyone takes their business to her, mention my name, and she'll lower the asking price."

The owner took back ten percent of the night's earnings and nodded at the new deal.

"You'll know when my girls are here. They'll have one of these." She pointed at the *bakeneko* tattoo.

A couple of hours before dawn, Takana wished to smoke from the *kiseru*, but without the special tobacco, she settled for another cigarette. She walked to Sōkichi's *dōjō* and sat down against the wall next to the gate. Her *kasa* provided enough cover from the light rain. She finished the cigarette, then dozed for an hour.

Sounds came from the *dōjō* at pre-dawn. The students woke up for their morning chores. Takana made herself visible by the gate. A student saw her and went inside for a moment. He came back with three other students, including Sōkichi. They both acted as if it was like any other visit, so the students were none the wiser.

They gathered around her with their wooden swords. Takana held up her hand when Sōkichi handed one to her.

"Thank you all for your help yesterday. Here are the four *ryō* I borrowed, and one for the training session this morning."

She exchanged the coins for the sword, then got used to the weight of it in her left hand. They frowned at her stance being backward.

"Go as hard as usual. I only ask that you be careful of my shoulder. It's still healing."

She earned more bruises than usual, thanks to being out of practice and clumsy with her left arm. At least they aimed away from her previous wounds. Except Sōkichi. The blatant targeting annoyed her.

Then he whacked her back shoulder. She cried out at the pain and fell to her knees. She caught herself from grabbing at the throbbing, itchy, burnt flesh. The three students turned on Sōkichi, chastising him for hurting her. He said nothing, but he stepped forward to loom over Takana while the students gathered around her in response, protecting her from whatever he planned to do next.

"An enemy won't choose to avoid your injuries," he said, then held out his hand to help her up.

The young students recoiled as if they'd been struck, then apologized to Takana for patronizing her and failing to prepare her for a real fight. They returned the coin for the training session because of their failure, then bowed deeply to their *senpai* before running back to the *dōjō* to finish their chores.

Takana tilted her *kasa* back and met Sōkichi's stoic stare.

"I'm glad you could teach everyone a valuable lesson, but I'm less effective the longer this takes to heal."

"Yes. That's the point of injuring your enemy."

"You sound like Tomoe-*sensei*. I don't mind you fighting rough with me, Sōkichi-*san*, and I get what you were trying to do. But talking as if we're enemies... Taiga did that to me. He meant it to come from a playful, mocking place, at first. You mean it to come from a protective one. It doesn't matter where it comes from. I—...I don't ever want us to grow to be enemies, so...please don't treat me like one."

He breathed deep, then bowed respectfully. Takana returned it, then relaxed.

"I hoped I wouldn't have to ask this, but are you coming back to the estate with us?"

"I didn't presume."

"Sōkichi-*san*... I'd like you to come with us."

He correctly sensed the sparks building between them; Takana speaking plain, being vulnerable. He moved closer, but she flinched when he went to put his hand on her shoulder. He persisted, laying a soft touch on her skin. His hands, like hers, were rough from swordplay, but he had a gentleness hidden behind his stoic exterior, beneath his fingers. The throbbing from his hit dulled, and, after a moment, his touch soothed better than the poultice the doctor had placed on the burn.

Takana took off the *kasa* and looked around for Fusa to pop out of nowhere again. Sōkichi betrayed a laugh. She was glad he'd be smiling for the attempt. The timing was perfect. The rain had stopped, and the clouds on the horizon split for the sunrise. The light spread across his face; she yearned to be those rays, touching his lips.

"*Senpai*! Breakfast is ready!" a student shouted from the gate.

The student waited for a response, more oblivious than Fusa. Sōkichi sighed and asked Takana if she wanted him to bring a couple of rice balls to the city gates. He said he'd gather his things and meet them there. She nodded and lit a cigarette to bring down her fluttering emotions.

Fusa and Shinkichi waited by the gate. Fusa held up her hands, displaying them to be empty.

"I'm so sorry, Takana-*san*. I lost your dice while we were practicing in the alleyway. They fell into a horrible-smelling hole."

Takana sighed. The trick dice could only be purchased from a shop in Edo. It was a long journey for something so small, but she needed to make the trip soon anyway, to get enough for all the girls, although they weren't exactly cheap.

Fusa naïvely held her arms out for a forgiveness hug. The strange girl's charm bewitched Takana and she couldn't help the urge to give her exactly what she wanted. Takana leaned in. Clumsy little fingers attempted to deposit the dice between her belt and lower back.

"Ah, you were so close, Fusa-*chan*."

Fusa cursed and took the dice back to continue practicing, at least until Sōkichi arrived. When he did, bearing rice balls, Fusa devoured hers before the others took their second bites, then walked ahead with Sōkichi as Shinkichi lagged behind a few paces with Takana.

"How'd you do last night, Takana-*san*?"

"Enough to pay back a debt, buy some dice, food for the estate."

"I did pretty well, myself. Found a drunk *yakuza* thug with a scar on his cheek asleep outside a bar. He had a lot of *ryō* on him."

"Funny how things work themselves out sometimes, Shin-kichi-*san*."

Chapter Twelve

Principles

Onna-musha: The female warriors who fought alongside samurai in battle. They were trained for offensive warfare, whereas onna-bugeisha trained for defense of the home and village. There is evidence of countless women warriors throughout Japanese history, ruling and leading clans and even the country, yet some historians dismiss nearly all accounts as fiction or exaggeration despite archaeological evidence that suggests otherwise. The relatively peaceful Edo period would see a significant downturn in the status of the onna-musha, as samurai battle companions were no longer concerned with war, but marriage, homes, and chi ldren.

July 1, 1708
On the *Nikkō Kaidō*, Tochigi Prefecture

TAKANA COLLAPSED AGAINST A TREE trunk with her arm covering her eyes. Everything hurt. Sweat soaked her clothes. Her hands were puffy and throbbing, almost unable to grip the wooden sword. Fusa and Shinkichi practiced sleight-of-hand in the distance, and she could barely focus on them. The rest stop had turned into anything but when she challenged Sōkichi to another duel.

Sōkichi frustrated her. Again. She could always count on him not to hold back. But somehow, since the decision to join them, he put more into his swings. Or was it her body crying out that it needed rest? Was he trying to push her to that realization? Was it only another lesson?

Back on the road, Fusa talked while hiding the dice.

"Why are you fighting so much, Takana-*san*?"

"Before my father's debt destroyed our lives, that's all I did with my free time. Fighting with Tomoe-*sensei*. I guess...I don't know what else to do with my free time."

"I can think of a couple things," Fusa said, tossing her head towards Sōkichi further up the road.

"That would be great, if we stopped getting inter-*rupt*-ed. What's the second thing?"

"Hmm?" Fusa hummed innocently while the dice disappeared from her hands.

"You said a 'couple things.'"

"Oh. Well, I didn't want to bring this up around the others, but...you could, maybe...you know, take a bath? More than once a week?"

"What are you talking abou—" Takana stopped herself after taking a whiff beneath her arm.

"Combine that with your burnt skin...I mean, I wasn't the cleanest *yūjo* in the *yūkaku*, but I know men might have paid a little more for me if you and I were the last ones in the lineup. Plus, you smoke. Your clothes don't get washed but, what, once every two weeks?"

Fusa slid her hand down the frayed cut of the kimono across Takana's torso, lightly touching Takana's cleavage on the way. Takana rolled her eyes and pulled the dice out of the little pocket in her *sarashi*.

Fusa smiled even though she'd been caught again.

"Nice try, Fusa-*chan*," Takana said as the dice disappeared from her fingers and back into Fusa's. "Do I really smell that bad, or was that all part of the trick?"

"Almost nothing smells worse than those hay stalls, Takana-*san*. But, you know, the principle of taking baths more often wouldn't hurt anyone."

Back in the estate, Takana luxuriated in a bath. She talked to a group of the former prostitutes who were also enjoying the spacious, natural *onsen* that pumped in from the rich mineral springs of the mountains. They reacted with shock and awe at her plethora of bruises, new and old. They got smacked around in their former occupation, but rarely by objects such as wooden swords. Or fire. Skin-on-skin left far less damage. It brought Takana great joy to be the one to tell them they would never have anyone smack them around again if they stuck with her and learned how to roll dice.

Chiyo disappointed with the news that she'd allowed the *rōnin* to take payments in "other forms" when they ran out of *ryō* to keep them on as protectors. Takana handed most of the take from her dice game over and told Chiyo there would be plenty more coming—she was never to use the girls in that way again.

Takana gathered every girl, along with Shinkichi, and explained her expectations for them going forward. To end the speech like no *oyabun* before her, she promised to never ask them to do anything that made them uncomfortable.

Now that she and Shinkichi had brought enough *ryō* to leave the estate well-stocked for a couple of weeks, Takana planned to leave for Edo to pick up dice. She'd earn on the way and back so they'd be set for the fall. She'd check in with Natsu at the Inn as well. Shinkichi would work on securing a fence closer to the estate. She didn't have an idea yet for what to do with Sōkichi.

Takana searched the building for him unsuccessfully. She asked one of the girls who would be much less shy about bursting in on him to check the bath. Taking advantage of the facilities while the girls had all been at the meeting was her last best guess. However, he wasn't in there, either.

Her outer clothes were being washed, so she only wore a fresh *sarashi* and half-length *hakama*. The rain had picked up again. The wet season neared its end, but still had about a week to go. She couldn't wait for everything to dry out. Mud stuck to everything.

A trek to Edo in the muck nearly put her off, but she needed to get the girls earning as quickly as possible. Takana tied on her *kasa* to keep relatively dry while she searched for Sōkichi outside.

Electricity coursed through the air. A thunderstorm passed overhead. A lightning strike flashed across the sky, illuminating Sōkichi standing in an open area behind the main building. He practiced with one of the wooden swords among the perfectly landscaped maple trees and moss-covered statuary.

During a powerful downswing, the thunder rolled over them, unzipping the rain. She approached him slowly. She meant to ask him his plans while she was away in Edo, but it was difficult talking in the deafening downpour. More lightning and thunder punctuated the carefully manicured grounds.

She might have questioned it before, but after his new "lessons," it was an opportune training condition. Battles didn't often wait for perfect weather.

Takana spied another wooden sword leaning against one of the trees. She retrieved it and gave it a few practice swings to get used to holding its wet hilt. One of the swings had some power behind it, and Sōkichi turned at the sound of it cutting the rain.

His eyes went to her *kasa*.

He was right. It wouldn't always be there to protect her. She'd become so reliant on it that she hadn't practiced without it in years. She leaned it against a tree, then pulled out the *kanzashi* holding her hair up. She threw it into the mud by the *kasa*, stabbing the earth. Her raven-black hair fell to her upper back and clung to her shoulders as it soaked in the warm rain, turning lush, dark purple.

Takana pressed the attack. He wasn't caught off guard by the advance as much as she'd hoped. She tried distraction.

"Sōkichi-*san*, we need to talk about what's next," she shouted into the pouring rain.

He struck her thigh. She'd only succeeded in distracting herself. She shook her head and focused on the fight. No matter what she wanted his answer to be, that didn't matter in a battle, either. Once the final thought of her attraction to him disappeared, she got through his defense. She hadn't entirely expected the move to work. Their torsos collided as her sword arm went by his. Her hand cascaded down his wet chest, then dropped to his belt and tore it off. She backed away with the sword raised.

His robe parted and hung soaked to the sides. He flung it off and prepared his stance to go again. Without her *kasa*, it was only fair he only had on his *hakama*, though she inadvertently caused a new distraction for her eyes. Takana tossed the belt over her shoulder and charged. They both "died" many times as Takana dusted off old moves she hadn't attempted since Tomoe-*sensei* taught her, switching things up with her left hand when she could. Sōkichi didn't need to try new moves—his strength and agility were difficult enough to penetrate.

Despite hitting him several times, she wasn't doing nearly the damage he did to her. If they were in a real battle, she'd have been skewered countless times, while he'd die by a thousand small cuts. Rage began to take over. She thrust and swung wildly, hoping to hurt him as much as she'd been. With each reckless step she took forward, he took back. As he easily parried her moves, her vision reddened.

She lunged forward for a stab, but he sidestepped and hit her in the back of the right shoulder again. The thunder overwhelmed her cry. She clenched her teeth and stared daggers into his eyes. It infuriated her on another level that he only stood there, expressionless as usual, as if it was nothing, as if he wanted her to think of him as her enemy.

Her outburst of pain changed to a guttural growl of ferocity. Instead of coming at him with honor, she threw the blade through the air. He wasn't expecting the blade to have left her hand. It hit him square across the upper stomach. He doubled over from the blow to his diaphragm. She closed the distance and shoved him into the mud on his back.

While she stooped to pick up the blade, he grabbed her ankle and pulled. She fell on her back next to him. She reached across her body to the sword, then rolled back to elbow him in the side. Finally—a yelp of pain.

Takana swung her leg up and over his hips, then plunged the sword into the mud by his ear. Still no smile. No fear. How could he feel nothing when she felt so much? She pulled back her right arm, pain be damned, and made to punch some emotion into him when he caught her fist centimeters from his face. He rolled over, putting her back into the mud. She struggled beneath him, kicking out her legs, trying to knee him between his.

She bit the hand that held her wrist, then reached over for the sword again. He rolled off her, which pushed her closer to the sword, but the force covered her front in mud, too. She got back to her feet and ripped the sword out of the ground while grabbing up a handful of muck. He was already in his stance, waiting for her to come at him again.

Takana flung mud towards him. When he turned his face away, she swung the blade across his back as hard as she could manage with her injured shoulder limiting her strength and pain tolerance. It made a strong *whapping* sound, and his grunt of pain was satisfying.

As he fell to his knees, she hugged around his back with one arm, similar to the way Natsu had killed the old man threatening Fusa. She brought the other arm around to go for the throat, but his hand again caught her wrist. He pulled her around to face him. On his knees, their eyes were level and within centimeters of each other. He was still maddeningly neutral. Several sequential strikes of lightning lit up the courtyard.

Traces of a small smile curled on his lips, and it was contagious. The rain dissipated and the thunder grew more distant. Takana's face burned at a chorus of muffled giggling coming from the veranda, but she committed to not getting interrupted again.

Takana washed the mud off her body and out of her hair, lowered herself into the part of the *onsen* where the water level reached her neck, and faced away from the door.

"Okay, Sōkichi-*san!*" she called.

While he washed the mud off, she focused on the water healing her shoulder's fresh bruises. The private *onsen* was her dream come true. Even though she had to share it with a gang of former prostitutes, she was glad to have it. Takana admonished herself—the women were so friendly and grateful; she needed to stop referring to them by their old profession.

The calm water rippled into her back as Sōkichi entered. He sat down behind her, and she leaned her back into his, molding to his musculature. They balanced themselves so they rested on each other equally, and Takana dozed as if she were sitting in a comfortable chair.

"You were saying something about what's next?" he startled her to full attention, breaking the blessed tranquility of the silent bath.

"Right. I didn't know what that might be until out in the courtyard. I've practiced at *dōjō* all along the *Nikkō Kaidō*. The women are going to need protection when they begin their dice games. Would you be willing to recruit guards for us? We're going to need one for every dealer, and I'd like to move away from unknown, dangerous *rōnin* protecting us here."

"I can start as early as tomorrow."

"Avoid Utsunomiya, please. I like the men at that *dōjō* but I don't want word spreading to the clan about where their stolen prostit— their former employees are. I don't suppose I need to mention that I'd like for your recruits to be the type you'd trust to leave alone with any of the women."

"Of course."

Takana lifted her hand up over her shoulder to rest on the side of his neck.

"You know, the type of man that can take a bath with a woman and not once steal a glance or fake a groping fall."

His hand reached up to cover hers. They held there as Takana dozed again.

When they finished their soak, they were red-faced and sweating. Sōkichi exited before Takana followed. He went to bed in the room closest to the entrance with Shinkichi. The other rooms were shared by the women. The doors remained open, so she got to hear all the giggling as she passed. It was mildly irritating, but she couldn't help feeling a little lighter as she walked. People acting happy for her was a new sensation.

Her mother had placed two *futon* in the largest room at the end of the hall. Chiyo turned to face Takana as she laid down.

"Was it everything you hoped for?" Chiyo asked.

"What?" Takana blushed and turned away from her mother's bemused smile.

"Fusa-*chan* shared the story of your battle in the courtyard. Maybe she...embellished? Sōkichi-*kun* is quite handsome. I'm so hap—"

"I don't want to talk about it, *kaasan*," Takana said as her skin's temperature rose again, almost hotter than in the *onsen*.

"Suit yourself. I can get more details from any of the other girls that enjoyed the performance."

"I'm not one of your whores. You don't need to know the details of that part of my life."

Chiyo sighed and turned away. Takana was miserable on the *futon*. The blanket weighed heavily in the humidity. She got up and walked to the door before pausing.

"I'm sorry, *kaasan*. That was rude of me. I've only recently come into friends and getting you back. I've developed edges. I'd...be happy to talk to you later. I love you."

"I love you, too, Ta-*chan*."

Takana went outside to find somewhere to sleep on the ground that had an overhang to protect from the light rain.

Chapter Thirteen

Marks

Kunai: A basic tool in the hands of a craftsman or farmer; a multi-functional weapon in the hands of a martial arts expert. Most commonly associated with shinobi and mythologized as a throwing weapon only, they could be used in myriad ways in ranged and melee distances, attached to ropes and poles, and concealed in several places.

July 3, 1708
Oyama, Tochigi Prefecture

WHILE NATSU SPOKE WITH THE last of the potential clients of the day, Takana sat across the table and smoked a few cheap cigarettes. The taste and smell didn't matter as the cloud that hung throughout the Inn was too thick to discern a single scent. Thanks to Takana's play with the restaurant owner, and some of the other places she stopped on the way back to the estate, Natsu had been busy weighing, rejecting, and accepting job offers of all kinds.

What worried Takana were the looks from many of the male mercenaries at the other tables cast their way. Some of them didn't seem to appreciate so much traffic going to the new girls' table, while others stared with a dangerous longing. Despite Natsu's black eye, she was still the loveliest of all the female mercenaries. After witnessing a small portion of her handiwork at the estate,

Takana would have liked to believe Natsu was in absolutely no danger. But then again, she'd had the element of surprise.

The last client left after Natsu said she'd get back to him. Takana offered a cigarette, to which Natsu sneered.

"It's bad enough I have to breathe in this room all day."

"Are you taking breaks outside?"

"Sure. How's the estate coming along? You look like you're finally gaining some much-needed weight."

"I'll feel better when we get rid of that *rōnin* protection. I have Sōkichi-*san* recruiting guards as we speak. Anyway, I'm heading to Edo tomorrow for the dice and the other thing. I might look for some tobacco, too."

"Tobacco is everywhere. Why waste the time and expense?"

Takana took out the *kiseruzutsu* and explained its significance. Natsu handled it respectfully while looking it over, then slid it back across the table with her brow furrowed.

"Are you okay, Natsu-*san*?"

Natsu's tight lips quivered for a moment before she waved her hand and cleared her throat.

"I've got some local jobs lined up. They'll be easy to take care of solo. I can do them at night anytime this week. You've got about eighteen hours of travel to Edo, right?"

"Yes, if I don't stop. But I've got several restaurants to visit on the way. There are a lot of dice games between here and Edo."

"I've got a better idea—there's a job I received yesterday. The pay is significant enough that you could skip all the stops to Edo. You and I could do it together, since it's on the way south."

"Will I need a *kunoichi* outfit to match yours for this job?"

"Not if we're careful."

They lay side by side on their stomachs, peering over the ridge of a roof in Koga. The meeting spot remained clear of activity.

"Should be any time now…" Natsu whispered.

"Do you have weapons and gear hidden all over the country?" Takana asked as she took another look at the bow at Natsu's side.

"My clan plans for everything."

"Are they going to be okay with you taking things from the caches?"

"They send new members through the country once a month to re-stock when necessary. There's nothing to worry about, except this damn meeting not happening."

The cicadas' buzzing died down once the sun had set. Without the insect's music drowning them out, footsteps came from opposite directions to converge near a spot along the wall under them.

Natsu nocked an arrow but kept low against the roof. Takana counted then lowered herself closer to Natsu. She motioned with her fingers that there were eight men below, four to each side. They picked up bits and pieces of their conversation.

"…Extra protection…clan lost half…one night…Kochiya clan breaking…"

Natsu nodded that she was ready. Takana pulled down four *kunai* from her *kasa* and returned the gesture. They crept over the roof to the edge, then let loose. Natsu's arrows were instant death—she was as much a master with the bow as the *tantō*.

Takana's *kunai* hit the right spot in the neck of one man. The other three on Takana's side had turned to run before she buried more *kunai* in the back of the two trailing men's knees. Natsu put down three of her men before her fourth started running.

They both grasped the edge of the roof and lowered themselves to the ground.

"Save yours or mine?" Natsu asked as she nocked the last arrow.

"Mine."

In a blink Natsu's straggler hit the ground; the arrow had found its mark through the back of his heart. Takana used her *wakizashi* to put an end to the two she'd crippled. She wiped the blade onto their clothes and collected her *kunai*.

"Nice and clean. Good work, Takana-*san*."

"I can't believe we took a job from a *yakuza* to kill the *yakuza* of two other clans."

"I'll take any job that pays me to kill more of them. And the more chaos it causes all of them, the better."

A yell came from the direction of the man they purposefully let live to spread the word.

"Your wish has been granted, Natsu-*san*."

Four more men, plus the man they'd let escape, ran towards them, *katana* in hand. One party must have had reserves in case negotiations had gone sour. Natsu pulled an arrow out of the first man she killed and let it fly through one of the charging men's head. Takana unsheathed her *katana* and readied herself for when Natsu ran out of arrows again. The next one whistled past Takana's *kasa* and took another man down.

The last man they'd killed at range was too far away for Natsu to reach before the men would be on them. Takana put her back to the building to keep from being surrounded. Natsu cursed as her third arrow narrowly missed the target. One of the men chased after Natsu while the last two stood diagonally on each side of Takana's defense to corner her.

The men charged at the same time, their blades held high above their heads, coiled for lethal downward strikes. Takana sidestepped to her left, blocking the left man's swing. She grasped the hilt of her *wakizashi* and in one fluid motion the blade found a new sheath in the man's back. She let go and backed up for the other man's recalibrated attack. Instead of a downward motion, he slashed horizontally. Takana flung herself backward below the blade's reach, caught her fall with her right hand against the ground, and thrust the *katana* in her left straight up into the man's chest.

Natsu rounded the corner of the building with the last man, holding her *tantō* to his neck.

"I had a feeling you'd forget to leave one alive," Natsu said, then growled in the man's ear: "Tell your clan this was the work of the Matsuba clan. We're coming for all the business in the city. And if you run for reinforcements, I'll make sure someone *else* will be the last one alive to deliver the message."

The man nodded and ran after she let go.

"What proof do we need to get paid?" Takana asked while cleaning both blades and returning them to their scabbards.

"A head from each clan."

"Do you really have to carry them all the way back to Oyama?" Takana's lip curled in disgust, remembering the mess in the bag she'd rescued for that headhunter.

"No. The Matsuba representative is meeting me along the road with our payment. He only wants to see them. And don't think I didn't notice you just tried to pawn that off on me," Natsu said in a good-humored tone.

"Okay, fine. Please tell me you have a bag before I start cutting."

Natsu pulled two head-sized bags from her back pocket. After the gruesome work was finished, they walked towards the road, each with a package in hand.

"How's Fu-*chan*?" Natsu asked. "Has she asked about me?"

"Um...no. Not really."

Even after seeing Natsu break down at the estate, it was still odd to see her lose her smile.

"I wonder...if I scared her...after what I did..."

"Mm... Maybe, but nothing seems to get her down for too long. Like you. Except I've seen you sad twice already today."

Natsu took on a far-off look and stopped talking. Normal conversation seemed strange while carrying human heads, so Takana didn't press the matter. When they reached the designated road, Natsu said the contact would reach them close to midnight. Takana lit a cigarette to cover the pungent smell of the heads.

"Natsu-*san*," Takana started after processing the question about Fusa, "when I get back from Edo, why don't you take the supplies and money back to the estate? I'll sit at the table for a couple days."

The brazier by the wall they leaned against didn't light up Natsu's face nearly as well as her smile did.

It was easy to guess which man was their client—no one had passed on the road for about an hour; no one traveled the road that late if they could help it.

"Keep your hand on the hilt," Natsu whispered to Takana before calling out the man's name to draw him over.

He approached, nodded, then asked to see the contents of the bag.

"Good. I recognize both of them," he said, then handed over a bag of *ryō*.

"Hey, you want any more *yakuza* dead, we're the mercenaries to talk to at the Inn," Natsu said.

"How many did you kill in all?"

"Twelve."

"Twelve?" The man shook his bewildered head. "I think I underpaid you."

"Consider it our introductory rate. Do you mind if I ask why you hired us to do that?"

"*Oyabun* wants to expand by starting a war between the smaller clans. Thin out the competition."

"Why not form an alliance?" Takana asked.

"Too expensive. You're much cheaper. And after the massacre with the clan that was joining the Kochiya clan in Utsunomiya, a lot of the heads are rethinking that strategy to expansion."

Takana's cheeks warmed up. She hadn't only ruined Tetsuo's alliance, but inspired bloodlust in the remaining clans, too.

"Mind if I count the bag?" Natsu asked.

"Please do."

Natsu turned her back to empty the coins on the low wall. The man pulled a *tantō* from beneath his robes and made a move for Natsu's back. He was fast, but not enough to outpace Takana's quickdraw, slicing through his wrist with her *katana*.

"*Arigatō*, Takana-*san*~," Natsu sing-songed without turning around, her back getting spattered by blood.

The man's shock kept him quiet for a couple seconds. Takana sheathed her blade, then moved behind him and put her hand over his mouth before he could scream the pain out. Natsu finished counting and put the coins back in the bag.

"At least the count was honest." She smiled at him. "I'm sure you thought you'd make your *oyabun* extra happy by getting the job done *and* keeping the payment. It's too bad. We could have done some important work together."

"Last man standing; let him spread the word?" Takana asked.

"No."

Natsu slashed the man's stomach open and stepped aside before his intestines could spill onto her *geta*. When his muffled screams stopped and his body lost all tension, Takana let him drop.

"If we're all done here, I'm heading to Nakada to sleep, then I'll get to Edo tomorrow."

"I look forward to seeing you in a few days, then," Natsu said. "Um, Takana... -*san*..."

Takana waited, but Natsu looked like she didn't know how, or even what, she wanted to say, and the way she almost dropped the honorific from Takana's name was unexpected.

"I hope you find your grandfather's tobacco."

Natsu bowed quickly and turned up the road.

By the time Takana arrived in Edo, all the *ryō* she'd collected at the towns along the way weighed her down. She appreciated Natsu's idea to skip dice games because of the *yakuza* payday, but Takana didn't have it in her to pass up chances to earn, debt or no debt.

Being back in the large city after so long was even better because she had her own money to spend. She ate foods she only dreamed of tasting before. There were accessories she'd always wanted—arm bands, bracelets, rings, hairpins to control her bangs and side hair. She visited four tobacco shops before finding her grandfather's special blend. She didn't care how much the clerk marked it up and bought two pouches.

After picking up the dozens of dice she'd ordered through a courier service—one third real, two thirds trick—she ambled the streets of Edo, smoking from the *kiseru* with languid enjoyment. She had one more task to accomplish before she'd hire a horse to carry the weight of her spoils back to the estate.

One of the jobs she did for the clan when she traveled to Edo every six months was to pick up *irezumi* supplies for the Utsunomiya *yakuza* tattoo artist. Inside the shop, she asked the owner if he knew of any *deshi* she could talk to within Edo. He directed her to the office of a tattoo master known for training *deshi* before they could be considered artists.

The master relayed to Takana that two of his apprentices were ready to move out to open their own shops, so she requested to meet them. The first refused to work for a woman. The second, Genjirō, was more amenable when she got to the part about marking many attractive young women. After he agreed to her offer, she negotiated terms with the master to let him leave Edo.

Genjirō's first order of business was to buy *irezumi* supplies from Takana's former contact while she hired two horses. After loading up, they began the journey north on the *Nikkō Kaidō*. Takana treated him to eating and drinking at the restaurants in which she hosted games on the way to Oyama, making back all she'd spent in Edo.

The burden of carrying so much coin was always a challenge, horse or not. But now that the money belonged to her, it was easier to bear. The debt hanging over her head had been replaced with prospect, excitement for the future. Still, she couldn't help feeling guilty on the road for all the superfluous spending in Edo. The rich, expensive food almost made her sick, and the wastefulness that twisted her stomach into knots didn't help. The opulent *onsen* visit she'd taken wasn't as relaxing as the cheap, public bathhouses. The only thing that still felt natural was sleeping outside in alleyways, and smoking.

But even the smoking was different. She bought two pouches of the special blend; smoking more of it walking around Edo than she had in the whole year prior. She neglected to buy the cheaper cigarettes that had, up until then, helped bridge the times she could justify bringing out the *kiseru*.

Takana had always found what pleasure she could in the mundane, but once her greatest pleasures became everyday occurrences, they began losing their appeal.

In Oyama, Takana relieved Natsu at the table like she'd promised. Before Natsu could make for the estate, though, they had to retrieve their coin from the private area of the Inn where all mercenaries were allowed to keep their earnings. They deposited their takes and the mistress removed ten percent of what was inside each week, with a man that followed her around with a ledger. Two guards posted outside the coin room and one in the deposit area. Once the mistress made her rounds, the mercenaries were allowed to take out the remainder or store it there.

There were no rules for the coins left in the deposit boxes when a mercenary died. The Inn still took their take, then left the remainder inside for the incoming merc to claim. Takana appreciated a little more Natsu's insistence that they become partners and ditch the "three favors" deal, as the partnership already proved to be far more fruitful than she'd imagined. In a bit of luck, the lecherous mercenary who'd left them his table had also bequeathed a couple dozen ryō to Natsu and Takana's startup business.

Adding their take at the Inn tripled the weight of the coin Takana earned since leaving the estate—all spending included. While she gathered the coin from their box, a stocky woman bumped into her from the side as she reached for her own box. Not expecting hard contact, Takana dropped her coins all over the floor. Takana pursed her lips and looked up in time to see the woman subtly let her hand slip, dropping her small number of coins on top of Takana's pile.

"Oh, I'm so sorry about that!" the woman said.

She bent down to scoop up coins into her box. Takana recognized what she was doing. Before she could push the woman away from the pile, one of the guards put a hand on the woman's shoulder.

The guard stood taller than Sōkichi, and had nearly the same musculature. She held a *naginata* as tall as her, with a blade at the end larger than her head. Her expression did all the talking necessary. The stocky woman let go of the coins, then stood back in shame.

"You back up, too," the guard said to Takana, then called out for the man with the ledger in the other room.

"What's going on, Chise-*san*?" the man asked.

Chise explained the situation and asked for an accounting of both boxes. Takana glanced at the woman, still hanging her head.

"Hey," Takana whispered, "does that really work for you?"

"First time I've tried."

"Why are you trying to rob me?"

The woman only stared at Takana, unsure how to answer.

"I'm Takana. My partner is Natsu. You've seen her downstairs, I'm sure."

"Hana."

"Tell me what you needed the money for so badly and I might not hold it against you," Takana said.

The mercenaries in the Inn weren't well-versed in partnerships, but surely the woman understood it was better to hold neutrality with other tables' members than to harbor a grudge over a petty misdeed.

Hana hesitated, then opened up.

"One of my best clients was working in the Kochiya-*kai*. They're having some kind of turmoil in the last couple of weeks, and the jobs stopped coming. I'm falling behind on my responsibilities."

"What's happening with Kochiya?" Takana asked, trying to sound like she'd never heard of that clan before.

"Power changes, defectors, transfers, suicides. All of this is hearsay. I only had contact with one of their lieutenants."

Takana abhorred the guilt piling on since leaving Edo. The news of her former clan in shambles was like a new debt she'd taken on inadvertently. She didn't want the feeling to follow her to the estate, so she tapped on the shoulder of the man with the ledger and nodded towards Hana.

"Give her the last merc's share, please, then come get me downstairs when you're done so I can take the rest."

Hana sputtered and couldn't get a real word out. Takana gave a weak smile as she left the room and sought Natsu to share the news of their minor loss.

Chapter Fourteen

Too Easy

Naginata: Also called "reaping sword," the naginata is a polearm with a large, curved blade at the end of a long shaft of wood. It is iconic to the onna-musha and features prominently in many tales of women warriors. The weapon may have been in use since the 12th century. It is said that the naginata is not a work of art or offering to gods as many other revered weapons, but equipment used only for combat, belying its effective and deadly reputation on the battlefield.

July 6, 1708
Oyama, Tochigi Prefecture

NATSU LEFT FOR THE ESTATE with Genjirō and two horses weighed down with coin and supplies while Takana sat at their table in the Inn. Genjirō had made a comment to the side that if the other women were as beautiful as Natsu, he might lower his fees. He laughed until Takana considered it aloud and he realized he should have kept the joke to himself.

A waitress provided Takana with a handful of cigarettes and a platter of rice balls. Mercenaries glared at her whenever her table had a line of prospective clients. Spreading the word through the region's restaurants had been so easy; had none of them ever thought of it?

The variety of requests she received were jarring at first: a farmer wanted her to kill the vermin decimating his crop. A *kabuki* actor requested a personal guard while he walked the city at night. A merchant needed something priceless in his shop to be hidden before he was visited by his *yakuza* creditors. Many *yakuza* asked for assassinations. A desperate woman clinging to her marriage begged Takana to sleep with her husband as a gift to keep him from leaving her. A former noble wanted an escort to Nikkō so he could pay respects to his ancestors without fear of being robbed along the way.

By the second half of the day, it dawned on her how much money she had to pass up. It was incomprehensible going from giving away every coin she'd ever earned to her clan, to having people line up to give her loads of it for some surprisingly mundane tasks.

Takana didn't have much time to absorb the goings-on of the Inn, not with so many clients wishing to speak with her. When there was a pause in clientele, she went outside to smoke on the veranda. Hana surprised her with a tap on the shoulder.

Hana bowed and thanked Takana for the unexpected assistance earlier. She said she would pay back the debt soon, but Takana shook her head.

"It was a gift, Hana-*san*. Or donation. Whichever sounds better to you. You don't need to pay me back."

"Is there nothing I can do for you, Takana-*san*?"

Takana considered Hana's eyes when she stopped bowing. It shamed her to beg, but there was a fear there, too. She must have known, just as well as Takana did, that nothing ever really comes for free. Simply telling the poor woman there was no debt wouldn't make it disappear.

"You said you lost your primary client from Kochiya, correct? I have an idea to replace the work I took from you."

"What are you talking about? *You* took it from me?" Takana realized what she said, then shook her head again.

"Sorry, I misspoke. To replace the work you told me was taken *from you,* why don't you accept some of my prospective clients? You'll pay my partner and me twenty percent as a finder's fee, plus the ten percent to the Inn, then keep the rest. We have enough jobs to keep you busy every day from here on out."

Hana couldn't believe the direction her life had taken from that morning. It seemed like she was being blessed instead of punished for trying to rob them. Takana told her to stop overthinking it and accept the terms. They bowed in agreement.

They sat at the table together, earning more angry looks. Takana ignored them and sifted through the job proposals, picking out the less-desirable ones to hand over to Hana. She chuckled when she came across the one she had planned to save for Natsu as a joke.

"How do you feel about sleeping with a man to save his marriage?"

As the day progressed, several mercenaries approached Takana to complain about rarely getting approached for jobs due to their placement in the back of the Inn. One of them even threatened to "end" her and Natsu for making their jobs harder, and that he'd get all the other mercenaries together to do it.

Takana compromised by offering them the same terms that she'd given Hana, who was out earning money as they spoke without ever talking to a client herself. Almost all of the disgruntled mercenaries accepted and took the job information. The threatening mercenary sat down at her table, unsatisfied with the idea.

"You really expect me to give ten percent to the house, and twenty percent to you? That's absurd!"

"One hundred percent of nothing is nothing. I'm giving you something you weren't earning on your own."

His anger dissipated as he thought about it. If he agreed to the terms, Takana decided she would give him jobs that didn't require too much thought. Eventually he bowed and took a job.

For the most part, the clients never sat down at a table unless they were invited. The last one of the day sat down without asking and eyed her tattoo.

"I recognize your mark. I've been to several of your dice games. I never thought I'd see a starving, dirty, *yakuza* errand-girl at one of these tables."

The faces of gamblers and *yakuza* thugs at the dice games all ran together in Takana's memories. The mechanics of the game were simple enough that she could do it in her sleep. She'd become so adept at using her trick dice she could do that just as easily. No dice game stood out from any other, except for the occasional bloodshed afterwards.

She pretended to at least recognize his face and asked what she could do for him after he introduced himself as Yoshimatsu.

"I'm running out of money thanks to games like yours, and I'm not getting paid by my *oyabun* for another month. I know of an artifact in a noble's house that would sell for enough that I wouldn't need to worry about income for six months. I've already got the fence set up; I just need someone to get it for me."

"If you know where it is, why don't you—?"

"One, I'm pretty clumsy. Two, it's my uncle's house."

Takana immediately had questions, but he interrupted before she could ask any.

"My family situation isn't important. I only need you to get the artifact. I'll pay you twenty-five percent of what I get from the fence. It won't be insubstantial."

Takana accepted and he relayed his uncle's location and guards' shifts. When he left, Hana came back from her job and showed Takana the count before she went to make the deposit upstairs.

"I have another job for you, Hana-*san*. See that man at the bar? *Yakuza* thug. I'm doing a job for him, but...there's something off. I can't put my finger on it. Please follow him, but don't approach him. I only want to know where he sleeps. For your help, you can keep the twenty percent from that job after you pay the Inn."

Hana nodded and went upstairs while Takana prepared to get back on the road. Yoshimatsu's uncle's house outside Nogi wasn't far away but the sun was almost setting, and she had preparation to do.

Takana watched the estate in the dark from a neighboring roof. Her hair lay damp on her shoulders from using the public bathhouse. She'd never be as lithe and slippery as Natsu, but her confidence was higher than it had ever been as she used Natsu's tips to espionage.

Takana staked out until the end of a guard shift, knowing they'd be sleepiest before getting relieved. There were only three patrolling the grounds. Even with their near-constant movement, there would always be a large enough gap for her to sneak through to the house. She scouted out the part of the grounds with the fewest bushes, trees, and sand to keep her movements as quiet as possible. Her loose gear and *geta* were all hidden back by the road.

She married the shadows while infiltrating the main house. A few residents slept in rooms she passed as she searched for the ornate plate. She found it in the *tokonoma* of an office. She'd seen more spectacular pieces, but its value came from being displayed in the Imperial Palace centuries before. There were two other plates on shelves as well, but it would be difficult to carry more than one in silence, so she ignored the greedy thought and picked up the one Yoshimatsu had described.

Back on the road with the stolen plate in hand, the uneasiness from the table grew. The job had been effortless. There should have been at least one more guard on the grounds, and one or two inside the estate. For a noble with other priceless art on display, she found it hard to believe she got out that easily. Or maybe it was all in her head and Natsu rubbed off on her more than she expected...

Yoshimatsu met Takana outside the gates of Oyama at dawn and said he'd come to the Inn after he fenced the plate. Outside the Inn, Hana waited, but before going into details about Yoshimatsu, she informed Takana that the mistress requested they meet and to not keep them waiting much longer.

When Takana went inside, the mistress and her ledger man were seated at her mercenary table. Takana asked if everything was alright, to which they invited her up to their office. The man introduced himself more formally there as Itarō.

"We see what you're doing, Gozen-*san*," Itarō said, throwing her off by using her surname. "What you've arranged with Hana-*san*, the jobs you're passing out to the less-successful mercenaries, the unofficial advertising…"

"Is there a problem? I thought there were no rules—"

The mistress held up her hand for silence.

"There's no problem with what you're doing. More jobs mean more income for the Inn. Happier mercenaries lead to less violence under our roof, fewer complaints in this office, and less bickering around the deposit boxes. More completed jobs lead to grateful clients spreading the word. These are all mutually beneficial outcomes for the Inn."

"The reason we brought you up here," Itarō continued, "is that we'd like to open a new Inn in Utsunomiya. This will broaden our reach into Nikkō to the west and north up the *Ōshū Kaidō* to Shirakawa. We'd like you and your partner Jingū-*san* to run the new Inn as mistresses."

Takana realized her mouth was open. She shook her head as if waking from a dream.

"We've only been working for a short time… I don't understand why you'd choose us for such an important undertaking."

"Jingū-*san* was one of the mistress's sisters among the *kunoichi* clans," Itarō explained. "She came here looking for a partner to carry out her revenge at the estate. She couldn't pay, though, so we told her she could hang around the Inn to find someone to work with, simply due to her connection to the mistress. We didn't let her do it for free, however. We asked her to keep an eye out for people of interest to help us prosper. She's been measuring you and your family. Jingū-*san* speaks highly of you all, though I'll admit she's forming new attachments that worry us."

Takana furrowed her brow. Natsu had been hiding even more than Takana thought. Her mind couldn't reconcile the fast, close trust the two of them shared with the knowledge that Natsu continued lying to her. The mistress sensed Takana's doubt.

"Natsu-*san* came up after my time, but she has a strong reputation among the *kunoichi* clans as being intelligent, loyal, and deadly. I would trust her with my life. When I saw her in Oyama after her trip to Utsunomiya with you, I sensed her burden had been lifted, and a new hope for life without revenge formed in its place. You gave that to her. She would die for you. You're perfect partners to open the new Inn, and you've already proven to be trustworthy with money and deals with the other mercenaries. We're confident with the coin you'll be pulling in once the Inn opens."

Takana imagined sitting in an office like theirs—people working for her, bringing her money through little effort on her part... That was mostly her plan with her new stable of dice dealers. Other than their initial training and an effective system for advertising, Takana planned to receive a percentage of their earnings without lifting a finger further. She was recruiting protection through Sō-kichi, so she could sit in that office without worry for the operation's safety.

The thought dawned on her what the scheme resembled; what she was actually building. More than his affection, had she secretly coveted Tetsuo's position as well? Was Tetsuo's spirit watching over her? Guiding her unknowingly? Takana resisted the urge to look over her shoulder, but her spine shuddered.

"This is a big decision for you, Gozen-*san*," Itarō said. "Think about it. Talk it over with Jingū-*san*. Until then, we want you to travel with Chise-*san*. She feels cooped up guarding the money, and she was impressed with the way you handled Hana-*san*. She'll share with you what she knows about this business, as well as protect the investment the mistress and I are hoping to make in you and Jingū-*san*."

Takana didn't know what else to say, so she bowed and went downstairs to the table to begin her day of offer-sorting. Yoshimat-su waited for her with a bag of money.

"That was incredibly fast. Your fence must have been so confident in your ability to get the artifact, he had the money ready to go," Takana said, raising an eyebrow as she counted out her percentage.

"I'm a persuasive man. The fence believed I'd come through. Now that I know you'll come through so expertly, I have another job for you. Much more lucrative."

"Want me to steal the rest of your uncle's artifacts?" She looked up to gauge his reaction.

"No. He'll be on high alert after the theft last night. What I need from you now isn't an object, but a person. There's a rival clan up in Koganei. We've engaged in some skirmishes over the last several months, trying to gain control of a few businesses and farms. My *oyabun* needs to know their plans for future hits. One of my brothers has been watching their headquarters for a month. There's a brief period of time when their *shateigashira* will be alone. I need you to subdue and bring him to the road, where my brothers and I will be waiting for the transfer."

"Sounds...expensive."

"Bring him to us, and we'll have two bags like this one—just for you, no splits."

Takana stared at the twenty-five percent she'd taken from the bag. The money in two of the bags would feed the estate for at least a year, even without frugality. That quick calculation pushed out her uneasiness. She bowed in acceptance of his terms. He said he'd meet her outside the Oyama gates with the information later.

Takana spent the rest of the day lining up jobs to give to her new mercenary partners while Hana described Yoshimatsu's house. When Takana finished and headed for the door, Chise stood in the doorway, blocking nearly all of it with her wide, muscular frame. She held her *naginata* proudly at her side and wore light plate armor. She nodded at Takana's approach and cleared the doorway to follow her out.

While getting the details for the abduction, Yoshimatsu dismissed Takana's comment that Chise would be taking her own cut from Takana's pay as none of his business. They parted from him and began the ninety-minute walk to Koganei north of Oyama. Chise didn't say anything; as a guard she was used to long periods of silence. Takana was accustomed to silence as she walked the road as well. She wasn't sure how well a relationship between two people that were content not to interact with others would work.

Silence while alone was easy. Walking side-by-side was another story. Initial small talk didn't seem to go anywhere until Takana asked to hold the *naginata*.

"Oof, this is much heavier than the one I practiced with. That was over a decade ago, too. I imagine no one gets near you with your natural reach and this thing."

"My days in battle are behind me, but that's still the case."

"Mm. Sorry, I didn't mean to make it sound like men avoid you. I was just saying—"

"Worry not. My feelings aren't so easily hurt. I may seem out of place in peacetime, but when I was the only woman in my unit, I got whatever I wanted and learned to get along with all of the men. It's *women* I'm more uncomfortable around."

"Oh. Well, I'm not sure you're going to like where I live, then."

Takana brought Chise up to speed on the estate and its new inhabitants. Soon they were in a position on the outskirts of Koganei where the *yakuza* headquarters were visible. They studied the entrance and exit points, then walked back through the city to discern the best escape route to the main road.

They used the local bathhouse after dinner to clean off the road smells and avoid spooking their target too soon. Chise wore dozens of scars across her body. The pain had left Takana's bruises, but they were in their end stages of healing when they're at their most colorful. That, combined with Takana's tattoo and burn scars, made a few of the other women in the bath leave abruptly. After only a few minutes of washing, the owner's wife asked them to leave to avoid losing more business.

Takana was used to that occasionally. For all the good the tattoo did to protect her, it got her kicked out of many places. Since she wore it publicly thanks to Fusa's half-*kimono* creation, she had resigned herself to being pressured to leave many more legitimate establishments than before.

Once they set up outside the *yakuza* headquarters to wait for their window of opportunity, Chise asked about the tattoo and the back of Takana's shoulder. After the explanation, Chise said she had a new respect for her after seeing all the bruises and hearing her story but didn't take the prompt from Takana when asked about her own scars.

When the right time arrived, they entered the headquarters through a back door. Chise was light on her feet and controlled her armor not to clatter. They made their way through the rooms. Each one was empty of not only people, but furniture as well. That nagging feeling of things being too easy pulled at Takana. She wished Natsu and Sōkichi were with her. Surely, they would feel it, too.

There was only one room left to check. It was bigger than the office, likely a meeting room. Chise slid the door open carefully. A man sat on a *zabuton* at a table with his back to the door. They slipped through and approached him.

Takana put her *wakizashi* to the man's throat and pulled on his shoulder so he wouldn't cut himself in a surprise reaction. His head lolled back, limp and lifeless. He'd been slashed across the neck already, but the wound had been cleaned.

"I've been set up..." Takana's voice trailed off before the *shoji* doors lining the walls all slid open simultaneously. Innumerable *yakuza* thugs burst into the room with swords drawn.

Chapter Fifteen

Battle Bond

Yubitsume: The yakuza custom thought to have originated with the bakuto (gamblers) whereby a member self-amputates their pinky finger. There are various reasons for the ritual, including apology, repayment of debts, surrender, punishment, and expulsion. The pinky grips a sword's hilt the tightest of all the fingers, the absence of which would cause one to not be able to hold the sword properly, forcing one to depend more heavily on the clan and the boss in battle.

July 8, 1708
Koganei, Tochigi Prefecture

THE DEAD MAN IN TAKANA'S arms had been left with his *daishō* attached to his hip. She threw her *wakizashi* into the closest thug, then pulled the dead man's and threw it into another one. The thugs backed up, surprised by her accuracy and lack of hesitation. A flicker of doubt ran across their faces. She unsheathed the man's *katana* and stood with her back to Chise.

Takana pulled a *kunai* from her *kasa* and felled another thug. The men shook away their fear, realizing that moving in slowly had been a mistake. They ran at the same time towards the two women. Chise swung her *naginata* around in a circle over Takana's head, slicing the necks of two thugs on both sides. Takana dove to the ground and cut the leg off one of them, then rolled behind the circle of charging men to give Chise more room to hold back her own group of thugs. Takana already stabbed through the back of one of hers.

She pulled another *kunai* and sent it through one of their eyes. More men pounded down hallways and crowded into the room. Takana suffered a cut along her thigh as she attempted to dodge a downswing. She ducked a strong horizontal swing that ended up in one of the other thug's chest. She stabbed the swinger swiftly, then moved to a wall to avoid getting surrounded. The room was small, the opponents were many, and the atmosphere was chaos.

A quick glance at the other side of the room showed several thugs dead on the *tatami* around Chise. Her armor deflected swings she couldn't dodge, leaving the assailants fully vulnerable to a counterattack. Takana had no such luxury except for her *kasa*.

Takana threw another *kunai* into a thug's neck and swung into the knee of one who got too close to her side. The men drew in on her fast. One stopped to rip a *kunai* from his dead comrade's head and threw it clumsily into the wall next to Takana. She returned it to the man's heart.

She sidestepped the next leading thug and sliced into his abdomen. The *katana* she'd grabbed from the dead man got stuck on the thug's robes, however. She wouldn't have time to pull her own *katana* out before she'd be pinned into the wall by the approaching five swords.

Chise bulled through the five men, using one of their dead as a shield. Takana let go of the *katana* stuck in the man's robes and unsheathed her own *katana* up through the chin of Chise's tailing thug, then hunkered behind her as Chise broke from the ambushers and made for a door. Someone cut into the back of Takana's left bicep, slicing through Fusa's creation. She pulled another *kunai* and threw it side-armed backwards into the nearest chaser through the hallway.

Chise stopped and turned around once they reached the end of the hall, pushing Takana to get behind her and watch her back. In such close, tight quarters, Chise's *naginata* kept the men at bay. The unfortunate men at the front got crushed between her and the men funneling into the hall from the back, unaware of the sudden roadblock in the hallway. Takana verified no one was coming from the other direction, then ran back through the room of the ambush to round on the men and take the line from the rear. The line of men backed away from Chise's advance and didn't look around until Takana had stabbed three of them. Chise easily cut through the rest as they stumbled over the dead behind them.

Takana's sigh of relief caught in her throat as someone grabbed her from behind. A *tantō* came across her vision from the side, but she got the back of her left wrist up to block it before it reached her neck. The bones in her wrist grinded against the metal but there was no spasm in her hand from the snap of a tendon. Chise charged towards them with the *naginata* in front. Takana tucked her knees up in a drop, pulling the man into a stooping position as Chise skewered him through the spine.

She helped Takana up, then led them back into the room to verify there could be no more surprises from behind. One of the men who hadn't been fatally wounded yelled as he threw one of the *kunai* into Chise's bicep between a gap in the armor. Chise winced as she yanked it out and handed it to Takana. The man crumpled to the floor after she returned it to him. Another *kunai* whistled through the air—from someone smart enough not to yell before throwing it. It sliced across the top of Takana's right breast, coloring the lower part of her tattoo in red. Chise was upon him before Takana could retrieve the *kunai* and return it in kind.

They ended any other thugs in the room that had survived. Takana retrieved her *wakizashi* and returned it to its scabbard. Her *sarashi* soaked in blood from the cut on her chest; the kimono's white-pink patterning turned red along her left arm. Her *geta* was slippery as blood trickled down her leg and congealed between her toes. She counted only two remaining *kunai* in her *kasa*.

They stepped carefully over the bloody terrain to the door they'd originally come through. Takana's vision blackened as something smashed into her nose, dropping her to her knees. Chise rushed forward and ended the man who'd hit Takana with a staff. His limp body hit with a muffled thud, but the echo of his staff against the hardwood floor was like a gong, summoning new opponents. More men streamed towards them from the main entrance. Chise held them at bay well enough while Takana tried to push past the incredible pain in her nose. A thug got around Chise's near-impregnable defense and was close to stabbing her in the back before Takana had a *kunai* sticking from the base of his neck.

She stood up, making sure her legs wouldn't wobble, then cried out so Chise would know she was coming from behind. Takana rushed past, slicing the air in a wide arc then backed up, forcing Chise to slow down and regain her breath. Takana was losing hers. She'd never had to fight for so long before, and her smoker's lungs were close to heaving. She couldn't afford to start coughing uncontrollably. Chise reached out occasionally to protect Takana's flank when she moved too far from center.

The piles of dead men actually helped the two regain their breath as the remaining pursuers had to step over or around their comrades. The sight of all the carnage gave some of them pause. One thug got over it and charged. He tripped over a body in his haste and impaled himself on a scabbard that had been sticking straight up from a dead body at a fatal angle.

While Chise and Takana moved backwards in a slow retreat down the hallway to the exit, the remaining men advanced with caution. They were smart enough to understand the danger of the chamber of death through which they trudged. One of the men picked up her *kunai* and threw it. A cough caught in Takana's throat, and she doubled over in time for the *kunai* to tear through her earlobe and cut along the side of her neck.

She cried out and dropped to her knees, playing up the minor injury. The front thug mustered new courage and charged. The *naginata* appeared above Takana's head and he ran into it before he could slow his momentum. Her hand closed around the *kunai* on the ground that had glanced off of her and threw it into the further thug.

She hadn't expected her arm strength to be so weak. It stuck into his chest, but not deeply. He pulled it from his robe and threw it back. Takana's reflexes were failing her. The *kunai* stuck into her side as she rolled to avoid it hitting anything vital. It didn't hurt any less for doing so.

A cry from behind them caught Chise's attention. A couple of men trapped them in the hallway, having run around the building to come in through the exit. Chise lowered to pick Takana up. Takana heard the sound of another fool running full steam towards that *naginata*. For the first time, Chise's strength also seemed to be lagging. The man's momentum caused her to fall into Takana's back. Takana tried her best to push back to make sure they both stayed on their feet. Chise used the momentum from Takana's push to lunge at another man.

Takana fended off a *katana* strike from the thug in front of her. The blow took even more strength out of her arms as the hilt of her *katana* vibrated. Never before had she almost dropped her blade from impact. She plucked the thug's eye out when his momentum brought his face too close to her. His anguished scream scared the few remaining men. In the clustered hallway it was hard to see past whoever was in front, but there was no mistaking what they heard. Takana seized the opportunity. If she waited even a second longer, she might not be able to find the strength to move again.

Ignoring the thug in eyeless agony, she threw his eye at the next man. He recoiled as it bounced off his chest and his discomfort turned to a shudder of death as she stabbed through his heart. She grabbed his *katana* before it hit the ground and put her legs into a throw that went through the neck of the next thug and touched the chest of the thug behind him. Takana charged over the bodies and threw herself into the dead man's torso before he could fall over. The *katana* finished going through the chest of the thug behind as they tumbled on top.

Coughs were building and taking over her lungs. She tried to at least keep her vision straight, but the pain in her nose was affecting that. Her injuries strained her energy and limits. The only thing that gave her hope was that there were only a couple more men in front of her. Chise made struggling noises behind her but didn't sound like she was down yet.

Takana tried to stand up, clasping her chest, but the next thug brought a strong downward swing onto her *kasa*. The broken *katana* that made up the protective structure of the *kasa* saved her head from direct damage, but she still felt the blow, the force jarring her neck. She cried out involuntarily and fell to her stomach. Her knees wouldn't hold her. She rolled to her side in time to see Chise switch directions and charge the thug that'd hit the *kasa*. Chise impaled him and the last man left on Takana's half of the hallway turned tail and ran.

Rapid footfalls came down the other end of the hall. The last two remaining men charged. Their eyes were on Chise's back as they ran with their swords held high. Takana reached out and tripped the front man who landed flush on his face over a dead thug's back. His arms landed in a way that his *katana* remained upwards, which was unfortunate for the trailing man that Takana also tripped, as it impaled him through the chest.

The last one alive within their vicinity was the man at the bottom of the impalement. He rolled over trying to get free of the dead men crushing him. Takana's cough betrayed how close she was to him, and he made her back up with the thrust of a *katana* he picked up from among the dead surrounding him. She took the *kasa* off and rolled onto her back, using it as a shield when the man got back on his feet. She blocked the first downward swing. The second swing sliced off her left pinky at the second knuckle.

That injury hurt most of all. She screamed and dropped the *kasa* so she could clutch her hand. The thug lifted the *katana* for a death-stroke when Chise's *naginata* burst through his chest, raining blood on Takana's face. Takana groaned through clenched teeth but was relieved that the last one was dead. That thought was cut off by a hellish scream from the middle of the hallway. The man who'd lost his eye crawled towards Takana while Chise struggled to pull the *naginata* out of the previous thug's chest, his ribs catching on some part of it. The eyeless thug reached Takana's legs, clawing along her body. His grip was horrendously strong, mauling her skin as he pulled himself up to straddle her.

He punched the side of her jaw, sending *hanabi* off in her eyes. Blood dripped from his eye socket onto her face. Coughing had sapped the last of her strength to fend him off. His fist found her broken nose and the world went black.

The humid night air was the first thing Takana felt, followed by the realization she was being carried by a pair of strong arms. Had Sōkichi found her? The passing braziers illuminated Chise's features.

"Where are we?" Takana whispered.

"Almost to a doctor."

"Someone you trust?"

"We fought together. I trust him with my life."

Takana fell in and out of consciousness. When she woke for good it was noon the next day. She scanned around the doctor's room and found Chise asleep, her armor removed. She only wore one bandage around her bicep. Takana peered down at herself. There were wraps around her thigh, side, chest, arm, neck, and ear. Her face was puffy and her vision was partially blurred by a bandage over her nose. A strange sense of loss weighed on her left hand. Upon closer inspection she realized her pinky was gone. The back of that hand's wrist had been slashed as well, so it was also wrapped.

She stared at her mangled hand. She'd worked so hard in her free time to get her left side caught up when her right shoulder was healing. Without her pinky, swordplay with that hand would be nearly impossible going forward—it was the digit responsible for half a grip's strength. She'd always scoffed at the *yakuza* punishment—as it reduced the effectiveness of the clan's own men. Why wouldn't they simply save that punishment for their enemies? It was ridiculous.

At the Inn, she'd realized she was dangerously close to becoming a *yakuza* in her own right. The missing pinky finger was the absolute last thing she would have ever wanted to pull her further into that cursed world. Through the pain of her injuries, she fumed at the *yakuza* dragging her back into their clutches, bit by bit.

A bout of coughing put pressure on her injuries, and the shocks of pain caused her to cough even more. The commotion woke Chise up. The strain on her lungs brought a panicked thought to Takana's mind. She got up from the *futon* too quickly and fell back as she waited for the dizziness to leave.

"What do you need, Takana-*san*? You shouldn't be moving so much yet."

"My *kimono*. Please bring it to me."

Chise did, and Takana rifled through the pockets. Her heart stopped pounding and she laid back in relief once she found the *kiseruzutsu*. She reached in another pocket for the special tobacco and held both tightly to her chest, then fell asleep again.

Takana and Chise journeyed back to Oyama in the early evening. Not wanting to cause a scene inside the Inn, Takana waited outside while Chise searched for Hana. When they both came out, Hana's hand shot to her mouth upon seeing Takana's condition. Takana had left behind her familiar *kasa* and let her hair hang down to cover her shoulders and half of her face. The blood soaked into her *kimono* and *sarashi* turned them pink, and all the bandages gave hints to the cut patterns beneath. The double black eyes and broken nose were the most gruesome part of the picture.

"What in the—?" Hana started before Takana cut her off.

"The *yakuza*. Take me to his house."

"Of course. He lives in Shinden, about thirty minutes north."

"Thank you, Hana-*san*. Do you feel like earning a little more before the night is over?"

Hana took Takana's condition in again.

"Am I going to look like you afterwards?"

"No, but someone else is going to."

Soon they stood outside Yoshimatsu's house in the dark. Instead of overpowering the lock on the sliding door, Chise smashed through it with a small statue from the meager garden in front. They found Yoshimatsu in his bedroom, packing bags with panic in his eyes. Chise leveled him with a punch, then tied his arms and ankles behind his back. Hana searched the house and confirmed they were alone.

"Please! They said they'd kill my wife if I didn't set you up!" Yoshimatsu cried. He swiveled his head around frantically to catch someone's eyes, which was difficult from the position they'd left him on his stomach.

Takana wasn't in the mood for a sob story, and kicked him in the face, knocking him out. She asked Hana and Chise to search the house for coin and valuables while she lowered herself to the floor in front of him, both to keep watch and to recover from all the strain of the constant walking they'd done since she woke up from the doctor's office.

Yoshimatsu regained consciousness after a few moments. Takana lifted his chin from the floor with the edge of her *katana*, straining her own level of consciousness. Her voice came out thick and far off.

"Who arranged all that?"

"Look, it might be hearsay at this point. I was approached by a clan that told me *they* were approached. They wouldn't give any more details other than the command came from Utsunomiya."

Takana seethed as Taiga's petulant face came to mind. It wasn't so much that she didn't expect he was capable of such treachery, but that he openly spat on her mercy.

Unsure if she was hallucinating how similar he looked to Taiga, Takana visualized painting Yoshimatsu's *tatami* red. She pressed the blade up into his throat. He only whimpered, afraid that speaking would end him. Chise interrupted by coming into the room with a bag of coins.

"Please," he begged and struggled to get away from the blade's point.

Against her hateful, near-delirious line of thinking, Takana released the blade's pressure and grimaced as she got back to her feet.

"Please, they'll kill her if I don't bring that bag to them."

"Why don't you take this to your clan?"

"The men that took my wife also said if I went to my clan, they'd kill both of us. You can see how we all ended up here, can't you?" he pleaded.

"I can't imagine they'll be well-guarded after what we did to their ranks in Koganei," Chise said. "Maybe we rescue his wife and keep the gold. Get something out of this damned situation..."

"I'll help," Hana said to Takana. "You gave me a second chance. Maybe…"

"You didn't just send a wave of *yakuza* thugs after us!" Takana lost her temporary calm. After the damage she'd taken, she didn't want to hear the possibility of chasing her losses—she was missing a damn finger! "And don't be fooled by his plea—she's a *yakuza* wife. She's not innocent just because she's a woman! I know many wives that deserve the same fates as their husbands."

Yoshimatsu looked hopefully between Chise and Hana, his eyes flitting fearfully back at Takana's furious expression.

"I'll bet that heist at his uncle's estate was a setup, too. Gave me a nice, easy task up front to whet my greed. It worked. He's set me up twice. You think I'm going to fall for it a third time? *Fuck* his wife!"

The pressure in her face from yelling brought the dizziness back. She backed up into a wall and leaned against it, sliding down to the floor as a few painful coughs broke through.

"My wife is everything to me! I'm not setting you up!"

"What were you packing?" Chise asked. "Planning to rescue her yourself before we came in? Escape with her before word got to the clan that your ruse was a failure? Your actions don't point to someone that's concerned about anyone but yourself. You're trying to tug at our hearts, so we won't take your money. Or kill you."

Takana sat in painful misery, dueling thoughts of mercy and vengeance playing out across her face. Chise stared at her for a few moments, then untied the man and picked him up, allowing him to see her in her full frame.

"Takana-*san* is merciful. You will take me to where your wife is being held, and I'll help her if you speak the truth. If I find you to be lying, you will experience Takana-*san*'s vengeance, through me. You will feel how two people survived your ambush."

"And I'll help. In either way," Hana added.

Takana laid down on her back. The spinning room began to slow.

"I'll stay here with the money. Keep him…slightly honest," she whispered as her body involuntarily plunged to sleep.

Takana woke stiff on the *tatami*, shaken by Hana, covered in bloody streaks. An equally bloody Chise stood over Yoshimatsu and his wife holding each other on the other side of the room. Hana helped Takana to her feet, then Takana grabbed the bag of money.

"Let's go." She motioned her head to Chise.

"Wait! That's all we have!" Yoshimatsu cried.

"Consider it your payment for the rescue job. It's half of what you promised for the ambush job, but I'll forgive that if I never have to see you again. If I do, I'm going to force you into paying back the other half or kill you. Whichever way I feel at the time. I suggest you don't test me. You don't seem all that lucky."

"What are we going to do?" the wife pleaded with her husband.

Takana followed Hana and Chise out the front door before she looked back one more time.

"Your husband knows a great place to find priceless artifacts. I'm sure you'll be fine."

Back on the main road, Takana gave the bag to Hana to divide appropriately in their deposit boxes at the Inn after giving Chise her share. Then she asked Hana to sit at their table and work with their alliance of mercenaries for a day or two until Natsu returned to Oyama. It struck Takana how discordant it seemed to have so many amicable people around her, yet things were always going so painfully, perpetually wrong.

On the road to the estate, Takana let a cigarette hang between her lips, but didn't light it. Several braziers along the way beckoned her to their glowing embers. Her mind begged her—the smoke would soothe her; heal her faster—it promised!

Replaying how closely coughing had almost gotten her killed, she settled for dampening them in her mouth before flicking them into passing braziers. When they were gone, she used the *kiseru* but without stuffing it with the special tobacco. It wouldn't have done any good, anyway. Blood had soaked into the pouches and ruined her supply.

She hoped the aroma would have survived, but it didn't mix well with the smell of rusty iron. She settled for taking dry tokes of air through the unlit *kiseru*, the hint of thousands of ashes over two centuries resting on her wanting tongue.

Chapter Sixteen

Regrets

Irezumi: The iconic tattoos of the yakuza, referring specifically to a particular tattoo styling, but has been adopted as a blanket term in modern times. All forms are applied by hand, using wooden and metal tools and special ink, and have been in use in Japan for over 12,000 years. It is painful, time-consuming, very expensive, and finding an irezumi artist can be difficult for many reasons. Tattoos were markers on criminals as punishments since the 4th century. It wasn't until the Edo period that they were slowly being considered as art.

July 10, 1708
Between Ishibashi and Suzenomiya, Tochigi Prefecture

AN UNUSUAL BIRD CHIRP CAME from the thicket as Takana and Chise neared the estate. Takana knew every bird call in Eastern Nihon. In the silence of her thoughts when she walked alone for eight years, it was all she had to keep herself sane sometimes. She nodded towards the thicket and Chise followed her inside.

Natsu's face dropped when she saw Takana's injuries up close. Tired from the walk, Takana sat down on the bedding Natsu had set up. Natsu wanted to hear the full story, but Takana didn't understand why Natsu wasn't sleeping in the estate.

Apart from that, Takana was more sinterested in talking about their business and the Utsunomiya proposition than what happened to her and Chise in Koganei, but Natsu kept interrupting. Her fingers would curl and move forward a couple centimeters for want of touching Takana's injuries, then catch themselves and go back to her sides. Takana grew annoyed at the questions and laid on her back. Chise mercifully filled in as many blanks as she could to satiate Natsu's concern. Natsu's hand finally came forward and folded into Takana's while listening to the story.

A few days before, Takana would have welcomed holding hands with her new friend. But anger over Natsu's continued deceit—that she'd been in league with the mistress the whole time—ruined the moment. Takana pulled her hand away and stood up.

"You lied to me, Natsu-*san*. Again. You used me for your revenge, and you used me to set yourself up at the Inn. Without the Inn, I wouldn't have been in that damn place. Without Chise-*san*, I would be *dead* right now! I wish I hadn't met you!" Takana blurted.

Takana could see Natsu's sorrow and regret painted all over her face. She was a master at omitting information, but she didn't hide her real emotions very well.

"I'm going to give you two some privacy," Chise said.

"No! No, wait," Takana said.

She lowered herself in front of Natsu so they could face each other as equals.

"I didn't...mean that. I'm just... Without you I'd still be drowning in debt. My mother, Fusa, all those women, they'd all still be slaves in the *yūkaku*."

Takana sighed and looked away. She wasn't used to friends, or explaining her feelings, or caring about anyone, even herself. All she had cared about was the *kiseru*—an inanimate object.

"I've never felt so...in tune with someone before. I can't understand why I trust you with my life when you've given me reasons not to, and...seeing you now... I see in your eyes I *can* trust you. I *want* to trust you."

A glimmer of hope shone through Natsu's misery.

"Tell me, right now—is there anything else you're keeping from me? Any more secrets?"

Natsu lowered her eyes and shook her head. Her shoulders shook, either from touching despair at the loss of a friend, or the sheer, overwhelming relief that she hadn't.

"Ok. I'm putting my life in your hands, Natsu-*san*. I'm *choosing* to trust you. Let's start over from here—forget what came before."

Natsu sniffed and wiped her eyes, then nodded. Takana stood and held her hand out. Natsu looked at it for a moment, then took it to stand up. They hugged for a brief moment, Natsu's orange hair brushing Takana's swollen cheek. Takana didn't care about the pressure it put on her injuries.

Chise cleared her throat. Takana gave her leave to head to the estate, and they'd follow soon. Once Chise left the thicket, Natsu busied herself with rolling up her bedding.

"So, how have things been going here? Did Sōkichi return yet? How do you think he'll react to...all this?"

Natsu's shoulders slumped when she mentioned Sōkichi's name, and she gave a smile that wasn't quite natural.

"He's got a bunch of recruits already set up outside the gates. They take shifts to guard the estate. None of them go into the dwelling without Sōkichi's escort. He's going out again tomorrow."

Takana hoped to improve Natsu's mood by changing the person of interest.

"How's Fusa-*chan*?"

Natsu sighed and looked away.

"You'll see her soon. She's always herself."

Takana put her hand on Natsu's shoulder. She winced and pulled it away.

"What's wrong?"

Natsu unwrapped her robes. The same as on Takana's front shoulder, Natsu had a bright new *bakeneko* surrounded by flames.

"I was the first. Genjirō's working on your mother today."

Takana studied the workmanship, impressed by the much greater detail he'd managed to incorporate than in her own. As Takana's face got closer, Natsu's skin around the tattoo flushed to a rosy pink. Natsu pulled the robe back on and tied the belt tight, then turned to pull a bag out of the hidden hole.

"I'm going back to Oyama. I'll see you...whenever."

Takana deserved the bit of coldness from Natsu. Why did she have to say all that earlier? Why did she feel the need to say anything at all instead of holding it in like she had always done before?

"Natsu-*san*," Takana said before she could duck out of the thicket. "At least travel back with Chise-*san*."

Natsu's head dipped.

"I don't need..."

Before Takana could respond to the cracking in Natsu's voice, Natsu disappeared out of the thicket and ran at full speed towards the main road.

Fusa hugged the last of Takana's energy out before she was sick of seeing people. She'd been wrong about Sōkichi's reaction. He wisely gave her space, but at least showed worry more than neutrality. She wanted to be alone with him, not around all the girls and her mother, and definitely not so soon after she might have ruined her relationship with Natsu.

Her stomach grumbled and she needed to smoke. Everyone's fussing over her appearance annoyed her. She'd been injured on the job—the difference was that no one ever cared before. After what happened in the thicket, she realized she liked it better that way. Other people's affections weighed as heavy as debt.

Takana wasn't used to the burden of other people's care, so she opposed it—punishing herself by refusing to eat, relishing the pain of her injuries and the craving of smoke that drove her to constant irritation. She wanted to be back in her old skin—her old dirty, ratty clothes. Friendless. Coinless. Starving. If she could have made one wish, it would be to sit once again next to Tetsuo while the sun set over the mountains, smoking her grandfather's tobacco in remembrance. They were the only two people that ever mattered to her after her life was destroyed by her father. She loved her mother, but Takana spent far more time with those two old men over most of her life.

Pretending to need the restroom, Takana left the gaggle of concerned women and brought a covering out of one of the bedrooms. She snuck outside the gates and around to the back of the estate, making sure none of Sōkichi's recruits saw her from their barracks.

While clutching the *kiseruzutsu* close to her heart, she lamented her losses—through everything that she had gained—before the throbbing of her body lulled her to sleep.

Takana took extra time to bathe. Several women offered to help her through the injuries, but her sour expression sent them on their way. Fusa was the only one undeterred, as she bathed and got into the *onsen*. She rested her chin on her hands at the edge, looking up at Takana, her usual effervescence tempered.

"Takana-*san*, I'm not sure what's going on. You're walking around here like Natsu-*san* did while you were gone. Well, she was normal until the recruits arrived with Sōkichi. But...she doesn't seem herself when you're not here."

"I can't speak for her. I think we have different problems. All I can tell you is I almost died the other day, and I'm not dealing with it as easily as I thought I would. I've been in duels before. I've killed people. This was..."

Takana trailed off and shook the memory of Koganei out of her head. Fusa frowned as naïvely as she smiled.

"What did *I* do, though?"

"Nothing, Fusa-*chan*. I can't explain myself very well. I can explain Natsu even less. I wish...caring about people didn't hurt so much."

Fusa gave an unsatisfied smile and got out of the bath. She left, then returned a few moments later with new dressings for Takana's injuries. Takana dried off and allowed Fusa to wrap her wounds. A tear fell down Fusa's cheek as she wrapped the stump where Takana's left pinky used to be.

"I'm so sorry," Fusa whispered once she finished with the last wrap.

"For what?"

"If you hadn't seen me come out of your father's house that night, none of this would have happened…"

Takana hadn't even considered that. She blamed Natsu for everything involving the estate, but Fusa was the real catalyst. Even before she followed Takana on the road, procured information from the headhunter, led them to the Inn… If Takana had never given Fusa that ryō… Hearing Fusa apologize for it hit Takana differently. She couldn't blame the poor girl. The mention of her father, though—the one person truly responsible for any poor, malicious decisions—boiled her blood.

Fusa recoiled from the rage seeping out of Takana—her skin turned hot and red, her expression hardened, and her body tensed, ready to fight. Takana calmed herself down after a moment, reacting to the fear in Fusa's eyes. She lay her hand across the back of Fusa's and squeezed.

"I'll never regret meeting you that night, Fusa-*chan*."

Takana spent the next two days hiding from everyone, either in the gardens or outside the gates. She wanted to sleep in the thicket like Natsu had but that would only keep her mood dark. Once the pain began to subside and the swelling in her face decreased, she decided she'd like to meet with Sōkichi when he returned with new recruits later in the evening. They hadn't spoken since she came back. Most people might have been offended by that, but she admired his patience and respect. It was like he could read her mind. She'd be with him when she was ready.

After a very small rice ball, only meant to shut her stomach up, Fusa brought Takana to a room and unfolded the *kimono*. It had been washed of the blood, and the left sleeve's cut had been sewn closed with a new janky line. The little frog had a new line, also. It smiled at her.

For the first time since joking about the unusual sex job with Hana, Takana laughed, and it came flooding out of her. She remembered her mother laughing like that when she saw the *kimono* back in the *yūkaku*. After the laughter slowed, she smiled at her friend.

"Oh, Fusa-*chan*, I love you."

The unexpected laughter and words seemed only to confuse Fusa.

"Well, I...I love you, too. But...what's so funny?"

Takana looked at the frog once more and the laughter started up again. She put the *kimono* on. It was like her soul had been washed and repaired alongside the gifted garment. She hugged Fusa in all her confusion.

"Are you getting marked?"

"I don't know," Fusa said. "Natsu was a statue while Genjirō worked on her. Your mother, though... It looks too painful."

"Remember I said it was optional, but it makes the dice games easier."

"That's not what Natsu said."

"What did she say?"

"That it marked us as fam—"

A commotion from the hallway, immediately outside the room, drowned out Fusa's speech.

"Don't go in there!" Chiyo yelled. "She'll kill you!"

The door slid open, revealing Takana's father, Iwakuchi, with Chiyo behind him, pulling on his dirty robes. He approached her. Takana's hand went to her left hip for her *katana,* but she wasn't wearing the *daishō*. He pinned her arms to her side. She resisted the deep, reflexive urge to headbutt him. Her broken nose and black eyes only barely kept her from knocking both of them out.

It took a moment to realize he was *hugging* her. She didn't understand and didn't care, wrestling out of his grip, pushing him into the *shoji* wall and almost sending him crashing through it. She pulled the *kanzashi* from her ponytail, sending her hair cascading down her back. The sharp end pressed into his neck hard enough to break the first couple layers of skin. Her face burned.

"Don't you *ever* touch me again! What are you doing here? How did you find us?"

"I recognized one of the girls from the *yūkaku* at the market in Utsunomiya. Since they closed the district down, I thought there must be a new one and followed her here. I saw your mother outside talking to one of the guards and—"

"You let him in?" Takana turned her fury to Chiyo. Most of the women were huddled in the hallway behind her.

"He broke away from us. I'm sorry, Ta-*chan*."

"I never thought I'd see you again, Ta-*chan*," Iwakuchi said, wincing when she pressed a little harder into his neck at the sound of his voice, at his use of the most familiar form of her name.

"You don't get to call me that anymore. I'm not your daughter. I'm *nothing* to you. You will leave my house *now*."

The wet in his eyes angered her further. Whether it was from genuine emotion, or pain from the *kanzashi*, the man wasn't allowed to feel—not before her, not after everything he'd done.

"You don't understand. There was a rumor from someone in Taiga's clan that they killed you in Koganei."

He'd be dead if she pushed even a little harder.

"How did you talk to them? Are you working for him?"

"No! I met the man in the public bathhouse. He recognized me."

Nothing he said soothed her rage.

"You led them here!"

Takana looked over her shoulder at Chiyo.

"Alert the men!"

"No! I wasn't followed! I didn't tell them anything! I really did think— I thought this was the new pleasure quarter!" he blurted.

With a mind of its own, her hand pulled the *kanzashi* back and cocked for a final stab through his throat. Before she could make final, life-ending contact, a strong arm hooked around her elbow to stop her momentum.

She looked up at Sōkichi's calm face. The pressure behind her own face loosened as the blood drained out. She looked back and forth between him and Iwakuchi, then lowered her arm. When

Sōkichi let go, she jammed the *kanzashi* into the wall millimeters away from Iwakuchi's ear.

Takana stormed from the room, growling at her mother to get him out of the estate, then went outside to vent at the recruits who'd let such a man get by them. They apologized and vowed to do better. Chise promised to whip them into shape.

Simmering down, Takana leaned her back against the gate and watched Chise put the men in formation. Soon Sōkichi stood by her side.

"I'm sorry for their lack of discipline. It won't happen again."

"With you and Chise training them, I believe that."

"Your mother is allowing him to stay through the night, then he has to leave in the morning."

Takana barked a laugh and shook her head.

"After everything he did to her... You know what? I can't be here. I'm going back to Oyama. Send a courier when you feel these boys are ready to guard the women on the road and I'll come back to see them off."

"You're going now?" Sōkichi asked.

"Yes."

She retrieved her gear and left the estate in a rush. Sōkichi wasn't anywhere to be seen. She grew even angrier at his absence. Couldn't he sense that maybe she wanted him to stop her? Or at least say goodbye!

Takana tromped up the road as the sky darkened, too absorbed in her frustrations to feel her injuries, nagging for better treatment. As she neared the section close to the thicket, a dark silhouette took shape. Holding up her lantern and drawing her *katana,* she approached the figure. It was only Sōkichi. She sighed and sheathed her weapon. Though he never expressed much, maybe he really could read her mind.

"Here to say goodbye?"

"If you're really leaving, then yes."

"What do you mean by—"

"I hoped to hear your story. Help attend your injuries. Make you whole."

"The last time I tried to tell the story it backfired. You don't need to know anything, anyway. It wasn't special."

"We both know that's not true. Your injuries tell most of the story, but I'd like to...hear more. I've never seen you so roughed up before—inside, and out."

"It doesn't sound like you're going to let any of this go. Fine. Here, follow me. I don't want to stand out in the open with the possibility of that cretin having *yakuza* following him."

She took his hand and pulled him into the thicket.

"I'll show you my wounds and you can discern for yourself what happened. Some of them are more permanent than others, so I guess you better get used to them."

Takana used the lantern to show him the injuries to her ear and neck. She illuminated her hand, then the cut above her right breast. Her skin temperature rose, as the anger from the last few days got pushed out by something else. She pulled her left arm out of the *kimono*, lowering it to her waist, then showed him the slash down the back of her bicep.

Her heart pounded as she anticipated showing the next injury, high up on her thigh. She untied the belt around the *kimono* and let it, along with the *hakama*, fall to the ground. Then she lifted the lantern to show her broken nose and black eyes.

Sōkichi inspected the angry bruising. Or was he looking into her eyes? It was hard to tell with the lantern dropping to her side slowly—just as slowly as his face grew closer to hers, and his hand touched her hip.

"Thank you for telling me your story. Now I know where to avoid touching."

Chapter Seventeen

Prices to Pay

Bushido: "The way of the warrior" was not only meant for the samurai, but as a complex set of Japanese values stressing honor, loyalty to country, and family above all. One of its principal values is a strict hierarchy, emphasizing obedience to authority. The samurai, yakuza, and individual families followed this code. Preserving a family's honor was worthy of fighting to the death. Ultimately, the individual is downplayed, no matter how much Bushido's tenets have been altered, translated, transposed, or recycled within Japanese society.

July 13, 1708
Between Ishibashi and Suzenomiya, Tochigi Prefecture

TAKANA WAS GLAD FOR THE warm, humid morning. She slept outside year-round, but never without any clothing. It gave her an involuntary shudder at the memory of the previous winter, rousing Sōkichi from his slumber. He stretched and reached for her neck, pulling her in for a kiss.

"Still leaving straight away?" he asked.

"I was going to, but I need to get my thigh re-stitched."

"I'm sorry about that."

"Don't be. It was a small price to pay for the night." Takana smiled, then sat up to shake the twigs and loose dirt from her hair.

She reached into the pockets of the rumpled *kimono* in a pile of both their clothes before remembering she was out of cigarettes. The empty *kiseru* would have to satisfy her craving while they dressed. Before leaving the thicket, they kissed again.

"I'm sorry I look so hideous," she said.

"Your looks don't define you."

"If you'd said that last night before all that, I wouldn't have believed you, and you'd have been sleeping alone. The real test is how long you'll feel that way. My nose is going to be crooked forever."

Sōkichi smiled in a way that answered her unasked question satisfactorily and led her out of the thicket. They held hands until the barracks came into view, then he parted to begin training the recruits with Chise. Takana continued towards the estate, preparing to apologize for her many displays of anger over the previous few days. At that thought she looked to the sky. It was a little after midday. If he was still inside...

She expected to find Chiyo in the bath, but instead found Fusa with a large contingent of the women. She showed them how to hide the dice without the benefit of sleeves, playing with their hair in different styles. In the dining room, Chiyo sipped tea, staring into space. Her *kimono* was open at the shoulder. Genjirō had done more work on it during the morning. She didn't notice Takana had entered the room until she sat down at the table and reached for the tea and a cup.

Chiyo smiled mischievously over a sip but didn't say anything. Takana took the silence and sighed over the warm beverage. Her mother's smile widened, knowing that sigh all too well.

"Whatever you think happened, didn't," Takana said.

"Mm-hm."

Chiyo's smile was infuriating. Takana didn't like that she could so easily tell what happened, but then again, she'd been the over-seer of the pleasure quarter.

"It was—..." Takana began, her mind yelling at her heart to shut up in front of her mother, but Chiyo leaned in like it was the most important news in the world.

Takana thought of how to finish her sentence without embarrassing herself when she registered familiar sounds she shared with Sōkichi the night before coming from a nearby room. It took a moment for Takana's tranquility to change to suspicion the louder the sounds got, then she recognized one of the voices.

Her hand went to her *katana,* but Chiyo rose and tried to keep her from unsheathing the blade.

"Ta-*chan,* he *paid*! Kiko was willing to earn. She's too clumsy with the dice, and she's worried you won't keep her around otherwise."

"It's not *Kiko* that needs to worry about being kept around."

Takana brushed past Chiyo and ripped open the door to the next room hard enough to knock it off its track. She pushed Kiko off of Iwakuchi. She regretted using force on the poor girl, but Takana's fury burned unrestrained. Instead of the point of the *kanzashi* sticking into his neck like the night before, she had his throat Buddha beneath a much longer, sharper blade.

"*Kaasan* said you were to leave in the morning. And this isn't the new pleasure quarter."

"I paid for—"

Takana took a coin out of her pocket and spiked it on his chest.

"Stop talking." Takana pressed the blade harder against his skin. "Get up."

Chiyo handed him his clothes. She looked at her daughter fearfully. Takana held back from the blade's edge of ridding them both of the worthless old man. Only her mother's presence kept her from ending him on the *futon* right then and there.

Once he dressed, she pressed the blade against his back and pushed him outside.

"Ta-*chan,* I have something for—"

"I said *stop talking*!"

Takana glanced at the wooden sword leaning against the veranda near the front steps. She sheathed the *katana* noisily, dramatically, hoping he would dare talk again.

"I promise you'll want to hear this!"

She cracked the wooden sword against his thigh, then bicep when he didn't start running. He stumbled into a sprint as she hit him across the back shoulder. Once he exited the front gate in a full run, she stopped chasing. The wooden hilt creaked in her grip. When she caught her breath and looked back at the veranda, many of the women had come out to watch the commotion. A couple of them seemed afraid, but most of them viewed her with respect. Takana wouldn't sell any of them out, and she would protect them from the wrong people. It was more than they'd ever come to expect from anyone before.

Takana thrust the sword's edge into the ground, then told all of them to get dressed and meet her out at the barracks.

Standing in front of clean, well-dressed men with Sōkichi and Chise at the head of their formation, Takana fidgeted under the realization that her clothes were dirty and frayed while her hair hung unkempt. At least the women weren't perfectly put together either, as they didn't have extensive wardrobes from which to choose anything from. All they had were the clothes they arrived in on the day of their escape and some meager garments Fusa had been working on. Chiyo stood in front of her women, ashamed for the morning's events.

Takana spoke loud enough for all to hear.

"I'm not sure what Natsu has already said to any of you about what we're doing here. I want you all to know, and always remember, you're here *voluntarily*. You're no longer chained to your old lives.

"However, if you were happy with your previous profession, and that's how you expect to earn your keep... I won't stop you. But there will be no *yakuza*. No gamblers. And that man I chased out of here this morning can never step foot inside our gates again! I'd prefer none of that was happening here anyway. Take it elsewhere, if you must.

"Otherwise, soon, most of you will be paired with a protector when you start your dice games. I think we'll increase the takes if the girls who are uncomfortable with the dice learn to push bets as temporary waitresses. Together you can influence the mood of the games. Come see me for how to do that. If some of you want to continue earning outside of the games, it's your choice. But you will communicate with your protector the times and locations of your activities so they can do their jobs.

"All I expect from any of you is ten percent of what you make, which goes to our home here. You keep the rest split equally between the two or three of you. Above everything else, I want to repeat—this is all voluntary. None of you are in my debt. You really are earning for yourselves, and the percentages really are that good.

"The last thing I'm going to ask of you is to get on Genjirō's priority list for your marks if you're ready to start working. I understand Natsu might have said it was mandatory, but it's not. It will significantly protect you on the road, though, and give you leverage with the restaurant owners to set up your dice games. If you fear the pain, no one here will look down on you or kick you out."

At the end of the speech Takana breathed almost as heavy as she had fighting alongside Chise. That was the longest she'd talked straight in her entire life. The women fidgeted as the heat of the day neared its uncomfortable climax. She dismissed everyone and sat down against a tree to rest her strained smoker's lungs.

Soon Chise joined Takana, though she remained standing.

"That old man gave me a message for you."

Takana barked a laugh and shook her head.

"I don't care what he had to say. Forget the message."

Chise ignored her. If there was anybody who wouldn't flinch at Takana's fury, it was Chise and Sōkichi.

"The *daishō* your old *sensei* gifted you, that he sold off without your permission—he knows where they are. He gave me the location."

"Trying to buy me back, no doubt."

"Maybe so. I'm only the messenger. Do with this information what you will."

As was her nature, Chise seemed content not to elaborate without prompting.

"...Where are they?"

"Lake Chūzenji. Above Nikkō."

"We get a lot of job offers around Nikkō. If the place is nearby, maybe I'll take a look."

Instead of traveling back to Oyama alone, Takana brought along the most advanced protectors and dice rollers, introducing them to restaurant owners along the way, then leaving them to work. She also brought along Fusa and Shinkichi, in case she needed support to talk to Natsu.

Shinkichi had taken Takana's order for a new *kasa* outfitted with the protective broken *katana* blades and a new arsenal of *kunai* to the blacksmith in Utsunomiya, after she'd arrived at the estate without her old one. He arrived with it only an hour before she was to leave for Oyama, to her relief. Placing it back atop her ponytail recovered a missing piece of herself.

Fusa and Shinkichi played with the dice together, but Fusa had become more than adept in Takana's absence. Soon enough they used it as an excuse to touch each other in the open. They also went off into the forest together during rests along the road. Takana asked them to help her learn sleight-of-hand without the use of her left pinky whenever the two of them weren't absorbed in each other, which wasn't often.

Without tobacco or Sōkichi, Takana's irritation grew the closer they got to Oyama. Iwakuchi managed to embed himself in her mind so subtly by merely passing on a message. Losing dexterity in her left hand didn't help her mood, either.

Nearing sunset on the third day since they departed the estate, they arrived at the gates of Oyama. Takana noticed a familiar *yakuza*, hardly older than a teenager. He had been one of the lowest ranks in the Kochiya clan before her escape. He met eyes with her from the front of a shop and before she could say anything, he ran off.

Taiga would know his plot in Koganei had failed sooner or later, but it unsettled her to see the domino get knocked over. To get her mind off worrying over potential retaliation, she imagined the blowback from the *yakuza* clan he'd duped into their deaths. She wondered if he'd undersold her skills—made it sound like an easy payday. Though if that was the case, why send so many thugs? They didn't know Chise would be there. In that light, he'd flattered her in a way that the false compliments in Tetsuo's office couldn't achieve.

With the low rank spotting her, she pondered proactively taking back her mercy...

Outside the Inn, two *samurai* stood at the entrance with the young *yakuza*. She expected him to run to Taiga, not confront her directly—

"That's the woman who stole my uncle's priceless plate. I'd recognize that tattoo anywhere."

Takana narrowed her eyes, running through the possibilities of talking her way out of the half-false accusation. She had stolen the plate sure enough, but could she convince the samurai that he only knew that because his yakuza clan had hired her to do so? The man would surely deny it, but would he be able to provide proof of his relation? Would the samurai care to confirm such a thing? If it slipped that the plate was little more than a setup to lure her into a subsequent death trap, there was no way they'd believe her story, so she opted to keep her mouth shut altogether.

She'd killed *rōnin* before, but the *samurai* were part of the city's police force. Even if she wanted to escape or fight, her injuries would hold her back. She'd gone through too much to risk her life so soon after starting a new one.

"Take these, Fusa-*chan*," Takana whispered as she handed over her *kasa*, *kiseruzutsu*, and *daishō*. "You and Shinkichi get away from me."

Before Fusa could question it, the *samurai* approached Takana with their hands on the hilts of their *katana*. Takana held her arms out, then they felt around her *kimono* for any other weapons. She winced as they got too rough around her injuries. Once they were satisfied, she fell in between them as they walked her through the streets to the open-air jail made up of several iron cages with hay lining the ground.

They pushed her into an empty cage and locked the door. She had to stay on her hands and knees or lay down thanks to the low ceiling. An administrator came over to the *samurai* and they talked over the situation. The *samurai* departed, then the administrator knelt down beside the cage to address her.

"For theft, considering the value of the item, you have two choices: you can stay in this cage for thirty days, or get out tomorrow morning after thirty lashes performed in the city square."

"I'll—"

He held up his hand.

"Think it over. Give me your answer at dawn."

Why would anyone choose the latter? After arranging the hay to be more comfortable, she laid back and welcomed the chance to sleep. To Takana's chagrin, so many thoughts ran through her mind that she couldn't close her eyes for more than a few seconds. Opportunity and ability never played together like they should.

Once the city went to sleep, the stars hypnotized her through the bars. She thought she must be asleep when everything turned black but realized that her eyes were still open. A dark shape blocked her view on top of the cage. The shape pulled off its mask. In the low light of braziers, strands of burnt orange hair fell through the bars.

"Hello, my pretty, bruised friend."

Natsu reached a hand through the cage as far as it would go and Takana grabbed it. Their hands remained together for minutes without a word spoken.

Finally, Natsu let go and put her mask back on, then rolled off the top of the cage to crouch in front of the door. She inserted a pin into the lock and clinked around with it.

"I'll have you out of here in a moment," she whispered.

"Wait. I need to be able to do business in this city. If you break me out, they'll throw me back in again and extend the punishment."

Takana explained her choices.

"You'd really sit here for thirty days?" Natsu asked.

"You'd really let them lash you and scar you up?"

"Well, if you're determined to wait here, I'll run the Inn and send couriers to the estate. I'll come by every night and let you know what's going on."

They held hands again through the cage in assurance. Takana squeezed, hoping to convey her gratitude. As they broke contact, Natsu disappeared in the shadows around the brazier's light.

The first week proved relatively easy. The jailers occasionally threw other women into the cage with her. Most of them got out the next day for their petty crimes. One woman scoffed at the lashes threat and showed off her back. She was gone the next day as well.

Midway through the second week, shortly before midnight, the administrator and another man stood outside her cage. The mystery figure kept himself blocked from her view, and her cage was too small to maneuver to a better vantage point.

"Two *ryō* for an hour. You can't hit her or leave any marks."

The man had the same build as Sōkichi. Takana's heart sped up at the thought that he'd come all the way to Oyama to see her. She'd missed his touch so much since leaving the estate.

The lock clunked open, and the man crawled into the cage. He lifted his face in the dim light. Takana crawled backwards to the corner.

"I've missed you, *ane-san*."

"*Kuso yarō!* Stay away from me!"

Taiga smiled with equal parts malice and amusement, making her skin crawl.

"I can commute your punishment—get you out of here tonight. I'll take you back to Utsunomiya and together we'll strengthen the clan."

"Have you snapped? You've tried to kill me twice since you killed the *oyabun*—your own father," Takana spat the last word. If anyone had felt the loss of a family member in Tetsuo, it'd been her, not his blasphemous son.

"All you've done since leaving is proven to me just how much I need you by my side. You're worth so much more than—"

"Shut up. I'd rather die than go back to the clan."

"That was going to be my second offer, for what you did to me in my office."

Taiga pulled a *tantō* out of its scabbard from the small of his back and crawled closer to her.

"Wait, wait! When you put it *that* way, *ani-ki*, what choice do I really have? Besides, you've been keeping up with me, haven't you? I can't change my ways—earning and fighting—what does it matter who I'm doing it for, so long as I get to keep doing it."

Taiga smiled again and sheathed the blade.

"I'll arrange your release with the administrator. Then we can go home."

"Wait, Taiga-*kun*. I'm sorry for my fearful reaction. After everything we've been through and you pulling that *tantō*, I panicked. But...I really did think about what you said to me in *oyassan's* office. Maybe...we really are meant to be together..."

His sharp expression faltered, and his brow lifted into a show of lovestruck relief. Simply saying his name with the confectionary affectation attached to it made him malleable.

"Taiga-*kun*, I don't want to wait until we get to Utsunomiya. Why don't we take advantage of what you've already bought?"

He undressed quickly for a man on his hands and knees. Takana kept his attention by tracing her finger up her leg, then hooking her thumb on the waist of her *hakama*. She pulled it down, teasing a few centimeters at a time. His eyes seemed to grow hungrier at the sight of her bandaged thigh. He crawled to her with no sense of seduction. He kissed her neck and had nearly lowered his weight on top of her before she put her hand to his chest.

"Please, Taiga-*kun*," she whispered with as much passion as her disgusted mind would allow, "slowly. I've...never been with anyone..."

He naïvely believed that and backed off of her. He seemed to have a terrible blind spot to her seductive voice.

"I do know some tricks from spending time around the pleasure quarter, though. Turn around, my love."

He nodded and turned around. She pulled him back to her chest, wrapping her legs around his thighs and running her hand over his musculature. The other hand went to her hair, where she hid the small *kanzashi* Natsu had smuggled in for protection.

She grabbed a handful of his hair and pulled his head back, then put the point of the *kanzashi* to his neck.

"You lying b—"

"I showed you mercy before, *ani-ki*. You repaid me with Koganei. I'm only sorry this has to be quiet, because I would have enjoyed showing you how I survived all those thugs. Do me a favor this time and don't piss in my cage."

She bit his ear, then pressed the blade harder into his throat.

"Hey! Let him go!" A lantern illuminated the scene from outside.

A guard put the end of his *katana* to the back of her neck through the bars. She let go of Taiga and put her hands in the air. He swung his elbow around and hit her in the jaw as he moved away from her. He didn't have a lot of leverage in his position, but it sent fresh shockwaves through her still-healing face. Taiga rustled out of the cage after dressing as fast as he could. The guard grabbed the *kanzashi* from her hand.

The administrator rushed to Taiga and apologized for the disturbance.

"I should say so. What kind of service is this? I want my money back."

"I do apologize, sir, but there are no refunds."

"Fine. Here's three *ryō*. Add thirty more days to her sentence."

"Yes, sir," the administrator bowed as Taiga straightened his robes and left. He looked back at her one last time, like she knew he would.

Why had she wasted time twisting the *kanzashi* by trying to shame him, rather than simply stabbing him with it? She had been so determined to kill him after Koganei, if she ever saw him again... Takana would see to it that there would be no more words between them the next time she had him within a sword's length. There would only be blood.

Chapter Eighteen

Ghosts

Daishō: The two blades that make up the set of a longer katana and shorter wakizashi. The most iconic set of weapons in Japanese history. Over time they have gone in and out of legality to carry around in public. Many families display a set in a katana kake as art and decoration in their homes. It is considered bad luck to unsheathe a blade unless it is used immediately, and there are complex rules for gifting, carrying, and displaying them. A gift of blades could often be interpreted as an ill omen—symbolizing the severing of a relationship.

August 17, 1708
Oyama, Tochigi Prefecture

BY THE MIDDLE OF THE fifth week in the cage, Takana's small cramps increased in intensity and frequency. Natsu worried over her during their visits each night, but Takana was determined not to let Taiga win. He wanted her to choose the lash or live without being able to earn for an extended period of time, which hit her unexpectedly. Why did she care about losing money during the short sentence?

She could deal with the small space—it was more protected than anywhere else she slept during her travels. She could deal with the once-per-week baths—that had been her frequency of bathing until recently anyway. The food tasted horrible, but Natsu brought the finest rice balls the Inn provided, and Takana even noticed a little weight gain.

Takana's body had nearly healed. The guards allowed Fusa to bring fresh linens and poultices. Takana had to apply them herself, and the guards leered at her once Fusa left, but she didn't care. They hadn't tried to touch her with anything but their eyes since her imprisonment, and that was more than she'd originally expected. Taiga appeared to be a one-off visitor, no doubt seeking her out after the young *yakuza* reported back to him about her manufactured imprisonment.

As the weeks dragged on, Takana noticed other parts of her body were changing. Her breasts were getting sore, and along with her weight gain, required daily rewrapping of her *sarashi*. The cramping in her abdomen wasn't normal. Even though she couldn't do anything in the cage outside of light exercises she recalled from her training with Tomoe-*sensei*, occasional bouts of fatigue plagued her.

One night during the sixth week, Takana grew so tired she slept through Natsu's nightly visit, even though it was the only thing she looked forward to and kept her motivated enough to ignore the call of the lash.

The next day, Natsu came into the jail without her *kunoichi* outfit, wearing her usual traveling gear. Takana forgot how lovely her orange hair looked in daylight.

The administrator met Natsu and talked for a short time, then they came to the cage. Natsu handed the man five *ryō*, then bent down and put her hands around the cage bars.

"You've proven your point, Takana-*san*. I'm getting you out of here. The administrator will strike your imprisonment from the record so no one will arrest you in Oyama for the same crime, but we'll owe him a favor. I've given him first priority if he ever comes into the Inn seeking our services."

"Oh good. I was afraid it was going to be a different kind of favor."

The administrator pretended not to hear the comment while unlocking the door. Natsu furrowed her brow at the inside dig but said nothing. Takana crawled out and stretched. The male prisoners expressed their disappointment at her release in groans as she walked by. She had convinced Natsu to bring them the premium rice balls at night in exchange for turning away whenever she needed to dress her wounds, rewrap her *sarashi*, or bathe in their view.

In the crowded streets of Oyama, Takana couldn't express to Natsu how much she appreciated her support during the imprisonment. Without being asked, though, Natsu led Takana to the only place she wanted to be in the world—the bathhouse. She paid an extra *ryō* to move up the *yakuza* hour and have a brief time to themselves.

Before undressing, Takana hugged Natsu in silence for a minute. Natsu took the embrace, smell and all, but once they broke away, Takana quickly went about taking her first proper bath in six weeks.

Afterwards, on the way to the Inn, nausea struck. She ran into an alley and vomited. Natsu stood behind her, holding Takana's damp hair away from her face and rubbing her back.

"I think I can guess what you and Sōkichi were up to before you came back to Oyama," Natsu teased.

"What are you talking about?" Takana asked as she spit out the last of the bile.

Natsu shrugged, but her smile said enough of what she really believed.

"My *sensei* once told me about women skipping the moons after battles. The violence and stress... It's probably a combination of the fight in Koganei and living in that cage for over a month. When I was starving myself over the last decade, I skipped several as well."

Natsu raised her eyebrows in thought, then nodded that it could be possible.

"Come on, partner."

When they entered the Inn, cheers from most of the estate's residents greeted them. Takana's friends and her mother waited to meet her at her table. The mistress stood at the top of the stairs and nodded down at her, then indicated they had one hour to use the main floor before she would open it back up for business.

Takana was overwhelmed. It had only been a few short months ago that she had no friends, no home, no freedom, no prospects beyond an eternal struggle to pay back a debt that wasn't even hers—now she had the world.

Takana ran outside and fought back tears on the veranda. She knew she earned it, but she still didn't believe she deserved anything. She didn't understand why they all liked her so much, besides her mother.

Since she'd been virtually forced to quit smoking after the attack in Koganei, her sense of smell and taste had improved. Natsu offered to smuggle her cigarettes in the night, but Takana took the opportunity during her imprisonment to cut ties with the habit. The hay smelled worse every day that passed until release. It was worth it, though. She smelled Sōkichi before his arm wrapped around her—the light sweat and then the heat of his skin. He leaned against the rail with her without saying anything. She kissed his hand, then his lips. They went back inside and spent the rest of the hour catching up on their enterprise.

Fusa hung back during the reunion, canoodling with Shinkichi. Takana expected Fusa would have been the first to hug her like a child as she'd done before. As the partygoers departed to restaurants for their dice games and her mother went out to find an inn with vacancy, Fusa finally came to Takana after retrieving the *kasa* and *daishō* from one of the game rooms.

"Thank you, Fusa-*chan*. Where's—?"

Fusa hugged Takana tight. Natsu smiled at them from their table.

"I'm glad to see you, too, Fusa-*chan*, but...where's the *kiseruzutsu*?"

"The what?"

Takana put effort into keeping calm.

"My grandfather's pipe and case. Where are they?"

"Oh! Are you sure you gave those to me?"

Takana squeezed the bridge of her nose.

"I really don't think you gave them to me, Takana-*san*. Why don't you check your pockets?"

"I just got out of jail! I gave them to *you*! Of course they're not in my pock—"

Takana thrust her hands into the pockets of the *kimono* sleeve to show Fusa how ridiculous the idea was, when her fingers brushed against the familiar casing. She pulled it out and lifted the lid in disbelief. The *kiseru* safely resided inside as always.

"How did—?" Takana started before Fusa's pursed lips burst into laughter.

"Shinkichi taught me that!" Fusa said after the laughter died down. "You didn't feel it while I hugged you? I didn't think I'd be *that* good yet."

Takana playfully slapped the side of Fusa's arm, then hugged her again.

"Thank you for protecting this, Fusa-*chan*. I love you."

"I love you, Takana-*san*."

Takana bowed to Shinkichi as he guided Fusa outside. Natsu's smile had disappeared by the time Takana sat at the table next to her.

"What's wrong, Natsu-*san*?"

"It's nothing."

"Yes, it is—"

"Not now. Look at all the customers outside with their eyes on our table. The mercenaries, too. I've doubled their output while you were away. We've got three deposit boxes upstairs now, and some of theirs are close to needing a second. The mistress has a new rack on order."

"Any movement on the Utsunomiya Inn?"

"Not on the location, but they've officially released Chise to work directly for us."

Takana nodded as the Inn filled with business.

It became apparent that something pushed Takana to travel to Nikkō. Four new jobs presented themselves before the day finished that started on the way and ended there. She would have been happy to ignore Iwakuchi's message. She had the *daishō* Sōkichi gifted her. While the set that Tomoe-*sensei* had given to her upon completing her training and turning twenty was beautiful and crafted by the finest blacksmith in the region, they served the same function as any other. Besides, the set was mostly decorative. To-moe-*sensei* and Iwakuchi had said it was bad luck to unsheathe them unless she really needed to use them, so they sat on the *katana kake* exclusively until they were pawned off.

"You seem uneasy, Takana-*san*," Natsu said as they found an alleyway in which to sleep. "If you don't want to go to Nikkō there are plenty of mercenaries we can send there."

"I have something personal to do. I was hoping to avoid it, but...I'll drive myself mad thinking about it otherwise. I need to go if only to never think about it again."

Natsu nodded as if that was all she needed to hear. She didn't ask follow-up questions or probe for further meaning. Sōkichi did the same thing. Takana appreciated it very much but didn't like that Natsu still wouldn't explain certain things to her. She wasn't lying, but purposefully avoiding talking about things wasn't much of a difference in Takana's mind.

Since she volunteered to accompany her to Nikkō, Takana hoped the trip would be a good opportunity to learn more about Natsu. Part of her wanted to only go with Sōkichi since they hadn't seen each other for over six weeks, but it would be safer to travel in a group. Takana knew she shouldn't be taking risks with Taiga alive and actively seeking her.

While she contemplated bloody revenge on the remaining Kochiya clan, her nausea came back. She got up and ran to the end of the alley and emptied her stomach.

"You okay?" Natsu asked after Takana returned.

"Yeah. I wonder what I ate recently."

Natsu reached for Takana's abdomen unexpectedly.

"Still cramping?"

"Yes."

"You'll probably be okay in a few—uh, weeks. Maybe a little worse before you get better."

"Should I see the doctor before we go west?"

"I don't think you're 'sick' but if it will make you feel better, sure."

Takana laid on her side. Natsu lay behind her, spooning into her back. Natsu put her arm around Takana's waist, fingers hanging in front of her belly button.

"The nights are getting a little colder," Natsu whispered.

She nuzzled into Takana's hair and fell fast asleep, her breathing warm and pleasant against the back of Takana's ear. Natsu's sudden, familiar touch might have been uncomfortable before the imprisonment, but after their bonding each night, Takana found it natural and enjoyed it for something more than warmth.

They gathered Sōkichi and Chise from the estate a few days later and began their journey west into the mountains. Chise chose to guide Takana to the location Iwakuchi gave her and protect the Inn's two investments as the mistress had asked of her. Takana believed Natsu might be even more dangerous than Chise and didn't need protection, but Takana had grown to enjoy traveling companions and didn't argue.

They completed a couple of the jobs enroute, stealing an artifact here, assassinating a *yakuza* thug there. Natsu's *kunoichi* skills made it too easy. The other three were glorified lookouts while she finished the jobs.

On the first night, Takana slept next to Sōkichi while the other two gave them distance. It was almost as comfortable and restful as sleeping next to Natsu had been—Sōkichi was admittedly less soft, but much warmer. She was getting spoiled—she hadn't slept by anyone in her life. It was always alone in her own room, or in alleyways. In the previous two months she'd slept beside Fusa, Natsu, and Sōkichi—all different in their own way.

The next day Sōkichi and Chise volunteered to chase off a small clan of highway robbers near Imaichi. Natsu and Takana took up positions near the road to steer the robbers away if they happened to run towards town. While they remained on alert, Takana broached the Fusa subject with Natsu.

"I thought you liked her very much. Why does your expression change around her?"

"I don't want to—"

"You never want to talk about it. But Fusa is going to be with us all the time. I need to know what your problem is with her before it gets any more complicated."

"It's... It doesn't even make sense to *me*," Natsu said with a wistful look into the nearby forest. "She reminds me so much of my older sister. I was never as close to anyone as her. When those *yakuza* butchers destroyed my family, in the moment I didn't understand what was happening.

"That night, I lost everything. I was broken by those men, and I had nothing to carry with me when they burned it all down. But the memory I'm most haunted by was—it was my sister's face as they forced themselves on her. I realized—later—her pain wasn't from what was being done to her, but what they were going to do to me... Knowing she couldn't stop them..."

Takana had no frame of reference for that kind of pain and hoped she never would, but she sympathized with the notion of having nothing to carry after the tragedy. She didn't know what she would do if she really lost her grandfather's *kiseruzutsu*. At least she'd always had that to ease her subsequent hard life.

"When Fusa fell into your arms after you saved her from that old man in the estate..." Takana mused.

Natsu wasn't telling the whole story, but Takana couldn't possibly grasp the turmoil Natsu must have been going through—confronting the release of sisterly attachment alongside something deeper that released upon being that savior—so she didn't press the matter.

A little better understanding of Natsu was enough for her.

Having extracted Natsu's most painful memory, Takana let the other part of the equation go, and instead of trampling on Natsu's admission with awkward talk about understanding and empathy, Takana simply grasped Natsu's hand and went back to watching the road.

Another wave of nausea cut through any lingering awkwardness between them, and Takana rushed behind a tree to empty her stomach. When she came back, Natsu put her hand on Takana's shoulder.

"How's the cramping?"

"Not as bad lately. I hope this is the end of it."

Natsu raised her eyebrow wryly.

"Have you told Sōkichi-*kun* yet?"

"Told him what?"

Natsu chuckled and shook her head. A commotion came from the forest as two men ran towards the road, looking backwards every few meters. Takana and Natsu squared to them, putting their hands on the hilts of their blades. The men saw them and turned south, away from Imaichi. Soon Sōkichi and Chise came from the direction of the fleeing men and joined Takana and Natsu. They collected their fee from the Imaichi police force and continued deeper into Nikkō.

Once they completed the final job, they hiked up to Lake Chūzenji. Takana had worked around Nikkō many times but had never had a reason to go to the lake. Down on the flat plain of the *Nikkō Kaidō* there were only rivers and trees while the mountains loomed in the distance to the west and north. She didn't have as much experience climbing the steeper roads.

Could she have made the hike when she was still smoking? It was far from easy, even with improving lungs. They stopped near the top to enjoy the tall, powerful falls that emptied into a river running down to Nikkō. Sōkichi guarded the women's supplies with his back to them as they bathed in the cold-water basin. The brightness and un-dulled quality of the new tattoos on the shoulders of Natsu and Chise made Takana jealous. Once all their co-workers were inked, Takana would get hers either touched up or have a new one added to the other shoulder.

The women traded places with Sōkichi. Natsu teased him that Takana would have joined him if the water wasn't so cold. Reinvigorated by the respite, the four continued the climb to the lake carved from the ancient eruption of a volcano. Opulent residences dotted the shore of the lake—mostly the second and third homes of nobles in Eastern Nihon.

It made sense that a rich noble had purchased her *daishō*. According to Iwakuchi, Tomoe's gift was more expensive than the *kimono* her mother had purchased for her after completing formal education. Takana often wondered how her life would have been different if Iwakuchi had been an actual noble and not merely left in control of the wealth her grandfather and *his* father had earned through careful, pragmatic business with all strata of commoners, nobles, and criminals.

Nearing the location Iwakuchi gave to Chise, Takana realized she didn't have a plan for buying it back. All they had was the money from the Imaichi police and the small amount they took from the estate for meals and public baths. Of course, Natsu could solve any problem in the night that money couldn't buy during the day, but Takana would rather it didn't come to that.

Unlike the other residences they passed, the one that supposedly housed her *daishō* was small and unadorned. There was a large rocky courtyard that had many well-used targets and effigies scattered throughout.

"Stop," Natsu said to the group, then moved around the courtyard, safely disarming a plethora of unseen traps.

Watching Natsu work in the dying light of dusk, it was clear that if Takana had journeyed there alone, she would have died before reaching the center of the courtyard. Only a *kunoichi* could have survived.

Natsu nonchalantly knocked on the entrance of the small residence and motioned for the other three to join her. Even though Takana had witnessed Natsu disarm so many traps, it still unnerved them to make their way across the courtyard.

No one answered the door. Natsu and Chise split up to look through windows while Sōkichi went to study the traps. Takana watched him as he moved about the courtyard. If she had kept her attention on the door, she would have heard it slide open. The homeowner placed a blade up against her throat and pulled her backwards into the house. Two skillful kicks knocked her *geta* off her feet from behind, then she was dragged and thrown to the musty *tatami* past the entryway.

The assailant shut and locked the door, then glided so quickly back to Takana that she was unable to get up on her elbows or scream for help. They flipped Takana's *kasa* off with the *katana* blade before pointing it back at her throat. The homeowner also had a large *kasa* covering their eyes, lifted just enough to see Takana's face.

"Gozen-*san*?" the woman asked, incredulity washing over her face.

Takana couldn't believe her eyes.

"Tomoe-*sensei*?"

Chapter Nineteen

Skewered

Yama-uba/Yamamba: There are countless variations of the mountain crone throughout Japan. They often have unkempt hair, torn and filthy clothing, and a mouth hidden beneath their hair. They are cannibalistic, monstrous, and cunning in disguise. Travelers and merchants were most often their victims. Eerie examples of yama-uba phenomena are the sounds of festivals and cursing coming from mountains, and weeping c ming from rivers.

August 21, 1708
Lake Chūzenji, Tochigi Prefecture

TAKANA SCRAMBLED OFF HER BACK, onto her knees, bowing deeply in apology to her former master. She begged forgiveness for their trespass. Tears of embarrassment and confused nostalgia played out while her forehead touched the *tatami*.

A loud commotion came from the front door as Chise and Sō-kichi crashed through. Tomoe squared up to meet them before Takana shouted at everyone to stop.

"Where's the *kunoichi*?" Tomoe asked.

Natsu slipped in from a dark area of the residence behind Takana. She held her hands out. Tomoe huffed and slid her *katana* back in its scabbard.

"Your traps are as old-fashioned as you look, lady," Natsu teased.

"Skilled as you are, *nēsan*, I'll wager you've never beaten your masters in the *kunoichi* training grounds."

Natsu smiled at being caught out and shrugged. Takana sat up on her knees, taking in her master. She'd aged well, not hiding her wrinkles or elegant gray hair with creams or dyes. Though it had been almost ten years, she was nearly identical to the last time Takana had seen her. There were no stooping or slow movements to her frame. Tomoe could take all four of them on and not break a sweat.

Sōkichi and Chise introduced themselves, even without knowing why Takana had called off their attack in the declared cease-fire. Though she wasn't nobility, Tomoe's appearance and posture commanded immediate respect from Takana's fellow warriors, Natsu's light teasing aside.

Tomoe motioned for Takana to stand up. She did, but on her feet, she bowed from her waist, parallel to the floor. She didn't want to meet Tomoe's eyes out of shame for their intrusion, and more so, shame that she could no longer explain it. Surely it wasn't a coincidence...

Tomoe lifted Takana's chin.

"What are you doing here, Gozen-*san*?"

"I didn't know this was your residence, *sensei*. I was sent here for something, and no other information was given. I would never have trespassed, otherwise."

"What were you sent for? I'm afraid I don't have much..."

Tomoe gestured around the room that conveyed very little aesthetic beauty other than minimalism.

"I fear I've been manipulated," Takana said, her words quiet and restrained as she worked through the vexing turn of events. "The reason I came all this way... It was Iwakuchi's attempt to earn my forgiveness."

"Your father? Why would he—?"

"He's not my father. He's nothing. I'm...ashamed to have come here for something so immaterial as the *daishō*. If I'd known it was your home... I never would have shown my face. I've been so full of regret—to have lost your gift to that man's desperate debt payments. I should have protected it more carefully. I am deeply sorry, *sensei*."

Tomoe cleared her throat and formally invited everyone further into the home. She started a fire that they all settled around, helping to prepare skewered fish, rice, and vegetables. While they cooked dinner, Tomoe went into a back room, then came back with the ornate *daishō* she'd gifted Takana.

"I don't understand why you have them," Takana said as she held them in her hands once more, shaking in reverence. "Iwakuchi claimed he sold them in the city."

"He probably never told you... I didn't buy these for you. In the last few years of your training, his payments nearly stopped. I didn't have the money I was making near the beginning of your lessons. Still, he wanted something to commemorate the end of your training. He bought these with his rapidly dwindling coin and gave them to me—to give to you. In the end he gave them back to me and demanded I at least reimburse him for their value."

"You're right, he never told me any of that. Do you think that's the reason he sent me to get them? To prove he isn't a selfish, debt-addled, useless cretin?"

Tomoe took several bites of dinner before answering.

"That doesn't make sense. He knew what these were. Go ahead and unsheathe them."

Takana did as asked. Even in the low firelight she could tell the color of the metal was off. It was cheap, poorly smithed, and dull. They'd break instantly in a duel, useless but for the gorgeous painting on the scabbards. Takana had been so awestruck by the wonderful artwork at twenty years old that she never unsheathed them, hoping to preserve their value and craftmanship inside the scabbards. She had also believed that superstition about only ever unsheathing them when in great need.

"If he meant this to be a peace offering of some kind, I would consider it a slap in the face," Tomoe added with a hint of disgust. "He may be those things you said, but he's not an idiot. He would know *you would know* their worth simply by looking at them."

Takana's rage began to boil. What had been the point of his errand? Suicide-by-angry-daughter? Too much of a coward to do it himself? He must have known she would come back down the mountains hellbent on making him pay for wasting her time. After her repeated efforts to rid herself of his pestilence—all the threats to his life—why would he instigate her?

She had missed something. Forgot...

Natsu snapped to attention over her bowl of rice. Within a blink she disappeared out the back door. The rest of them stood, grasping the hilts of their weapons. Chise and Sōkichi went to opposite sides of the door they'd broken down and peeked around the frame.

"It's too bad your friend disarmed my traps..." Tomoe muttered.

"We'd be dead if she hadn't," Takana whispered.

A loud whapping sound came from the front entrance. An arrow stuck out of the loose armor protecting Chise's shoulder. She ignored it as she and Sōkichi backed up from the wood and rice paper. More arrows exploded through the walls. They ran back to Takana and Tomoe, centered in the living area.

"All those traps... Do you get attacked often, *sensei*?"

"I've never been attacked since I moved here."

Even deep into the house, an inhuman scream blew in from across the courtyard, followed shortly by another one, then indistinct shouting. Takana ran out the back door and around the building. The moonlight shone over the house and courtyard, but the forest itself was devoid of light.

An injured man ran out of the blackness, holding a broken bow and dragging his leg. Takana readied a *kunai*, but a *shuriken* flew from the forest into the back of his head. More men ran into the courtyard, afraid of the darkness and the *kunoichi* haunting it.

Chise and Sōkichi charged out of the entrance and cut them down as they kept looking over their shoulders. Takana and Tomoe joined the fray as more men flooded out, half in fear of the forest, half to meet their opponents in the open field. Arrows fired out, hitting targets, allies, Chise's armor, Sōkichi's loose robes, Tomoe's house, and Takana's *kasa*.

Whenever Takana turned in expectation of arrows coming from the same direction, the only thing that came out were the marksmen getting chased into the open by Natsu. After a short time, arrows came more often and precisely as the remaining archers found protected firing places instead of panicking into the open battle.

"Into the forest!" Tomoe shouted.

They followed her lead, taking away the archers' advantage of far-off cover and easy sight lines. Any man who hadn't fallen to their blades but were left in the courtyard stayed out there, petrified of unseen death.

The group quieted their movements and split up. They came across panicky archers too afraid to move, understanding they were going to die whether it was in the dark or out beneath the moonlight. Whenever one stood up to run, he rustled the forest's detritus and met a quick demise. Takana heard the strong, single blows of Sōkichi's *katana*; the surprised cries from impalement by Chise's *naginata*; Natsu's *shuriken* slicing the air and landing wetly, firmly into flesh; Tomoe's breath releasing in controlled bursts as she expended efficient thrusts and slashes.

Takana ignored the panicked breathing of the men she chased; the pleading when they tripped and she stood over them; the useless twang of a bow string in the dark hitting nothing but tree trunks—she cut them all down without mercy.

She imagined every other one to be Taiga or Iwakuchi; their malicious expressions molding into the faces of the men whenever she'd catch them eye to eye. One or both of them were behind this. As thoughts whirled in her mind, sporadic with adrenaline, she remembered Iwakuchi mentioning that Kochiya *yakuza* he met in the bathhouse.

Iwakuchi sold her out; the bastard sent her to her death.

Even if he hadn't intended it—knowing what awaited her at Tomoe's house—he had knowingly sent the estate's most experienced warriors away on a goose chase. Tomoe was right—he wasn't a stupid man. The estate was only guarded by recruits. Her mother trained as an *onna-bugeisha* decades before but had no reason to practice in the time since she'd settled down, devoting herself to her daughter's upbringing, education, and culture.

Taiga was wiping Takana out and using Iwakuchi to that end.

Her fury exploded at the realization, increasing the savagery of her hand. She wanted to hear them beg; to cry; to apologize. She heard Taiga and Iwakuchi's voices in the pleading, and it made her lustful to silence them.

Dripping with warm blood in the night air, Takana's body hummed with retributive ecstasy.

An orange glow from the courtyard illuminated the forest's edge. The men who'd been too afraid to go back into the darkness mustered the courage they needed as the light from the house fire grew wider.

Chise and Natsu screamed in unison. It wasn't in a painful, panicked voice. It was the horrifying, ethereal voice of the *yama-uba*, the mountain crones with cannibalistic tendencies. The men stopped venturing into the forest at those blood-chilling shrieks and ran back into the courtyard. Sōkichi and Tomoe chased after them, cutting them down.

A few of the stragglers stopped at the edges of the hottest flames, trapped, and were impaled from behind by Chise. Natsu and Takana emerged from opposite ends of the courtyard, stabbing anyone who hadn't suffered mortal wounds and were only crippled or too frightened to run away.

They met in the middle but kept their attention to the forest. Natsu's body tensed as Takana heard a bowstring draw back. It came from somewhere unreachable, further up in the trees. They would be aiming for Natsu, the primary threat; the one who'd cut down so many of their fellow archers. Without a thought for herself, Takana shoved Natsu aside. An arrow hit her *kimono* sleeve, thunking into something hard and pulling her to the ground with its momentum.

Two more arrows fired from different directions. One glanced off her *kasa*, hitting hard enough to knock it off her head to Natsu's feet, and the other went through Takana's *bakeneko* tattoo, the shaft stopping halfway so it stuck out of both sides of her shoulder. Natsu raged and grabbed Takana's *kasa*. She ran with it in front of her for protection to the edge of the forest and threw the *kunai* into the darkness in the direction the arrows had been loosed.

Two bodies crashed to the forest floor. A bowstring twanged from above, but the arrow landed somewhere heavily, uselessly in the darkness. A man cried out. A body struck the ground, and the same voice cried out again.

Natsu pulled the man into the courtyard, holding his bow against his neck to drag him despite his flailing legs. Takana registered the arrow sticking out of her shoulder as her adrenaline plunged. Sōkichi and Chise kneeled at her sides. Natsu tortured the man for information in front of all of them. She didn't work her way up from smaller injuries; she went right to the worst pain she knew he would survive without passing out, using a chunk of Takana's bamboo *kasa* to extract information. Once he mentioned Taiga, Natsu ended him.

Takana didn't know if it was Natsu's method of swift torture or the nausea that'd been accompanying her the last week that made her vomit, but she did so all over Sōkichi's *geta* and the lower part of his *hakama*. He didn't flinch, but put his hand to her face, comforting her and showing she had nothing to be ashamed of.

Tomoe asked Chise and Sōkichi to pick Takana up. She sliced off both ends of the arrow so smoothly and skillfully with her *katana* that Takana barely noticed that the shaft had been touched.

"Come, there's a doctor at the other end of the lake near the main trade hub."

Takana responded to her master's command, doing her best to put one leg in front of the other. She only made it a few feet before her legs turned boneless, and she collapsed in shock.

Takana apologized again, more embarrassed than she'd been when trespassing on Tomoe's property.

"What do you have to be sorry for, Gozen-*san*?" Tomoe asked, standing on the opposite side of the doctor as he wrapped Takana's shoulder.

"I'm a worthless warrior. I learned nothing from you. Every scar is a disgrace to your efforts. You wasted over ten years training me, and for what!"

Tomoe put her hand to Takana's forehead and smiled.

"Gozen-*san*, you misinterpreted the goal of my training. It was never to be the most skillful warrior or kill the most enemies. Survival—it's all I wanted for you. I saw the writing on the wall when your father stopped paying me. I saw where your life was headed, and I did the best I could with the short time I had left to help. Watching you save your friend's life in that battle, the selflessness... You learned more than I imagined a rich, spoiled only-child capable. I'm proud of you."

The doctor left her side, and Natsu materialized from the shadows to grasp Takana's hand.

"I'm thankful for you, my pretty, skewered friend."

Natsu stooped down to briefly kiss Takana on the lips, then backed up. The action surprised Takana but was so quick—and not entirely unwelcome—that she didn't have time to react.

"I need to go back to Tomoe-*sensei's* residence. I'll meet you all at the estate."

"Everything's burned down—" Tomoe started, but Natsu had already dissolved into the shadows.

Tomoe shook her head and backed away for Chise and Sōkichi to flank the sides of the table. They both conveyed with their eyes all they needed to. The battle strengthened their bonds. Chise put her hand on Takana's uninjured shoulder and smiled, then walked away. Sōkichi remained and kissed her much longer than Natsu had. She felt through his lips all his relief and concern.

Takana replayed the battle in her head and remembered the thoughts she'd had about the estate being unguarded. She sat up, ignoring the pain in her shoulder.

"The estate!"

While she threw on her *kimono*, she told her companions why she thought the estate was in danger. As they made to leave, Takana noticed her left sleeve felt off. There wasn't the familiar, light tugging of weight from a certain pocket. She thrust her hand through the fabric in a panic.

It wasn't there.

The poor stitching had torn through the back of the sleeve, ripping out the pocket lining.

Intense, burning wetness built up in her eyes. Two thoughts crowded into her grief-stricken mind—if she hadn't pushed Natsu out of the way of that arrow, it would still be in her pocket; and if Fusa had put even a little more effort into learning how to sew properly, it would still be in her pocket.

Takana turned her rage on herself for the selfish thoughts, valuing an object over both of her closest friends. She cursed herself as they hurried down the mountain. Her body was numb, but her thoughts were vibrant with pain. The hole in her soul—the last remaining artifact of her grandfather, lost—hurt worse than the hole in her shoulder.

Chapter Twenty

Bumpy Road

Hara-kiri: Self-disembowelment that is less honorable than seppuku, though the two terms are often conflated to be the same thing. The result is the same, but hara-kiri simply refers to the action of cutting the stomach without the sense of ritual, tradition, and honor associated with seppuku. Women had their own form of the ritual, called jigai, but was performed without assistance by slashing the jugular vein instead of the abdomen.

August 23, 1708
Between Ishibashi and Suzenomiya, Tochigi Prefecture

TAKANA SHAMBLED THROUGH THE BURNT ruins of the estate, her body beyond tears, her mind unable to digest the overwhelming remnants of what lay before her. She took no solace in the fact that most of the women were out on the road with their protectors when it happened. Those lucky ones trickled in with their hauls only to discover that all their friends who'd volunteered to tend the estate had been slaughtered and burned. One of them was missing. Their communal fortune had been stolen before the rest of the estate went up in flames.

Staggering through the bones of the structures, Takana kept coming back to her mother's corpse. She died shielding one of the youngest, for all the help that had been for the poor girl. Takana cursed herself for that stupid, bitter thought. It was how she felt about her lost *kiseru*. She hated herself for it. Her mother had sacrificed herself for someone, no matter her relationship to that person, no matter the thought of how successful that sacrifice would be. Takana brought shame upon herself for finding any way to fault what her mother did. Had she no honor left in her?

Takana didn't have the words to comfort an inconsolable Fusa. Shinkichi did the heavy lifting of being there for her, because Takana wasn't up to the task. Several of the protectors cursed their survival, lamenting they weren't there to protect anyone. Sōkichi, Chise, and Tomoe met with each of them, helping them to understand their roles and to guide their rage and sorrow towards the enemy. All of them came away more determined.

Takana wished she could internalize what Tomoe said to her after they'd come upon the estate still on fire, but she'd tuned her out. The quiet crackling of embers, the smoldering timbers of the home she'd earned, was too deafening to hear anything about recovery or perspective. Sōkichi's normally comforting touch felt cold and lifeless whenever he'd find moments to reach for her.

She didn't know what Natsu thought, because she was gone. Natsu had come into view on the road, as Takana took in the horrors of the estate. When they made eye contact, Natsu paused, then ran away. Perhaps she saw in Takana her younger self and couldn't bear to look upon it.

Takana didn't have any thoughts of malevolence towards Natsu for that. Takana had that urge as well once she came across her mother's body. But something kept her around the estate. She wanted the survivors to lash out at her. She wanted punishment, no matter from who—the dead could rise, and she'd let them drag her to Hell. She wanted Taiga or Iwakuchi to come out of hiding and kill her once and for all; she wouldn't even defend herself if they did. She just wanted all the bloodshed to be over...

She pushed her despair aside in brief bouts of mania, attempting to provoke the survivors to yell, scream, cry, even harm her by exclaiming how it was all her fault. She told anyone who listened what mercy had bought her, her deceased mother, and their friends and coworkers. If only they'd all been smart enough to stay away from such a dirty, criminal vagabond who'd entertained delusions of grandeur for a better life, a better home for all of them.

Takana envied Fusa's naïve nature and lack of decorum as she grieved openly. Her tears were raw and untwisted by guilt that she was even allowed to shed them. Their coworkers were drawn to Fusa, to protect the most innocent of all of them. Jealousy of Fusa's grief—of all the ridiculous, demented thoughts to have—was the final straw. Takana didn't deserve to be their friend, least of all their leader.

In the evening, she waited in the thicket until most of those remaining would be asleep in the new makeshift barracks that the protectors had constructed to keep their minds on a positive task as the women wept for their family. Takana slipped out of the thicket and went to the road. Out of sight of the barracks and estate, but not more than a few minutes' walk, she took off Fusa's *kimono* and folded it neatly before setting it in the grass next to the road, then laid her *katana* across the fabric.

Standing in the middle of the road, she slipped out of her dirty, bloody, tattered *hakama*. She folded it, too, then kneeled down on it over the dirt. Only white linen around her waist and chest were left. She unsheathed her *wakizashi* and held the hilt in one hand and the edge with the other. It was a little too long for what she intended, and she didn't have a cloth to keep from slicing off her fingers on the follow-through. If she went in far enough, though, it wouldn't soon matter.

Takana rubbed a hand over her stomach, tracing where she'd drag the blade with her fingernail, leaving a raised pink line to guide the cut. She wondered what would go through her mind as she attempted to earn some honor for her life—her last thoughts. What did *samurai* feel on the battlefield after failing their *daimyo*? Not all of them chose the path of honor. Many became *rōnin*, wandering around wearing their dishonor and disloyalty with no remorse. Some of them seemed haunted by the choice, but they valued living more than honor, nonetheless.

Takana's world crashed down on her. Her thoughts wouldn't allow her respite or consolation. There was no life worth living left to seek. She wouldn't be like those cowardly *rōnin*. Her action would mean something to the people that tried comforting her but must secretly hate her. She didn't buy their outward support or soothing speeches about sacrifice and leadership. They must assuredly blame her as much as she blamed herself. She would prove to them she understood that—her life for their justice.

As she rubbed her hand a few more times over the decided path of the blade, a small rise in her lower abdomen caught her attention. It confused her—she hadn't eaten anything since the interrupted dinner at Tomoe's residence, and she'd vomited all that out. She shook her head at the distraction. She wasn't going to be knocked from her path to honor so easily. The bulge was her grief turned into stones, carried around in her stomach. She would cut them out for the world to see.

Takana held the blade out, allowing the tip to draw blood near her hip. She took several deep, stoic breaths. If she cried out, it would destroy everything she meant to accomplish. She would be swift and silent, but if she lingered, she would end her own suffering with a slash across the neck. With the last few breaths, she concentrated on how good it was to breathe, knowing it would be her last breath ever taken, unburdened by pain.

She extended her arms for the thrust. Muscles tightened.

A flash of metal hit the hilt and sent the blade flying out of her hands, clattering into the grass. A *shuriken* stuck out of the hilt.

Footsteps approached from the side of the road, but Takana stared at the hilt, comprehending what had happened. Wetness dripped onto her thigh and brought her out of her trance. Her left palm was sliced open, but not too deeply to disable her remaining fingers.

"With all the death around you, your answer was to end two more lives?"

Takana sighed and relaxed for the unbearable tension in which her body had been locked. She looked up at the stars exploding from the purple mist of the galaxy, rotating around her.

"What are you talking about, Natsu-*san*? All the death ends with me. Everyone else can live their lives free of danger."

"There's no such thing," Natsu said as she sat down close, letting their thighs touch. She reached across and felt Takana's abdomen. "You have something more to live for yet."

Natsu caressed Takana less medically and more lovingly. Takana assumed she'd been checking for collateral damage, but she stayed away from the bloody cut.

"Where have you been?" Takana asked, changing the subject.

"Do you even have to ask?"

"I suppose not. What kind of security has he set up outside the headquarters?"

"It's formidable, but nothing we can't overcome. I already paid off the *samurai* to look the other way. They only asked that we don't burn the place down."

Natsu stood and offered her hand for Takana. She took it, then looked again at the *wakizashi* with the *shuriken* sticking out of the hilt. The gravity of what she had chosen to do struck her all at once, and great sobs choked their way up her throat. Natsu wrapped Takana in her arms and allowed her to release everything she'd bottled up since the smoke of their destroyed home had filled her lungs and clouded her mind with sorrow.

Once she found her control and sniffed and wiped away her sadness, Takana gazed into Natsu's eyes. It was as close as Takana had ever been to another person: partners in business, veterans in battle, their families ripped apart by *yakuza*; their lives saved by the other. Takana leaned in and kissed her on the lips. It wasn't brief, but there was no arousal in it. Natsu had done so much for her without asking for a thing in return. Holding hands and hugging didn't feel like they conveyed enough how much Takana appreciated her friend. It simply felt like the right thing to do.

Part Three – Bloodlines

Chapter Twenty-One
Rewards

Ojigi: Bowing is fundamental to Japanese society, thought to originate between the 5th and 8th centuries from Buddhist roots. Bowing became closely affiliated with samurai but evolved into our contemporary understanding of the concept during the Edo period. Angle and length of bow connotate countless meanings in virtually every setting and strata of Japanese life. Entire manuals have been written on the proper bowing etiquette as it has evolved through the centuries.

August 27, 1708
Utsunomiya, Tochigi Prefecture

TAKANA OCCUPIED THE CENTER OF the road leading to the front stairs of the Kochiya-*kai* headquarters, her *katana* drawn and held at her left side, squared to the entrance. Blood from her sliced palm dribbled down the shaft, forming a puddle beneath her *geta*. Most citizens gave her a wide berth and went about their business, while others stopped to watch whatever threatened to unfold. Many shifted restlessly as she stood there; a statue of retributive intimidation, her eyes covered by her *kasa*.

A rat's nest of hair hung along her upper back. Arrow pieces stuck in the *kasa*. Her exposed shoulder-wound leaked into her *sarashi* and made a mess of her tattoo. The blood of the men who attacked them at Tomoe's residence decorated her torn *kimono*.

Residual char from the estate streaked her *hakama* and calves. Dust clung to any place that wasn't caked with bloody mud. She had only bathed in violence since the journey to Lake Chūzenji.

Her stomach threatened to expel the small amount of food she ate before the walk to Utsunomiya. Takana had been standing out front for long enough without drawing the attention of the *yakuza* inside. It was time to instigate before she grew any weaker. Natsu and Sōkichi had warned her about the course of action after Natsu finally unblocked Takana's denial, and Takana had shared the news with him but no one else. However, nothing was going to stop her from ensuring that when the baby arrived in the world, Taiga would not be in it.

"*Ani-ki!*" Her voice broke at the end. The street paused and silenced itself.

The bitchy *yakuza* wife who manned the front poked her head out, then disappeared. Taiga appeared from the mouth of the entrance and smirked down at her. He shook his head and laughed.

"I never lied to you, *ane-san*. The things you and I could do together... After everything, I still want you by my side. I always will. Won't you finally see reason? Or are you that determined to die, like a dog in the street?"

Takana lowered the *kasa*, inviting Taiga to run at her from the stairs. Footsteps indeed pounded down the stairs, but it was a stampede of the last remaining Kochiya clan. She peered up again to see Taiga hadn't moved at all. He wore a venomous smile and unearned confidence while his men circled around her back and flank wielding blades. Onlookers backed away from the rising conflict.

"Finally, I can see for myself how you keep surviving," Taiga shouted down to her over the clamor of men. "If you survive *this*, I'll free you from this feud."

"I'll free myself, *tonchiki*," she muttered. Her loose, pinky-less grip squelched against her blade's hilt.

The men all looked up at Taiga, waiting for his final command. Getting bored with Taiga's pomp and unearned self-satisfaction, Takana turned the blade of the *katana* by her side. The *yakuza* thugs were yanked back by hidden arms in doors, windows, and alleyways that had set up around her well before she arrived. Their throats were cut in unison, spraying the road and Takana's feet in red as she began her march.

She focused on the sound of Taiga's *geta* as they escaped back into the headquarters. He hurled the *yakuza* wife, and she tumbled down the stairs. Takana stopped her roll halfway down. The wife braced for Takana to run her through on the steps, but Takana only continued up and into the building she knew so well.

Taiga had emptied every available *yakuza* from the building with his opening gambit; he had no more protection. Takana didn't expect the slime to willingly face her, so she planned to trap him. Natsu and Sōkichi had set up beneath the balcony and would have already climbed up at the sound of shouting and thunderous footsteps from the front.

Takana stalked the hallways to the main office. She took a deep breath and threw the doors open. Natsu and Sōkichi's hands went to their weapons, then relaxed.

"He didn't come through here," Natsu shrugged.

Takana cursed and turned around, running to check rooms she never assumed he'd hide in. Inside one of the lieutenant's rooms, a *tatami* tile lay slightly askew in the corner. Takana pulled it aside to reveal a trapdoor leading to an escape route through the foundation. She hopped down into the hole and crawled after her target. The tunnel emerged into the city and was completely hidden from her force in front of the building. No one could have seen where he went.

Takana sighed and sheathed the *katana*, then met her clan while they consolidated the bodies in the road. They looked to her for guidance. She tossed her head in the direction of the city square, then grabbed the weeping *yakuza* wife by the elbow. They dragged the remnants of the Kochiya clan, painting the road on the way.

They piled the corpses in the square. Fusa brought the surviving women of their clan through the streets that connected to the square, each hauling a bucket of liquid. The *yakuza* wife pulled a cigarette from an inside pocket. She shook as she lit the end of it in a brazier and watched the solemn procession.

The women doused the corpses with the liquid. Men on the edges of the crowd of onlookers mustered their courage to attack. Takana recognized many of them as belonging to other Utsunomiya clans. Fusa poured her bucket in a line from the pile of corpses to Takana's feet. She bowed and threw the bucket behind her. Her expression wasn't naïve anymore. If she hadn't been on Takana's side, Fusa's vengeful determination would have scared her.

Takana raised her voice to address the crowd.

"The Kochiya clan is no more! I offer fifteen *ryō* to anyone who brings me Taiga Kochiya alive, ten if he's dead. If anyone harbors him or assists in his escape from the city, this will be your fate."

Takana plucked the cigarette from the wife's trembling lips, ignoring the intense, sudden craving it stirred in her, and used it to light the long, thin candle she used to use for her own cigarettes. She knelt to the trail Fusa had made and put the flame to the oil. Everyone watched in silence as the fire raced towards the pile of bodies. She left the candle on the ground and stood.

Handing the cigarette back to the wife, Takana glared into her eyes.

"You have until midnight to get yourself, your children, and the other Kochiya wives out of Utsunomiya. If my clan sees any of you within the walls after that, they'll kill you on sight."

As the fire raged in the square, Takana gathered the women of her clan.

"Spread the word from here to Nikkō to Shirakawa—the Utsunomiya Inn is open for business in the former headquarters of the Kochiya-*kai*."

Natsu met Takana at the top of the stairs, shaking her head.

"We turned the place upside down. Our gold isn't here."

"There should be plenty in Oyama, and it won't take long to build a new fortune here."

"Good point. So, are you finally ready to bathe, my pretty, smelly friend?"

Takana nodded, but instead of using the opulent bathhouse within the headquarters, she went down the road to the public one. Her desecrated tattoo inspired fear in the woman in the lobby, who let Takana in without paying. Many of the women in the bath were unfamiliar to her, but their faces wore the same level of fear. With Natsu, Chise, and Fusa at her side with their clean *bakeneko* tattoos, they were given all the space in the bathing area, then the bath itself. They finally allowed themselves to relax for the first time since meeting Tomoe.

Back on the streets, Natsu, Chise, and Fusa's tattoos were covered. Still, with Takana as their spearhead and her tattoo on display, the people in the streets parted for them. Takana led them to a local seamstress. She disrobed from her *kimono* so the craftswomen could inspect it and requested two dozen be made in the same fashion—with the right half of the torso exposed. She promised to pay upon completion and the owner didn't question her.

Outside, Natsu excused herself to Oyama where she'd lay out the details for the Utsunomiya Inn with the mistress and collect their pay. Genjirō, their tattoo artist, had been housing in Suzumenomiya, between their estate and Utsunomiya when the incident happened. Fusa volunteered to collect him together with Shinkichi. Chise followed Takana back to the headquarters where Sōkichi enlisted some of the protectors to pull down the sign hanging over the entrance.

No longer fearful of eyes on her and Sōkichi, she kissed him in front of the men. They good-naturedly cheered at the triumph of the day and the deserved display of affection between their strong leaders. Chise bowed, then ventured into the headquarters to begin preparations to accommodate the coming influx of mercenaries and clients.

Sōkichi directed his men to recruit at all the *dōjō* in the city which had previously been off-limits to avoid drawing the Kochiya clan's attention. Takana then led him to the balcony in the back with its view of the mountains to the west. She relished the quiet between the buzz of cicadas, until she and Sōkichi were puncturing the silence together.

Takana sat on Tetsuo's *zabuton*, surveying a map of the region marked with each restaurant they ran dice games through. Fusa sat by her side at the head of the table, taking mental notes to pass along to the women where they could seek new restaurants and business partners. While Takana ran her finger along a new path to the north, Fusa put her hand over Takana's.

"I'm so sorry for your mother, Takana-*san*. I wish I could have thanked her more formally for asking me to leave the *yūkaku* to follow you."

Takana raised her eyebrow.

"You didn't follow me of your own accord?"

"Not at the time, no. I was scared to death of you. But she said if you were going to refuse her birthday gift, she was still going to give you something. She asked that I shadow you."

"I'm sorry, Fusa-*chan*. I thought you were already free. You aren't in my debt, and I apologize if that's all that's kept you with me."

"Are you—? ...Sometimes I think you're dumber than me," Fusa smiled, then put her hand over her new tattoo.

A knock at the office door interrupted them. Fusa started to get up, but Takana put her hand on her thigh.

"You're not a servant, Fusa-*chan*."

Takana opened the door to find Sōkichi standing behind a well-dressed man with silver streaks in his hair and beard. He bowed respectfully and she invited him in. Sōkichi closed the doors behind him while Takana pulled a *zabuton* out of the closet. She set it in front of the desk for the man, then she and Sōkichi joined Fusa sitting on the other side of the table.

"I was hoping we could speak in private, Gozen-*san*," the man said as he looked back and forth between Fusa and Sōkichi.

"My partners are my equals. Anything you say will be shared with the other two that aren't here. Privacy doesn't matter in this office."

The man nodded, then introduced himself as Manhachi, the first lieutenant of the Kameya clan, headquartered in the northeast section of the city.

"You made a loud declaration in the city square last week, Gozen-*san*. I know of your connection to the Kochiya clan. The *oyabun* is intrigued. Taiga has made loud declarations of his own at the regional clan meetings, claiming that he killed you—*three times*. Each time he sounded more and more certain based on the number of men he sent for you. Your declaration is the one we *heard*.

"The oyabun isn't a fool. You're formidable and cunning. You've taken significant chunks of resistance out of the outside clans that agreed to send men on Taiga's errands. Rumors of your *Bakeneko* clan's money-making prowess and deadliness are spreading. I was impressed by the foot traffic in the building while your man led me back here."

Takana held up her hand to pause his annoying flattery.

"Manhachi-*san*, before I ask you to get to the point, I want you to learn to break the habit of looking at the only other man in the room. Yes, Sōkichi-*san* is our equal, but you're talking to all of us, not him alone. If you wish to do business with us, you'll need to get used to dealing with women. Now, please continue."

Manhachi bowed and apologized to all three of them, then shifted to continue as she'd requested. Takana didn't blame him for defaulting to address Sōkichi, more so she was pleased with his lack of hesitation to adjust to the new rule—taking her word on the matter as law to begin with was promising.

"The *oyabun* wishes to work together. He knows most of the other clans in the region will challenge your new presence, regardless of your display in the city square. They might even be harboring Taiga. In exchange for ten percent of your operation, the *oyabun* is prepared to speak as your proxy in the clan meetings and provide intel and protection to keep the other clans at bay."

Fusa shifted and stiffened her back.

"I want to hear all this from the *oyabun* himself. No offense, Manhachi-*san*—you're very polite and I hope you'll be his intermediary going forward. But not until the *oyabun* gives his terms to my clan *personally* will we enter into any form of alliance. And he will agree to...*eight* percent."

Takana raised her eyebrow to Manhachi, trying not to laugh, as he looked at each of them in turn to determine whether she was serious. He bowed respectfully and agreed to deliver the message. Once he left and they could no longer hear his footsteps in the hall, Fusa fell back on the *tatami*, shaking with laughter. In a rare show of emotion, Sōkichi laughed with her.

"I could barely hold it in—he had no idea whether we were serious or not! That was the most fun I've ever had!" Fusa said after getting herself under control.

Takana smiled, pleased that Fusa was enjoying her new, unfamiliar power.

"Even if he agrees to the eight percent," Takana said, "I'm not going to hold our ledger responsible for calculating out such a difficult number. We'll allow ten percent as a goodwill gesture if he agrees to your terms."

"We never discussed what the clan would be called. It will be difficult to do business without a title," Sōkichi brought up to the table. "I assumed it would be the Gozen-*kai*, but after you discussed us as equals, that wouldn't work. He called us the *Bakeneko* clan. Bakeneko-*kai* doesn't quite roll off the tongue, but I believe it fits."

"I love it," Fusa said.

"You're the bosses," Takana grinned, powerless to hold back how much Fusa's energy affected her.

Sōkichi bowed to both of them and excused himself to commission a carpenter to build their new sign. Fusa scooted closer to Takana and grabbed her hand again.

"I heard something yesterday, Takana-*san*," Fusa whispered.

"Why are you whispering?" Takana whispered back, gesturing that there was no one else in the room.

"I don't know if you're keeping it a secret. But in the bath, one of the girls noticed your body's...change. May I feel it?"

Takana leaned back and pushed the *hakama* down to expose her abdomen. Fusa ran her hand over it, then frowned at the healing cut near the hipbone.

"What—"

"I banged against a railing."

"Ouch. I'm so happy for you, Takana-*san*."

Takana smiled and put her hand on the back of Fusa's head.

"Um, the reason I wanted to confirm... Are you and Sōkichi going to...you know...get married?"

"We haven't talked about that at all..."

"Oh. Um, Shinkichi-*kun* asked me to marry him two days ago. I told him I wouldn't give him an answer until I could ask your permission. If you were going to tell everyone of your baby, I didn't want to distract from that announcement with my news."

"Ask my—? Why would you need *my* permission?"

Fusa looked away, ashamed.

"I don't have a family. I have no dowry to give to him."

"If he's expecting one, then you don't have my permiss—"

"Oh no! No, he didn't ask. I just thought that was what happened? How it's always been..."

"Fusa-*chan*, I'm not interested in how things have always been done. If your decision hinges on my permission, then I grant it—so long as he's marrying you for you and expects nothing else in return. And don't worry about my situation. In fact, I'll personally set up a dance hall and recall all of our clan for you to make your announcement."

Fusa professed her love and thanks, bowing deeply several times as she made her way to the office doors.

Takana looked forward to something their clan could do together that wouldn't end in bloodshed.

Chapter Twenty-Two

Understanding

Oyabun: The head of a yakuza clan, literally means 'foster parent.' It's not difficult to see how they could be seen as pseudo parents to the organization. Members of the yakuza traditionally cut their family ties and transfer loyalty to the oyabun. Some heads of clans were so famous as to be considered folk heroes.

September 8, 1708
Utsunomiya, Tochigi Prefecture

WHILE THEIR CLAN CELEBRATED FUSA'S engagement in a rented dance hall, Takana guarded the entrance with Tomoe. Protectors worked in short shifts to patrol the grounds, then got their chance to join in the revelry. Regardless, Takana was paranoid that something would ruin the evening. She hastened the meeting with the Kameya clan to request that they gather and provide her with intel on the other clans' whereabouts.

At the meeting, the *oyabun* accepted their ridiculous grab for eight percent. She offered to add the two percent back, using it to leverage a commitment from him that he wouldn't let any other clan know about their alliance. He promised to be in touch before the next clan meeting. He would attain the Bakeneko-*kai*'s proxy to disguise as his own vote, as long as it didn't clash directly with his business. If that happened, he further promised to negotiate with them in good faith.

In her own show of good faith, and to test his word, she extended an invitation for the Kameya clan to send a representative to the engagement party. The *oyabun* sent Manhachi, who brought the happy couple a small bag heavy with coin, and a list of homes in the city that would be vacant in the coming months; quality lots far away from the crowded, fire-prone *yakeya* housing close to the city walls.

Takana had purchased Iwakuchi's old residence in those very *yakeya*. She still slept outdoors, in a different alleyway throughout the city every night, but she visited the house once a week hoping to find him squatting in it. He deserved no less than to die in the squalor he'd bought himself with her and her mother's lives.

Tomoe and Takana reminisced about exercises they used to do while Takana grew up. Now that she had practice and experience, Takana wished to know more about the philosophy behind everything, and Tomoe seemed happy to pass on her knowledge. Tomoe reacted to being around the clan as Takana had when she first started living with everyone at the estate. She'd grown so accustomed to living alone that it was uncomfortable to be around people, even people who liked her. But as the night went on, and guests brought them servings of sake to ease the evening chill on their watch, Tomoe seemed to soften.

Tomoe sniffed the light breeze and smiled.

"Your *kunoichi* approaches."

Takana looked up, forgetting to hide her excitement, but she couldn't see Natsu anywhere. After a few seconds, Natsu emerged from the shadows and came up the path in the half-*kimono* of the clan. Her high, orange ponytail and bright tattoo stunned.

"Easier to smell an uncovered armpit. I'm not impressed, *sensei*," Takana teased.

"I'll send out another guard to take my place," Tomoe chuckled and went into the dance hall.

Takana hugged Natsu tight, always thankful when she returned from Oyama safely.

"You've nearly ruined Fusa's night, my friend," Takana said. "Every time one of us walks into the hall, her hopeful look is crushed when it's not you."

"I'm sorry. I'm having issues with a merchant in Oyama who couldn't meet a deadline he was supposed to hit before I left. I gave him another week but the argument with him delayed my departure."

Takana expected Natsu to hurry inside, but she only stood there. Natsu grasped Takana's hand and simply stared at the front door. Comforting words failed to materialize. Takana couldn't guess how Natsu felt about Fusa reminding her of her older sister, and the apparent attraction she had for Fusa mixed beneath that.

Not wanting to see her friend hurt, and hoping to relieve whatever tension was holding Natsu back from entering the doorway, Takana leaned in and kissed her cheek. Natsu turned her head in surprise, and Takana found herself going back to land on her lips, firm but gentle, reassuring. The air between their faces was warm against the night. The gesture was comfortable, but lingered, and as Takana pulled back she felt something different: a draw to stay.

"I...uh..." Takana managed, unable to explain herself.

The door slid open, jolting the two of them to step back from each other. Sōkichi and Chise came out. Chise walked around the hall to relieve one of the protectors, while Natsu and Sōkichi bowed to each other and passed. Natsu's face glowed red when she straightened, then she departed into the hall. Takana grabbed Sōkichi's hand and stood with him at the top of the stairs. She gave him a kiss before turning around in his arms and leaning into him.

"Don't you want to spend more time in there?" Sōkichi asked. "You've been out here more than anyone else has."

"Let Fusa and Natsu have their moment. I need to be out here—if anything happens to anyone in that hall tonight..."

"You don't trust our people to feel that weight the same as you? We all saw the estate. None of us want to see anything like that happen again. Go on inside. Even though she looks overjoyed to be with Shinkichi-*san*, Fusa never looks as happy as when she's with you and Natsu together."

Takana sighed in agreement, although she only wanted to sway in Sōkichi's arms for the rest of the night. Still, she appreciated him turning her around and ushering her towards the door.

Miraculously, no one attempted to attack the hall all night. The clan exited slowly and wobbly, having gone through dozens of *sake* bottles. Many protectors had their arms around the women, taking their "protection" to a different level as they disappeared into the early morning darkness together. Takana chuckled to herself as Manhachi walked out side-by-side with Tomoe. Finally, Natsu came out between Fusa and Shinkichi, her arms hanging around both of their shoulders, unable to walk straight from the *sake* that she wasn't used to. *Kunoichi* could be trained to tolerate poisons, but apparently not so much booze. She'd become everyone's favorite part of the evening for the short time she was there.

Takana put her fingers to her lips as that thought was true for her as well. At the top of the stairs, watching everyone trickle off, she tried to understand why that was. Sōkichi slipped his arm around her, and they watched their clan depart together.

"Which alleyway are you sleeping in tonight?" he asked.

"Well, I'm still wide awake. Did I tell you we have this dance hall until dawn?"

Sōkichi smiled and swooped her up in his arms, then carried her back into the hall.

Several weeks after the party, the *oyabun* of the Kameya clan sat as an intermediary between Takana, Sōkichi, and Chise, and a rival *yakuza* thug that the Kameya clan had captured after he killed one of the Bakeneko clan's protectors. The thug explained what had transpired in the streets. The protector was off duty and playing games of chance at a local restaurant—one that offered a safe room for *yakuza* of rival clans to play in the same place.

Throughout the course of the thug's story, Takana recognized he had been played by the dealer and wait staff, though they weren't a part of her clan. They marked the thug and the protector as rivals and played them off each other the whole night. Many drinks and lost coin later, in the deserted streets of Utsunomiya, the thug challenged the protector to a duel. The thug claimed to win fair and square.

Sōkichi took umbrage that the thug stole the protector's *daishō* and coin purse from his dead body. The thug made a dismissive comment about spoils going to the victor. Takana lived by that creed not so long ago, too, but she kept her own opinion sealed.

The Kameya *oyabun* said one of his own men was at the game, and his account corroborated the thug's. Takana nodded. She knew what her verdict would be; she was more interested in Sō-kichi and Chise's decisions. She also knew the *oyabun's* game: testing their clan. Would her companions make the correct de-cision—mark themselves as strong leaders, or pursuers of petty personal conflicts?

Sōkichi bowed to the *oyabun*.

"My heart breaks at the loss of my friend, but this young man may go. I only ask that the *daishō* are returned to us. They were issued for his duty and were not a personal possession."

Chise agreed.

"If he'd come at our man without announcing himself or chal-lenging a duel properly, this would be different. As it is, it wasn't murder. Let him go."

Takana nodded and bowed to the *oyabun*, signaling her agree-ment. He returned the gesture and snapped his fingers for a lieu-tenant to let the thug go *after* returning the *daishō* to the front door of the Bakeneko-*kai* headquarters.

"Respect, fairness, and mercy, even for your enemy. That *yakuza* belongs to the clan most angry at your presence. Killing him would have sent a powerful message. What you've decided is even better. He'll spread word of your actions throughout the city. Even if his clan comes at you or me, that man and his closest friends within the clan will remember this."

They bowed and turned to leave. The *oyabun* asked Takana to stay behind for a moment.

"Gozen-*san*, I know your clansmen are equal, but this information I have is personal to you."

Takana excused herself from her partners and returned to sit near the *oyabun*.

"I know Manhachi-*san* suggested Taiga might be hiding with the other clans, but we've been unable to find evidence of this. I believe Taiga has fled the city."

Takana waved off the information.

"He'll turn up. He always does."

"Well, I didn't want you to think we weren't still looking; that you weren't getting your money's worth in our alliance."

Takana bowed in thanks.

"Do you know who runs the restaurant those men were playing at? And who protects it? Can you get me a meeting with the owner and their clan representative?"

The *oyabun* bowed and promised to look into it, as well as serve as intermediary.

A week later, the two sat on one side of the office, while Takana and Fusa sat on the other. They bowed to the two men. Fusa laid out an offer to have a Bakeneko clan dealer run the games every other week. The clan protecting the relatively new restaurant was the youngest clan in the city after the Bakeneko clan. Fusa offered them the use of their personal tattoo artist, Genjirō, free of charge to make up for the lost income.

Tattoo artists were expensive and hard to find outside of Edo. The clan member said he'd speak to his own *oyabun*, but he believed it would be an amenable response. The restaurant owner appreciated the lower percentage of the take that the Bakeneko clan expected, and the promise they could easily fill his rooms with patrons and gamblers alike to increase the overall take.

Fusa left to spread the word to clients of the Inn about a new restaurant she recommended in the city. The other two men left shortly after. With only Takana left in the room, the Kameya *oyabun* relaxed. He was a few years younger than Tetsuo had been. His eyes were nearly as kind. He pulled out a pipe and lit it, then offered her a toke. She shook her head, but he noticed her breathe the smoke in deeply anyway. It was woodier than her favorite smell... She thought?

She couldn't pinpoint the smell of her grandfather's tobacco anymore. A fluttery panic rose as she recognized she hadn't thought about him since the estate burned down. Escalating breaths caught in her throat as she forgot the exact shape of his beard, no matter how hard she concentrated on it. In fact, concentrating made it worse. Whenever she had that feeling, all she needed to do was grasp the *kiseruzutsu*. Thrusting her hand into its empty home in her sleeve amplified the panic.

Takana hyperventilated. The *oyabun* got up and opened a window, then guided her to put her head outside. He rubbed her back as she got her breathing under control. His eyes lingered on her burgeoning baby bump, but when she looked into them, they seemed to understand that her reaction was more than sense-sickness.

"Kochiya-*san* and I built our clans together," Kameya said. "There were minor arguments between us, but we were both stronger for our alliance. We arranged once a year to travel alone and meet at a different mountain *onsen*. We had a rule, to talk about everything but business—except he was fond of talking about *you* these last few years. He told me your family's story when you came under his clan, what—eight...nine years ago now? He regretted not setting better boundaries between you and Taiga.

"When Taiga mocked you by forcing you to get that *bakeneko* tattoo, Kochiya-*san* was furious. When you turned the tables by getting the frog tattoo on the other side, signifying your ability to earn, he never felt prouder of you. Then he *respected* you for your earnest efforts to pay back your father's debt, outearning most in his ranks. And the fact you did it all on your own, without guidance on how to earn your way..."

Takana sniffed. She never had a choice but to honor her father. It was *expected*. She certainly hadn't been doing it out of the kindness of her heart to help the *yakuza* clan that enslaved her and her mother. Still, it was rejuvenating to hear the words from someone other than Taiga, knowing she wasn't being manipulated by the cretinous scumbag. After her attempted suicide, it meant everything to her to know that Tetsuo had truly respected her; that she was seen with honor by *someone*.

"I thought about this all week," Kameya continued, "your damaged tattoo mesmerized me while I watched you handle your business. I thought back to a curious comment Kochiya-*san* made during one of our recent retreats—that you had a penchant for a particularly expensive tobacco. Tetsuo didn't like it that much, but he always remembered it from his dealings with your grandfather and it sounded like it brought him great comfort to keep around. It is a stretch, but I thought, as his protégé, you might share that with him as well.

"I...apologize that I couldn't remember the brand, but he described its smell to me, since he knew I loved smoking more."

Kameya pulled a pouch out of his robe and placed it in Takana's hand. She brought it to her nose and inhaled the aroma. It was so close, but not quite the right smell. Still...

She embraced Kameya as her grandfather's beard returned to her memory. Tetsuo also came back to her. He thought of her as his protégé? If only he'd said something...

Even if she were being manipulated in that moment, she would be eternally grateful to the man for helping her reclaim her lost grandfathers.

Chapter Twenty-Three

Honor

Seppuku: Ritual self-disembowelment whereby the beginning is the same as hara-kiri, but there is most often someone close to decapitate the person for both mercy and ensuring the person does not die alone. There is far more honor in seppuku—that one is willing to die for a cause, in apology, in punishment, in atonement, in losing a master or family, and m any other reasons.

October 12, 1708
Utsunomiya, Tochigi Prefecture

THE MISTRESS AND HER LEDGER man, Itarō, from the Oyama Inn, sat in the Utsunomiya Inn's office with Takana and Natsu, introducing them to a new record keeper they hired from Edo. He'd scoffed at the job Fusa and the women had done keeping the records since opening and complained about the work cut out for him, but Takana detected pleasure behind his voice at getting to untangle the financial knots.

Because individual *yakuza* made up such a large percentage of both Inn's clients, Takana invited Kameya and Manhachi to the office to sit in on the meeting and see for themselves how lucrative the business was. Separate from the ten percent they kicked up to Kameya from the Bakeneko clan's side dealings, Takana offered him five percent of the Utsunomiya Inn's take in exchange for spreading the word to allied *yakuza* clans about the Inn's location and effectiveness—as well as his continued protection and service as intermediary between the clans.

Their final topic of discussion was the selection process for mercenary tables. Takana and Natsu forbade the "anything goes" method for gaining employment in their Inn. Whenever a table opened, the established mercenaries would be required to monitor prospects. It would be on the prospect to take as many jobs as possible at no charge to the clients—which the mercenary would vet, supply, and verify upon completion. The most completed jobs earned the table. Takana and Natsu hoped that the new system would encourage the acceptance and execution of jobs that commoners and peasants would never be able to afford, and mercenaries would otherwise refuse. The only stipulations were the exclusion of nobles and *yakuza* clients, and assassination or theft contracts during prospect weeks.

Petitioners lined the road to the Inn during those times. The Inn's reputation and prestige grew in the region so rapidly that Takana considered buying a new location in order to hire more mercenaries.

The mistress seemed intrigued and giddy to get back to Oyama for her own trial runs, starting with the vacant table formerly occupied by Takana and Natsu. She sent one of the women to hire horses for their ten percent haul, and paid Sōkichi for the use of his protectors on the *Nikkō Kaidō*.

Takana had been seated when everyone came into the office, so when she stood up to follow them out the door at the end of the meeting her bump caught the mistress's eyes for the first time. She fussed over Takana's work ethic stressing the baby, which was entirely unexpected in contrast to the mistress's usual cut-throat demeanor. Takana imagined if she were Fusa, she'd be just as into it, but getting excited about the baby wasn't up her alley.

She wished she could do a better job hiding the bump so people on the streets would also leave her alone. Her anonymous, lonely life kept calling to her, reminding her how much simpler those times were. Sleeping outdoors and bathing in public helped decrease the anxiety from working around so much opulence, but that feeling would never completely go away.

Everyone in the meeting gathered at the bottom of the stairs of the Inn's entrance and were soon joined by Chise, Fusa, and Sōkichi to exchange respect and goodbyes. Tomoe also came out to say a personal goodbye to Manhachi.

Someone approaching them up the road caught Takana's attention. A familiar woman led a horse with a person seated atop, their hands tied behind their back and a sack over their head. Behind the mount stood four young men carrying a large box on two poles.

"Kiko-*san!*" Fusa cried and ran for an excited embrace.

After the estate burned and everyone came in from the road, they were unable to account for one woman, but they couldn't guess who it was because of how badly most of the bodies were burned. Kiko stood before them, the only survivor of the massacre. The last time Takana saw Kiko, she'd shoved Iwakuchi off her and chased him out of the estate.

Fusa and Kiko walked the horse to the gathering, then handed the rope to Takana.

"What is this, Kiko-*chan?*" Takana asked.

"Takana-*san,* I could never earn for the estate the way you wanted us to, and though you allowed us to sell ourselves if we chose, I could tell you didn't want that, either. I... When you went to Nikkō, I went to Ishibashi and sold myself. I wanted to earn and bring back coin and hoped you would never ask where it came from.

"On my return to the estate, there were men with weapons and torches on the road ahead. I hung back and hid in that thicket by the road. Before long, the men ran away. I watched the estate burn behind them. I was frozen. I couldn't help anyone. I felt more useless than before. If I'd had a *tantō* in that moment...I would have..."

Fusa hugged Kiko again as tears trickled out. Natsu joined Fusa in consoling her. Kiko shook, reliving her grief and shame. Takana was no stranger to that despair. After a few moments, Kiko sniffed and straightened her back.

"But when the men fled back to the main road," Kiko continued as she looked up at her prisoner on the horse, "I recognized this one. He and three others carried out that box."

Kiko motioned to the four young men to bring forth the box. They set it down and opened it, revealing all the stolen money from the estate. Takana closed it to avoid gathering citizens from eyeing it. She stepped beside the horse, looking up at the prisoner with the bag over his head.

"Whatever she's saying isn't true!" the man's voice was muffled through the bag, and he squirmed on the horse.

He stopped moving when Takana pulled her *katana* from its scabbard, allowing him to hear every centimeter of steel slide out of its home. She used the tip of the blade to grab the loose part of the sack, then removed it with a flick of the wrist.

Iwakuchi blinked the sunlight away, then lost all color when he looked down at Takana's expressionless face. Sweat dripped and his breathing sped up as Natsu, Fusa, Chise, and Sōkichi joined her on both sides of the horse.

"I followed the money," Kiko said from behind Fusa. "He and the three other men took it to Suzumenomiya. I watched their comings and goings over a couple months. He murdered the others gradually, hiding their bodies in the early morning. When it was clear he was the only one going in and out of the hiding place, I approached him and lied about who I was. He didn't recognize me, even after—it doesn't matter. He was too drunk most of the time.

"I gained his confidence after a couple weeks and got him to drink enough to black out. I tied him up and found these four boys to help haul the coins here. I... I promised them I'd pay them when we arrived..." Kiko trailed off.

Sōkichi pulled coins out of his robes and paid each of them before dismissing them. The mistress, both ledger men, Manhachi, and Kameya listened in rapt attention. Takana wasn't sure she wanted them to know Iwakuchi was her—

"Your father denied he had anything to do with the massacre of my friends on the whole ride here," Kiko said. As she gazed upon him the sadness drained from her face. Malice replaced it.

Takana closed her eyes and breathed. As soon as she saw his face, she tried to find a place in her heart that would allow her to let him run away. Give him one more—final—threat, deadlier than all the previous ones combined. With all eyes on her, knowing what he'd done and who he was to her, that was no longer possible.

Even as she concluded what she must do, a heavy weight formed in her chest. She hoped she could follow through without shedding a tear, but a lump already crawled up her throat. Hoping an infusion of anger would push it back down, she put herself into action.

Takana reached up to Iwakuchi's elbow and yanked him off the horse, only barely allowing him to escape a complete fall. She needed his arms to remain unbroken.

Kiko moved the horse away from everyone. Yet again, the whole city watched Takana, gauging her decisions. In one agile motion she sliced the rope holding Iwakuchi's arms behind him. She walked around to stand before him as he scrambled to sit on his calves. He looked up at her, his eyes growing wide as they passed over her stomach.

"Ta-*chan*, are you—?"

"No, Iwakuchi. I eat too much."

The weight in her chest compressed further when she dropped the honorific from his name. His hopeful, desperate smile disappeared, replaced by the saddest smile she'd ever seen in her life.

"That's good, Ta-*chan*. I'm glad you're finally eating well."

He knew she was lying, and that he deserved to be lied to—he had no right to claim the role of grandfather to a child whose mother he'd sold. Takana reached for anger again. She couldn't let pity for him muddy her actions. If he could accept his own disgraced status, why couldn't she? Takana's resolve solidified: there was only one way for him to reclaim all that he had squandered.

"Your actions led to the deaths of our friends. You killed *kaasan*."

His hand shot up to his mouth.

"No! No, I didn't see her! I hung behind. I only told them where to find the gold. She's...gone?"

"Gone. She died protecting a petrified girl. Even if you didn't kill her yourself, none of that would have happened if you hadn't sold us out. I should have killed you when you first forced yourself into our home."

Iwakuchi bowed with his forehead touching the ground over and over as he apologized, blaming Taiga and the Kochiya clan for manipulating him from the moment he was spotted in the public bath. Taiga had told him Takana's debt was clear and hung a new one over Iwakuchi's head.

"Enough!" Takana cut him off. "It shouldn't matter to you, anyway. Once you sold me and *kaasan*, you gave up the right to consider us family. She was another person for you to use in the end, no different than any of the other dead bodies in the estate you didn't care about."

"Please, Ta-*chan*! You always act like I wanted to be in debt! That the decision to sell you was made lightly! Ask Tomoe-*san*! I tried everything I could think of to get the money before the debt came due!"

"Don't bring other people into this. Tomoe-*sensei* would never have suggested selling your family to the *yakuza*."

Takana wasn't actually sure about that. She glanced up slightly to see Tomoe. Tomoe sensed the question and affirmed Takana's statement with a slight head shake that no one else saw—everyone was too absorbed by the spectacle before them.

"Please forgive me, Ta-*chan*. Let me go. I'll run away and never come near you again."

"If Kiko hadn't brought you before me, you wouldn't have ever returned? You would have hoarded our estate's stolen money? What about when you inevitably lost all that wealth, too, Iwakuchi?"

Takana exhaled, then used the tip of the *katana* beneath his shoulder to lift him from his low bow but kept him on his knees.

"Your crimes against my family are too great. You spit on the efforts *kaasan* and I put into paying off your debt. You've dishonored my friends, my family, your wife, and your former daughter. There's only one way to earn it back."

Takana untied the *wakizashi* sheath from her belt and held it out over his head. He winced as if her next move was going to be to run him through. Instead, she dropped the weapon to the dirt in front of him. She took two steps away, turned her back, and relaxed her stance. The rest was up to him.

The road was silent despite the number of onlookers. A light breeze picked up, swaying the bamboo and trees to fill the city with pleasant sounds that one wouldn't normally be able to hear over the din of city life. Loose strands of hair blew across her face as she waited for his decision.

Takana's ear pricked up as the *wakizashi* was lifted from the dirt. She heard his trembling breath as he grasped the hilt tighter. The blade scraped against the scabbard as they separated. She imagined him staring at the blade, the weapon weighing heavier and heavier with each passing second.

She had one final thought as she heard his effort to extend the blade out—she was his only daughter, his only living family. Perhaps he wouldn't have betrayed the estate if she'd accepted him back as easily as her mother had. And what if Taiga really had manipulated him? It seemed to be the only thing Taiga was actually good at...

Why was it easier to give Taiga and other criminals her mercy than it was to forgive her own father? She never gave him a chance to make it up to her.

In the end, *she* had failed *him*.

She had to put an end to it—and damn all the spectators that judged her decision-making.

"*Chichi-ue!*" she cried out and spun on her heels in time to see the blade thrust into his stomach.

She no longer cared that the city watched as a sob broke through her composure—releasing grief for a father she'd already lost a long, long time ago. He pulled the blade across his abdomen, stoically, only the smallest bursts of pain escaping from his clenched teeth. Veins pressed out on his forehead. She could see them pulsing against his skin.

Iwakuchi pulled the blade out and thrust in again to complete the *hara-kiri* ritual. Takana pulled out her *katana* and stood to his side, raising the blade back behind her head.

She completed *seppuku*, ending his misery and bestowing the honor of not dying solely by his own hand, alone in the world. The *katana* clattered to the ground as his head rolled away from his crumpled body towards squeamish onlookers. Without looking behind at her friends, family, and business partners, she ran.

The ceiling rotated around as Takana stared at it in the dark. She was dizzy in more ways than one. Her lower back hurt from laying on it too long. Two stomachs cried out for food, though she would have given almost anything to have a cigarette instead. Her father's old home smelled awful, even with the window open.

She despaired in the hours after killing Iwakuchi for giving in to spectacle, revenge, anger, and old hatreds. If she'd stopped him one second sooner, she'd still have some connection to her old life. Now both parents were gone, and she'd lost the *kiseruzutsu* at Tomoe's burned-down residence. She had Kameya's thoughtful gift of tobacco, but it wasn't the correct aroma.

She contemplated a trip to Edo to pick up as much as possible while clearing her head, then considered how the walking distance would affect the baby. That tobacco was the only thing she could cling to anymore to remember her family, though. Thinking about the baby made her sob again and she put the left *kimono* sleeve over her eyes.

The baby would never know a loving grandparent as she had. Her grandfather had such an outsized effect on her life that she couldn't imagine how she would ever give her baby that sort of figure to look up to; to learn from; to emulate; to share memories and stories; to link hundreds of years of history. Her child's heritage would be nothing but blood, debt, cheating, whore houses, tobacco, crass riches, and needless death.

A dream Takana'd had years ago came to her. Before things really became bad between her and Taiga, her dream gave her a baby from him. She'd humored the idea, happy only for the fact that the baby would have such a wonderful grandfather in Tetsuo.

She snapped out of her pointless remembrance to realize she didn't know if Sōkichi's parents were alive or not. If they were, perhaps they would be something for their baby that she couldn't offer with her own bloodline. Or maybe Tomoe could fill the grandmother role? Takana's mood lifted as she thought of what a wonderful set of aunts the baby would have in Natsu, Fusa, and Chise. It would be doted on by the whole clan. It might actually end up being the luckiest baby born in Utsunomiya. Takana's broken heart began to mend.

Takana lifted herself up to relieve the strain on her lower back before the door slid open. Her hands went to her hips, but she'd dropped her weapons before she ran. She sighed in relief as her friend slipped off her *geta* and came into the house.

"How did you know I would be here, Fusa-*chan*?"

"It's the first place we met, and the only thing in the city that was your father's. We've been searching for you all day, but this occurred to me as we checked the former pleasure quarter."

"Mm."

"Here, I brought you a rice ball. I knew you wouldn't eat after all that. It's been hard enough getting your ribs to stop showing even after your appetite 'increased' lately."

Takana bowed in appreciation and took the rice ball. Fusa ate one of her own.

"Sorry if you were expecting more. I'm eating for two now as well."

Takana put her hand to Fusa's abdomen, struck speechless.

"I'm not that far along yet. Things started changing last week."

"I'm so happy for you and Shinkichi-*kun*! Have you told anyone yet?"

"No. With yours on the way and everyone giving you extra attention, I didn't want to—"

"*Please* tell everyone. I don't want the extra attention at all. You can have all the attention in the world. Take it from me," Takana half-begged.

"Okay. I'll tell everyone at the next clan meeting, then."

Fusa beamed, and her good mood brought Takana out of her dark thoughts.

"Come on, Fusa-*chan*. Let's get out of this place. There's a new restaurant opening up the road. That rice ball wasn't nearly enough."

Chapter Twenty-Four

Curiosity Piqued

Ane-san: Elder sister in familial terms. Very few women are acknowl-edged in yakuza clans, except for the wives of the bosses, who are referred to as ane-san, regardless of age in relation to the speaker.

November 17, 1708
Utsunomiya, Tochigi Prefecture

TAKANA SAT COMFORTABLY ON A cushion, half-naked, with her *kimono* and *sarashi* loosely held over her chest while Genjirō worked on her back. Natsu laid out perpendicular to Takana's side, propped up on her elbow, resting her head on Takana's belly with a big smile.

"It's kicking my ear, Takana-*san*," Natsu said. "Whatever it is, it's going to be a fearsome warrior."

"Or not. Maybe it's trying to hug its favorite aunt."

"I can work with that just as easily."

Takana smiled, then winced at Genjirō's scraping. He'd finished embellishing her literal burn scars with fiery orange ink and start-ed new artwork from the edge of the flames to the opposite shoul-der. The creature in the image was a clean take on the *bakeneko*, one unmarred by burns, cuts, and perforations.

While he worked and Natsu looked close to falling asleep next to her stomach, Takana gazed across the office to the *katana kake* that mounted the *katana* and *wakizashi* her father had used to regain his honor. Sōkichi had gathered them from the road and commissioned a *kake* to be built that matched the artwork on the scabbards. It was placed in the *tokonoma* alcove on the wall behind the desk. He never cleaned the blood off the blades or hilts, promising a powerful message to any who met in their office.

Chise and Sōkichi had also taken care to treat Iwakuchi's body respectfully so proper funeral rites could be observed. His ashes were placed in a shrine next to Chiyo's in Takana's private room in the Inn, though she rarely went in there except to be alone with Sōkichi, and, once, in a charged moment with Natsu when they argued over how to handle an unusual contract request.

Once they'd each extinguished their arsenal of arguments, the silence that fell between them sparked. Having closed the distance while they were shouting, Takana found herself breathless and only a foot apart from Natsu's flushed face. A rush through her chest compelled Takana to transfer one passion into another, when Chise opened the door to check on all the shouting.

Natsu and Takana stared at Chise, then each other, then laughed it all off. Since then, Natsu looked for any excuse to be around Takana, alone or not. She found little ways to come into contact—letting their knees touch beneath the desk when listening to proposals in the office; the backs of their fingers brushing together in passing; prolonged touches of Takana's abdomen, using the baby as a pretense—Takana not only tolerated it, but grew hopeful that Natsu would keep it up; maybe even turn it into something more.

The closest they came to explicit contact that could no longer be excused as friendship was in the public bath, during the *yakuza* hour late at night. They almost never went in alone—Chise or Fusa or any number of the other women had to use the bath at the same hour now that they all wore tattoos openly. That night, though, nearly everyone in the clan worked out on the road.

It was Natsu's custom to avoid eye contact with other women in the bath, often turning her body and eyes from the groups. Takana noticed her staring at the bathhouse's corners, but when that odd behavior got any of the women talking, Natsu adopted closing her eyes to feign relaxation. With no one else in the bath, Natsu sat next to Takana for the first time, using the baby bump as an excuse to get that close.

Takana enjoyed the smooth feel of Natsu's thigh against her own. Their bodies grew pink during the close, naked contact. They sweat far more than the bath would cause on its own, anticipation building. When their eyes met, Takana's face burned, and her breath quickened. It warmed her further that Natsu reacted the same way.

When they'd kissed before, they'd done it without hesitation, leaving no doubt that it was meant to be anything but friendly. In the bath, Takana moved slower towards Natsu, hoping for something beyond; to explore that spark she felt at Fusa's wedding party. Their lips brushed before a trio of women made a commotion outside of the entrance curtains. They parted and turned their backs to each other as the wives of some of the other *yakuza* clans came in. The women paused, regarded Takana and Natsu, then went about their business.

Natsu leaned into Takana's back, and Takana returned the balance, relishing the close skin-to-skin contact, making the best of what they missed out on the moment before. Their hands, hidden from view beneath the water, found each other. As the women laughed and got in on the other side of the bath, Natsu's hand left Takana's and purchased the side of her thigh.

The hot bath steamed out of her ears, so Takana announced she'd get out first. The *yakuza* wives saw Takana's belly and fussed over her, eagerly sharing stories—some good, most bad—of having children within *yakuza* families. As Takana reluctantly gabbed with them near the exit, Natsu left the bath. She put her hand on Takana's burn scar, caressing along her back as she passed, too quick for the wives to notice. They asked Takana why she shivered, and she used it to complain about standing in the cold air naked and excused herself.

Takana couldn't find Natsu the rest of that night. She lay awake next to Sōkichi's sleeping form, imagining what would have happened if they hadn't been interrupted, or if she'd come upon Natsu afterwards, assuredly alone.

While Genjirō neared the end of the tattoo session, Takana ran her fingers through Natsu's burnt orange hair as she slept.

She'd thought about what happened in the bathhouse many nights since. Takana wasn't sure if she could ever vocalize her feelings. She loved Sōkichi, and had been with many men on the road during her Kochiya years—mostly as a way to infuriate Taiga even if he never knew—but she'd never been attracted to a woman before. She couldn't say she was now either, even with her feelings towards Natsu pushing towards the surface. She felt nothing seeing Chise, Fusa, her employees, the *yakuza* wives, or any other women in the public bathhouses. She loved Fusa and Chise, almost naturally as if they were real sisters. But it was different with Natsu.

It was *Natsu*—not simply an attraction to a woman. That was the best explanation Takana could think of if she were ever confronted about it.

Takana spent hours thinking about what that confrontation would be like, and whether or not she should take the mystery out of it and admit her feelings to Sōkichi, if only to lift the weight on her conscience. He seemed so understanding since they'd first met outside his *dōjō* many years before; she allowed herself to hope he would understand her new attraction. But whenever she thought she had summoned the courage to tell him, words failed her, and she changed the subject.

Genjirō finished, then whispered over Natsu's sleeping form. He updated Takana on any information he learned from his free work on the other *yakuza* clan, who had proven to be quite chatty around him. She thanked him and he departed with his tools.

Takana remained motionless, staring down at Natsu's face, letting her doze as long as she wanted. Her touch, as inconsequential as the side of her head resting on Takana's belly, getting pummeled by her baby, served to soothe the pain on her back and helped tune out the world.

In Kameya's office before an essential regional meeting, Takana sat across from him as he smoked some of the tobacco he'd given her from his own *kiseru*. She enjoyed the smoke as it filled the room but declined his offers to smoke along with him—the intensity of it would surely make her nauseous. The quiet atmosphere calmed her, preparing her for the meeting ahead.

Shortly before it was time to leave for the offsite dance hall, Kameya went to a closet and pulled out an impressive set of *daishō*. He laid them on the desk and sat back down, then motioned for her to try them out. The artwork was understated, and the blades were far more than ornamental in sharpness and strength.

"Impressive," Takana said as she sheathed them and put them back on the table.

"They're a gift, Taka-*chan*."

Unease crept up on her. Kameya had never referred to her that way before, and the only people in her life who had were Tetsuo and the blacksmith.

"*Oyassan*, I can't accept a gift from you. The tobacco was enough."

"I realize you will never again wield those blades used in your father's ritual, and I haven't seen you with a set since. You need protection when you walk these streets. Not all the clans are happy about your presence, as you will learn tonight. I insist you take them."

"I don't know what to say. You've given me a great gift already. I can afford to buy new *daishō* anytime I want. I just need distance—from blades... For a while."

"I can understand that, but I insist again that you take them. Any more refusals and I will take it as an insult." Kameya was stern, but with a slight smile.

Takana tied them to her belt, keeping an eye on the way Kameya looked at her. It was different than usual.

"Is there any way I can talk you into postponing your participation in the meeting? Until you're...less vulnerable?"

"I appreciate your concern, *oyassan*, but I won't be alone. And I have your protection, right?

"Right?"

She didn't appreciate his reluctance.

"You must realize, I have alliances with clans that consider you their enemy. It's a delicate balance to work with your proxy alongside my interests, let alone keeping my alliances intact."

"I don't plan to speak unless spoken to, except for my one request."

"I can pass that request on for you."

"You're looking at me like so many others lately—like I don't know I'm pregnant."

"If you persist," he sighed, "you can't say I didn't speak up. If something happens to you..."

Takana stood up, getting annoyed at his riddles.

"If you know something, say it."

"I don't, Taka-*chan*. But you know how *yakuza* are—you're the exception, not the rule. They resent you. There's never been a woman at the head of a clan. They want what you've earned for yourself, and they want far more than the small bites you've given me."

Takana wasn't sure what lurked behind his sudden lecturing, and *really* didn't appreciate his use of the word "small." He could have made the speech at any point since they first met. If what he hinted at was true, she was in as much danger out in the streets as she would be at the meeting.

She departed the Kameya headquarters and met Tomoe and Sōkichi outside the dance hall where the meeting would take place. The heads of the clans arrived in circles of their best men. They entered the halls alone, leaving the men outside to wait. Many set up games or challenged each other to duels using wooden swords.

Nearly all of them sneered at the Bakeneko clan, and they all had something to say indirectly, loud or in whispers, about a female head of a clan, and a pregnant one at that. Most of them were creatively filthy and violent in their declarations of how they'd like to treat her when she was alone.

When Kameya arrived, he motioned for Takana to follow him inside. Manhachi came over and told them there was only one seat, so Sōkichi would need to wait outside with the rest. At the entrance, two neutral guards appointed by Edo bosses that weren't part of the regional clans directed them to surrender their *daishō*. Takana handed her new set to Tomoe and went inside.

When they sat at their designated seats at the long table, it was clear she was the youngest in the room. Everyone wore expensive robes while Takana wore her regular half-*kimono*. At least she had it thoroughly washed the day before and allowed Fusa to style her hair more formally, instead of the ponytail she favored whenever she wasn't wearing her *kasa*.

Nearly all the men on the opposite side of the table took long looks at the exposed half of her torso, but because of the position of her mangled tattoo in proximity to her right breast, she couldn't always tell which they were more focused on. Either way, she was pleased they were so clearly distracted, like she preferred the men at her dice games. Distracted men were easier to manipulate, or fight, if it came to it.

The meeting began in a cloud of mixed tobacco smoke and clinks of *sake* bottles. Many men seemed reluctant to bring up business around her. She waited patiently while several of them stuttered through what they wanted to say. Some of the younger ones spoke louder, contemptuously, almost violently, though without directing anything specifically at her.

Takana swayed to a sense of appreciate for Kameya's warning beforehand—if she had been expecting him to put himself on the line with the others, she would have been disappointed and hurt. It was a great advantage to know she was there alone. Luckily for her, she only wanted to discuss one topic. She was content with her business dealings continuing to go through Kameya behind the scenes.

Once they'd all argued and negotiated for their pet causes, Kameya held his hand out to her. She straightened once every eye settled on her.

"Gentlemen, when I eliminated the remnants of the Kochiya clan, I announced in the city square a reward for finding Taiga Kochiya. There were onlookers of every class there, including many of your brethren. I find it extremely hard to believe there wasn't a greedy soul among all those people that didn't want to give him up for such a sizeable amount of gold."

"What are you insinuating?" one of the calmer men asked.

"One of you is hiding him, and you've got the lid on your organization closed tight. I wonder what the reward price will need to be to get any of your poor, low ranked thugs to hand me Taiga?"

Several heads didn't appreciate her aspersions and attempted to shout her down, but she wasn't interested in any of them. Those who were tight-lipped and avoided eye contact would be the culprits... Unfortunately, there were almost as many of them as there were loud protestors.

"Many of your men are my clients. I'll spread the word to every clan in Eastern Nihon of a new reward—one that *can't* be ignored. Even your lieutenants won't be able to resist my offer."

"Name whatever price you want, *kuso ama*," one of them cursed. "Why would we care?"

"Because your low ranks will begin attacking any other clans they believe to be harboring Taiga for a shot at that reward. It will start a war. Eliminate large parts of your ranks. Decrease your earning ability. Frankly, I don't give a damn what happens to anyone in here but for a few unnamed individuals..." She let her words trail off to inspire discord.

Men pointed at others, accusing them of being in league with her, or worse, sleeping with her. When Takana stood up, the room quieted down.

"I don't want that path. I want *Taiga*. He's worthless to you. Don't fall for whatever lies he's told you. That's how Tetsuo—his own father—found his throat slit. Just imagine what Taiga is willing to do to anyone else, if they come between him and what he wants. Whoever is harboring him doesn't have to admit it to this room. You all know where I operate. Bring him to me and I will reward you with long-term business. I'll even pay you the reward I offered at the fire in the square as a show of good faith. I know how greedy you all are—you won't even have to involve your men if you want to keep it quiet. I'll keep your secret if you wish.

"This is the best deal you're going to get for someone that's not worth protecting. That's all I have to say. Once I have Taiga, I'm open for business to all of you. Until then, all deals I have with some of you will be put on hold."

In the cacophony that followed, Takana sat down and waited for Kameya to meet her eyes. She bowed her head slightly to indicate his business with her was safe. Once the meeting ended, most of the younger men left quickly. What surprised her were the number of heads who had their business curiosity piqued. They seemed like they were able to look past her gender, realizing greed paid better than hate.

She acted respectfully but told them she meant what she said. Taiga first, business second. However, she looked forward to dealing with all of them once her interest was seen to and she could devote herself to making them all richer than ever.

Takana's feet ached the longer she stood with the mumbling old men. When they finally seemed to be satisfied, she bowed as deeply as her back would allow, then sat back down to rest as they left. Soon she was the only person in the hall. She wondered idly why Tomoe and Sōkichi hadn't checked on her yet, but maybe the guards were still holding people outside until the very last person exited the meeting. She wasn't entirely sure of the protocols yet.

At that thought, a commotion echoed down the hallway. Two thumps hit the floor outside, followed by footfalls running to the dance hall. A man she'd never seen before entered the room with blood splashed on his robes, his *katana* red and dripping in his hand.

Takana stood up as he ran towards her, shouting to intimidate her. He made himself an easy target if she had her *daishō* on her, but those were outside with Tomoe. He lunged as if to impale her swollen belly. She sidestepped, and in the same motion, she shot her hand to her hair and pulled out the *kanzashi* holding her formal hairstyle up. She stabbed it into his sword hand, causing him to yelp and drop the *katana*. Her left hand already lowered between the two of them and she caught the hilt mid-drop. She let go of the *kanzashi* and put both hands on the hilt, since her lost pinky provided no leverage, then made an upward swing that sliced through his torso. She brought the blade down across his back as he fell face-first onto the table.

Another man ran into the room and paused at the sight of the first man's failure, his blood sprayed all over Takana's face and torso. The man held his *katana* up shakily as Takana's eyes met his and narrowed into slits. She let him see what she thought about someone attacking her baby.

She motioned for him to fight. He gathered his courage and ran at her with the blade held high. Holding the *katana* in both hands still, Takana brought it up and over her head, then threw it in a straight line through the charging man's chest from meters away. His momentum carried his body into hers, collapsing on top of her. The hilt of the *katana* she'd thrown pressed over the top of her belly. Pain exploded from her, his weight on her making it all the more impossible to breathe. Afraid of bringing harm to her baby, she gathered a burst of adrenaline and flung the dead man off of her.

She looked down at where all the pain was coming from and gasped at the blood. There was no way to tell if the blood was hers, the attackers', or whoever's blood they'd come in already covered with. Tomoe and Sōkichi ran into the room with their weapons drawn and bloody.

Whether in relief or shock, her head fell back to the *tatami* hard, and she blacked out.

Chapter Twenty-Five

Cold Blood

Haiku: Short form poetry, most famous for its syllabic pattern of three lines of five, seven, and five syllables. There are many different styles of traditions that have evolved within Japanese and other languages. Most often they will use nature as their subject. Haiku first emerged in the 17 [th] century but did not become known by that word until the 19th century. Liberty is taken within this book to use the term haiku even though that word would not have specifically been used in the 18th century. Hokku may be a suitable term, but that was as part of an opening stanza to a much larger genre of poetry which only over time became its own form of poetry referred to as haiku.

December 1, 1708
Utsunomiya, Tochigi Prefecture

ONLY FUSA WAS ALLOWED TO fuss over Takana's injury whenever the heads of the Bakeneko clan convened in the mornings. It took considerable arguing from everyone—even slightly forceful handling on Sōkichi's part—to keep Takana contained in the headquarters. They bid her stay in her private room or the office, while she convalesced from her broken rib, and wouldn't allow her to sleep outside or walk to the public bath.

She hardly slept and went as long between bathing in the opulent bathhouse as she could get away with before Natsu or Fusa commented on her smell. After a couple weeks and a few natural remedies, she slept better and her attitude on bathing more often took hold when Natsu stopped trying to make physical contact as often.

Since Takana spent most waking hours sitting, Genjirō was able to finish her back tattoo. While she stared down at the angry purple bruising above her belly, she thought about expanding the tattoos. With weeks to be still, she commissioned Genjirō to work on a full-length sleeve down her left arm.

During the day in the office, Takana and any combination of her companions listened to client disputes with mercenaries, mercenaries' complaints against other mercenaries, and commoners begging for help outside of prospect weeks.

The latter was easy. Sōkichi and Fusa's hearts were too kind to hear their pleas and do nothing, so they would offer their services for free. Natsu handled disputes and complaints, almost always making the same decisions Takana would. Chise spent most of her time stationed throughout the headquarters, standing guard with whichever protectors weren't out on the road.

Two weeks after the meeting in which Takana broke her rib, Taiga had been handed over by one of the men she placed in the top five of most-likely-to-harbor-Taiga after measuring all the present heads. Kameya presided over the swap as Takana gave the man double the reward she had offered for bringing him in alive, and immediately opened talks to mutually beneficial business.

Takana paid the city *samurai* to keep Taiga in their jail until such time as it didn't hurt her to sleep anymore. Once she had him, and Kameya spread the news to the other clans, nearly all of them—even some of the men who'd been openly contemptuous of her at the meeting—wanted to meet with her over the course of her many rib-healing weeks.

She could tell easily enough when the offers of alliances were genuine, and which were opportunistic and would be fraught with tension—likely to break at the slightest provocation. Kameya's comments on clans' temperaments and history supplemented the latter assessment.

Kameya continued to prove himself well worth the ten and five percent she paid him from her two businesses. She looked forward to his visits, especially when it wasn't as intermediary. He often joked that he only wanted to keep an eye on Manhachi and Tomoe, even though he spent all his time entertaining Takana's company. Soon Kameya opened up, telling her about his family and the world outside of the *yakuza*. He wanted to arrange for a private winter retreat for the two of them so she could enjoy a mountain *onsen* before the baby would be born, and he could reminisce on his annual visits with Tetsuo that Taiga had taken from him.

What increasingly frustrated Takana with each passing week was the lack of identities of the men that had killed the guards outside the meeting and tried to assassinate her. There had been even more men trailing those two that Tomoe and Sōkichi had dealt with before finding Takana in a pool of blood.

One night the week following the attack, Sōkichi opened up to her how the sight of her on the floor with so much blood covering her belly had nearly broken him. It frustrated him just as much that none of the clans copped to sending the assassins. It didn't help that each man was an independent mercenary—they wore no tattoos or carried anything identifiable among clans like insignias on *daishō* scabbards.

Another night, their sensitive pillow talk became tense when Sōkichi scolded her for attending that meeting in the first place.

"It's been weeks since that happened. Why are you getting angry about it now?"

"As your belly grows, I think about it more."

Though it pained her to sit up from the *futon*, she pushed through it so she could look into his eyes.

"You and Chise are the only people that don't fuss and coo over me. Your understanding of my boundaries has always been what I love most about you. Is this what I have to look forward to the heavier I get? Fuss over the baby all you want when it comes out. *I* don't need or want that kind of attention from you."

"You put our baby in danger, Takana. If that *katana* hilt had struck you a few centimeters in the other direction..."

"But it didn't. Do you think I took that hit passively? I'm aware of my surroundings. I'm protecting it with all my ability."

"I don't want you putting yourself in harm's way, period. That's my only point. Stop meeting with the dangerous *yakuza*. Let me, Chise, or Natsu do that for you. Assassins are still out there."

"If they get through this Inn, with all our guards and all of you in their way, maybe they'd deserve that victory. I've stayed inside like you asked, now stop talking about it and go back to your usual emotionless self so I can sleep."

If her rib didn't hurt, she would have fallen back hard on the *futon* and turned her back to him. Neither of those positions were comfortable. In fact, nothing was comfortable in their room. She didn't like sleeping in the same space as her mother and father's shrines. Or on a *futon*. Or under a roof.

Takana stood up and dressed, wincing as she tied her *sarashi* around her chest, and a harness beneath her belly for more comfortable movement—a gift fashioned by a frustrated Fusa when she couldn't convince Takana to stop moving around so much. Takana didn't feel like putting on the *kimono* and only slipped on her half-*hakama*.

"You can't be serious..." Sōkichi said.

"I'm going to the toilet. I'm sorry for what I said. I know you're not emotionless."

Before waiting for his response, she slid the door shut behind her and left the headquarters after grabbing Kameya's gifted *daishō*. She put a hand on one of the protector's arms as she passed and smiled at him in the brazier's light. He asked if she needed an escort, to which she clicked her tongue. He nodded and stood back at attention.

The end of fall had brought colder nights, but her skin loved it. She hated being boxed inside a room at night. The only season she excused it was the dead of winter. All she needed was a little hay, a light wrap, or even her *kasa* if there was nothing else at hand. Without any of those, she'd sleep next to a brazier in areas of the city that weren't patrolled by *samurai*.

But sleep wasn't what she sought; it would be nearly impossible after arguing with Sōkichi anyway. All she'd do is lay there and think about it for the rest of the night.

If anyone had asked her for a reason why her *geta* took her to the jail site, she wouldn't have been able to come up with one. The guards knew she had paid for Taiga's imprisonment and let her pass through the gate. He sat in a corner of his cage. Sleep had also been eluding him.

The door of the cage was the only solid part. She leaned her back into it and sat down, relieving her tired feet and back. From that angle, Taiga could only see her legs. She expected him to say something or move, but he did neither.

"I don't know why I'm here, *ani-ki*," Takana whispered.

After a few silent moments Taiga spoke up.

"Here to gloat. To tell me I deserve this for doing the same thing to you in Oyama. To show me how you continue to live better the farther you get from your father's debt, and I've moved in the opposite direction."

"Do you regret any of your choices? Or only that you're here, at my mercy again?"

Taiga sighed and moved so his back was to the left of the door. His warmth radiated against the back of her right arm.

"Do you regret not becoming my wife, *ane-san*?"

Takana knocked the back of her head against the door and stared at the North Star.

"I know it seems like there should only be one answer to that question, but...I once dreamt of having your child..."

Taiga shifted in the hay.

"Not for *you*, *tonchiki*. For Tetsuo. He deserved better than you."

"What do you know? You weren't his real family. He always treated you differently."

"It was easy to earn his respect. The fact that you never did only speaks to your pitiful efforts, not a soft spot he may have had for me."

"You were a tool to him. When you began working for us, he boasted about breaking you in; making you his concubine."

"Your attempts to hurt me are working as well as your attempts to kill me. You're a sad, pathetic child."

"What I am won't matter when I'm standing over your corpse."

Takana turned around on her knees, grabbed his hair, then banged his head back against the bars.

"You killed my mother. You killed my father by using him against me. You killed Tetsuo because he protected me, because you were jealous. You killed the memory of my grandfather when your assassins broke and lost my *kiseru*. I have every reason in the world to kill you. Do you want to know why I'm *allowing* you to live?"

He struggled to get away from her grasp, but she pulled again, banging his head a second time, harder, her nails raking into his scalp.

"Every day you live is another day of losing face for failing to kill me. You're a pariah. You have no one left to hide behind, no one left that's willing to protect you. I want you to live with your cowardice—a better torture you could never dream up."

Taiga slipped out of her reach. He chuckled while he rubbed the back of his head. In the faint brazier light, he observed the loose hairs tangled in his fingers.

"You aren't as respected as you think you are," he said. "I don't have to be outside this cage to hurt you."

"What are you talking about?"

Taiga threw a handful of hay in her direction and laid down away from the door. One of the *samurai* guards came around the cage and asked her about the banging sounds.

"It was nothing, sir. Give this one to the end of winter. I'll bring the payment tomorrow morning."

Takana woke up in an alleyway somewhere between the jail and the Inn covered in a dusting of snow. Her skin glowed reddish pink and her teeth chattered as she stretched and yawned. When she emerged onto the road, Fusa and Chise were on their way back to the Inn. She shouldn't have been surprised to run into them. Takana had been too sleepy to remember they were going to see off a dealer and protector that morning. Dice games expanded north at a good pace.

"Are you crazy, Takana-*san*?" Fusa yelled, then pushed Takana to move faster through the cold towards the warm embrace of the Inn's bathhouse.

"What were you doing sleeping outside?" Fusa once they relaxed in the water.

"I couldn't sleep inside."

"Your eyes are starting to turn purple. I know it's hard to get comfortable enough to sleep with your rib, even with the medicine, but we need to come up with *something*."

"Worry about your own health, Fusa-*chan*. Stop pestering me."

Chise's meditation broke and Fusa recoiled at the sudden attitude. Takana sighed and looked up at the ceiling.

"I'm sorry. Irritation is building up in me lately... I hate staying here all day, every day. I haven't been able to exercise, to practice, to play dice. I want to smoke an entire pouch of my tobacco. Even if I try pushing past the rib pain, there's always some other discomfort; my feet hurt all the time. In this state I can't relieve stress with Sōkichi or Na— ah–avigate all our new clients properly. I've been on the move for nine years. This whole situation is horrible."

"I wonder if I'm going to complain so much when I'm as pregnant as you," Fusa mused.

Takana smiled trying to imagine Fusa complaining about anything. It didn't fit.

After the bath, Takana took up her position behind the desk again. She waited for people to visit, wearing her *kasa* and a new *haori* to keep her warm. Even with the temperature drop she never tired of looking out at the trees and mountains and didn't want to close the balcony doors. She worked on calligraphy and *haiku* for hours before Chise came into the office with a shabby peasant.

"She says she overhead something you'll want to know. Could be very lucrative," Chise passed on the information.

Takana nodded. Chise said she'd heard a couple *yakuza* raising their voices when she walked past the mercenary room and wanted to check on them—she'd be back in a minute.

The potential client introduced herself as Kunō.

"What can I do for you, *nēsan*?" Takana asked while motioning Kunō to sit in front of the desk. "What did you hear?"

She wore dirty, stained clothing and smelled like she'd gone a week with no bath; a smell Takana knew well. Kunō stared at her lap, hardly looking up beneath her shawl.

"I heard of a cat who escaped its master this year. Depressed, near despondent, the master decided to stop waiting for the cat to come back and offered a reward so high everyone in the city wanted to find the poor thing."

"I see. This sounds like something any one of my mercenaries could have handled. Why bring it to me?"

Kunō continued as if Takana hadn't asked the question, her voice taking on a sinister quality that made Takana's skin tingle.

"I heard this cat ran to a new master, one far richer than the old one. He lavished the cat with gifts and gave it the whole region to roam and be content."

Unease crept up Takana's spine and she shivered involuntarily. A curl of a smile appeared from the side of Kunō's mouth.

"The new master may have been richer than the old one, but the old one still had a reward worth giving anything up. He wouldn't settle for a new pet. He wanted the old one, pretty, agile and...heavy as it may be getting."

"Did the new master give the cat up to the old one?" Takana whispered through growing dread.

"Not yet. The old master would like to keep that reward if he can—something to rebuild with. He knows where the cat is—why pay for something he can get himself?"

"And you?" Takana asked. "Did the old master pay you to fetch the cat for him?"

"He paid for that and more. He told me he was so betrayed by the cat, he didn't want it returned alive. All he wants is two heads to display, a warning to all future pets who believe they can escape from their rightful owners."

"Two?"

Takana wasn't going to be able to reach the *katana* on its stand behind her. She took a deep breath, bracing for how much it was going to hurt to defend herself. Kunō pulled a long pipe out of her sleeve, brought one end of it to her lips, then blew. Takana lowered the *kasa* to protect her face and chest, and the billowy *haori* sleeve to protect the rest. The dart got caught in the bamboo layer of her *kasa*.

Her free hand shot up beneath the rim of the *kasa* and pulled down a *kunai*. She looked up enough to see through the slit between her *haori* and *kasa*. Kunō reloaded the pipe with another dart. Takana threw the *kunai*, not prepared as well as she thought she'd be for the pain in her rib. The *kunai* glanced off Kunō's shoulder, only tearing fabric. She blew another dart that stuck into the dangling fabric of Takana's sleeve.

While Kunō reached for another dart, Takana pushed herself up from the *zabuton*, hands on knees, and thumped across the desk. She pulled another *kunai* and fell on top of the woman with her shins pinning the legs down and holding the blade against her neck. Takana took care to keep from laying directly on her belly.

"What did he pay you for this?"

When the woman didn't answer immediately, Takana pushed the blade harder against her skin, trickling out blood.

"Takana-*san*!" a blessedly familiar voice yelled from the balcony.

She and Kunō looked over to see Natsu coming inside, drawing her *tantō*. Kunō gained leverage in the distraction and brought her knee up to smash Takana's stomach. Takana lost all sense of vengeful pride and rolled off to the side to protect her baby before Kunō could connect directly. The hit didn't hurt so much as cause her mind to think of the worst possible outcome. She winced and cradled her belly, ignoring the rib pain. Kunō deftly got back on her feet to face off with Natsu, the fat cat no longer the threat in the room.

Takana peered up from her belly to see the women clash. Their movements were equally graceful, as if they'd trained together.

Chapter Twenty-Six

Holding Back

Enmaku-dan: Smoke bombs used by shinobi, one of their most-employed tools as a diversionary tactic or as a means of a quick escape. Often made from an eggshell filled with gunpowder and other ingredients that could increase flash, the plume of smoke, and potentially irritate eyes. Heavily contributed to the notion that shinobi were supernatural beings.

December 15, 1708
Utsunomiya, Tochigi Prefecture

NATSU TRIED CORNERING THE ASSASSIN, but she was too quick and aware of Natsu's intentions. Kunō made a run for the balcony, but Natsu tackled her to the ground. Kunō's reflexes amazed as she grabbed Natsu's hands in hers, keeping the *tantō* from slashing across her neck. She spun beneath Natsu's body and brought her legs around Natsu's arm.

Natsu threw her weight to the side to avoid getting her arm locked between the legs. Kunō straightened her legs out, bending Natsu's arm in an unnatural position. The *tantō* clattered to the *tatami* as Natsu let go, trying to keep her arm from snapping in half.

Takana picked herself up through the excruciating pain. She pulled the dart out of the *haori* sleeve and walked gingerly in the two *kunoichi's* direction as they wrestled on the ground like snakes.

Kunō gained the upper hand, raining fists on Natsu's head while her legs held one of Natsu's arms to her torso.

Kunō rolled her back to Takana. Takana grabbed Kunō by the hair and put the dart in front of her face.

"Let her go. I know this is poisoned."

Kunō immediately let go. Natsu rolled away and got back to her feet in one lithe motion.

"Are you okay, Na—?" Takana started before Kunō shot her hand up to grab Takana's wrist.

She was much stronger, easily pushing the dart back towards Takana's neck. Takana whimpered at the quick reversal. Natsu growled to get Kunō's attention, and her eyes turned to deadly slits.

Natsu lunged to stab at Kunō with the *tantō* but got kicked back. Takana stopped fighting against the dart and dropped it out of her hand. In the same breath, Kunō let go of Takana's wrist and punched her in the face, sending an explosion of *hanabi* off behind her eyelids. Takana staggered and fell into the *katana kake*, sending fresh pain into her back as she landed on top of the wood.

Struggling recommenced between the other two while Takana had an awkward time getting untangled. Her pained belly was nothing but in the way, and her rib sent strong signals that it would shut her down if she didn't stop exacerbating the injury. Her nose was broken again. But it looked like Kunō was getting the upper hand on Natsu, even though Natsu was the one holding the blade.

Takana's *kasa* had fallen off her head when she crashed into the *kake*. She reached for it and pulled another *kunai* out. Natsu grappled so Kunō's back faced Takana. The next throw wouldn't miss. As she threw it, Kunō twirled Natsu around. The *kunai* hit Natsu's back.

She cried out but the *kunai* fell to the ground. It stopped at the back shoulder bone, much to Takana's relief. Kunō took advantage of Natsu's surprise, slinking behind her and wrapping her arms around her neck. She squeezed and Natsu's breathing grew desperate.

The first dart stuck out of the top of the *kasa*. Takana yanked it out and concentrated on how much she wanted to kiss Natsu at least one more time. She threw the dart into the exposed calf beneath Kunō's tattered rags.

It took Kunō a second to realize what happened. She looked back at her calf and screamed before letting Natsu fall to the *tatami*, gasping for air. Normally Takana would have grabbed the *katana* from the ground and ended the nonsense in a matter of seconds, but she was exhausted and hurt all over. As she only tried to take a step forward her body betrayed her; she had nothing left.

Takana kneeled down. Natsu coughed on her hands and knees. Kunō picked up the *tantō* that Natsu had dropped and took a step towards Natsu's back when the office doors burst open. Chise didn't take more than a quick glance to see where to aim her *naginata* as she charged towards Kunō.

Kunō reached into her sleeve and pulled out a ball. She threw it into Natsu's side and thick, white smoke engulfed her. From Takana's viewpoint she could see Kunō escape out onto the balcony and over the rail while Chise charged and tripped over Natsu, falling face first on the other side of the smoke.

Takana laid down on her back and closed her eyes, trying to put out all the little fires throughout her body with sheer willpower. It didn't help all that much. Chise pulled Natsu out of the smoke and laid her down next to Takana, then excused herself while she went to sound the alarm among the protectors and find Kunō.

When Natsu's coughing stopped, she rolled over to prop herself on her elbow, then put her hand on Takana's stomach.

"How's the baby?"

"I don't know. Let's send Fusa to fetch the doctor."

Natsu looked into Takana's eyes and smiled.

"I can't believe you threw a knife into my back."

Takana remembered the wish she'd put into the dart before she'd thrown it. Natsu's smile sent Takana's heart pounding just as hard as it had been in the heat of battle. She grabbed the fabric around Natsu's collar and pulled her closer.

"Let me apologize, my pretty *kunoichi*."

Takana understood Sōkichi's anger, but no matter how much Takana tried to convince him she had gone out of her way to sit still, bored in the office, he wouldn't stop shouting at her recklessness. She shouldn't have let Chise out of her sight; she should have told Kunō to come back later when Natsu or Sōkichi could supervise the meeting; she should have shut herself in her room unless she had an escort. He went on and on with all the things she was doing to put herself and their baby in danger.

His anger boiled over when she explained that it was Taiga who'd set up the assassination attempt. In contrast, Takana wasn't as angry as she knew she should be. Internally, she loved foiling Taiga again. That little bit of happiness, and how she felt after kissing Natsu for the first time in earnest desire, nearly took all the pain away. Plus, part of her was beginning to like Sōkichi's overt protectiveness—a nice change of pace from his sometimes-annoying stoicism. It had a multiplicative effect to go along with Natsu's kiss.

That evening Sōkichi wanted to take their argument straight to Taiga, which he exclaimed with his hand firmly grasping his *katana*. Takana told him if anyone was going to end Taiga, it would be her. She put on the *daishō* that Kameya had gifted her, and they walked down to the jail together, hand in hand. On the way, as she held the hilt of her *katana*, she thought about the *kunoichi's* words... And then it struck her further—how did Taiga get enough money to pay for a *kunoichi* mercenary? She'd thought he was all bluster in the cage about hurting her. Did he send the *kunoichi* after that or was the plan already in motion? Did he really put out a city-wide bounty on her? She couldn't wait to squeeze the answers out of him, if she or Sōkichi didn't simply end him immediately.

Takana's stomach sank at the sight of two dead *samurai* guards outside the entrance of the jail. Sōkichi's grip on her hand tightened. She stopped and pulled him back.

"Wait. Maybe going in there isn't a good idea."

"I'm glad you're finally listening to me. I'll stay here to make sure he doesn't escape. Go find Chise and Natsu and send them here. Don't come back with them. Stay in the Inn with Fusa and Shinkichi. Go!"

Takana nodded and kissed him.

"Don't you go in there by yourself, either. Wait for Chise and Natsu!" she called over her shoulder as she went as fast as she could manage, hand beneath her belly to prevent the skin from tearing and supporting the harness holding it up.

She found Chise coming out of the bathhouse and informed her of the situation. When they started for Natsu's room, Takana remembered that Natsu had set out to meet with one of her *kunoichi* contacts in order to put a stop to the assassination attempts by offering the guild a doubled reward over what Taiga offered.

Chise put her hand on Takana's chest at the front door and pushed her back.

"Where do you think you're going?"

"To back up Sōkichi. With Natsu gone—"

"I happen to agree with Sōkichi. You put yourself in far too much danger to—"

"We're wasting time, Chise-*san*!"

Takana ducked beneath Chise's arm, which wasn't much more than a light bow since she was so tall, and went down the stairs while tying her *kasa* back on. Chise grumbled and ran ahead to slow Takana's unreasonable pace and take up the lead. When they reached the jail, a *shuriken* stuck out of the ground where she'd left Sōkichi. Along the road to the jail, several more *shuriken* followed, a trail forcing Sōkichi into the jail area.

Raised voices came from the other side of the log-fenced walls. Takana and Chise entered to find more dead *samurai* guards. All the prisoners shouted from their cages and pointed to the back of the jail area.

They emerged from the cluster of cages to find Taiga with his back to them, holding a *katana*. It looked like two *kunoichi* were holding Taiga in place, but when Takana's perspective shifted as she approached, she could see around Taiga's body; it was an illusion. They were really holding Sōkichi against a pillar, his arms tied behind it and the *kunoichi* holding his head back by the hair.

Both *kunoichi* wore their full black outfits and hooded masks. One of them was wobbly on her feet.

"Come any closer, *ane-san*, and I'll run him through!" Taiga yelled without turning around.

Takana gave herself the same wish—to be with Sōkichi again—and pulled a *kunai* from her *kasa*. She threw it into the back of Taiga's sword hand. He dropped the *katana* and pressed his hand between his legs. Takana's rib brought her to her knees again while Chise ran at Taiga's back. He got up from his whimpering to run and climb to the top of a cage. One of the prisoners reached up through the bars and tripped him on top. The sound of his body hitting the metal was hollow, echoing and painful. Taiga cursed, gathered himself, then jumped over the fence which led to Utsunomiya's countryside.

The wobbly *kunoichi* brought a *tantō* to Sōkichi's neck. Before Takana and Chise arrived, they had tortured him with a lash across his chest, and badly beaten his face—no doubt a mark of Taiga's jealousy.

"Kunō, stop!" Takana cried.

The steady *kunoichi* paused and asked how she knew Kunō's name. Takana ignored her and continued appealing to her unstable partner.

"I know you're poisoned, Kunō. Let me help you. You don't have to die."

The other *kunoichi* took off her mask. Her beautiful face held an expression of genuine concern for Kunō.

"Kunō-*san*, we'll never get back to the alcove in time to concoct the anecdote. Why didn't you tell me?"

"Shut up, Aoi-*san*. If we kill them the clan gets the reward," Kunō said as she pushed the blade harder against Sōkichi's neck.

Takana rose to her feet and dropped her *daishō* and *kasa* to the ground. She held her palms out as she approached slowly.

"Kunō-*san*, we have a doctor that can help you. Even though you tried to kill me, you were only doing what you were hired to do. I don't hold it against you," Takana said. "Your sister Natsu Jingū is negotiating with your clan to pay you double to call off the kill. Please, let him go."

Kunō ripped off her mask and vomited behind the pillar. Aoi untied Sōkichi and attended to her sister. Chise supported Sōkichi's weight as he nearly passed out from the pain. Takana picked up her weapons and led them all to the doctor. She banged on the door until a lantern's glow approached from the other side. The doctor whined at them waking him so late at night but relented and allowed them inside when he saw the blood soaking through the tatters of Sōkichi's robes and the color of Kunō's face.

Takana eased Sōkichi onto a *futon*, then she and Chise gathered supplies as instructed by the doctor while he mixed materials for an anecdote. The *kunoichi* detailed the type of poison they used as Takana and Chise cleaned Sōkichi's wounds. When the basics of care were administered, the doctor instructed the three relatively healthy people to go outside.

"I think I'm destined to never heal this damn rib, Chise-*san*," Takana muttered while rubbing the spot above her belly. "And my damn nose…"

Chise huffed and shook her head. At least she hadn't reached the point of lecturing Takana, too.

"Why don't you let the police know what happened at the jail?" Takana asked Chise. "Then get some sleep. I'll stay here. You can…send a protector by," she added, trying to appease everyone's worries.

Chise nodded and disappeared up the road through the darkness. Aoi leaned against the corner of the doctor's building and smoked a cigarette. Takana stood close to her to breathe in the smoke. Aoi offered a drag, but Takana shook her head. Aoi went back to staring out into the darkness.

"How did Taiga get word out of that jail and secure a contract with your clan?" Takana asked.

"One of the *yakuza* clans sent a representative. They approached us on his behalf."

"No clan is representing him. That doesn't make any sense."

Aoi shrugged and stepped on the cigarette.

"Can you describe the representative's tattoos?"

"It's not like he approached our clan with his robes off. But I did see a little bit peeking through from his chest and neck."

Takana's hand tightened around the hilt of the gifted *katana* as she listened to the pertinent details of the tattoo.

After a while the doctor came out to let them know how Sōkichi and Kunō were doing, then allowed them inside to monitor his patients while he went to bed. He grumbled the whole way out of the room about how Takana's enterprise made him busier than he ever wanted to be. Takana held her tongue that he never complained about the money, knowing full well the burden of a prosperous business.

In the morning, Takana prepared food with Aoi and asked questions about the *kunoichi* clan. She intimated that they must be pretty hard up for money if Kunō was willing to die for whatever reward Taiga promised. Aoi confirmed that peacetime had hit their clan as hard as the *samurai*, but at least the *samurai* were hired on as police forces. The only clans making any real money were the *yakuza*.

"You obviously don't have any problems working for *yakuza*," Takana mused. "But they're fickle and dishonest. Every one of them. You can trust my clan, though. None of us are actually *yakuza*. I have more work than mercenaries. We offer protection, bathhouses, and restaurants along both roads to Edo, plus two Inns through which to operate. I hope you'll take Natsu-*san* with you to your clan leaders to work out the details."

"That's probably not a good idea," Aoi sighed.

"What isn't a good idea about all that?"

"The Natsu-*san* part. We have a history, she and I."

While they waited for the rice to cook, Aoi talked about their training together, years past. Natsu was loved by nearly all of their clan. Aoi confided that Kunō had only been trying to subdue Natsu because it would have broken her heart to kill her in Takana's office. The *kunoichi* fought each other relentlessly during training but would never turn on each other outside of their enclaves.

"You're afraid a line has been crossed?" Takana asked.

"Kunō-*san* told me Natsu-*san* wasn't even trying to hold back. Tell me, Takana-*san*...are you two in lo—?"

"Shh!" Takana shushed and checked that Sōkichi hadn't woken up.

Aoi followed Takana's fearful look, then smiled as Takana's face burned.

"I thought so. Kunō-*san* said she'd never seen that look in Natsu-*san*'s eyes before. But I had. In the enclave, she had a bully. One of the girls hated all the friendly and...let's say...*loving* attention Natsu-*san* earned. She endeavored to make Natsu-*san*'s life hell. She found out about Natsu-*san*'s family and the tragedy surrounding her...and used it as a weapon.

"I told you *kunoichi* don't turn on each other *outside* the enclave. But I saw that look in Natsu-*san*'s eyes during a training exercise. The bully's life was nearly ended. The act was something far worse than could ever be dismissed as an 'accident.' Natsu-*san* was dismissed from the enclave for a period of time, but never came back when her exile was finished."

"You were saying you had a history with her?" Takana asked as she plated the food.

"I'm ashamed of what I did to earn that look from Natsu-*san*. She was one of the best of all of us. I never should have said what I did about her family. I deserved the scars she left on me. I'll bring your proposal to my clan, but Natsu-*san* won't be necessary to make it happen."

Aoi paused and lowered her voice when Sōkichi stirred to the smell of food.

"I regretted for so long pushing Natsu-*san* out of our clan's arms because of my own pettiness. I'm at least glad to see that she's since found her way into yours."

Takana nodded and brought a tray of food to Sōkichi's bedside. While they ate together, she contemplated how she was ever going to reconcile her feelings for him and Natsu.

Chapter Twenty-Seven

Discontent

Onsen: Hot springs covering nearly every part of Japan from north to south along the volcanic country. Renowned worldwide for their many health benefits related to their various mineral contents. Even today, many onsen operators will ban bathers with tattoos, but there are some who will allow it. There is a middle ground where small tattoos that are covered by a patch or plaster can enter. Tattoo rules are specifically to keep out yakuza and other criminals from using the facilities—they would need to find a tattoo-friendly onsen or get their own. Mixed bathing was traditional until the West arrived.

January 9, 1709
Utsunomiya, Tochigi Prefecture

AS WINTER GREW COLDER AND snow covered the mountains, the Bakeneko clan earned more than ever by allowing the *kunoichi* to take all the jobs that the Inn's mercenaries couldn't or wouldn't handle. Happy to be employed, they were so efficient at completing contracts that the imbalance of clients to workers evened out. The long lines decreased, but the work still kept everyone busy.

Takana hated it.

She was surrounded by so much money, she ran out of things to dream of spending it on in order to expand the business. The next project to invest in would be expansion further north, west, and into Edo, but to what end? For all the good it did to have opulent furniture and decorations throughout the Inn, all Takana wanted to do was sleep on the balcony—her compromise with Sōkichi on sleeping outdoors.

She had the best *daishō* money could buy in all of Utsunomiya, replacing the set Kameya had gifted to her and now sat on display in one of the other rooms. She'd sent couriers to seek her grandfather's special tobacco, resulting in a chest full of it that she couldn't even smoke until the baby was born since attempts on her life could come at any time, and the potential coughing fits were a mortal liability. Her tattoos were finished, and Genjirō had moved on to expanding her clan's displays, jealous as they were with Takana's gorgeous *irezumi*. The constant income they paid him did nothing to dent their fortune.

The other thing Takana had come to hate was Natsu spending more time in the field and visiting the *kunoichi* clans. Takana understood it but grew jealous the longer Natsu was gone. She saw how close the women warriors were whenever she was around any of them—except Aoi. Was their close bond only because of Takana's proximity to Natsu at the time? Takana must have been like any of the dozens of anonymous *kunoichi* that Natsu gravitated towards since their alliance.

As the weeks went by, Takana took to reinforcing her love for Sōkichi, pretending her increasingly public displays of affection were to fuss over his injuries. He grew more present and protective the larger her belly grew. Her rib had finally healed after being forced at length by Fusa and Chise to spend more time sitting still, and she joined with Sōkichi nearly every night as a means to keep herself distracted from Natsu's absence. Their *futon* sparring increased so much that he told her he needed breaks a couple times a week at least.

Natsu herself wasn't distant with Takana when they were in the same room. She still wore her wonderful smile and didn't change the way she talked to Takana, but she wasn't blind to how Takana was getting closer to Sōkichi and appeared to take that as a sign to back off. If they could ever be alone together, Takana would tell her that wasn't her intention, but they never got the opportunity. Everyone was on high alert around Takana after all the attacks, and with her ninth month of pregnancy approaching, none of her friends were taking chances anymore, escorting her everywhere and never leaving her alone in a room.

She had money, protection, shelter, love, and deep friendships. It was all suffocating her. She needed to get away.

The road called.

Takana sent word to Kameya that she was ready to travel to the mountains for the *onsen* trip he pined for. On the morning of departure, she left a note in the office that she was fine and didn't need to be followed. If she had told anyone that face-to-face, she would never manage to get out of the building.

To avoid alerting the protectors, Takana escaped through the hidden exit that Taiga had used when they took over the head-quarters. Crawling woke up muscles she hadn't used in a while, even though she had to go slower than she would have liked, care-ful not to scrape her belly against the ground. She was invigorated by sneaking to the entrance of the city walls to meet Kameya.

They both wore thick *haori* and their *daishō*. Takana gave him a pouch of tobacco to smoke as they hiked towards the mountains. She walked behind him to smell the aroma drifting on the wind. His old, slow legs were perfect to keep pace and avoid stressing her own tired feet. He needed many blessed breaks as they traveled.

Though the silence was meditative and glorious during the hike, sometimes Kameya began talking about Tetsuo, which led to memories of Taiga and the former Kochiya clan. Takana believed he talked more to himself, since he spoke in such glowing terms about the clan that ruined her life. She expected him to be more tactful on that sore subject, even if their journey was bringing those memories flooding back. But then again, Tetsuo was the main thread that had brought them together. Perhaps Kameya didn't know what else to talk about besides their old friend and tobacco. Takana wasn't sure what to talk about otherwise either, although she would have been content in silence all the same.

The deeper they hiked into the mountains; monkeys began out-numbering humans. Several *onsen* were filled with them. Takana envied their easy outdoor living, lounging in baths all day. The monkeys cleaned each other's backs and didn't backstab them.

When they kicked up a fuss if she and Kameya got too close to their *onsen*, it was only to create space, not to harm or kill.

The higher up the mountain they went, the monkeys and their *onsen* grew scarcer, until eventually they came upon their destination—a private *onsen* that Kameya had borrowed from the head of one of the Edo *yakuza* clans. No road led to it, and there were no other structures for kilometers through the surrounding forest. The snow covering the single-roomed building and the *onsen* area was breathtaking. It was the only type of luxury Takana ever wanted: smoking and soaking all day.

She knew what to spend her money on after only a few minutes in the wonderful isolation. She couldn't wait to bring her future husband and child to their own private mountain *onsen* someday. For a brief moment she imagined someone else joining her.

She pushed the thought away. That ship was sailing in the opposite direction.

Takana prepared their dinner while Kameya filled the room with smoke. Her grandfather once brought the family to a similar place, but it hadn't been quite so secluded. She recalled it had been shortly before his death and the rapid disappearance of their money as her father mismanaged their inheritance. It was one of her last memories of being truly happy, before the dark clouds of debt overtook them.

Chiyo's burnt body and Iwakuchi's headless corpse came to her through the smoke of the food and tobacco. Kameya noticed her far-off look and asked if she was alright. She blamed her watery eyes on the thick cooking smoke, to which he nodded and went back to his writing.

"What are you writing, *oyassan*?" she asked.

"Instructions for Manhachi. When I leave and get back to the main road, I'll have a courier deliver it ahead."

Takana wondered if he wanted to be caught out. He was usually more careful in his words.

During dinner Kameya talked about his life, increasingly unfiltered. It began to feel like he was transcribing his life to her, in hopes she would chronicle it or pass it along. His most bitter regret came from never bearing children, though he'd tried his whole life.

Kameya apologized for talking endlessly; that their trip brought out such strong feelings that he couldn't contain them. Takana agreed. It'd only been a few hours and she was swimming in memories. She wondered if, and faintly hoped, the *onsen* would cleanse her of her haunted past.

After dinner they enjoyed each other's presence in silence. Kameya continued writing and Takana worked on some new *haiku* that the trip and all the nature around them inspired. She recited a few to Kameya when he begged her to share, then brought a few tears to his eyes with her own thinly veiled threat:

Shishi Oyabun

Shihai-shimashita

Neko taosu

Before midnight, Kameya asked that they enjoy the *onsen* together—the darkness would cover them. She agreed and told him to follow her out after a minute. Takana walked with a lantern through increasing snowfall to the edge of the *onsen*. She slid off her *daishō* but unsheathed the shorter *wakizashi* and put it in the water, then stripped down and placed her clothes on top of the scabbards to hide the missing hilt.

She blew out the lantern and climbed in. There was absolutely nothing in the world quite like the warm water in the falling mountain snow. She relished the sensations. Kameya came out not long after and placed his lantern on a rock behind where he sat into the water, ensuring she couldn't see his face, but he could see hers.

He leaned back and relaxed, taking in the serene environment as she had, sighing contentedly. Takana sighed with him, but she was far from content.

"Why did you finance Taiga's revenge against me, *oyassan*?" Takana asked.

She was glad she couldn't see his face. It made her resolve easier to maintain if she didn't have to gauge further manipulation behind his kindly, wrinkled mask.

"I told you how barren it felt—not having children. Tetsuo allowed me to help raise and bond with his only son. He was a good boy until he met you."

"Funny. *I* was good before I met *him*."

"It's obvious that you both bring out strong feelings in the other. It's regrettable that those feelings are like opposite ends of magnets. Tetsuo confided in me he hoped one of you would be the stronger person, apologize and amend, and you'd be able to give us grandchildren we could spoil through the ends of our lonely years."

"Taiga could have been with countless concubines; gotten any wife he wanted. Why me?"

"I've long suspected your grandfather hid his affiliations from you. Tetsuo thought as much and respected your grandfather's wish to hide such knowledge from his family. Before his unexpected death, he had hopes of marrying you to Taiga, to ensure your family's financial stability for the rest of your lives.

"Your father, however, didn't want you to live out your life as a *yakuza* wife. He dreamed you'd go out into the world with your martial training and make something better of yourself, unconnected to your grandfather's dealings or our clans. He attempted to juggle those alliances once your grandfather passed, never telling those closest to him how he was losing his fortune. When he became desperate enough, he endeavored to renegotiate the deal your grandfather wanted. That deal had been more financially motivated than anything else, however, and he had nothing left to leverage.

"He went into further debt with other *yakuza* clans who weren't as patient as Tetsuo and me. Tetsuo was merciful enough to buy them out from the other clans, absorbing all the Gozen name's worth. He let you and your mother work under his protection to keep up the pretense that had already been set. More than he hoped to preserve your grandfather's legacy that your father was so rapidly destroying, he thought it was a fair enough arrangement. With time you and Taiga could grow fond of each other naturally, and through your work, you'd earn yourself the dowry your father squandered."

Little drops plinked, mixing salt in the warm, pristine *onsen*. She'd misjudged her father so catastrophically. If he'd only talked with her about it *once*... Did he fall into a drunken, abusive spiral because he had been deemed expendable in his father-in-law's legacy as an utter failure?

If Takana had known, she would have worked off his debt from a place of love, rather than contempt bred from societal obligation. She would have made a better effort to keep him sober and productive. If she'd ever looked further into the tale that he sold them into slavery, a lie reinforced by Taiga and Tetsuo, she would have attempted to destroy the Kochiya-*kai* far sooner.

That thought startled her and she realized why he'd kept silent for nearly a decade—if she'd sought revenge while she was young and inexperienced, she'd only have succeeded in getting herself killed. Her father must have known her far better than she'd thought—would her younger self have been able to resist forceful closure of the debt?

The web of lies surrounding their situation and her hate for her worthless, deadbeat father had protected her from seeking justice; acting rash...

In the dark ripples of the *onsen's* surface, Takana's face distorted to that of her father's—she remembered how he'd looked when she lied to him about being with child. He had smiled in knowing, content that she had broken free of the tethers from which he'd been unable to untangle their family. Takana had become her own woman.

"Why did my father do Taiga's bidding? Send me to Nikkō and betray my location and the estate?" Takana sniffed, not knowing how much more she could take.

"I don't know what your father was thinking, but I can tell you that Taiga told him his debt wasn't paid. He used that lie to manipulate Iwakuchi. Taiga promised not to harm you or your mother as conditions for giving you up—your father wasn't lying about your mother's death surprising him...

"I was so ashamed of Taiga that I convinced another clan to bring him to you, even though I was the one protecting him."

"You knew all this, and you let my father die? He killed himself right in front of you!"

"It made things going forward less complicated—"

"Less complicated? So why break Taiga out of jail?"

"I expected you to finish him like you did Iwaku—"

"Don't talk about him! I didn't know... If I'd known all this..." Takana lifted her hands out of the water, unsure what to do with them as misery threatened to choke her.

"I've grown fond of you, Taka-*chan*, much like Tetsuo. But the longer you left Taiga to languish in jail, the more I resented you for not allowing him to regain his honor; to save face for his transgressions. You dragged it out for no reason. You either want him dead or you don't. The humiliation was cruel and unnecessary."

"So, you've brought me up here to talk sense into *me*? End *his* misery? I just found out I needlessly killed my own father, and you want me to feel sorry for *Taiga*? I see where he got his little speech skills from. Trying to blame other people for his actions... I can see the part of you that helped raise him."

"*Sense* is why I brought you up here. I hoped to talk you into accepting and marrying him, before he arrives here tomorrow with half of my men."

"*Kuso ossan!*"

"How quickly you lose respect. I'm trying to save you; giving you a future that won't include attempts on your life. A future for your child once Sōkichi is dealt with—a future it won't get to have if I don't prove to Taiga you've turned over a new leaf by tomorrow."

Takana lowered her head, scowling at his delusion. The rage in her body surpassed the heat of the water.

"I can't wait to meet him tomorrow," she growled. "It will be an immense pleasure showing him your head. Only you're not going to earn your honor back through *seppuku* like my father. And neither will Taiga. I want to thank you for sending so many of your own to their deaths in these mountains. It will make it that much easier when I wipe the rest of your clan off the face of the earth."

"In your state? Are the Gozen delusions hereditary? It's for the best, then; Taiga's line won't inherit such absurdity as well. I won't make the same mistake as Tetsuo. When it finally comes down to choosing, I won't pick you over my son!"

Kameya lunged forward, aiming for her neck. He reached her and squeezed. His hands were stronger than she'd expected for his age. She clenched her teeth and neck in a grotesque smile that grew wider and more satisfied as his grip tightened.

Then it weakened. He looked down into the black water, unable to see the blade that had slid through his stomach.

Takana rose out of the water and pointed at the deformed *bakeneko* tattoo on her right shoulder. His eyes moved slowly across the ragged artwork. When he looked back at her face, her eyes flashed, and her lip curled. Satisfied she'd made her point, she ripped the blade across his abdomen below the surface. The expensive steel slid through easily. Bloody bubbles of internal air and gore rose to the surface. She pushed him off her blade, then used the end to guide his floating body to the side in the direction of the water's flow, then lifted him over the side.

The final knowledge of what she'd done to her father hit her all at once, rending her soul, and she wept.

When she ran out of tears, she ducked her head under the water to wash her face. Something large splashed into the other side of the *onsen*. Takana burst up with the *wakizashi* drawn back for a quick stab, expecting to see Taiga across from her. The silhouette of the person in the water didn't match his, though. It had a high ponytail and—

"Finally! I was freezing out there watching you talking with the old man, and then all that *crying*!"

A laugh burst out of Takana as she tossed the blade behind her. She waded across to hug Natsu tight, feeling her cold body heat up in the water. A strong desire to kiss her was tempered by the realization she had been in the warm water far too long. Instead, she whispered in Natsu's ear.

"Warm up and meet me inside by the fire, my friend."

Chapter Twenty-Eight

Heart to Heart

Makibishi: The Japanese version of caltrops, used by shinobi. Could be thrown like shuriken or placed on the ground to pierce the soles of feet. Often made of six or eight pointed spikes, sometimes serrated, and occasionally coated in poison.

January 15, 1709
Mountain retreat outside Nikkō, Tochigi Prefecture

THE FIRE PIT CRACKLED IN the middle of the room as Takana laid out in a corner with only a thin robe covering her. She'd been in the *onsen* too long and the fire wasn't helping her cool down. Natsu took her time in the water, then settled close to the fire when she came inside. She explained how easy it was to pick up their trail when she saw Takana's note. Manhachi told Tomoe that Kameya left for the mountains, so that clearly wasn't a coincidence. With the slow travel of a pregnant woman and old man increasing in elevation, Natsu caught up quickly and simply followed the pipe smoke the rest of the way. Even carrying a large bag of supplies hadn't slowed her enough to lose the trail.

"We thought your note could have been planted by Taiga or you were going after him yourself. In case Manhachi's confession was a lie, all of us spread out to find you. Chise-*san* is on her way to Oyama. Sōkichi-*kun* went to the thicket and old estate. Fu-*chan*'s been searching the city. Tomoe-*san* is keeping tabs on the Kameya clan in case the old man got back before you."

"I'm glad it was *you* that found me," Takana whispered. She needed to figure out where they were with each other, once and for all.

"No point in whispering, Takana-*san*. I'm glad you had that old man under control. When he lunged for you, I was ready to throw a *shuriken* through his face, but your head was blocking my line of sight."

"Mm."

Takana didn't feel like repeating any part of her conversation with Kameya. She enjoyed the silence as her body cooled. Once the air had sufficiently reversed her temperature, she crawled closer to the fire and laid on her side so she could admire Natsu's lovely face.

"Why have you disappeared so much recently, Natsu-*san*? I...I've missed you...so much..." her voice trailed off.

"I've been searching for someone."

"A former *kunoichi* lover?" Takana didn't expect her jealousy to creep out like that.

Natsu frowned, then smiled again, like there was still a secret behind it.

"No, my friend. An artisan. Someone to repair something that saved my life."

"What's so hard to repair that any artisan in Utsunomiya or Oyama couldn't take care of it?"

"Something that may be too old to fix. Do you understand how hard it's been finding that person? I've been in Edo far more than I care to be."

It was Takana's turn to frown.

"What are you going on about? What is this thing?"

Natsu crawled over and lay behind her, pressing into Takana's back from her chest to her feet. Something hard at Natsu's chest stuck into Takana's back. Natsu leaned away to pull something from her light robes. She pressed her chest into Takana's back again and wormed her arm between Takana's elbow and torso, holding out a box. She couldn't immediately see what was on the box because of the fire's shadow, but its size was unforgettable.

Takana reached for it with trembling fingers, daring not to get her hopes up too much. Once relieved of the box, Natsu's hand went to Takana's belly and caressed back and forth. Takana hardly noticed, as she creaked open the box. Her grandfather's *kiseru* was there, intact and repaired from when it was broken in two and lost outside Tomoe's former residence near Lake Chūzenji; when she'd saved Natsu from that arrow.

Takana's vision blurred as she felt along its shape—getting reacquainted with its length and texture. The repair was so artfully done she couldn't feel a crack or chip. It hadn't even needed a layer of paint to hide the damage. The *kiseruzutsu's* damage was a little more obvious due to the holes that had to be patched, but as she turned it in the light, despite the extremely slight feel of the patchwork, the paint-over looked exactly as she remembered it to the finest detail.

Takana replaced the *kiseru* in its home and snapped it shut. She laid it off to the side, then laced her fingers through the back of Natsu's hand and sniffled quietly. She knew what she wanted to say but words died in her throat when her lips tried to part. Natsu didn't spoil the moment by talking, allowing Takana to absorb the magnitude of what her friend had done for her.

No.

They weren't friends anymore.

Their hearts were one. *Kokoro no tomo.*

Takana used her free hand to part her robe, then guided Natsu's hand over her heart. It bumped against Natsu's palm with increasing speed and strength. Takana held Natsu's hand firmly as she rolled over on her back. The robe fell off her sides.

They didn't need to say anything. Natsu reached for Takana's other hand and pulled it to her own heart beneath her loose robe, and the conversation came full circle. Takana released Natsu's hand and touched her face. She pulled Natsu's smile to hers and determined their conversation wouldn't end there.

Takana leaned against a tree, shin-deep in snow and nearly blinded by it. A gray sky peeked through the forest canopy, threatening to dump even more in a few minutes. The wind picked up speed and blew ice crystals between the trees. She held branches with plenty of pine needles to cover her as footsteps crunched only meters away. The snow picked up as she hoped it would after the last man passed by. The wind whipped through and disguised her footsteps.

A bird call pierced through the wind from the flank—a call non-native to that part of Nihon.

Takana got up carefully with a *tantō*, tightened the harness supporting her belly, and stepped in the tracks of the passing men to avoid unnecessary crunching. The man in the back walked slower. She enjoyed the likelihood that he'd been versed in the results of all the previous ambushes Taiga had sent after her. She wouldn't disappoint the legend.

She was able to get her hand over his mouth before a splash of red hit the snow in front of him. She lowered his body to the ground, the wind muffling all sounds of slight struggle. She crept along diverging footprints, picking off the stragglers.

As they got closer to the building, cries came from the men in the front line. Takana hid behind a thick tree capable of covering her *kasa* behind its trunk. The lead men had stepped on Natsu's supply of razor-sharp caltrops spread throughout the various paths towards the building.

Through the wind, Takana heard the whistling of arrows, raining down on the men behind the crippled front line. As they'd anticipated, a few of the men broke free of the group and ran back the way they'd come. Takana put her back to the trunk and pulled *kunai* from her *kasa*, sending the blades into the backs of the fleeing men.

One of the men heard the bodies falling behind him and turned around, spotting Takana behind the tree. She feared he would shout and give away her position but as his mouth opened an arrow skewered his neck. She looked around the trunk and watched the men who weren't fleeing spread out and nock their own bows.

Takana crept from tree to tree, getting closer to a pair who were busy looking up into the canopy. They'd never be able to see

Takana's white-clad *kunoichi* angel. However, one of the pair saw well enough the angle that the arrow had stuck into his comrade's throat. Takana hurried behind the one still standing who aimed up in Natsu's direction. She slit his throat, then grabbed his bow and both of the men's quivers.

Takana moved away from the rest of the group as they cowered to look up in the trees. Natsu joined her in a thicker-forested area. Takana handed over the second quiver to increase Natsu's arrow count.

"How good are you with that thing?" Natsu whispered, pointing at the bow Takana had picked up.

"Not very."

"Okay. You can still distract them. Fire a few arrows around them. Keep them confused. If you hit one, all the better."

Takana put her hand on the side of Natsu's white-masked face and nodded before they parted again.

She found a safe spot with three trees close together, then fired an arrow to distract a group of three men who were huddled and strategizing. One found an arrow in his neck from Natsu before he could even turn to look where Takana's arrow had landed. Another ran off in the direction of the arrow that killed the first one, while the third man ran in her direction. She lined up her shot between tree trunks.

She thrilled at the impact her arrow made in his chest, but it wasn't a kill shot and it didn't have power enough to knock him down. He staggered but continued running to her position. She dropped the bow and waited for him to round the corner so her *katana* could finish the kill. Once dispatched, she picked up the bow again and moved to a new position, creating a wide berth between her and the building since the remaining men flocked to its relative safety.

Takana hunted down the men who'd tried limping to cover after stepping on the caltrops. Their blood led her straight to them. Each of them held their crippled feet in despair as she silenced them for good.

Takana found a wide tree to hide behind closer to the building, turning around to make sure no men snuck from farther out. When she believed the two of them had done all they could to herd the remaining men into the smaller areas around the building, she moved to a position closer as well.

Several took cover inside while a few bravely stood outside. One came into the range of her *kunai,* and she threw it into the side of his neck. Natsu wasn't too far away, as a few *shuriken* flew past Takana's tree and found their marks in the other two men. They screamed at the non-lethal pain and staggered back towards the door. Takana stepped out from the tree and put an arrow in one of their backs while Natsu's arrow finished the other. Their bodies crashed through the sliding door of the building.

Natsu appeared behind Takana and put a hand on her lower back as if to say she'd be relieved soon, then broke off to a different tree. She looked back at Takana and nodded. They pulled a few smoke bombs out from their pockets and threw them into the open door. White smoke poured out, almost obscuring the structure into the snowy mountainside.

They rushed to either side of the opening and waited for the men to blunder outside where they would meet Natsu's *tantō* and Takana's *katana.* The smoke cleared after a minute, then they snuck inside, leaving the four bodies of those that had tried escaping the smoke behind them. Two men were left, cowering in the corners of the main living space.

Takana would have normally cut them down with the blade, but with her protruding belly she didn't want to risk getting that close to cornered animals. She and Natsu lifted their bows and fired from a safe distance.

They searched the small building, checking each closet. They found no more men. Takana leaned back into a wall and sat down, letting her feet and back recover while she regained her breath. Natsu sat next to her and pulled off her mask, her fetching orange hair clinging to her face by sweat.

Takana flung her *kasa* to the other side of the room, letting her hair fall loose. They both put their heads to the wall, where they were drawn like magnets to lean against each other in balance. Natsu grabbed Takana's hand, and they sat like that for several minutes in silence.

Takana thought of something just then, and whispered a clumsy *haiku* about the red-crowned crane and dedicated it to Natsu:

> *Watashitachi*
> *Zuttoisshoni*
> *Tanchōzuru*

Natsu's infectious smile broke into laughter. Takana couldn't help laughing along with her, though she wasn't sure what was so funny.

"It was lovely, Takana," Natsu said when the laughter died down. "That was five, seven, *six*, though."

"Well, I made it work anyway. No one else in the world has such a *haiku* dedicated to them. It's one of a kind…"

Laughter again. In a life Takana had only ever expected to be punctuated by battle cries, she was blessed by Natsu's laughter, and she never imagined how good it would feel to hear her name without qualification beyond her future husband. She kissed the back of Natsu's cold hand, then leaned over for a quick kiss on the lips.

"Don't get *too* sappy with me, my poetic friend," Natsu got up, then offered her hand to help Takana to her feet. They walked hand-in-hand towards the wreckage of the entrance.

"Think the old man's blood has cleared out of the *onsen* yet?" Natsu asked. "I've always wanted to be with you in something other than those damn public ba—"

Natsu stopped at the opening. She gave a stiff stagger, one foot forward and one step back. A rod of bright steel in the front of her, red-coated blade exploding from her back.

Takana's world slowed down. An arrow whistled from outside, then found its home in Natsu's chest with a heavy thud. Takana pulled out her *wakizashi* and grabbed the collar of the *yakuza* on the wrong end of the *katana* sticking from her lover. She pulled him back from Natsu and slid her blade through his eye, screaming like a *yama-uba*, drowning out the man's own pained screams. Natsu hit the floor limp and ungracefully, a state Takana never thought she'd witness from her flawless *kunoichi*.

Twisting the blade and pushing him through the opening as a shield, she searched for where the arrow had come from. Another whistled from the tree line and stuck into the back of the shield, silencing him for good. Making a note of where she saw the arrow fly from, she dropped the shield and backed away into the building.

The sight before her was impossible.

Natsu lay on her back. Her leaking eyes darted around frantically until they found Takana's. Takana collected Natsu's hands in hers as she knelt down. Their hands and eyes talked for what felt like ages but were only a few precious seconds.

Natsu's lips parted to say something, but blood trickled out of her mouth. Takana nodded that she knew what Natsu needed to say aloud but couldn't. It was agony to open her own mouth to say what she wished she could have said a thousand times more, for the rest of their lives.

"I love you, Natsu. I always will."

Natsu's lips twitched into a weak smile as her eyes stopped moving.

Takana brought their foreheads together. Droplets fell onto Natsu's still face.

An arrow whistled in through the opening, coming so close to Takana's head that wisps of her hair followed the passing projectile. She eased Natsu's hands onto her torso and cherished one last look into Natsu's eyes before closing the lids.

Another arrow missed her head by millimeters.

She rose slowly, unable to break her gaze from the captivating person before her. Another arrow grazed her belly. She didn't feel it, or care, even as a red stain spread over her *kimono*. She backed away from her *kokoro no tomo*, into the wall next to the opening.

"I'll be back for you," Takana whispered. "I promise."

Chapter Twenty-Nine

Bakeneko & Tanchōzuru

Tanchōzuru: The red-crowned crane is another iconic animal in Japanese lore. They symbolize longevity due to their life spans (both practically at 30-40 years and mythologically at 1,000 years), and fidelity since they are known to live with the same partner for life. Origami cranes are their most notable form in modern culture, but they have graced countless tapestries and other art forms for millennia. They are said to grant favors in return for acts of sacrifice. The red-crowned crane is the second-rarest species of crane and is endangered throughout the world. The most promising population restoration efforts are taking place in Hokkaido.

January 16, 1709
Mountains outside Nikkō, Tochigi Prefecture

AS TAKANA STUCK HER HEAD out, an arrow buried itself in the wall, nearly coming all the way through to prick her shoulder. Takana tromped out in the direction the arrow had flown with only her *katana* in hand. As her lovemaking with Natsu the night before warmed her during the slaughter, her rage burned hotter. Snow didn't stick to her wind-blown black hair or exposed belly through the tear in her *kimono*—it melted before touching her.

Through her state of heightened concentration, she faintly heard a bowstring stretch and twang on the wind. Knowing where it was coming from and hearing its whistle approach, she put her left hand out to protect her chest. He was a good archer, and Takana knew exactly where he'd be aiming—for her unrequited heart. The arrow found bullseye into her palm, its velocity stopping to leave the shaft stuck halfway through her hand. She never broke stride as she stalked straight toward the archer's position.

Though she hadn't seen him, she was certain he hadn't run off. She would have heard the snow beneath his feet. She did, however, hear him fumbling for another arrow from his quiver. Moving along a different angle, she saw the top of the man's head as he nocked another arrow from behind a tree. Her pace remained steady.

She wanted him to remain overconfident of his easy target and not run away. Chasing through the snow with her aching feet and swollen belly would be impossible—not that she wouldn't try if he did turn tail. The bloody cat and mouse games were over.

They were only a few meters apart when he straightened up and pulled back his bow. An evil grin crawled across Takana's face. Taiga loosed the arrow and she turned her body. It burrowed through her mangled tattoo. The painful impact caused her to drop the *katana*, but she kept pace toward him, uncaring. His eyes grew wide with horror that nothing was stopping her—maybe nothing *could* stop her. Her grotesque smile never wavered, the corners curling deeper like a bared cat's grin, so pleased to be reunited with its rightful master.

Taiga screamed as a gust of wind blew Takana's hair off her shoulders in a thousand directions. She never broke her stare into his frightened eyes as she backhanded him with her left hand. The arrow skewering her palm pierced through both his cheeks and out the other side. He tried to turn away but with the arrow in his face he only succeeded in pulling her down on top of him.

She let him struggle against the arrow, delighting in the mangling of the venomous lips he'd so often wielded against her. She relinquished the hope of ever using her left hand again and wrenched the arrow, twisting it through the tendons. In his panic Taiga grabbed the feathered end of the shaft and ripped it out of his face, flinging Takana's hand away with it. Blood sprayed across Takana's demonic face and colored the white snow.

She backhanded the arrow into his side, but it grazed a rib and only tore his skin. He punched her in the face, knocking her off of him. She fought through the pain of her unhealed, broken nose getting hit again, involuntary tears, and flickering blackness as Taiga scrambled to his feet. He made to kick at her belly, but she turned so he only connected, albeit painfully, with her hip bone.

Takana waited for him to try again, then backhanded the arrow into his thigh. He cried out and jumped away, nearly pulling her shoulder out of its socket before he tore the arrow out. She rolled over onto her knees and rose back to her feet as he ran away from her. At the sight of the hand she'd willingly sacrificed for disfiguring Taiga, a moment of clarity came to her—what else was she willing to sacrifice to catch him? Was the pain she put him through worth all the damage she would sustain to achieve it? What state would she be in if the chase lasted too long?

A gust of wind blew through her hair again, carrying a scream from ahead. Takana looked toward the building, nearly out of view through the whipping snow, and followed the scream.

"*Arigatō*, Natsu-*san~*," Takana whispered, in a soft, sing-song voice.

She found Taiga writhing on the ground, a caltrop sticking out of his foot. Takana whistled to get his attention—so he could watch her fearlessly grip the end of the arrow sticking out of the tattoo he had commissioned for her as a mocking joke and yank it out with her right hand.

Taiga crawled back on his hands, panic and fear increasing with each step she took, deliberate and slow. Something stuck up, gleaming from the snow behind him a few more meters. She angled him towards it, thankful for Natsu's continued assistance. It wasn't lost on her that Natsu was paying back Takana's help in overcoming her own familial tragedy and subsequent revenge.

Taiga wailed as his hand went through the barbed caltrop. He curled on his side in his pain, too overwhelmed to address all the threats around him; too absorbed with the rope around his neck to notice the executioner standing over him. Takana stabbed the arrow down towards his heart. He jerked around and the shaft snapped between his ribs before it could reach its intended destination. She thrust the jagged broken arrow through his stomach so his damn ribs wouldn't keep getting in the way.

The snapped wooden end took far more strength to break skin. She stabbed several places along his torso ineffectually, getting high off his pain and weakening resolve. She put a strong, final plunge into his gut and let go. He moaned and rolled in the snow in agony.

With all the mobility she still had in her left hand, she grabbed Taiga by his shoulder, pinning him down to face her. As she moved closer, lowering her hips onto his, the fabric over her pregnant belly soaking up the blood gushing from his stabbed abdomen, she saw a flicker in his eyes—one last confused look of hope, as she mounted him like they might have as lovers. Takana determined to give him all the love she had left to offer: she gripped the arrow sticking out of her hand, ripped it out, and penetrated his neck.

Then again.

And again.

Their fated union was finally complete.

His arteries painted her face, *kimono*, arms, and belly before she was done and long after he stopped moving.

She let go of the arrow and sat back on her knees. She hadn't realized she was hyperventilating until the numbness subsided and she acknowledged the cold air ripping through her lungs. Her breath slowed and she regained what wits remained. Her left hand sent lightning bolts of pain through her arm as she tested each useless finger. Only her thumb wiggled, but it didn't hurt any less.

Takana surveyed the day's carnage. Taiga's blood steamed and melted the snow around him, but after a minute froze over. She felt the blood covering her frosting as well. She stood up and shuffled back to the building. Her feet fought her the whole way, but they'd thank her soon enough.

With the last of her strength, Takana lowered herself and Natsu naked into the *onsen*. It had been quite difficult to drag her across the snow, but Takana was determined to give Natsu her last wish. Though Takana held onto some shred of sanity, it heartened her too much to feel Natsu's cold body warming, fantasizing that she might come back to life through the *onsen's* vaunted healing powers.

Takana held out for as long as her body would allow the heat, then brought Natsu back inside the building and started a new fire. She painstakingly dried and cleaned Natsu's body, then dressed her in the clan's *kimono* that she had worn as she tracked Takana to the blessed, cursed place.

She tied Natsu's hair in her signature high ponytail and propped her comfortably on a *futon* next to the fire. Takana lay next to her and put her arm across Natsu's torso, then drifted in and out of consciousness, recalling every moment they'd spent together.

It struck her that she'd only known Natsu less than a year, but it felt like they'd known each other a lifetime. It leveled her that she didn't have some sort of memento to keep her beautiful memories of Natsu alive. She had her grandfather's *kiseru*; the *daishō* her father had used to earn back his honor; and the two pairs of trick dice her mother had given to her before Takana set foot on the road for the first time.

Takana sat up in a panic and tore through Natsu's bag for something—anything—that she could keep. But there were only weapons and clothing. Nothing that carried Natsu's essence. Takana looked around the building for anything she might have overlooked. Then she wracked her memory for anything Natsu would have kept in either the Utsunomiya or Omiya Inns, but nothing came to mind. Natsu traveled light and had no personal belongings of significance.

It also hit Takana then that she had been showered with gifts her whole life—the *kiseru* from both her grandfather and Natsu, special treatment from two *yakuza* bosses, Fusa's "fashionable" creations, all the *katana*, unexpected and deep friendships, her mother's love and dice that fueled years of debt-recovery, her father's clumsy protection, and entire estates that came into being only because she had met Natsu in the first place.

Natsu had nothing since she was ten years old. Her forlorn looks at times made complete sense as Takana realized how much had been taken from Natsu and virtually nothing returned to her. Hot, silent tears spilled as Takana cursed herself for not realizing all that until it was too late.

She lay down again and caressed Natsu's cheek, despairing at the situation. Natsu's head lolled to face Takana. Her ponytail caught Takana's attention. Takana smiled and kissed Natsu's cold lips.

"Thank you again, my sweet friend."

Takana cut Natsu's ponytail and set it aside, then put her own hair up in a ponytail before cutting it off, too. She married the locks together in a tight braid, using their hair ties to complete the ceremony. None of it was easy with only her left thumb and right hand at the end of a bad shoulder, but she persisted—the task and its necessary pain was even more important to her than ending Taiga had been. The bundle went into a free pocket between the *kiseru* and dice in her *kimono*.

She kissed Natsu's forehead, cheek, and lingered on her lips one more time, then imagined all the gifts, material and intimate, she would have loved nothing more than to shower her great friend with over countless years, until she drifted to sleep.

Takana woke in the morning to shouting from outside. Two of the voices were blessedly familiar. She rolled over to share a last moment alone with Natsu.

"*Ohayō, tanchōzuru.* That's still six syllables, I know. But we'll always be together as they are. I'll never forget you in a thousand years."

Footsteps crunched through the snow outside the entrance. Sō-kichi shouted for her. Kunō shouted for Natsu. They were both relieved when they came into the building and saw Takana gingerly get up. Sōkichi's eyes widened when she removed the blanket to reveal her blood-soaked *kimono*.

She reassured them that only a small amount of it was her own. Takana got up and stepped away for Kunō to discover Natsu wasn't only sleeping. Takana relived the final realization that it was over when Kunō wailed at the loss of her *kunoichi* sister. Takana wept into Sōkichi's arms, letting out everything that had pent up for so long. His hand lingered on her shorn hair for a moment before squeezing her tight.

Tomoe joined them shortly after, pulling Manhachi into the building with his hands tied behind his back.

"Alright, I showed you how to get here. You can untie me now."

"You said it was only going to be Kameya and Gozen-*san* up here," Tomoe said. "Who sent Taiga and all these men from your clan? The old man? Or was it *your* idea?"

"The *oyabun* was sure he would talk Takana-*san* into marrying Taiga, but he wanted Taiga to have insurance when he got here in case she refused. It's not hard to see what her answer was..."

"Tomoe-*sensei*, how attached are you to Manhachi?" Takana asked as she left Sōkichi's arms to give Manhachi a deadly stare.

Tomoe smirked at him.

"He did nothing to dissuade any of the Kameya-*kai* from this course of action. What do you want to happen here? I don't think he'll willingly commit *seppuku*."

Manhachi fell to his knees and begged for his life. Takana made a quick gesture with her head. Tomoe nodded and beheaded him with a flash of steel so quick that Takana could have sworn the *katana* never left its scabbard.

Sōkichi hiked to the nearest town to rent a couple of horses while Tomoe and Kunō dressed Takana's injuries. Takana had done what she could with fabric from Natsu's bag but doing everything one-handed, a damaged shoulder, and no pain-relieving herbs made for a messy result. Once they finished, Kunō went outside to collect all the caltrops to protect the incoming horses.

Tomoe watched without expression as Takana sat down and cradled Natsu's body.

"Tomoe-*sensei*," Takana whispered as she began rocking a little bit, "did you know my father was only trying to protect me from the *yakuza*?"

"Yes, Gozen-*san*," she answered.

"All those bad things you said about him in your home... All those things I always said about him around you—you were protecting his lie?"

"Yes."

"Why didn't you stop me?" Takana snapped. "You knew! And you let me force him into *seppuku*!"

"You gave him the greatest gift," Tomoe shrugged, her eyes lazily settling on Manhachi's body. "He earned his honor back and—"

"*Fuck* honor! He could have had a grandchild. He would have been *everything* to it. I could have helped him; the baby would have helped him. He needed my forgiveness!"

Takana hugged Natsu tighter as she sniffled.

"Were it not for this child, I'd commit *hara-kiri* right now..."

Tomoe closed the distance across the room remarkably fast and slapped Takana, then pointed in her face.

"*That* would be unforgivable. It would spit on *all* he did for you. Don't ever let me hear that word from you again, Gozen-*san*."

Takana dried her tears in Natsu's shorn hair with a final embrace, then lay her back down carefully, lovingly in the *futon*. She got up in front of Tomoe but nearly fell over in her weakened state. Tomoe steadied her, and Takana straightened her back.

"*Sensei*, as flawed as his execution was, my father sacrificed my love for him, to protect me from the *yakuza*. That was the wish he died for. Now I wish to see his will through, one way or another. I've ended the Kochiya clan once and for all. Will you help me end the Kameya?"

Takana spent the last month of her pregnancy sequestered in her private room, on the order of all the Bakeneko clan's leadership. She spent the days healing and having a new tattoo added from the back of her neck down to her calves. Normally such a large tattoo would take over a year to complete, but Genjirō had progressed rapidly from his training in Edo, and with the long days spent sitting in a room with nothing better to do, it developed much faster.

A red-crowned crane danced with the *bakeneko* along her shoulders, and Genjirō artfully integrated the *haiku* she had improvised for Natsu in both the literal kanji and visual language of the two legendary creatures.

When he was completing the written aspect, Genjirō had to stop himself from laughing and ruining his artwork when he noticed the *haiku* had the wrong number of syllables. His laughter in that context reminded Takana of Natsu's laugh, and she found a small measure of happiness that she thought had died in the mountains.

When she wasn't wincing at the pain in her hand, shoulder, belly, nose, and from the *irezumi* work, she contemplated and meditated on the three shrines in the room. She squeezed the hair bundle during particularly painful moments, invoking her memories through touch, just as she had done before through the smell of her grandfather's tobacco.

Fusa passed time talking and gossiping next to Takana as her own baby bump continued to grow. Their relationship had strained as Fusa adjusted to married life and Takana spent so much time with Sōkichi and Natsu. The long, boring days in front of the shrines allowed them to re-strengthen their bond. Takana tried her best not to laugh at the little outfits that Fusa sewed for the two babies. She also tried her best not to cry whenever Fusa brought up a memory of Natsu. Takana wondered if that feeling was ever going to go away. Considering how attached she was to the memory of her grandfather, she chuckled at the ridiculous notion that she could possibly forget Natsu.

Chise, Sōkichi, and Kunō provided regular reports on the activities of the Kameya clan in and around their headquarters. Tomoe maintained her cover inside, pretending to be despondent that Manhachi hadn't returned, all the while listening in adjacent rooms for how the remaining members handled the power vacuum of their *oyabun* and his *shateigashira*.

The leadership of the Bakeneko clan never went anywhere alone anymore, even when traversing the Inn. Takana wished they'd instituted that policy before—that she hadn't been so stubborn herself when others had tried.

The baby was due any day. Takana came out of her room for a rare appearance in the office and listened to the leadership of the clan and *kunoichi* lay out their plan for taking the Kameya headquarters and ending the existence of its ranks. Fusa reminded them all to spare the wives so they could escape the city with their children. Chise reiterated the terms of the contract to the *kunoichi* that they'd split everything valuable found inside down the middle.

They planned meticulously until the sun set, then spent another hour preparing their outfits and weapons. As she watched, listened, and approved the course of action with her clan, Takana inwardly thanked Taiga for being such an impatient idiot. If he'd done more than throw bodies at her and crossed his fingers, he might have accomplished something. He went through faceless *yakuza* thugs like Iwakuchi went through the family fortune.

Under cover of darkness, the clan and *kunoichi* left the Inn for the Kameya headquarters. Takana stood on the balcony and stared off into the mountains. Fusa joined once everything in and around the Inn fell silent. They leaned on the rail with their elbows touching. Takana appreciated that Fusa recognized the quiet moment didn't need to be interrupted by nervous talk.

Without looking away from the mountains she held her hand out over the rail, open-palmed and wordlessly inviting. Fusa put her hand in Takana's and they enjoyed the silence for a long while.

Fusa couldn't contain herself anymore and she wept as she had when Chise had carried Natsu's body into the Inn. The two of them embraced and Takana stroked Fusa's hair while she let it all out.

"I'm so thankful I met you, Fusa-*chan*," Takana whispered. "We never would have found her if it wasn't for your kind heart on the road to Oyama. You're the best of all of us."

Fusa sniffed and wiped her eyes after breaking the long embrace, then turned to go into the office.

"Where are you going?"

Fusa looked over her shoulder and smiled.

"To fetch the doctor. Didn't you feel all that water splash our feet?"

Chapter Thirty

Brushstrokes

Nigi-mitama: Gentle spirits who brought good fortune and protection; a spirit representing the soul of a dead person. Ancestors and respected elders often take the form of nigi-mitama. Animals, objects, natural features, and other phenomena could be inhabited by these spirits as w ell.

June 1, 1709
Utsunomiya, Tochigi Prefecture

TAKANA GOZEN SAT ON A *zabuton*, smoking the special tobacco from her grandfather's *kiseru* while influential *yakuza* sat at spots around a long, rectangular table in the center of the dance hall she owned. Her stomach was satisfied with the many courses she had served at the gathering—only one early course was of rice balls. She sat informally on one foot while holding her arm up with the other knee. Many of the men didn't like her casualness, but their whispered complaints lessened the more she let the slit in her *hakama* slide off her leg.

She forbade the rest of the men from smoking their own tobacco so the air wouldn't be tainted by any aroma other than her own. However, she did pass around one of her many pouches so they could at least smoke that with her.

There were countless distractions for the heads and lieutenants of the region's *yakuza* clans—opulent food; expensive tobacco and *sake*; waitresses wearing loose, flowy robes that showed too much when they stooped over to serve all the food and drink; Takana's own loose wardrobe. She had pretended to be too hot and slid her blood-stained *kimono* down to the waist. The men all got an eyeful of her tattoos over her back, shoulders, left arm, and front torso—all depictions of cranes and demonic cats, with several *haiku* weaving in and out of the unforgettable imagery.

She wore her hair up in a loose, short ponytail. Only her white *sarashi* covered any part of the tattoos, and several men leered and cajoled her to show them more out of "purely respectful curiosity." Sometimes she played coy, and sometimes she pretended to fan her cleavage by pulling on the *sarashi* back and forth—both routines kept their attention throughout the night.

Before their post-dinner *sake* could be brought out, Takana juiced the men's anticipation by offering use of her full stable of former prostitutes; a goodwill gesture to unite the clans. She had the women parade around the room while the men yelled out vulgar, creative desires for their bodies. Once the women exited, Takana asked that the men quiet down.

"I want to personally thank you all again for meeting tonight. There was too much bad blood coming to the surface after the end of the Kochiya and Kameya clans. I know we all want to move past the bloodshed and get back to business. Some of you have come to understand how good I am for business. Many of you remain skeptical, however.

"Tonight was a small taste of what you've lost by refusing my offer of alliance after the Kameya clan was destroyed. I hope you've seen the error of your obstinate ways."

One of the men frowned and interrupted.

"Why are you talking that way?"

"Hmm?" Takana raised an eyebrow.

"You speak as if there's no chance to change our minds."

"Did I? Oh, I do apologize for that. Since having the baby I've been cooped up in my room. While recovering I've been creating dozens of *haiku*. I often get the tenses wrong in order to force the syllables to work. I find myself screwing it up out loud occasionally, too.

"Now, I've ordered the finest *sake* from Fushimi in Kyōto. Once we've toasted the end of the meeting, you're free to enjoy my entertainment for the rest of the night."

Takana snapped her fingers for the large *sake* bottles and cups to be brought in front of her. While the movements of the beautiful waitresses around her distracted the guests, she slipped her fingers into the little pocket over her cleavage and pulled out a pinky-length, thin glass vial with a powdery substance inside. She skillfully kept the vial out of view with her right fingers.

She requested her most voluptuous waitress to pour the *sake* from Takana's left, while she used her right hand to hold the cups and pass them out. She emptied a few doses of the powder into specific cups, all while the men stared at the waitress's stooped chest. She had another waitress take the cups to pre-defined spots that Takana had instructed before the meeting took place.

Once all the cups were passed out, Takana raised her own.

"Let us toast to the excision of bad blood, and the forging of our new alliances."

Takana drank hers quickly, then watched each man drink theirs. After that, she put her hand to her ponytail and pulled it tighter. Three men from various spots at the table nodded and left the room in a hurry.

"Where are they going?" one of the remaining men asked.

"Those men have been by my side since I started my business. Their clans will benefit from their foresight for decades. The rest of you…you've supported Kochiya. You participated in Taiga and Kameya's efforts to assassinate me. My spies have told me many interesting things about how you all planned to try your own hands at ending me; to take what I've built for yourselves. You scheme and machinate to attack me, my leadership, and my employees.

"You whisper honey to me, then shout threats when I'm out of sight. Nothing you say or do will make me trust you. Some of you have even threatened the life of my child—as if I didn't already have enough reasons to end you…"

The men tried to clamber to their feet, but the ones with the cups she'd spiked doubled over and vomited onto the table—they were the strongest-looking men in attendance. Several men made moves towards her before *tatami* mats from the edges of the room flung open. Bakeneko-*kai* protectors came out of the crawl spaces led by Sōkichi, Chise, and Tomoe, weapons drawn. Kunō came out of the kitchen, followed by the *kunoichi* waitresses. Aoi brought in the rest of the *kunoichi* that had been masquerading as prostitutes.

While blood painted the table, floors, and walls, Takana emptied the spent tobacco from her *kiseru* and stuffed it with a new pinch. She blew out a long, satisfying cloud of smoke as blood rained around her, then drank the remnants of one of the *sake* bottles.

When the last cry of the attendees came at the end of a blade, rapid footsteps came from the entrance. A long stream of *yakuza* thugs poured into the room, most of them meeting their ends only a few feet away from the room's opening. Several managed to get through but fell all the same.

Sōkichi helped Takana to her feet and handed her a *katana*. The shouting, charging *yakuza* got closer and closer to the center of the room. Takana pulled Sōkichi's robe and kissed him. They parted with a smile before joining the fight.

June 1, 1719
Utsunomiya, Tochigi Prefecture

A ten-year-old girl slid the door to Takana's bedroom open without warning. Takana and Sōkichi broke apart beneath the blankets. The girl ran to the *futon* and crawled between them, clutching at Takana. She hugged the girl tight and kissed the top of her head while Sōkichi caressed her shoulder.

"What's wrong, Natsu-*chan*?" Takana whispered. "I think you're getting a little old for this..."

"*Kaasan, chichi-ue*, I felt it again. I thought I heard something in the shrine room when I was getting water. I went inside but no one was there. I looked at the shrines and I felt a breeze lift my hair, but— But there are no windows in that room!"

Sōkichi smiled and shrugged at Takana.

"That room is haunted!" Natsu cried.

"I think you're right," Takana said. "But those aren't evil spirits. They're your family. They would never hurt you. When you feel that breeze, they're telling you they love you very much, just like your father and me."

"Chiyo-*chan* said it's a demon when I told her about it last week," Natsu whimpered.

"Well, I'll talk to Fusa-*obasan* and Chiyo-*chan* tomorrow. We'll tell them the truth. Those spirits are their family, too."

"I don't understand..." Natsu trailed off.

"You will, baby. Someday..." Takana whispered.

Sōkichi ran his hand along Natsu's hair, then Takana's cheek, before yawning and turning over to sleep. Takana touched his back and whispered they'd try again the next night.

The next day Takana leaned her chin on her good hand at her desk. She smiled as Natsu practiced calligraphy. Takana loved how Natsu wasn't deliberately using *wabi-sabi* in her brushstrokes, but it was coming out perfectly imperfect anyway.

With her lame left hand only able to hold a brush between her thumb and palm, Takana absentmindedly painted her own imperfect *haiku* while handling her and Natsu's hair bundle. Her orange feline friend interrupted often, and Takana ran her good hand over the middle-aged cat's back and bobtail.

Sometimes when the husbands were out training or traveling to far off *dōjō* to recruit more employees, Takana would spend the whole time with Fusa and their children. While Fusa sewed clothing for them, Takana painted Fusa's back with a dry brush and new *haiku*, having her guess the words. That led to an awkward conversation with the girls on the meaning of Fusa and Takana's tattoos, and why they were forbidden from ever getting them in the future.

While Tomoe trained the girls in self-defense, Takana and Fusa guided the girls to use brushes and words over swords and shouts. Laughter and tears were more powerful and everlasting than rage and blood.

"You forgot a stroke there, Natsu-*chan*," Takana smiled. "Without that stroke, it's meaningless."

Natsu puzzled over what she missed.

"Leave it. Your teacher would think it's meaningless. But what you did is still beautiful. Come over here, baby."

Takana waved for Natsu to come around behind her. She loosened her *kimono* and shifted it down so Natsu could see her entire back tattoo.

"Do you see the *haiku*? The one between the *bakeneko* and *tanchōzuru?*"

Takana delighted in Natsu's hand tracing the brushstrokes, studying as she read.

"It's wrong. The syllables are wrong."

"You're right. If I had written that in school, I would have been reprimanded by my teacher. But it has endless meaning for me. It's *everything* to me, just like you are. It doesn't matter that it's 'wrong.'"

"Is that what you were trying to show me the other day? When you said my flower arrangement was 'too perfect?' And how you said Fusa-*obasan*'s *kimono* design was 'perfect' even though she can't keep lines straight?"

Takana chuckled.

"Yes. Rules are important, Natsu-*chan*, but sometimes we only achieve greatness by breaking them. Knowing when to break them is the real art."

Natsu continued tracing with her fingers, expanding her curiosity to the whole tattoo.

"I don't like the scary cat."

"You're not supposed to. It's a warning."

"Warning against what?"

"Why don't you ask me about it later? After last night I don't want to give you more nightmares."

Natsu wrapped her arms around Takana's neck.

"Is that really true? Those ghosts are my family?"

Takana nodded as tears threatened to trickle out. She recited the *haiku* on her back to conjure Natsu-*san*'s laugh and brighten her mood.

Her daughter's laughter at hearing the *haiku* that wasn't a *haiku* filled Takana with new joy. She kissed Natsu's hands and brought her around for a tight embrace.

On her way to meeting Sōkichi in their bedroom that night, Takana passed the shrine room and heard a small voice inside. She peeked through the door to find Natsu speaking with the three shrines, telling them about mostly mundane aspects of her day. Takana choked up knowing in her heart how the three people in those shrines would have listened raptly to their granddaughter and niece go on and on about anything.

When Natsu stepped out of the room, Takana scooped her up in a big surprise hug. She asked Natsu to talk to them every night before bed from then on, and, starting the next day, Takana would begin to share their stories with her in exchange. Natsu said she wasn't scared anymore, "even when the spirits touched her hair again." Takana smiled and kissed her before guiding her back to her room.

After she and Sōkichi enjoyed a rare, uninterrupted time together and he was snoring away, Takana put on a light robe and walked out to the balcony. She lit a new pinch of tobacco.

The trees were stone-still and silent without a breeze to move them. Takana looked up at the stars, then lingered on the mountains around a place she knew.

She whispered *haiku* to her lost family as smoke lingered around her shoulders.

An ethereal wind answered.

THE END

Glossary of Japanese Vocabulary

Ama – Pejorative for a woman, similar to 'bitch'

Ane-san – Wife of the head of a *yakuza* clan

Ani-ki – Older brother, often used among *yakuza* to refer to others in the same clan

Bakeneko – Hiding behind the appearance of a cat is the fearsome, legendary demon capable of haunting its home, shapeshifting, possessing humans, throwing fire, waking the dead, and devouring its master

Chichi-ue – Father, formal

Chō-Han – Centuries-old Japanese gambling game played with dice. Literally 'Even-Odd'

Daimyo – Lords serving as vassals to the *shogun*

Daishō – A set of swords, comprised of the longer *katana* and shorter *wakizashi*

Deshi – Tattoo artist, apprentice-level

Dōjō – Practice, training, and study hall for martial arts

Dorobō – Thief

Dōshin – The third-highest rank of the *samurai* police force

Edo – Modern-day Tōkyō

Futon – Japanese-style bedding

Geta – Footwear made of wood, sometimes with elevated risers

Gomen-nasai – I'm so sorry!

Gyoza – Japanese dumplings

Haiku – A poem of seventeen syllables, in three lines of five, seven, and five syllables. Traditionally evokes images of the natural world

Hakama – The lower half of traditional robes

Hanabi – Fireworks

Haori – A traditional jacket that goes over robes or *kimono*

Hara-kiri – Ritual self-disembowelment. Less honorable, more painful, and lonelier than *seppuku*

Hashi – Chopsticks

Irezumi – *Yakuza*-style full body tattoos

Itai! – Ouch!

Kaasan – Mother, informal, affectionate

Kangan – Eunuch

Kanzashi – Sticks that hold hair up

Kasa – Cone-shaped hat

Katana – The longer of the two blades in a set of *daishō*

Katana kake – The stand that holds up a set of *daishō*

Kimono – Traditional female dress

Kiseru – Tobacco pipe from the Edo period

Kiseruzutsu – Ornate casing for *kiseru*

Kokoro no tomo – Same-sex soulmate, platonic or romantic

Kunai – Throwing dagger

Kunoichi – Female *shinobi*

Kuso! – Japan's most versatile curse word

Naginata – Pole-arm-type spear with a curved blade at the end

Nēsan – Informal address of an unknown woman, such as a waitress

Nikkō Kaidō – One of two major highways that connected Nikkō to Tōkyō (Edo)

Obasan – Aunt

Obi – Ornate, wide belt tied around a *kimono*

Ohayō – Good morning

Onna-bugeisha – Warrior women trained to defend the home or village

Onna-musha – Warrior women trained for offensive warfare

Onsen – Hot springs

Ossan – Old man, disrespectful

Otanjōbiomedetō – Happy birthday

Oyabun – Head of a *yakuza* clan

Oyassan – How to refer to the *oyabun* within the ranks of the *yakuza*

Rōnin – *Samurai* with no lord, or wandering ex-*samurai*

Ryokan – Traditional Japanese-style inn, often opulent yet minimalist in design

Ryō – Oval-shaped gold coins from the Edo period

Sakagura – *Sake* brewery

Sake – Alcohol made from fermented rice

Sakura – Cherry blossoms

Samurai – Warriors serving a *daimyo* as a soldier or village as police, exclusively portrayed as men but evidence suggests there were women as well

Sarashi – Plain cloth or linen, often used to bind breasts, among other uses

Senpai – Elder (in profession or study)

Sensei – Instructor or doctor

Seppuku – Ritual self-disembowelment followed by merciful beheading

Shakuhachi – Japanese flute

Shateigashira – Second lieutenant in the *yakuza*, beneath the *oyabun*

Shinobi – More commonly known outside Japan as *ninja*, but *ninja* would not be in recorded use until after the 19th century, derived from Chinese-influence. *Shinobi* has been in use since at least the 8th century and is the original Japanese term.

Shoji – A door, window, or room divider, consisting of paper sheets and a lattice frame

Shuriken – Throwing star

Sofu – Grandfather, informal, affectionate

Tanchōzuru – Red-crowned crane, deeply embedded and revered in Japanese culture, synonymous with loyalty, fidelity, and good luck. Said to live for a thousand years and mate for life

Tantō – Long dagger

Tatami – Traditional flooring material in Japanese housing

Tokonoma – A recessed alcove on a decorative wall in Japanese architecture

Tonchiki – Jerk, cretin, dumbass, dimwit, etc.

Tsujigiri – "Crossroads Killings." An act when *samurai* would "test the sharpness of their blades" on peasants. Largely outlawed in the Edo Period

Wabi-sabi – The art of using imperfection in order to achieve perfection

Yakeya – Nickname for Edo period common housing with a propensity to catch fire

Yakuza – Japanese organized crime organizations

Yama-uba – Cannibalistic mountain crone from Japanese mythology

Yarō! – Bastard!

Yūjo – Edo-era prostitute

Yūkaku – Edo-era pleasure quarter

Yukata – Bathrobe, or lighter, informal version of *kimono*

Zabuton – Square pillows for kneeling on the floor

Takana's Haiku

Shishi Oyabun
Shihai-shimashita
Neko taosu

=

You lion bosses
Though you dominated all
Toppled by a cat

Watashitachi
Zuttoisshoni
Tanchōzuru

=

You and I will be
Together, forever one
Just like the red-crowned crane

Special Thanks

I want to thank a certain Lounatic, a great critique partner and friend. He introduced me to my editor, Ollie Ander, who keeps me excited through the long, lonely process of writing, even when I feel like giving up. I appreciate her tough editing that doesn't seek to discourage or insult, but to educate and improve the work. I'm not sure if I could have completed this without Lou and Ollie's encouragement.

Thanks to my alpha- and beta-readers for their patience reading early drafts and providing valuable feedback.

Apologies if I can't mention every person I'm thankful for—I would be the guy at the Oscars without a prepared speech because I would never have expected to win, and actually mean it.

About VB Scott

I've traveled to many places in the world, but none so wonderful in nearly every aspect as Japan. Its history, culture, language, and people are endlessly fascinating. Living in Japan has been the highlight of my entire life.

I enjoyed writing this book so much that I intend to write a five-book series set along the *Gokaidō* (The Five Highways connected to Edo).

If you enjoyed Revenge of the Bakeneko, please consider leaving a rating and/or review, as this will go a long way to ensuring more books in this time and setting will continue.

I write in several genres and would love nothing more than for you to follow me as I release more stories that I hope you'll enjoy.

My handle is vb_scottwrites on Threads, Instagram, X, TikTok, and Facebook.

My email address is vbscott.writes@gmail.com